Ellie and the Shadow Man

Ellie and the Shadow Man

Maurice Gee

faber and faber

First published by Penguin Books (NZ) Ltd in 2001
First published in Great Britain in 2002
by Faber and Faber Limited
3 Queen Square, London WC1N 3AU

Printed in England by Clays Ltd, St Ives plc

A CIP record for this book
is available from the British Library

ISBN 0–571–21092–9

1002825683

T

2 4 6 8 10 9 7 5 3 1

For Nellie

Contents

House 4

THE OVERBRIDGE had been for Ellie more than just a way of crossing the lines: it marked a transition from a state of easiness into unease; which was stupid because she was just as bossy and loud — two words she used with some pride of herself — on the school-and-friends side as the home. But there, on the Willowbank, the two-storey house, the swimming pool and tennis court side, she often felt a disturbance in her mind as if something submerged was running against the tide. It was not exactly worry, for she was too sudden and eager for that, but a kind of watchfulness that made her pause inside, even as her voice and her movements went on.

Just be yourself, then nothing can go wrong, her mother advised; but *she* didn't know the things that could happen, in tiny ways, to alter the look in someone's eyes or shift the angle they stood on as they talked to you. The mothers over the bridge were the worst for that altered stance, the fathers not so bad. They could grin as well as smile, and ease up in their language, and sometimes they gave a lurch or a jut of the chest as though she made a heel-kick inside them. She recognised it instinctively and quietened down.

Halfway across the bridge she dropped a gob of spit between the railway lines, then looked around quickly to make sure no one had seen. The boys in the third form at Hutt Valley High had claimed that spit would sizzle if you hit the overhead wire, and they told a story about a drunk who peed from the bridge and his cock and balls had been burned off. They had looked hungry using those words and Ellie had understood that she was chosen as the sort of girl you could talk smut to. She had punched the worst of them in the chest so hard he had doubled up and had to hide the tears on his cheeks.

Her mother had shifted her from Hutt Valley High to Willowbank School when Ellie told her, a move that lost Ellie most of her friends. Paying private school fees trapped Mrs Crowther in two jobs, which made Ellie guilty and beg to be shifted back, although she had come to like Willowbank quite well.

'Ellie's the sort of girl who can be happy anywhere,' Mrs Crowther told the hostel matrons.

That's not true, Ellie wanted to say, even though it was meant as praise — her mother always praised her and ran down almost everyone else — but she saw why people might agree, and was puzzled by the unhappiness of so many of the girls she knew. They made a virtue of feeling sad; and now and then Ellie wondered if being blonde and blue-eyed and overweight, and being a woman early — too early, one of the matrons said — disqualified her from the feelings girls were supposed to have. Jealousy and envy were two more things she did not feel.

'She's a jolly sort of girl,' one of the nicer mothers said, which seemed to deny Ellie any feelings at all and even deny that she had brains in her head, while Ellie knew she was clever and sharp and had two ideas for every one her friends could produce. She could read books that bored them and know why the characters did what they did, even when it took place hundreds of years ago — why they gave each other up even though it meant they would stay lonely all their lives. She could leave the movies understanding why this person had been cruel and that one submissive, instead of thrilled by how gorgeous they looked and how long they had kissed for. She could draw. She could paint. Jolly, indeed.

'A wee bit on the boisterous side,' another woman said. 'And a wee bit crude.'

Boisterous was better, although it had something to do with her size and what the gym mistress called her early development. That meant her breasts. As for crude, those mothers should hear how dirty-mouthed their daughters could be in their Willowbank voices. Sometimes they made Ellie blush.

Being foul-mouthed was shallow, she thought, wheeling her bicycle down from the bridge. And lying was shallow and made you smaller. It chipped off part of who you were by making the other person less. Ellie had learned that from lying to her mother. She had not felt whole again until she confessed, which she did in a straightforward way so neither of them would get emotional. 'Thank you for telling me,' her mother said, and they both felt better; and Ellie felt rounded out again.

She did not believe she had to protect her mother but stand beside her and not be budged. Mrs Crowther needed support if she was to keep going. Ellie felt no burden and no hands holding tight. Her mother made decisions and had rules Ellie did not like, but kept them separate from her love, which she wore like a skin. (Ellie had tried to paint it as an aura or glow in the parent portrait they had done at school, but could not prevent it from spreading like a rash.)

She looked back past the railway station at House 4, where she had left her mother in bed with two hotwater bottles and a lemon drink sweetened with honey. One of the other matrons would look in. Ellie had insisted on that. The nurses were in Wellington at a Saturday class so there would be no hard heels on the stairs and no 'Mairzy Doats' on the piano. Her mother would have silence, aspros, lemons, a warm bed, a darkened room. I've done all that, Ellie thought, satisfied, although the Saturday class was only luck.

She rode up Oxford Terrace towards Waterloo. There were fewer people on this side of the bridge and more cars, bigger cars: bigger houses, more trees, taller trees. There were shell-strewn drives and flower beds shaped like diamonds and fences made of tortured iron.

Lawns mown so close they looked in pain. Blinds that made the windows seem like pages in a notebook, unwritten on, and the houses empty. Ellie preferred the way her side of the valley seemed to teem, although she didn't always like its noise — and none today, for her mother, please. She sometimes said she liked its untidiness better — the peeling paint and weedy paths and hydrangeas out of control — but the truth was she thought of it as a kind of backside. West of the lines was the made-up, combed and dressed side of the valley, while on the east, out beyond Cambridge Terrace, it was as if someone was showing his bum through a hole in his trousers. One day she would like to stand on the overbridge and draw both sides, but give them a twist, and show somehow that that was part of this and this of that. Because, she thought, it's true, isn't it, we're the same — and was overwhelmed by the knowledge she had found, before it just as quickly went away.

By the time she reached Angela's house, muddy clouds, wet along the edges, had swelled up over the mountains. A little puffed-up northerly was blowing, too warm for rain. She did not want the day to be cancelled, not before she'd played a couple of matches, not before the fruit salad and cream. It would be terrible to ride home to empty old House 4 before she and Angela had beaten Heather and Sue, before she had been paired with a boy, even if they lost their game. And before she'd eaten some of the chicken sandwiches Angela had promised.

She watched the clouds anxiously. They lay still, then seemed to shrink like scummy froth on a beach. She turned into Angela's drive — crackling shells — rode along by flower beds at the side of the house and dismounted at the big double garage, where a car and a yacht on a trailer gleamed like treasures in the gloom. There were no other bikes. She blushed at hers — a man's bike — and the way she'd had to swing her leg over the bar. Then she was blasé, remembering her mother's advice. She freed her racket from the carrier and bounced it on her knee.

'Ellie, you're the first,' Angela cried. She stood in the glass door as though in a frame, displaying herself — to little effect, Ellie thought (a phrase she'd learned recently, and liked). Angela was bony but smooth, and her attractiveness was in her skin, and in her eyes, which were dark blue, suiting some poetic word: dewy perhaps. Ellie liked Angela up to a point.

'Come and meet Mummy. Come inside,' Angela said.

Ellie leaned her racket on the wall. She did not want it in the house where people might see how old it was. The woman in the room was standing back, keeping out of the sun, but was coloured like a fish in a bowl — though upright of course, which made the likeness wrong. Like a seahorse perhaps. Ellie stepped inside and smiled brightly, got her words in first: 'Hello, Mrs Prime.'

'It's Ellie, from school. My tennis partner,' Angela said.

'Hello, Ellie, I'm glad you could come,' Mrs Prime said. She had a quick-moving smile, like a ripple, like a shiver. It lit nothing up, just moved her mouth. 'You must be hot after riding. Do sit down. Angela, get your friend a drink.'

Ellie sat, remembering to keep her knees together. 'You've got a lovely house,' she said. 'Lovely garden.'

'Oh, it's a place to live,' Mrs Prime said. She had a bendy neck and collarbones whiter than the rest of her skin. Lovely hands, lovely lovely hands, white and fine and rounded and perfectly smooth, and pliant, elastic, as they lit a cigarette. Bits of people, parts of people, sometimes astounded Ellie, noses, mouths, kneecaps, as though they were slumming and should go back where they belonged. Mrs Prime's hands belonged on a film star or a princess; and Ellie felt sorry for her that she could not live up to them, although she tried. Tried with her voice and her way of posing herself.

'Angela tells me that you live at the YWCA,' she said.

'Yes, my mother's a matron there, in the dental nurses' part. It's House 4,' Ellie said.

'That must be interesting.' She showed no interest but gave a sideways glance, and Ellie knew she was curious about how a hostel matron managed to send her daughter to Willowbank School.

'We have some fun there,' Ellie said.

'They have peeping Toms,' Angela said, coming back with a glass of lime cordial.

'Not any more. We haven't got anyone now.'

'He used to steal scanties off the line,' Angela said.

'Really, Angela,' Mrs Prime said.

'He's caught,' Ellie said, blushing again. 'He was only fifteen. He was a loony.'

'He had hundreds of pairs —'

'Angela, it's not a topic I care for. Have your drink, Ellie. And tell your mother I admire her pluck.'

'Yes?'

'She must work hard.'

'She does. She's got a day job too. She does the wages at the biscuit factory. I help at the hostel. I take out the linen, stuff like that.'

'Remarkable. Now here are some more of your friends, Angela. I think perhaps you should start playing now.'

Heather, Sue, roly-poly Barry, tall Rex with the small eyes whom Ellie had met once before at a school dance, where he'd ignored her. Darryl, Catherine, Mattie, Faye. A shy boy called Robert, who whispered and blushed and furtively smoothed the front of his shorts, although there was no bump there that Ellie could see. If her luck went the usual way, he would be her partner.

The court was at the back of the section and was surfaced with grit that got in your shoes. They played short matches, best of five, boys' doubles first, then girls'. There was hardly time to get going, Ellie found. She and Angela beat Heather and Sue three love, and Ellie didn't have a serve, which made her grumpy. Serving was the best part of her game. She could belt her first one down as fast as any of the boys and would have liked to play singles against them, especially Rex — ace him if she could. That would make his little eyes pop open. He had long legs and calves with interesting muscles, fat then thin, long then short, jumpy calves. They were the best part of him, better than his face.

'It's getting dusty, Daddy. Will you sprinkle please?' Angela cried.

Mr Prime fastened a hose to the garden tap. He walked through the girls at the court entrance, holding the nozzle rudely, which had to be unintentional, then signalled Angela to turn on the tap. A drizzle of water wet the gravel. He did not look like a lawyer, more like a coalman, Ellie thought, with black eyebrows joining in the middle and red-splotched cheeks. Were they drinking spots? He undulated the hose like a snake, making the girls squeal as they jumped out of the way.

'Do be careful, Harold,' Mrs Prime said from her wicker chair. She sat with three mothers by the rock garden, away from the players so as not to interfere. They wore summery dresses and floppy hats.

This is like the pictures, Ellie thought. It's like waiting for something bad to happen or someone dangerous to turn up. There should be music.

'Harold, that's enough. You'll make it muddy.'

'Right,' he said, and coiled the hose.

'Thanks, Daddy. Mixed doubles next. It's me and Rex versus Ellie and Barry,' Angela cried.

That was better than the shy boy, Robert, who still seemed worried about his pants. Barry was a hard hitter and Ellie liked that: it was her style. He got around the court fast for a fat pink boy and rushed to the net at the wrong time. His game could be described as impolite — the gym teacher's word for Ellie's. She liked the way he hit his smashes straight at Rex's long legs, ruining the dignified style Rex liked to play. She did not expect they would win, because they made too many mistakes, hit the net, hit beyond the baseline, but she liked the way Barry grinned at her and cried, 'Hard luck,' and 'Ah, not quite,' when she missed the line by a yard or two.

'Let's rush them. Go for it, eh?' he said on the last game. It was two-all. Ellie was serving. She had almost decided to be careful because she'd never beaten Angela before, in singles or in doubles, but she liked his eagerness and said yes; and kept to it, whacking down her second serve as fast as her first, which made Angela cry out, 'Hey,' as though shots like that were against the rules. That would teach her for nodding smugly at Rex and creeping up slyly to the net. Ellie put some top-spin on her next serve, something that mostly didn't work, and made Rex hit a backhand into the umpire's stand. Then Barry nipped in for a lucky netcord. Suddenly it was forty-love.

This must be against some sort of rules, Ellie thought. She saw Mrs Prime watching with shaded eyes from under her hat, and Mr Prime hook-fingered at the wire, and someone in a glistening coat walking on the lawn.

'Serve straight at him. Get him in the middle,' Barry said, meaning somewhere else. Ellie liked his dislike of his friend. She served: a fault.

Barry ran back from the net. 'He creeps right up. Do your second hard,' he whispered.

'I might miss.'

'So what? Have a go.'

She wondered later how she knew — wondered if it *was* knowledge — that if she lost the point Rex and Angela would take five in a row and win the match. It was laid down like counting, which nothing could turn aside, and yet she could subtract it by throwing up the ball and hitting hard. She seemed to have seen everything that would follow.

'Double fault,' said long Rex, sweeping a downward-pointing horn of hair from his forehead.

'Come off it, sonny boy,' said a voice.

'What?'

'It was in by two inches. Do you want me to come and show you the mark.' The man in the glistening jacket had a widow's peak as sharp as a pen nib and white hollow hospital cheeks and a white thin nose. He turned his face to Ellie and gave a wink.

'You keep out of it, Hollis,' Angela said.

'Ask the umpire,' Hollis said.

'Yes,' said the shy boy, Robert, sitting where he didn't want to be, on the umpire's stand, 'good serve. Game and match to Barry and Ellie, three-two.'

'We won,' Barry cried, throwing up his racket and catching it. He shook hands with Ellie.

'Fluke,' Rex said. 'Anyway, it was out.'

They walked off the court. Ellie went to the drinks table and poured herself a glass of ginger ale. Her left shoulder turned hollow when the man in the leather jacket joined her from that side. She ignored him while he poured himself a drink.

'Thanks,' she said.

'That joker's a cheat.'

'I knew as soon as I hit it it was in.'

Strangely, like a picture in an IQ test, he changed from a man into a boy. He had a sick face and a crabby mouth. 'You sweat a lot for a girl,' he said.

'It's hot,' Ellie said. 'Anyway, who are you? Where's your motorbike?'

'Do I look like I've got one?'

'You look like a milkbar cowboy,' she said.

'It's better than pansy white pants.'

'Do you mean Rex?'

'All of them. You too.'

'You don't know what colour my pants are.'

She should never have said that, but he'd made her, by suddenly sneering after helping her win.

His face made another change, older again, experienced, and she found herself thinking that he'd been some place she'd never been.

'What are you doing here? You're not playing tennis,' she said.

'I could if I wanted to.'

'Are the Primes your friends?'

He made a couple of laughing sounds, chipped off something hard in his chest. 'That's my mother' — Mrs Prime. 'And my old man' — Mr Prime. 'Angela's my sister.'

'You're kidding.'

'She's never told you, eh? They're ashamed of me.'

'Why?'

'Don't ask me, ask them.' He drank some lemonade. 'If you want my advice, you're a bit too floppy to play tennis.'

'What do you mean?' — although she knew.

'Girls should stop when they get too big.'

'Ha ha,' she said, furious.

'Just trying to help. Hey, I'm glad you beat my sister.'

He put down his glass and limped away. *Limped* away. His hip seemed to do all the lifting, and his foot slapped down as flat as a dinner plate. He went around to the back of the court; sat on a stone seat in the shrubbery; lit a cigarette. Ellie wanted to follow. She wanted to sit with him. Ask why he limped. Share his cigarette. Say things that weren't part of a game.

She went into the house and washed her face, which glowed like a heater. She wished she could be as cool as Mrs Prime. Switch off my face, she thought, wondering if it would leave her all bendy necked and snobbish and cold. She saw how her mother would be in a house like this — a mixture of delighted and afraid. She would love the bathroom, though, as clean and white as the Primes who washed in it — except Hollis, if that's his name: he doesn't look clean, Ellie thought.

She went back to the lounge, walking like a thief. There weren't even any smells — though she had got a whiff of tobacco breath from Hollis and something sumpy from his jacket. She wondered if he had hurt his leg on a motorbike; and the thought of abrasions made her cross her arms on her chest. Floppy, she thought. She hoped that whatever he had done it had hurt. 'Hollis' too. That was a stuck-up name, worse than Angela.

The light in the room faded as a cloud crossed the sun. The colours went out of the pictures on the wall. They were ones she'd seen in the art room at school, framed reproductions: the irises by the Dutchman, Van Gogh, and the French one by the river on a Sunday afternoon with the people and the water and the trees all done with dots. That was clever, and she wanted the sun to come out and light it up again, because somehow that day was this and the artist could just as well be here. She thought she would try painting a picture with dots: the tennis court, the wicker chairs, the women in their hats.

Mr Prime was standing outside the french doors, unaware of her. He looked brown-bearish, unclean, and she saw that this family was broken in two parts. Hollis saying 'my old man' instead of 'my father' showed that they were on the same side. She saw the players on the court over Mr Prime's shoulder, and the non-playing girls and boys lounging in a group. Mrs Prime and her friends conversed in their chairs, with Mrs Prime's lovely hands stretching and folding like seagull wings. Mr Prime made a sound in his throat: a creaking thud, a closing door. 'Well, dumb ox, you married her.' He gave a little laugh, half a sob. 'Whoa,' he said, or was it 'Woe'?

Ellie crept back to the bathroom. She released her ponytail and retied it. That's terrible, she thought. Her own father had felt no pain like that. She thought of him as happy, although he was dead: happy then, when he was alive, not happy now. She could not imagine an after-life for him and had no picture of a person she might meet, even though her mother had photos showing what he looked like. Over-weight, which was where her plumpness came from. Her colouring was his too, less pretty than her mother's. 'Damn you, Dad,' she said; then, 'Sorry, didn't mean it.' The apology failed to work as it usually did, because she was disturbed about the Primes. 'Poor Angela,' she whispered.

When she looked out the door again, Mr Prime was washing his car by the garage. She walked across the lawn to her bike and took her handkerchief from her cardigan draped on the bar.

'What sort of car is it?' she said.

'A Mercedes.'

'It's nice.'

'It's a way of getting from one place to the other,' Mr Prime said, echoing his wife.

'Is that your boat?' she said, peering into the garage.

'Yes. *Surprise*. I don't get to sail her much any more.'

'Whose wheelchair is that?'

'My son's. It used to be. He hasn't needed it for years. Ellie. Is that your name?'

'Yes.'

'Don't waste your time with me. Go and talk to the boys.'

'OK,' she said and turned away. She thought he was a feeble sort of man and that he should limp like his son; and she wondered what the wheelchair had been for, what injury.

Hollis was still on the seat at the back of the court with his arms spread out and his head pillowed in a shrub. He had his legs splayed in a way that would surely offend his mother. Ellie went along the near end of the court and around the back, through the rock garden, aware of Mrs Prime watching. I'm breaking rules again, she thought, but anyway I'm being myself.

'Shift your arm, I want to sit down.'

'Be my guest.'

It was like the movies: good lines, nice and snappy. She felt sharp in her mind.

'How old are you?'

'Who wants to know?'

'I'm Ellie Crowther. That's my name.'

'How old are *you*?'

'I'm fourteen. Nearly fifteen. And if you say jailbait I'll slug you.'

He grinned at her. It made him crooked and dangerous: crooked teeth.

'I'm not kidding,' she said. 'I punched a boy at school once and made him cry.'

'There's no boys at Willowbank.'

'When I was at Hutt Valley High. Do you go there?'

'Do I look like a schoolkid?'

'What do you do then?'

'That's my business.'

'I suppose you think it's fun being rude? What sort of name is Hollis anyway?' It was not a question but a hit. She thought she should leave it there and walk away.

But instead of getting angry Hollis sighed and closed his eyes.

'I find a good seat and some dumb sheila parks herself.'

'I'm not a sheila and I'm not dumb. What's wrong with your foot?'

'Jesus,' he said.

'Are you crippled or something?'

Ellie saw she'd gone too far. He was older than she'd thought and looked as if he might answer in a language she did not know. But it was his tone that was utterly strange: 'Go away.'

Drops of rain struck her arms and face. Rain made a wall at the garden end. The tennis boys were grabbing chairs as the ladies fled. It was as though Ellie had done it, turned the day around with her stupid questions. The girls ran, white as chickens, for the house.

'You'd better put your bike in the garage,' Hollis Prime said.

'Aren't you coming?'

'I'll stay here. It's my bath.'

'You're mad,' she cried.

She ran through the rain and saved her bike. Mr Prime was sheltering in the garage.

'He won't come in. He's just sitting there.'

Mr Prime put his head out into the rain. 'Yes, well, he's best just left alone.'

'What's wrong with him?'

'Do you mean down here' — he tapped his leg — 'or in his head?'

'It's my fault. I asked him was he crippled.'

'It's a reasonable question. In fact, he is. He's had polio.' He looked outside again. 'My son knows how to get attention.'

Ellie stepped into the rain for a moment, watching Hollis through the wire-netting. He had unbuttoned his shirt and thrown back his head and was washing his face with his hands. His leather jacket had blackened and taken a beetle sheen. He opened his mouth and drank the rain.

The girls in the french doors swayed like lilies. 'Hollis, come inside,' Angela screamed. He spread his arms along the back of the seat. She slammed the door and jerked the drapes across.

Ellie stepped back into the garage. Mr Prime had gone to his yacht and was running his hand along the curve of its bow. The rain on the iron roof rushed like a train.

Ellie dried her face with her handkerchief. Her racket was outside getting ruined, unless one of the girls had rescued it. She did not care; and did not care about Hollis Prime. He might have had polio, she thought, but he's a mutt. He's trying to make himself the most important thing. Sitting there was saying, Look at me.

I won't, Ellie said.

Mr Prime was leaning on the yacht with his cheek on the hull. His eyes were closed. In the house people would be eating chicken sandwiches and fruit salad and cream. Ellie wanted to be there. She watched for a break in the rain, then saw Hollis Prime limping to the french doors. He opened them, took a handful of the flowered drapes and dried his face. He stepped inside and closed the door.

'Hey,' Ellie whispered, 'I'm here.'

After a while the rain eased. She fetched her racket from the side of the court and rode home. Leaning her bike in the coal-shed, she thought she should put a smear of coal-dust on her forehead, the way Dolores sometimes did for penance, although with her it would be for anger and disappointment. Instead she slammed the door. Then she walked around to the milkbar by the Prince Edward and bought a meat pie and a candy bar. She ate them walking home so her mother would not know.

Mrs Crowther's headache had not gone so Ellie offered to do her switchboard duty.

'No, Mrs McDermott owes me one,' her mother said. 'What you can do, take a glass of ginger water along to Dolores. She's got her pains.'

Ellie knocked at the door, even though it was her room as much as Dolores'. For three years she'd had to sleep on the fold-out sofa in her mother's living room but with the newest intake had been allowed to share a bedroom with one of the nurses. Dolores was a fluke. Dolores was a marvellous piece of luck: so beautiful, so sulky, so extreme. Ellie loved to watch her, and smell her too, pick fragrances out of the air, name them, covet them, as Dolores got ready for a party or a dance. 'It's an education,' Ellie said, when Dolores objected, which she did insincerely because she liked people noticing her.

'Ginger water,' Ellie whispered, creeping to the bed.

'Put it on the table,' Dolores said, equally soft, and with such an air of suffering Ellie felt she should applaud. Mrs Crowther, in her darkened room, waited out her headaches but Dolores played her cramps like a movie.

'There's some light between the curtains. It's like a knife,' she said.

Ellie shut it out. 'Can I get you some aspros?'

'They're no good. Not for me.'

Ellie grinned, hoping her teeth did not gleam too brightly in the dark. 'When did you come home?'

'Twelve o'clock. In the rain.'

'Yes,' Ellie said, remembering Hollis Prime drying his face. He must have come into that room of pink and white girls like a dog shaking itself after a swim. Black dog, she thought, seeing his teeth. His hitching walk and slapped-down foot were out of step with everything she'd known, and she wondered how badly he hurt. Did polio hurt? And why had being crippled seemed romantic when what it really did was twist you round and torture you — and maybe even make your teeth grow crooked? Make you cruel and stupid, maybe?

'Can you get me a cold flannel?' Dolores whispered.

Ellie wet a cloth in the bathroom and brought it back. 'Drink your ginger water,' she said.

'It's no good. I don't know where your mother gets the stuff.'

'Her mother used it. It works for me.'

'It might for kids.' Dolores wiped her face and hands with the flannel. 'My feet are burning, Ellie. Will you wipe them?'

23

'Come off it.'

'Please. It hurts when I bend.'

Ellie washed Dolores' feet, roughly at first, then with enjoyment, feeling their bony shape and warmth. They made a pale gleam in the darkened room and were independent, cut off by a long distance from Dolores' face. Feet, feet, Ellie thought. She'd never been aware of how interesting they were, what a life they led. She wiped between Dolores' toes.

'That's enough.'

'You've got some rough bits on your heels.'

'Don't, it tickles. Give me my ginger water now.'

'Can I paint your toenails?'

'No. Go away, Ellie. I want to rest.'

Ellie sat on her bed. 'I met a boy today.'

'I'm not interested in boys.'

'What I think, though, is he's not a boy. I think he must be about nineteen.'

'What does he look like?'

'Dark. Good-looking. When he smiles.' She almost said he looked like James Dean but it wasn't true. She was startled to find that the crooked bits in Hollis's face were the bits she liked. None of them would fit on an actor's face. 'He's maybe twenty. I sat with him and we talked.'

'Three cheers.'

'He stayed out in the rain and got wet.'

'What is he, a nutcase?'

'It was —' Ellie thought for a moment — 'defiance. He wears a leather jacket. It got soaked.' She was getting closer to his crippled leg, but would not mention it, not because it spoiled the picture but from a sudden loyalty.

'Like I said, a loony,' Dolores said.

'No he's not,' Ellie answered calmly. 'The trouble is . . .'

'What?'

'I don't know how to see him again. How do you, Dollie? How

do you make a man take you out?'

'Your mother wouldn't let you, with someone twenty.'

'I could say he's sixteen.'

'He hasn't asked you yet.'

'No. I suppose he won't.'

'Someone twenty wants you-know-what.'

'Not necessarily,' Ellie said. 'He might be —'

'What?'

'Above it.'

Dolores giggled. 'Above the waist. I bet I know why he spotted you.'

'Shut up, Dolores,' Ellie said. 'And wash your own feet.' She went out and closed the door hard, but smiled as she went along to her mother's rooms. It was true he'd noticed her for that. She hoped that not going inside for sandwiches and dessert had made him wonder where she was. Then she thought of his crippled leg and frowned. It seemed like more of her bad luck.

The rain started again and kept on softly through the afternoon. Ellie stayed in her mother's living room and read a book, hoping that Angela would phone to find out where she'd gone. She kept on remembering that Angela wasn't really a friend, just her tennis partner, and that she didn't like her much. She was boy-mad and talked all the time about new dresses she had bought. Ellie could not see that she had time to wear them all.

The dental nurses came thudding in from town and started their run on the bathroom. Mrs Crowther got up and went about sighing. She sent Ellie to the dairy for an *Evening Post* and sat drinking tea and making pencil circles around advertisements for houses she would never have enough money to buy. It made Ellie sad, then guilty after a while, as it always did. There might be enough money if Mrs Crowther didn't have to pay Willowbank fees.

'Dinner time, Mum.'

'I'll come a bit later. You go on.'

'How's your headache now?'

'It's getting better.' She smiled at Ellie. 'Thank you for looking after me.'

'That's all right. It's good practice.'

'What for?'

'Life. Didn't you say it's a headache most of the time?'

'Oh Ellie, I don't mean all the things I say.'

Dolores was sitting on her bed yawning. 'I went to sleep.' She was rosy, swollen faced, and smelly with sweat and bad air. Her little golden cross on its chain had worked sideways out of her blouse. It made her lopsided and tarty, which was not what a cross should do.

'You don't mind if I air the room?' Ellie said, pulling back the curtains and raising the window.

Dolores grabbed her towel. 'Wait here till I wash. I'm coming to dinner.'

And I'll bet you go to the dance, Ellie thought. So much for cramps.

The clatter of plates in the dining room made little flashing lights, sparks of electricity in the air, and if you tried to paint the scene you'd have to show conversation hanging over the tables, grey like plasticine but tinsely with bits of laughter too. How could that be done; and how could you show the smells of food, as well as the food itself and all the women eating? There was too much of everything.

Although she was allowed to sit with the matrons, Ellie followed Dolores to a table where two other dental nurses sat. They were Presbyterians and said grace, but switched to excited talk so fast when it was over that Ellie almost missed the change. She was careful with religious girls; she watched her language. Some of them even objected to damn.

These two, Alison and Wendy, were going to a church dance not in a group as they usually did, but separately, each with a boy in a car.

'Make them park underneath a street lamp,' Dolores said.

'Oh ha ha, Dollie's getting jealous,' Wendy said.

'Peter and Tony have both got good morals,' Alison said. 'So pipe down, Dollie.'

'Do you want a tip, Alison?'

'No, I don't.'

'Don't eat cabbage before a dance. It'll give you bloat and he'll think you're pregnant.'

'I'm shifting tables,' Alison said.

'Me too.' Wendy followed her.

'Why do you have to get them all worked up?' Ellie asked.

'They make me sick. Good morals,' Dolores said.

'They probably do have, at a church dance.'

'Sure, Peter and Tony and all the saints. I can't eat this muck. I'm going to grab the bathroom.'

Ellie sat alone, eating stewed plums and custard, which made her remember the fruit salad she had missed — fruit salad with cream. She wondered if Hollis Prime's leather jacket was ruined, or would it dry out? Infantile paralysis was polio's other name. That meant children got it; but Hollis must have been older because it was 1954 when the schools were closed. She remembered doing schoolwork at home, and a girl called Muriel in her class who had caught polio, although not badly. Back at school, no one wanted to share a desk with her. They pretended they could see germs hopping over, and ran to the taps and washed their hands if they had to touch Muriel in folk dancing. Ellie blushed lightly, remembering her part in it. She wondered if Hollis Prime seeming less clean than Angela meant anything.

'Ellie,' Mrs McDermott said, stopping at her table, 'are you going out tonight?'

'I thought maybe the pictures. Mum will be all right.'

'Do you think you can do the switchboard seven to eight? I can come along then.'

'Yes, no trouble.'

'We won't tell your mother. She needn't know.'

'Yes, that's fine.'

'Good girl.' Mrs McDermott rolled away, smiling because she would have time for the quiet ciggie and glass of gin that were essential to her well-being, she claimed. Ellie liked Mrs McDermott, who could easily get sacked for gin.

She walked along to the switchboard room at seven o'clock and settled in front of the board with a feeling of efficiency and control, brought about by the pins and cords and sleeping lights. She was a pipe or conduit, something electrical that messages passed through. Calls came for women in House 5 and House 7, and she listened long enough to know that they were going on dates, the lucky things.

She had not brought her book because of interruptions. Instead she made pencil drawings in her small sketch pad. She drew Rex going knock-kneed as a tennis ball skidded between his feet. One of the things she thought she might be when she left school was a newspaper cartoonist, or even better someone who drew jokes. She sketched the sad boy Robert holding his tennis racket against the front of his shorts. She had danced with a boy like that at a school dance. He had left her suddenly halfway through a waltz and she'd wondered if she was meant to think it was her fault. If she drew him she would call it: *Me and my big troubles.* She could not think of words for underneath Robert, he was too sad, but she went back to Rex and made a speech balloon: *It's against the rules.* Then she drew Hollis Prime. He was easy. Everything was crooked and sharp: teeth, nose, that little pick-axe of hair called for some reason a widow's peak. She put him on the stone seat in the rock garden, with his legs wide like scissors, but then was stumped by the crippled one. First thing — was it withered up or swollen? Second — was it the left or the right? It made her impatient with herself. If you drew people, you had to really look. It seemed to mean that she was no good. Worse that that, if she hadn't looked properly there was no reason for him to look at her.

That's bull, she thought. The face had Hollis Prime perfectly — sneering, bad tempered, crooked, cruel.

A call came for Dolores: her man friend who drove a Jaguar. He was supposed to be a well-known footy player and spoke as if he was in the All Blacks already: 'Dolores Wood.' No 'please'. 'Hold the line,' Ellie intoned. She wished she could tell him that Dolores called him 'My bloke with the ears'.

'Get off the line, Ellie,' Dolores said.

'Oh, sorry.'

She drew the footy player with quilted ears, then rubbed them out and turned them into real cauliflowers. *Save me from the caterpillars*, he cried. She wondered if she had the nerve to leave it on Dolores' pillow.

'Woburn Hostels,' she half-sang, professional.

'Can I speak to Ellie Crowther?' Angela said.

'Angela, it's me. I'm on the switchboard.'

'Where did you go? We couldn't find you.'

'I got locked out, so I went home.'

'No one locked you out. That's stupid. Anyway, there's someone here who wants to talk to you.'

'Who?'

'It's none of my business.' She gave a little giggle and Ellie could tell how excited she was. 'Here he is.'

'Ellie,' said a voice, 'it's Hollis here.'

'What do you want?' It was all that came into her head. Nothing else was there.

'I was rude to you today, so I wanted to say sorry.'

She managed to answer, 'That's all right.' She knew now what the girls at school meant by gooey inside — a sweet sick feeling like being overfed. She found herself pulling a face, but thinking at the same time: I love Hollis Prime.

'So, what are you doing?' he said.

'I'm on the switchboard in the hostels. Till eight o'clock.'

'The thing is, I thought we could meet. So I can say sorry properly, eh? Can you come out and meet me for a minute?'

'Yes,' she said.

'If you get off at eight o'clock, what about ten past? By Woburn station. My side.'

'Yes, all right.'

'I'll be in my car.'

'Car?'

'It's a Morrie Minor. See you there.' He hung up. She guessed it was to stop her saying no — which she began, just began, to want to do.

Mrs McDermott arrived. She wanted to gossip, but Ellie cried, 'I've got to get to the pictures, Mrs McDermott.' Lie number one.

She ran to House 4 and burst into her mother's room. Mrs Crowther was on the phone. The call must have come through the moment Ellie had left the switchboard. She was leaning back in her easy chair, smiling and smoking, and looked as if she'd never had a headache in her life, so it must be dumb taxi driver George on the line. She waved Ellie out of the room, leaving loops of smoke in the air. 'Yes, I'm feeling better. Yes, you can.'

'Pictures,' Ellie whispered, and went out. Number two; but she did not feel bad because she hated — no, she *despised* George, who seemed to think he could get her on side by winking at her, as if that was all he had to do.

She ran to her bedroom. Dolores was gone but the room was thick with smells of her; coloured with her too: broad slashes (her Chinese dressing gown on the bed) and tiny strokes (her lipstick, her eyebrow pencil, her used embroidered hankie which she'd shied at the dirty clothes pile in the corner and missed).

Ellie grabbed her towel and flannel and ran to the bathroom. She washed her face, unbuttoned her blouse, wiped her armpits. She'd shaved them for tennis with Dolores' razor and they felt like sandpaper, which made her feel experienced, then frightened her. She did not want to be experienced — just, what? Herself.

She hurried back to the bedroom, looked longingly at Dolores' lipstick, left it there. The ticking alarm clock said eight minutes past eight. She grabbed her jacket from the wardrobe and went out. Half of her was walking to the overbridge, the other half pulled backwards, not wanting to go — and which was real? She'd been out with boys, had even kissed them, but this was the first time it hadn't been a joke.

She saw the Morris Minor from the top of the bridge. It gleamed like a cake of scented soap. She felt that this time she was really crossing over, that the world really was in two halves; then — perhaps it was the familiar drumming of the boards — she found her balance and knew that nothing had to change, that she could just be interested, and that it was absurd — she was far too young — to believe she loved Hollis Prime. She didn't know Hollis Prime. What a dumbcluck name.

He leaned across and opened the passenger door.

'Pink's a funny colour for a car,' she said.

'The bloke who had it before me painted it,' Hollis said.

'How come you've even got a car? Did your father buy it?' She supposed he could take that as meaning did he buy it to make up for Hollis's crippled leg. But that didn't stop her, because suddenly she didn't like the look of him, which was a relief. He looked sly, and like a liar, and smaller than she'd thought, sitting with his hands on the wheel like a boy playing at driving a racing car.

'I suppose you get lots of presents?' she said.

'Jesus, I don't think I will say I'm sorry.'

'It's immaterial to me. Don't start the engine.'

'I didn't come to sit here.'

'I'll get out.'

'Get out, then.'

She smiled at him, pleased to be quarrelling, and pleased with 'immaterial'. She felt that a change had occurred when she used the word and that she was old enough to deal with Hollis Prime, order him not to start the car. She had no intention of accepting his invitation to get out.

'It's a nice seat. I'm comfortable. I might let you drive as far as Petone beach. As long as we're back here by half past nine.'

'Big deal.'

'That should be enough time for you to apologise.'

Then a set of images eliminated the game. She saw her mother sitting in her room worrying — saw her lighting one cigarette from the butt of another; saw herself sneaking past the door. She heard herself lying. It made her curl inwardly, away from Hollis Prime.

'This is dumb. I've got to go.'

'No, don't.' He put his hand on her arm, a grip without assertiveness but heavy with some need that she connected with his leg. It seemed like naked touching and made her shiver up the length of her arm into her head. Hollis Prime became good-looking again as though a change of light had shifted shadows on his face. It was like turning a corner. It was like a taste, a view, an opened bottle of scent, and she wanted to roll down the neck of his sweater and touch his throat.

'Do we have to quarrel?' he said.

'I don't suppose so. All right, drive. But I do have to be back by half past nine.'

They drove beside the railway line, where a unit went by behind the trees. Half a second and it was gone, heading for Waterloo and Upper Hutt. She felt the geography of the valley, from the mountains behind her to the harbour in front, making a frame around the car with her inside next to Hollis Prime. She touched his arm.

'Another leather jacket. How many have you got?'

'Two.'

'I like the black one better.'

'Yeah, so do I, but it got soaked. You've got to dry them slowly or they shrink.'

In Petone he stopped at a milkbar and bought two bottles of Coca Cola. People looked at the car because of its colour. Some thought it was stupid, she supposed. Old people hated it — she saw it in their faces; but she loved the soapy sheen of the bonnet and imagined that she looked glamorous, like a blonde, and Hollis in his jacket dangerous.

He parked on the foreshore. 'Do you want to go for a walk?'

'No, I like being in here. How old are you really? You don't have to lie.'

'Yeah, OK. I'm twenty-two.'

32

'I'm fifteen.'

'Fourteen, you said.'

'Fifteen in two weeks.' She tried to close the gap but it stayed dark and sinister. 'There's older girls than me.'

'Hey, we're out for a drive. You don't have to worry.' He had finished his drink and threw the bottle looping, like a knife, into the sand dunes. 'You look older than fifteen. You look about seventeen.'

That was a lie, unless it meant her breasts. The pleasure she had felt slid away, leaving a space where something that he wanted stayed hidden, yet was plain.

'Why did you have to get Angela to telephone?'

'I didn't know your number otherwise. Angela's all right.'

'Now it'll be all over the school.'

'What will? A drive in my car and a bottle of coke?' He grinned with half his mouth. 'Relax, Ellie. We'll just talk. How come you live in Woburn Hostels?'

'It's my mother's job. She's one of the matrons.'

'Where's your father?'

'He's dead. He was beheaded.'

It made him look at her properly. She felt the same control she'd felt with 'immaterial', and kept her father off, kept him at a distance: a shadowy figure, not with or without his head, whom she was grateful to for helping her.

'Yeah?' Hollis said. Then, a little primly: 'Please explain.'

'I don't remember him. I was only two.'

'Was it in the war?'

'No . . .' He moved in close, her father, whom she knew only from his photographs — wedding ones, where he was bruised around the eyes with happiness; dance ones where her mother in hairdo and dress was at the centre and he merely Brylcreem and long knobby hands; and one with Ellie, aged two, on his shoulders. She thought she could remember holding his head between her palms. 'He couldn't go to the war because of his leg. He broke it playing football and it didn't heal right so he walked with a limp. It was too bad for the army even though he wanted to go. Anyway, he died after the war. He could be a railway shunter with his leg.'

'A shunter?'

'It happened in the Wellington railway yards. He was on the footplate, and he got off to run ahead and change the points and he tripped over. His leg was weak. The engine went over the top of him. That was my dad.'

She could not remember him. Her strongest memory was of a woman in a hat with a pin that looked as if it went through her scalp as well as her hair saying in a voice meant to be soft, 'His head was lying there like a ball,' and someone else saying, 'Sshh.' She could not even now, against the evidence of the photographs — his angled brow and springing hair — believe that her father's head was not smooth and round. It sometimes made her grin at the thought of him.

'That's really crook,' Hollis said.

'My mother still cries about him,' she said, and wondered at her compulsion to tell him things that were none of his business. 'She's only young. She's thirty-four. She should be married, that's what she says. I think she wants more children except me, but sometimes she says I'm her whole life. Then she says, "I shouldn't have said that, forget it, Ellie." It's why she goes out with men who aren't a patch on my dad.'

Hollis opened a packet of cigarettes. 'Want one?'

'No thank you.'

He lit up and flicked the match away. She could tell that he didn't know what to say; and thought, Well now I've done it. I suppose he wanted necking and I've told him about my life, and there's plenty more. She grew sorry for him, stuck with someone he hadn't bargained for, and she could guess how it made him small in his own mind, as if she'd told him to calm down and start again.

She took a mouthful of coke. 'So,' she said, 'what about you?'

'What about me?'

'I've told you some of my stuff, so you can tell me yours, about polio' — because his crippling was the most important thing: where

34

sitting in the rain began, and using floral curtains to dry his face, and wearing leather jackets and driving a pink car. It was where trying to pick up girls who were only fourteen began.

'What makes you so damn nosey?'

'There's a difference between nosey and interested,' she said. 'My dad had a huge funeral. All the railwaymen in Wellington came. But I can't remember anything about him. Not one thing. I was too young. How old were you when you got your leg?'

'Eleven.'

'That's —?'

'1947.'

'Was there an epidemic? I remember 1954.'

'Yeah, schools got closed. Some people died, because they didn't have good treatment then, not like now.'

'What happened to you?'

'Nothing much. I got carted off. Then I was in a wheelchair. I wore calipers. I'm OK now.'

'Did it hurt?'

'Yeah, it hurt. The treatment hurt.'

'What's polio?'

'Are you dumb or something?'

'Some people die and some just get crippled legs.'

'That's the way it goes.'

She saw he was pleased to have found that answer — a movie line. 'Baby' would have sounded right at the end of it. If she wanted to be kind to him, she would leave it there, let him win what had somehow turned into a contest; but if she did, it seemed that she would stop liking him because he would have chosen to be small — just his face, just his clothes, just his car — and she wanted to stay on the edge of love and had to have him rounded out for that.

'What do calipers do? Are they those iron things that go round your leg?'

'I don't wear them. Not any more.'

'What do they do?'

'Stretch the tendons.'

'So, does polio make your tendons short?'

'It wastes the muscles. The tendons stop working. Jesus, Ellie.'

'Are yours working now? Will they get better than they are?'

'No, they won't.'

'So you'll always limp?'

'Sure. Satisfied?'

She finished her coke. The answer was yes. He had made himself almost complete.

'What causes polio? Is it germs or something?'

'It's a virus. They've got stuff you drink now. Salk vaccine. Too late for me.' He put both hands on the wheel and held it tight. 'You want to know the worst thing? It's my parents.'

'Why?'

'I don't mind being crippled. It's no big deal. But Mum thinks I'm spoiled. Like a bloody bike, you know, that's got a buckled wheel. She doesn't want me any more.'

'She doesn't say that.'

'She doesn't need to. She used to be all over me when I was a kid, but now she doesn't even like touching me. She's always telling me to wash my hands. She went along to school after it happened. Dad told me, so it's true. She accused them of letting me play with dirty kids. You know, germs.' He held out his hands. 'Polio is working class, not for Primes. Even though I was at Scots College, in the prep.'

Ellie swallowed. It was getting close to too much, even though it made him flash with colours somehow.

'Your dad's all right, isn't he?' she said.

'Yeah, he's all right. He's just unhappy. He wants to get away and he can't.'

'From your mother?'

'Yeah, from her. But Primes don't get divorced. Not when they're partners in Endacott Prime.'

'Is that lawyers?'

'Yeah. My grandad started it with old Endacott. I'm supposed to go there.'

'Are you at the university?' Ellie said, surprised. 'Are you being a lawyer?'

'Maybe. What dad wants to do is build a yacht and sail it solo round the world. The solo bit is the bit he likes.'

'He's got a yacht.'

'That's just a mullety. It wouldn't get him out past Barretts Reef.'

Ellie shrugged. She wasn't interested in Mr Prime. I'm sitting in a car with a lawyer, she thought. That was unreal, because of how young he was, and how he was dressed, and his crippled leg, and because it meant his head must be full of stuff, laws and rules, that couldn't possibly be there. He had seemed no older than her, talking about polio.

'Is there a sort of apprenticeship for lawyers?'

'I do clerking. I've got another three years for my LL.B.'

She saw him draw back from the conversation, saw a shift in his eyes as he decided that what he'd said recommended him. He stubbed out his cigarette in the ashtray.

'Ellie,' he said, and took her hand.

'No, don't.'

'Why not?'

'I came for just a drive.'

His edging close and touching her moved him away. She tapped her empty coke bottle on his hand. 'What do I do with this?'

In answer, he grabbed it. He put his arm out the window and threw the bottle into the dark. A fracture, a splintering, came from behind the dune.

'Hey, it must have hit my one. Pretty good, eh?'

'Fluke,' she said. She opened her door.

'Where are you going?'

'To find them. You can't leave broken glass lying on a beach.'

'Ah, come off it.'

Ellie peered at him. It amazed her how small and bent he could become. 'You seem like fifteen not twenty-two.'

'A bit of broken glass,' he complained.

'Kids play here, don't they? Did you hear about the broken glass someone hid in the sandpit in a playground?'

'I wouldn't do that.'

'Wouldn't you?' She walked away.

'Hey, wait on.' He turned on the car lights. 'That better?'

She went over the top of a sandy rise into a hollow so heavily shadowed she thought it was water. Hollis limped behind her, lit up at first, then dark.

'Have you got a torch?' she said.

'I've got my matches.' He tried striking one, but the wind blew it out. 'Shelter me.' He got a match going, cupped in his hands; released the flame long enough to catch a glint of bottles on the sand. The wind, coming up the beach, full of damp, made the flame flicker and shrink, but Ellie had the bottles sorted out. She crouched by them.

'Strike another one.'

'They've got a guy who picks up all the rubbish. Just leave it to him.'

'Down here,' she said. 'Where I can see.'

One of the bottles was unbroken but the other lay in pieces, some so tiny they looked like crushed ice. She picked up the large ones and stacked them on her palm.

'Leave the rest,' he said.

'Ouch.'

'Leave them, I said. Jesus, Ellie.'

'Don't swear. Keep the match close.'

She smelled his breath: cigarettes. She smelled the cow-dung odour of his jacket. The car lights shone over the top of the sand dune like a sunrise. Everything was strange, and she liked it, even the sticky blood on her fingertips. She burrowed under the tiny bits of glass and picked them up on a layer of sand.

'We can leave the bottle.'

'You're not getting in my car with that stuff,' he said.

38

'There'll be a rubbish tin somewhere. I'll go along to the wharf.'

She went past his car on to the footpath and walked along to Petone wharf. The sea broke with muffled thumps on the beach, and the running waves hissed. No stars in the sky, even down harbour over the Eastbourne hills. Wellington glowed far away. It trembled and was alive. She wondered how she would paint all this: the dim wharf like thigh bones, the lighted street, two pedestrians, two parked vans looking as sticky as lollies spat out, and Hollis creeping after her in his car with his white face pasted on the windscreen. You would show the mountains by the weight of paint and Somes Island by using its three lights. Oh yes, she thought, carrying knives of glass in her palms, feeling bee-stings in her fingertips. She was on some sort of edge and a whole new view would open out — and yet she was here in the thick of something: Hollis Prime, his car, his intentions; her need not to let him, her need to be back with her mother in House 4.

'Come on, Ellie, for God's sake,' he said.

'Wait on.' She was filled with her picture, which broke up when she emptied the glass into a rubbish tin. It made a clatter, with a ringing aftersound. She wiped damp sand from her hands on to her skirt, then realised she had marked it with blood. 'Damn.'

Hollis Prime blew his car horn. She climbed in, slammed the door. 'I've got blood on my dress.'

'I told you not to pick the stuff up.'

'At least no one's going to get cut feet.' She wanted him to acknowledge what she'd done, not just to please her but to show he understood. The rightness of it set up a humming in her mind, as though she'd answered perfectly in a test at school. He was like a snag in a creek, with the water running easily around him — a hook, a finger, immovable.

'Can we go back now?'

'It's not even nine o'clock.'

'My mother will be wondering where I am.'

'Does she keep tabs on you like a kid?'

Ellie smiled at him. 'Well, I'm not twenty-two.'

'Bloody fourteen. I should have my head read.'

'Yes, you should. If you want girls to do it with, there must be plenty, I suppose.'

It silenced him, although he kept on throwing looks at her as he drove.

'I'd end up in prison with you,' he said.

She found this exciting but sad. She wasn't going to let him touch her, not even to kiss, and could feel how he wanted to, and feel a wanting in herself. Everything that followed would be easy. She wondered if when they got back where it was safe, by Woburn station, it would be all right to have just some necking there. He was interesting and good-looking and had a way of lop-siding his face as though his crippling had an effect up there. And he was twenty-two, so he would know how. She found herself wanting to be touched; she felt how delicious it would be, and so much stranger, so much more out of this world, than when she touched herself, which happened too often now. And yet he was all wrong, cut off by rules and by her instinct saying no.

They drove beside the railway line and came to Woburn station, where he parked in the shadow of a tree. Ellie grinned, remembering Dolores' advice: Always make your boyfriend park underneath a street lamp.

'Thank you,' she said. 'You can tell Angela we had a drive and that's all.'

'Hey, you don't have to go yet. Sit and talk a while.'

She felt as if their ages were reversed: that he was fourteen and she was teaching him; and it amused her, and made her sad, that only half an hour ago she had believed she was in love.

'I've got Dollie's rules.'

'What's that?'

'You don't kiss on the first date.'

'Who's Dollie?'

'My room mate.'

'Tell her to keep her sticky beak out.'

He took her hand, and she allowed it but said, 'You should go for girls your own age.'

'Ah, come on, Ellie.'

'No.'

'You know what you are, don't you?'

'What?'

'A cock-tease.'

'Don't you talk to me like that.' She looked at his contracting, pointed face. 'Are you sure you're twenty-two?'

Yet she was excited by the word. Her hand had jerked away and she wanted to put it back.

'It's because of my leg, isn't it?' he said.

'Your leg's not important. I would have come out with you again but I won't now.' She felt like crying. 'You should get an older girl.'

He surprised her by sighing and turning away. He put his hands on the steering wheel, stared into the long road leading to Waterloo station. 'Yeah, OK,' he said, not in agreement but telling himself, it seemed to her, that he'd missed what he had wanted and could stop.

'Thanks for telling me about your dad,' he said.

'That's all right. Yours too. He should build his yacht and sail away.'

'Yeah, maybe.'

'And your mother should get a job. Mine's got two.'

'You really like giving advice, don't you?'

'Why not?'

He took out his cigarettes and lit one, watching a unit pull into the station.

'What I reckoned was, I'd get your bra undone tonight.'

'Is that all you're after? I thought you might like me.'

'I do. Sure I do.'

'Did you say to Angela about the bra?'

'Jesus, I don't tell my sister stuff like that.'

'You'd better not. Anyway, I'm going.'

She got out of the car and looked across the roof. Dolores was walking up the ramp to the overbridge.

'Hey, Dolores,' Ellie yelled. She leaned into the car. 'Blow your horn.'

'What for?'

'Go on, quick.'

He pressed the horn. Dolores looked around. Her face seemed white, her tan coat white and her hair inky black. She looked as if she was on a ship sailing away.

Ellie waved. 'Over here.'

'Who is it?' Hollis said.

'Dolores. My room mate. She's supposed to be out with her boyfriend. He's Bevan Yates, the footy player.'

'Is she the one with Dollie's rules?'

'Don't say I said that.'

Dolores came down the ramp, clack clack in her heels.

'What are you doing here?'

'I went for a drive. I thought you were going out with Bevan.'

'Never heard of him,' Dolores said. 'Who's this?'

'Hollis Prime. He's a friend of mine.'

Dolores looked at him hard — and Ellie saw him as though he had an outline inked around him: crooked, sneaky, selfish, somehow unclean in his tinny car. It seemed a judgement on her that he was like that and she said, 'He's the brother of a girl at school.'

'Yeah,' Dolores said.

'We went to Petone for a coke.'

'Did you? Why's he dumping you here?'

'That's what she wanted,' Hollis said.

Dolores grinned nastily. Her clothes seemed to crackle and her skin glitter. 'Well I've got news for you, buster, you're driving us home.' She opened the back door of the car and got in.

'Hey,' said Hollis.

'Climb in,' Dolores said to Ellie.

'It's only a couple of hundred yards.'

'A gentleman always drives you to the door.' She relaxed in the back seat, but said, 'They're mingy cars, these. Have you got a smoke?'

Hollis could not find a come-back. He took out his cigarettes, tapped one halfway out and offered it.

'Thanks,' Dolores said. She waited for a light.

Ellie got in the car. She would rather have walked but something was going on and she wanted to see, and maybe stop it. She wished she smoked.

Hollis struck a match and lit Dolores' cigarette. It's like the pictures, Ellie thought: his cupped hands, Dolores' cheeks reflecting while her eyes stayed in the dark, and the cigarette coming to life.

Dolores sat back. 'You know where we live,' she said, instructing him.

'Yeah, I know.' Hollis started the car and made a U-turn.

'Nice drive?' Dolores said brightly to Ellie.

'Yes, all right.'

'I've had a lousy night. I can't wait to get to bed.'

Hollis drove across the railway lines.

'It's round there,' Ellie said. 'House 4. You don't have to go right to the door.'

'Yes he does,' Dolores said.

'Stop here. Stop, I said.'

'Make up your minds,' Hollis said. He stopped the car at the entrance to Hawkins Street.

'Thank you,' Ellie said. 'Thanks for the coke.'

'You're welcome,' Hollis said, watching Dolores in the rear-vision mirror.

'You can take me right to the door,' Dolores said. She smiled at Ellie. 'See you in a minute.'

Ellie closed the door. She knew half of what was happening — and would think years later how moments gained or lost, delays, hesitations, words spoken in the wrong way, could be instruments for changing lives, and how her own life had changed that night, and Dolores', and Hollis's too. The *chunk* of the closing door, the pink car

43

moving away, were sound and image of that broken step and of forward motion regained.

Dolores got out of the car and waited for Ellie at the House 4 gate. Hollis drove away.

'Never let them sell you short,' Dolores said.

'No.'

Inside she stopped at her mother's door. She put in her head and smiled at her, smiled at George, who was sipping tea and eating broken biscuits Mrs Crowther had brought home from the factory.

'Hello, Mr Brownlee. Mum, I'm going to bed.'

George put down his cup and made a comic salute. For the first time she saw how shy he was — winks and salutes, both uncertain, both shy. After Hollis Prime he was suddenly nice; but she still could not see how her mother could like him seriously.

'Have you got a kiss for me?' Mrs Crowther said. She was not false like this when she and Ellie were alone. 'Had a nice night, dear?'

'Yes, thank you,' Ellie said. She kissed her mother's cheek, which had a lovely coolness and a powder taste.

'Off to bed, then.'

She wondered if her mother would smooch with George when they said goodnight. How could she with a man who had ridges in his skull and a line of hair on his throat where his shaving stopped? It was off-putting. Worse than off-putting, it was gross.

She went to her bedroom. Dolores was sitting on her bed, rolling down her stockings.

'I'll have an early night for once,' she said.

'What went wrong?'

'Do you know where he tried to take me? His flat.'

'Didn't you know?'

'I certainly did not. He had a bottle of Pimms all ready and waiting. I took one look and said, "No chance, Bevan," and I left.'

'What's Pimms?'

'A leg opener. So they think.'

'What if he was going to propose?'

'I'd never marry a clown like that. All I liked was his car. The first night I went out with him he asked me what it felt like getting seen with someone famous.'

'He's not.'

'He thinks he is. Anyway, goodbye Bevan. I was mad at first but now I feel really good.'

Ellie found her sketchpad and tore out Bevan's picture. 'I did that for you.'

'Is it Bevan? God, it is. That's really him. I'll post it to him, can I? What right has he got to think I'm that sort of girl?'

Ellie went to the bathroom, then got into bed. Dolores, wrapped in her dragons, sat leaning on her pillows, reading a magazine.

She's beautiful, Ellie thought. Everything is easy for her. It isn't fair — her hair, her mouth, her eyes and her long legs, with ankles you could hold in your hands: none of it fair. Hollis Prime had shifted like a train switching points.

It enraged her in flashes, then left her detached, pleased that she didn't have to bother any more. Going out with him would have meant doing it, and then she'd get pregnant — it always happened. The baby would be adopted and she'd end up as a waitress in a greasy spoon — that happened too. She was going to be much better than a waitress. As well as that, Hollis Prime had insulted her. She felt the flash of rage again, remembering it.

'You couldn't have, anyway. It's your period.'

'What?'

'Got in bed with Bevan.'

'Do you think I would have, Ellie? God, I couldn't touch the sort of ears he's got. And he belches and doesn't even say pardon. How old is that guy Hollis, do you know?'

'Twenty-two.'

'That means he's only after one thing.'

'He didn't succeed.'

'It's a pity he's good-looking. He looks like James Dean.'

'James Dean doesn't limp.'

'What?'

'Hollis Prime limps. He's had polio. You get that from not washing your hands.'

'Did he have it bad? I mean, how much?'

'Like he's got a club foot. It would be easy running away from him.' She smiled at Dolores to show it was advice.

'What does he do?'

'He's learning to be a lawyer, so he says. I'm going to sleep. Please don't keep the light on too long.'

She turned on her side with her back to Dolores. If she didn't stop talking she would bawl. She was closest to it when she was being nasty. It wasn't because she liked Hollis Prime, but a feeling that something inside her was being twisted, and it hurt. My heart is being twisted, she thought, then grimaced at the corniness of it. Not her heart: her eagerness — people always said how eager she was — and her openness. She felt that she had lost something and would be smaller from now on. She certainly wouldn't trust any boy.

Dolores turned a page in her magazine. You can have him, Ellie thought, and I hope it hurts. Then she thought of her mother and George, and started to cry.

Dolores sat beside her and stroked her shoulder, thinking, of course, all the wrong things.

In the May school holidays Ellie's mother told her that she and George Brownlee were getting married.

'When?' Ellie said, terrified.

'We haven't set a date. Sometime soon. I want you to be pleased, Ellie. I couldn't stand it if you weren't pleased.'

Ellie said she was. She acted being pleased, with exclamations and hugs; and cried with her mother, neither of them loudly, with handkerchiefs dabbing their eyes. She was not sure why her mother cried, unless it was from having failed. She must have wanted someone better than George. The houses she had put rings around in the paper were ones he would never be able to afford. Love, she thought, was out of it. Love was impossible. The only time she'd ridden in George's taxi she couldn't believe how badly it had smelled — beer, sweat, cigarettes, fish and chips, upholstery vomited on, and some sickly stuff he cleaned it with: humanity, she wanted to say, but felt it was a word with another side and George didn't fit. Now, she thought, he'll be my step-father. She prayed, almost formally, that she would not have to call him Dad.

She wanted just to shake hands with him when he called that night. Instead he caught her in a bearhug and she felt her breasts squashed against a man who wanted to be liked, only that, and wanted ease and happiness. She endured him, smiled, promised herself that she would try. He wiped his eyes with long sweeps of the backs of his hands. She expected he would always be kind.

'Where will we live?' she asked her mother.

'George has got a house in Brooklyn. We thought we'd live there. It's not very big, love, but maybe later on . . .'

Oh, later on, Ellie thought; later on never came. What would come was moving from House 4 and changing schools.

'There's Wellington Girls' College,' her mother said. 'You've never liked Willowbank much, have you?'

'No,' Ellie whispered. She could not explain that liking and not liking were made up of shifting parts and what mattered was being in a place, being able to stand there and be certain. House 4 and Willowbank were inside her as well as outside and she did not want them rooted out. They were part of the picture she might draw of her life.

'What's the matter, Ellie?' Mrs Nimmo asked on the first day back.

'Nothing. Why?'

'You don't seem your usual cheerful self.'

This sort of remark usually annoyed Ellie, because it seemed to say she was simple minded, with nothing more to her than a laugh; but Mrs Nimmo meant everything exactly — it was a principle with her — and Ellie had learned to listen to what she said.

She concealed that her mother was getting married; said they were moving to Brooklyn which meant going to another school. Mrs Nimmo was the person she would miss, leaving Willowbank. Mrs Nimmo with her darned cardigans, wrinkled stockings, lopsided shoes; with her haystack hair and spectacles mended with sellotape. Her name among the pupils was The Baglady — a term Jenny Dodson had brought back from America (Jenny's father was a diplomat). Ellie wondered why a school like Willowbank, where the first instructions she had had were to smarten herself up and tone herself down, kept Mrs Nimmo on, especially as she made no secret of being a communist. (Not the Russian sort, mind you, after 1956.) Her lessons were full of things in pairs: exploitation/hunger, empire/oppression, brotherhood/peace, with stories that seemed personal to accompany them. Ellie loved the way they balanced out and made her *see*. She left these lessons with her mind buzzing, and sometimes with an anger she could scarcely conceal. 'Now off you go,' Mrs Nimmo said, stating no opinion, 'off you go to Divinity.'

Ellie topped the class in Social Studies. She did well in English and French. But although she enjoyed the stories in Divinity she could never climb above halfway. She did not understand how she could have faith: it seemed to vanish out the door every time she turned her eyes in the direction it should be.

'Don't worry,' Mrs Nimmo said, 'you'll find your own way. I'll be surprised if you meet any sort of god waiting at the end.'

Mrs Nimmo could get fired for stuff like that. It was even worse than communism, in a church school.

'I bet I don't find any teachers as good as you,' Ellie said.

She went to the pictures several times with fat Barry, the tennis player — not really fat and not only a tennis player, but she was going through a spell of exaggeration, of smartness and verbal savagery — held hands with him and let him buy ice creams. He walked her to the door of House 4, where they kissed because it was a part of going out. Ellie was relieved when he stopped inviting her, although he could be funny now and then — saying how all the tough guys must have to learn slow-motion so John Wayne could get his punch in first — and wasn't scared of serious talk about the things he liked, brass bands especially, where he played the cornet.

She sat on her bed and watched Dolores getting ready to go out. Dolores in her dragon dressing gown — red, green, orange, black — which made her look cheap and expensive at the same time. Dolores smelling sudsy from her bath, then turning sweet — lemon tea with sugar — as she put her make-up on. Shaved legs that must be as smooth as velvet to touch. Pink silk scanties you could see a dark vee through. She sat at the table and cleaned nicotine from her fingers with a piece of pumice.

'What does his leg look like when he's got his pants off?' Ellie said.

'Don't be nasty, it doesn't suit you,' Dolores said. 'And I haven't seen.'

'Where do you go? He can't dance.'

'Curiosity killed the cat,' Dolores said. She grinned at Ellie. 'At least I don't get my toes trodden on.'

The Morris Minor waited over the road, with Hollis Prime smoking patiently. His face lit up then faded the way jellyfish swelled and contracted. He did not climb out and open the door when Dolores appeared, as Bevan had with a manly flourish; and did not walk her to House 4 when they came home, which seemed to show they were serious. Ellie could not quite see whether he lit her cigarette in his mouth, Hollywood style, then handed it over. Probably not. After a time people had no need to be phoney.

'Are you getting serious?' she said.

'Who wants to know?'

'Me, Dolores. I found him for you.'

'You did not. I found him myself. In fact, we met.'

'Have you been to his house?'

'God no. I'm not going there.'

'Why does he still live at home if he's twenty-two?'

49

'There's nothing wrong with it,' Dolores flared. 'Anyway, he's getting a flat.'

Ellie hummed the wedding march, although her throat was thick and she almost cried. 'Flat' filled her with envy. It was such an exciting word.

'But he's not a Catholic,' she said.

'Oh, shut up,' Dolores said.

Ellie watched them drive away. Hollis the Morrie Minor, she thought. It was better than Bevan the Jag. Cars weren't everything, in fact weren't much, and pink was more interesting than black. And Hollis Prime was a mystery; he was more than one thing — which Dolores, bloody Dolores, was finding out.

George arrived in his taxi to take Mrs Crowther to a little gathering — 'What's a gathering?' Ellie said — in Upper Hutt. George the Stinky Old Taxi, she complained. She sat in her bedroom and read a book. Later on she went to the lounge and sang out-of-date songs round the piano with half a dozen stay-at-home girls. 'Gimme a little kiss, willya, huh?' they sang. 'What is this thing called love?' 'Who's afraid of the big bad wolf?' 'Am I blue?' It struck Ellie after a while that nearly all the songs were asking questions.

The taxi and the Morris Minor arrived back at House 4 at the same time. It was almost as if they'd had a race and the little coloured car had won. Ellie, kneeling on her bed, watched through an opening in the curtains. George escorted Mrs Crowther in and didn't stay, which relieved Ellie of the awful suspicion that her mother was 'doing it'. The Minor sat alone, with heads melting into each other, big long kisses and, she expected, busy hands too. She would have to see if all Dolores' buttons were done up, and knew that she would look with an appalled sort of wonder at her hands, if they had been touching him down there. She felt guilty watching, and a bit sick, and lay down and pulled the sheet over her eyes.

The car door slammed and the Minor plugged away. Mrs Crowther padded out to lock the House door, which meant that Dolores had got inside exactly on the curfew. Ellie heard them murmur, heard them laugh, which seemed like a betrayal. Her mother should laugh only with her. Dolores came in and turned on the light.

'What's the time?' Ellie yawned, pretending to wake.

'One o'clock. I feel like staying up all night.'

'I don't mind as long as you turn out the light.'

She did not want it out because she wanted to keep on looking at Dolores. She was flushed. She was smeary. She was, Ellie decided, remembering a line from a song, on cloud nine. If you got close enough you would smell sex on her, if sex had a smell — which it ought to, and probably not altogether nice.

'How's Hollis?' she said. He must be different with Dolores from what he'd been with her. Twenty-two. The number turned him hugely older suddenly, and made her almost shrink with fear at where she had been, who she'd been with on that night. He was utterly strange. Dolores was strange. Stockingless, barefooted, down to her slip, hair unpinned — she was on the other side of something, the other side of knowing; and Ellie felt tiny in her ignorance, but still with a kind of newness that made her feel she had not lost.

'Do you know what his leg looks like now?'

Dolores laughed. 'What's a leg, Ellie. Don't be a dope. Hey, he was telling me about his mum and dad.'

'I've met them.'

'He does their voices. You should hear him, especially his dad — you know, stuck up.'

'I liked his dad.'

'When his sister has parties he likes to sort of work the girls into a corner and stand close.'

'Who, Hollis?'

'No, dumbo, his dad. He tells them jokes, and everyone thinks they're going to be dirty but they're not. His sister keeps on calling out, "Daddy, stop." Do you want to hear one?'

Ellie was wondering why she hadn't been invited to the parties. A wider gap was opening, with the Hutt Valley in halves tilting away and the Primes on the other side.

'There was this family of skunks,' Dolores said. 'There was Mummy Skunk and Daddy Skunk and two little baby skunks called In and Out.'

'No, don't,' Ellie said.

'Wait. Wait. One day In got lost in the jungle and Mummy and Daddy searched and searched but they couldn't find him. So little Out said, "Let me try," and soon he came back bringing In. "How did you do it?" Mummy and Daddy cried. "It was easy," Out said. "In stinked."'

'Ha, ha,' Ellie said.

'That's what they all did. They groaned. And the sister said, "Oh, Daddy, why don't you go and sit in your yacht?" He keeps a yacht in the garage.'

'I know,' Ellie said. She felt a revulsion from Hollis Prime. He should not have let Dolores think the yacht was a joke.

'His mother was an actress, did you know? She used to be in amateur plays, she was always the "ingenoo". You should hear Hollis say it. She had to get kissed on stage and Hollis's old man didn't like it. But then she had to be the older sister and then the maid and she got all snooty and she quit.'

'Stop talking,' someone called from the next room.

'Cheeky cow,' Dolores said.

She made a left/right wriggle out of her slip, shed her bra, stepped out of her scanties and was wrapped in her dragons before Ellie could see if her body had been used — if it had known pleasure. The ideas contended as Dolores grabbed her toilet bag and towel and left for the bathroom. Used by him for his pleasure, or by her for her own? That left his body out of things, but Ellie shivered away from it as something white and damp — all of him, not just his foot. She almost cried again, with a swelling and choking in her throat, because love must be different from what she had imagined, because she must be wrong, she could not know, and because Dolores was so happy.

Another thing she could not imagine was Hollis Prime and Dolores married, even in a flat. When she tried to see one of them — eating at a table, washing dishes — the other became hazy. They were like two colours that wouldn't mix. So what was going on with them, in Hollis's car? Was there time to look in Dolores' scanties in the corner to see if there were marks on them, if they were wet or something, or had grains of sand?

No, she thought; said it: 'No.' It was disgusting. If she crossed the room she would come back different: all dark and wrinkled, with nothing worth having of her old self left. It was something she knew, even if she could not know about love. Ellie hugged her chest. She turned over and faced the wall and pretended to be asleep when Dolores came in.

'Night,' Dolores breathed.

The soft happy whisper made Ellie smile, and she was suddenly happy herself, softened by it, expanded as though her edges stretched and took in spaces outside herself. She wondered at how up and down she was, tripping as though in gutters one moment and standing on hilltops the next. It's interesting, she thought, and wonderful.

How interesting everything could be.

Ellie rode her bicycle to church in the morning. She did not often go because she could not find a religious reason for being there. It was as though there were something she reached for but could not hold. It made her skin seem rubbery and her fingers thick. But then there would be singing, and the priest and the choir would float up from the floor and take an inward slant like strokes in a painting. The coloured light from the windows, the sound of the voices and the organ, upheld them — and that was weird enough to count as religious, she supposed.

The sermon was a snake writhing from the preacher's mouth. It changed colour — red, gold, blue, then black for the warnings about sin. As for communion, 'begone' was the word that came to Ellie as she knelt. She wanted to pick the wafer off her tongue and nip her lips closed with her fingernails.

She fetched her bike from the side of the church.

'Ellie,' said a bendy woman, tilting her long brow.

'Hello, Mrs Prime. I didn't see you.'

Mr Prime was standing back, turning his hat in his hands.

'I wonder if you and I could have a word?' said Mrs Prime.

'Sure. I don't mind.'

'You must forgive me if I seem to pry. But I feel that it's my duty as a mother.'

'Yes, all right,' Ellie said, although it was not.

'We — Harold and I — have to take Hollis's best interests to heart, because of his disability, do you understand?'

'It hasn't got anything to do with me, Mrs Prime.'

'Yes, I realise. But he's inclined to be secretive and you are in a position to know. Because of where you live. There is a girl there, isn't there?'

'There's hundreds of girls,' Ellie said.

Mrs Prime's eyes grew bright. A little self-enjoying smile raised the sharp corners of her mouth. 'What I'd like to know is her name. Angela has told me that you share a room with her.'

'Excuse me, Mrs Prime. I've got to go.'

'I'm not asking you to betray any confidences. But Hollis — well, you've met him. More than once, I understand.'

'He's twenty-two,' Ellie said.

'In some ways Hollis is a child.'

'Madeleine, I think we should call it a day,' Mr Prime said.

'In a moment. Her name is Dolores, or Dollie, isn't it?'

'I don't know,' Ellie said.

'And she's a Catholic?'

'What does it matter what she is?'

'And also she's a goodtime girl?'

'You've got no right to say that. Her morals are better than your son's. Angela shouldn't tell you stuff I say at school.'

'And you, young lady, shouldn't be at that school. As far as I can tell you're straight out of the Mazengarb Report.'

'Madeleine, stop it,' Mr Prime said.

'Somebody has to tell the truth.'

Ellie swung her leg over her bike. 'I think you're barmy. And so's your daughter. So's your son.' She rode a short way, then stopped. 'Dolores is too good for him.'

I'll never go back to that church, she told herself. Yet she was elated, riding again. She had answered back in a way that almost seemed inspired. Dolores *was* too good and they *were* barmy, the truth was like an angel sliding on a beam of light. The Primes were crooked people and Dolores was beautiful — and she was too; she saw it as a kind of revelation: blonde and blue eyed, round and smooth, like an illustration in a religious book. Mr Prime had blotches; Mrs Prime had knobs on the back of her neck; Angela was all boney, and had pimples for breasts, and thought that doing ballet and coming top in French and saying 'très intéressant' and 'pour' and 'avec' all the time made her better than anyone else. As for Hollis Prime, he was crippled, which was a judgement probably.

'Mazengarb Report,' she said. Her mother still kept a copy somewhere. The government had sent one to every household in the country after the scandal four years ago, when teenagers up the valley had been caught drinking beer and having sex, and ones in Wanganui were dancing naked in graveyards and using bottles of fizz to stop getting pregnant. Ellie had read about it in *Truth*, but hadn't got far with the Mazengarb Report. It seemed to be asking for more religious teaching in schools and better moral standards — and it was one of the reasons why her mother had been so quick to shift her from Hutt Valley High to Willowbank.

Ellie realised how badly Mrs Prime had insulted her. For the rest of the morning she kept stopping suddenly and exclaiming until her mother asked what was bothering her.

'Nothing.'

'Well, calm down, you're making me nervous . . . It's not George is it, Ellie?'

'No, it's not. I like George. He's better than some people I know.'

They went for a drive up the coast after lunch. The taxi smelled better, which was Mrs Crowther's doing. Ellie enjoyed the way the hills came down so steeply and almost tipped the road into the sea. They walked on Paekakariki beach, George and Mrs Crowther holding hands. It embarrassed Ellie and she ran ahead, swerving to keep clear of waves sliding up the sand. When she looked back, her mother and George seemed like a girl and boy, except for the sun on his bald head. The happy couple, she thought. She wanted her mother to be happy and wished that George was better-looking so he could make sure of it. It was impossible to believe they were in love.

Mrs Crowther waved her back. The wind was too cold for them. They drove to Brooklyn, where George showed Ellie his house. It dismayed her — so small and dark. She had wanted a bungalow on the side of the hill, looking at the mountains across the harbour, but this was in a gully where the sun was gone at three o'clock and other houses stared from across the street. Brown little rooms with lino floors. George had lived here with his mother, who had died two years ago but left embroidered proverbs and biblical texts hanging on the walls — everywhere, every room — and a glassed-in sideboard full of crockery that looked as if she had thought it was the Crown Jewels. The bedroom Ellie would have was only eight feet wide — she measured with her arms when no one else was in the room — and had a mouldy smell in the walls like toadstools growing.

George made tea. Ellie was surprised her mother let him do woman's work, but it turned out she wanted to talk.

'I know it doesn't look much, Ellie, but George is going to do it up. He's taking two days a week off, starting tomorrow. He's going to paint it cream with yellow windowsills and do the whole inside with new paper and put some carpets down. And next summer we'll build a sunroom on, and maybe you can have it as a bedroom, I don't know. He'll do it all himself, Ellie. He's a handyman.'

'A jack of all trades,' George said, rolling a tea trolley in. He looked so friendly and so keen and Mrs Crowther smiled so nervously that Ellie understood how much she could hurt them. It came in a surge, like a wave: she could overturn their happiness. Already she had done it with her mother a little bit, put her off balance by the stillness she had kept on her face; and she knew she must not give in to a kind of greed she felt to do it more. Yet she did not want the job of making them happy; it was not up to her — to pretend and lie. She did not like the house. She hated it. And George was too ordinary, too simple, too plain.

'We've decided to get married in August,' Mrs Crowther said. 'The house will be done up by then, won't it, George?'

'Just you watch me,' he said.

'So you can do the whole term at Willowbank. That's what you want, isn't it, Ellie?'

'Yes,' she said. Then she could not help herself, she started to sob.

'Ellie. Oh, Ellie,' Mrs Crowther said.

'It's not you. It's not what you think.'

'Tell me, love. Let me help.'

'It's Angela's mother. It's Mrs Prime.' And suddenly it was, by a simple transfer. Disappointment turned into anger and poured out: Dolores and Hollis Prime (not herself and Hollis), Angela's blabbing, Mrs Prime's snobbery, and worst of all the Mazengarb Report.

'She thinks I'm some sort of goodtime girl just because I talked to her son. She thinks Dolores is chasing him and she's no good because she's Catholic. And because she lives in the Woburn Hostels.'

'What's wrong with the hostels?'

'I don't know. They're lower class.'

'They're good girls there. They're Christian girls. I'm going to go and see her. She can't say things like that. What did she mean, the Mazengarb Report?'

'I don't know. She thinks I'm like Dolores, I suppose.'

'Wait till I get her.'

'No Mum, don't. I shouldn't have told you.'

'You should let people like that stew in their ignorance,' George said.

'Who's this boy Dolores is going with? Is he the one in the pink car?' Mrs Crowther said.

'Yes.'

'She's not doing anything bad with him, I hope.'

'No, she's not.' Ellie was not sure of it — or if what her mother supposed they were doing was bad.

'I think it's time I moved you out from her. She's too sophisticated for you,' Mrs Crowther said.

'No she's not, she just likes make-up. Mum, I'm all right now. Don't do anything, please. We've only got three months and then we can go.'

Mrs Crowther's face was still pale. 'How dare the woman?'

'She's wrong, Mum. I'm not like that, I promise you. Mum —' she saw a way of being finished — 'can I choose the colours for my room? Can I, George?' It was the first time she had called him that. 'I want to paint the ceiling orange, as if the sun's up there.'

'You can't have an orange ceiling,' Mrs Crowther said.

'And I want some of the walls blue and the others green.'

'Like the sky and hills,' George said.

'Yes, exactly. I don't want a carpet on the floor, just plain floorboards. And a mat.'

'Purple,' George said.

'No.' Ellie laughed. 'Brown, I think. I'll help with the painting. I'd love to help. I can take some time off school.'

'Not in your School Certificate year,' Mrs Crowther said.

'But if she came on weekends?' George said. 'You can both come. I'll need as much labour as I can get.'

'Well, we'll see,' Mrs Crowther said. Ellie could tell how pleased she was. A flush had come on her cheeks, replacing the white, and she grinned at George, who grinned back. Ellie wondered if she should go for a walk in Brooklyn and leave them alone.

Instead they drank tea, then drove to Woburn. Most of the nurses were doing prep in their rooms, but Dolores had left a note on Ellie's bed: *I won't be in for tea. Tell your ma I'll beat the curfew.*

'By ten seconds,' Ellie said.

She ate her meal at the matrons' table and mimicked the elocution teacher at school demonstrating vowels. It made Mrs McDermott laugh, but several of the others frowned at her cheekiness. Mrs Crowther had to say, 'That's enough, Ellie,' looking pleased.

Dolores came in at half past nine.

'How was it?' Ellie said.

'I've got a bone to pick with you.'

'Yes?'

'What's the idea of talking about me with his sister?'

'What happened?'

'His la-de-da mum thinks I'll get him in trouble. So he told her he was leaving. And he will. He's packing up.'

'Will you go with him?'

'I've got a course to do, remember? What did you tell her?'

'Nothing much. Just your lipstick and that. And shaving your legs. And your dresses.'

'That's not all.'

'I told her some of the stuff you said about boys.'

'Like what?'

'Like — well — she thinks to get a baby the boy has got to leave his thing inside the girl all night. So I told her what you said about spunk and stuff.'

'Just because I know doesn't mean I do it.'

'I didn't say that.'

'She's one of those little bitches who tells their mother everything. So mummy's bossing Hollis to stop him seeing me. Calling a halt is what she says: "It's time you called this whole mistaken episode to a halt."' Dolores smiled savagely, flashing her teeth. 'That's when he told her he was leaving.'

'Well, he should. He's old enough.'

'Don't get smart. I'm not pleased with you.'

She was pleased with something, Ellie saw.

'Did she say about being a Catholic?'

Dolores frowned. 'That's got nothing to do with them. Why don't you go to bed, Ellie? I don't want to talk to you.'

'OK.'

'You don't know how nice he can be.'

'No, I don't.'

'Drop dead.'

Ellie changed and got into bed. She turned her back because Dolores, in spite of being angry, still wanted to be watched. She's like an apple, Ellie thought, ripe and red on one side and black spot on the other. Not black spot for sin, of course, or anything like that, but for vanity and temper. Dolores was perfect in her way.

In the following weekends she helped George and her mother with the house, which meant she could not play for the Willowbank hockey team. The gym mistress lectured her on school spirit, but Mrs Nimmo, passing, winked at her. Ellie kept away from Angela Prime, who was suddenly growing tall like her mother and making actressy gestures with her hands. 'Quelle surprise,' Angela kept saying, and, 'C'est magnifique.' 'Isn't England the most important, Mrs Nimmo?' she asked. 'Why do we have to learn what Hindus eat?'

George took down his mother's embroidered texts and the matching photographs of his parents in black oval frames over the fireplace. He bought a painting from a furniture shop — a thatched cottage in a valley, smoke from the chimney, cows in a meadow, a workman trudging home, his wife and child waiting to greet him in the door. Ellie kept quiet. She helped him hang it.

'Up a tiny bit on the left.'

'I never thought I'd get married,' George said.

'Why not?'

'You get into a way of thinking, It won't happen to me. Mum kept on saying, "Why don't you bring home a girl?" I never could with her living in the house.'

'You should have gone to live somewhere else.'

'It's funny how you don't. How you get scared. And people make you do things without trying to. You can't bear to make them unhappy.'

It sounded pathetic to Ellie, and she said, 'I'll paint you a better picture than this one day.'

'Don't you like it?'

'It's too pretty.'

'I thought pretty was good.'

'Too pretty, I said. How did you meet Mum?'

'She got one of her migraines at work and I'd just dropped a fare off there, so I got the job of taking her home. It was luck.'

'A migraine's not luck.'

'Luck for me. I helped her inside and made her a cup of tea, and then I started coming back and we got friends. All I want to do is make her happy.'

'Don't you want to be happy yourself?'

'I will be. I am.'

Mrs Crowther came in. 'What are you two gabbing about while I work? Oh, George.'

'Like it?'

'It's beautiful.'

And goodbye mum and dad, Ellie thought, looking at the oval frames face down on a chair. 'Beautiful' annoyed her. Her mother only used it because she was happy and thought it was the sort of thing you said about a painting. She had no artistic sense; but she was trying, like George. Ellie hoped neither of them would try too hard. It would be interesting to see who ended up boss with each determined to put the other first.

She went back to the bedroom, where she was stripping the wallpaper, a job she enjoyed. It came off in heavy strips — I'm done for, it seemed to say — and Ellie felt cruel and satisfied. She imagined the new colours she would blot out the past with — this brown old dusty past where people grew scared and lived in oval frames and said what they believed with embroidery. George's idea of a purple mat might not be bad.

A southerly brought rain day after day. Crossing the overbridge, Ellie saw the wet suburbs stretching away: red slick roofs, brown tiled roofs, bare trees, black evergreens. The three-storeyed buildings of Lower Hutt appeared and disappeared in shifting curtains of rain.

The river overflowed and flooded a street of low-lying houses. Drains blocked and made a lake outside House 4. The nurses had to take off their shoes and stockings and hitch up their skirts and wade to the station.

Ellie went to Wellington after school to buy winter shoes. She hated walking around Kirkcaldies in her Willowbank uniform, and was sure the saleswoman was putting on an upper-crusty voice and giving little smiles of secret understanding. What was it they were both supposed to know that girls in different uniforms did not? I should tell her I'm leaving to be a waitress, Ellie thought. 'Ah oui, très intéressant,' she said, inspecting shoes. The saleswoman did not understand French.

At the station Dolores was not with the nurses getting on the unit, so Ellie waited for the next. Hollis Prime's pink car drove past the taxi rank to the parking lot. Ellie watched from the station steps. Dolores and Hollis were either telling jokes or quarrelling, the way they moved their heads, the way Dolores worked her hands. Telling jokes, Ellie hoped. She was in favour of happiness, and of anything that would upset Mrs Prime.

Dolores got out and slammed the door. A quarrel. She stalked into the station, stern and cold in her belted coat — sophisticated — and Ellie edged with small steps round a pillar to avoid being seen. She followed Dolores on to the platform.

'Fancy meeting you,' she said.

'Go away.'

'I've been buying shoes. Want to see?'

'No, I don't. And I want to sit alone if you don't mind.'

'OK.'

But in the carriage she took a seat beside Dolores. 'It's crowded,' she explained.

'Just keep quiet,' Dolores said.

The unit ran along the edge of the harbour on the earthquake fault line that always made Ellie imagine a tingling from pressures underground running up her spine. The unit could be swallowed in an instant. Dolores looked as if it would not bother her.

'How's Hollis?' Ellie said.

'Mind your own business.'

'He hasn't shifted out from home, has he?'

Dolores made an ugly sound, metallic, in her throat. In a moment she said, 'Flats are too expensive, if you must know.'

'I thought you said he was packing up.'

'Well, he's unpacked. All right?'

'Yes.'

'Is that enough information? Do you want some more?'

'No.'

'Just as well. Now leave me in peace.'

Hollis's car appeared in Oxford Terrace as the unit pulled in. He had driven fast.

'Dolores,' Ellie said, nudging her.

'I'm not blind.' She strode up the ramp but turned left instead of right.

Ellie looked back at Hollis Prime by his car. He was hunched and crumpled in the rain: miserable, monkey-like. She shrugged at him to let him know she sympathised, but wasn't sure he'd seen. She would have liked to go down and push him back into his car out of the wet, ask him what the trouble was, tell him it was childish to stay home with his parents, no matter how much it cost to rent a flat.

Dolores went into House 4 and into their bedroom. She took off her coat and shoes and lay face down on her bed.

'Can't you go somewhere? Just for once I'd like to be alone.'

'What's the matter, Dolores? I thought we were friends.'

'I haven't got any friends.'

'You've got me.' Ellie sat on the bed. She put her hand on Dolores' shoulder and stroked it for a moment, then slid her fingers under her hair on to her neck. Dolores shivered.

'Don't. It's cold.'

'I'm sorry you've had a quarrel.'

Dolores was quiet: a long moment that grew round and thick, coiling like a snake. 'It's worse than that,' she said.

Ellie took her hand away. 'Yes. I suppose you're pregnant.'

Dolores turned her head deeper into the pillow.

'How long?'

'Only two weeks.' She rolled on to her side and looked at Ellie, her face tear stained. 'But I'm never late. I've never been late in my life.'

'Wait till next month,' Ellie said. 'Mum says you can miss two or three times in a row.'

'Not me. I thought it was safe. We only did it when it was safe. Or I made him stop.'

Ellie stood up.

'Don't go all prissy on me,' Dolores said.

'I'm not. Have you told him?'

'That's what we were talking about. He doesn't know what to do. He just says wait, like you.'

'Get married,' Ellie said. It sounded like an order. She softened it. 'When you're sure.'

'I'm sure. It's like I've got something stuck inside me.'

'You shouldn't have done it,' Ellie said. *I* didn't, she added to herself. She was moving between cruel and satisfied one minute and wanting to take Dolores in her arms the next. Left and right — she couldn't stop turning.

'Get married,' she said again.

Dolores turned her face into the pillow. 'I don't think he'll ever marry me.'

'But he's got to,' Ellie said.

'You tell him. Tell his mother.'

'What's she got to do with it?'

Dolores sat up. 'I sometimes think him and me, we're only about her.'

64

'But she hates him, because of his leg.'

'Who told you that?' Dolores crossed her arms, making her shoulders small. 'I know what she'll try and make me do.'

'What?'

'Never mind. Just go away, Ellie, and leave me alone.'

'Are you coming to tea?'

'Do you think I can eat when I'm like this?'

Ellie went to her mother's room and showed her the shoes. She spoke carefully, enunciating, in case information should slip out. Dolores would be expelled, in a hurry too, if anyone found out she might be pregnant.

At school next day Ellie came top in a short-answer Social Studies test, which seemed a step towards a place where things might work out. She stayed behind to talk with Mrs Nimmo.

'Can I ask you a question?'

'Yes, of course.'

'It's private.'

'It won't go any further than me.'

'Well —' it was hard — 'is there something you can take if you've missed your period?'

'Oh Ellie, Ellie,' Mrs Nimmo whispered.

'No, it's not me. Truly it's not. I promise.'

'Which one of the girls?'

'No one here. That's a promise too. It's one of the nurses at the hostel.'

'Ellie, do you mean it? It's not you?'

'No, Mrs Nimmo, I've never done it. I'm not going to either, for a while.'

'Don't. Please don't.'

'I don't want to get pregnant,' Ellie said.

'Good girl. That's good. But — who is this other person? Why did she tell you?'

'I've got to keep it a secret. But she's upset. So if I can just tell her something to take . . .'

'Have you told your mother?'

'No, because —' she almost said 'Dolores' — 'this girl, she'd get kicked out.'

'How late is she?'

'Not much. A couple of weeks.'

'Tell her to wait until next month. It might be all right.'

'I did.'

'Ellie —' Mrs Nimmo ran her hands through her haystack hair. 'I'm not supposed to talk to pupils like this. I'd get the sack.'

'I'm sorry.'

'I really would.'

'I won't tell anyone.'

'Go to your next class. I need some time to think.'

'Don't worry, Mrs Nimmo. You can just forget it if you like. She's a Catholic, by the way.'

'Oh dear.'

'I wish things could be simple,' Ellie said.

She felt a hunger for simplicity, it would smooth things out and narrow them, instead of all the widening and mixing taking place — like a river rolling silt and trees and boulders down its length.

She went along to English — another test. One of the questions was: *'Oh —, —, wherefore art thou —?' Fill in the spaces and say who is speaking.* She felt sorry for Juliet, who had problems like Dolores, and did not like her being used in such a stupid way. Came top again, and was glad she would have good news for her mother that night. It did not seem there would be good news for Dolores.

Mrs Nimmo caught her by the gates after school.

'Ellie, come here.' They stood close together with overlapping bikes. 'Tell your friend — and this must go no further.'

'Yes, Mrs Nimmo.'

'I don't know how to get it and I don't know how much — but tell her to try stil boestrol.'

'What's that?'

'I don't know. Ellie, I know nothing. And that's all.'

66

'How do you spell it?'

Mrs Nimmo hissed. She leaned close. 'S-t-i-l b-o-e-s-t-r-o-l. I've got to go now. Ellie, I'm trusting you with my job.'

She rode away. Ellie felt like yelling 'thank you' after her. She wanted to tell Mrs Nimmo that her job was safe. And she felt that she should ask if stil boestrol was dangerous with a name like that.

She rode to the library and looked it up in a dictionary. All it said was: Powerful synthetic oestrogen derived from stilbene.

Stilbene was: Aromatic hydrocarbon forming phosphorescent crystal.

That was no help, although aromatic sounded nice.

Oestrogen was: Sex hormone or other substance capable of developing and maintaining female characteristics of body.

She could not see how it would help Dolores, who didn't need developing in that way. There must be chemical things she could not understand.

She borrowed some romances to celebrate coming top in English, but changed her mind about a travel book for her mother, who would have to stay home now that she was getting married.

'Top in English, top in Social Studies,' she sang when Mrs Crowther came in.

'Ellie, that's wonderful. Where in Maths? Where in Divinity?'

'They're next week. I just come top in the important things.'

'I must tell George. He's clever too, Ellie. He's very clever with his hands.'

That annoyed Ellie. She went to her bedroom and sat on her bed, where she sketched George with a tiny head and apish hands. He was tying a complicated knot. It was cruel and she crumpled it up when it was finished. She was sorry for her mother, having to find good things in George and point them out. Then she drew Dolores pregnant, dropping tears as fat as bantam eggs on her swollen stomach, but she tore it up and carried the pieces out to the boiler-room fire, as much because it was too sad to look at as from fear that Dolores would arrive unexpectedly.

She watched out her bedroom window as the nurses came down the ramp from the overbridge; and there was Dolores, striding in front as though leading, or as though pursued. Why must she always be alone? It was not just from her sense of superiority, but surely from something in her that said, or only whispered, the opposite. Her determination was so hard, so unnatural, and her contempt so overdone. Ellie felt a hunger to know the rest of Dolores' life, not just whether she married Hollis and had a baby and settled down, but how she grew old, how she turned into someone whose life had been happy or sad. She felt on the edge of knowing her own life, as though she might step through with Dolores, through a door, and find it there, wide and endless, on the other side.

Yet she was going to lose Dolores in a month, when this intake of nurses moved to another hostel and a new batch took their place. She would not even have her for the last few weeks of her own stay in House 4. Dolores had become, in only five months, the closest friend she had ever had. Now events were turning them out of each other's lives. The door that they might step through closed with a non-reverberative thump.

Dolores came in. 'What's this, an ambush?' She was flushed and windblown and out-doorsy, not the least bit like a goodtime girl. 'Oh, my feet,' she said, kicking off her shoes. 'I don't think I'll be a dental nurse, standing up all day.'

'No,' Ellie said. 'Did you have any luck?'

'No, I didn't. Just forget it, Ellie. I don't want to be asked.'

Ellie swallowed. This was hard. 'I talked with someone today,' she said.

Dolores turned sharply from the wardrobe. 'Not about me?'

'I didn't say any names. I just said I knew a girl who was late.'

'That's stupid. People can work things out . . . Not your mother?'

'No.'

'God, if you tell her —'

'I won't. This was someone who said — stil boestrol. I can spell it if you like.'

'Bugger you, Ellie. Just bugger you.'

'It changes your hormones or something.'

'Everybody knows that stuff. It doesn't work. You'll be saying gin and hot baths next.'

'No I won't.' She wondered what gin and hot baths did. 'I was trying to help.'

'Well, don't.'

'So — what can I do?'

'Just be my friend, that's all.' Dolores lay down. She turned her face to the wall.

'I am,' Ellie said. She sat on the bed, wishing she could hold Dolores' hand. After a while she said, 'I'll go away if you like.'

'No.' Dolores turned her face, pale and sharp. 'You don't understand. I'm a Catholic.'

'I know.'

'Doing things like that, taking stuff, it's a mortal sin. I'd go to hell.'

Ellie felt her mind shrink. Everything she might answer went away. She stroked Dolores' shoulder, and tried to picture hell, which hardly ever came up in Divinity. Jesus descended there in the Catechism, that was all. Ellie had not thought people really believed in it, just that it was something old, kept to add interest. Dolores' warm shoulder should be — was — a total denial of devils and all that horror stuff.

'I've got a headache now,' Dolores whispered.

'Shall I get you some aspros?'

'Yes please.'

Ellie fetched them from her mother's room and a glass of water from the bathroom. She watched while Dolores swallowed — her throat, the way it worked. There was no hell, she was sure of it; and she knew she would remember this moment all her life: Dolores, teary, beautiful; the water in the glass; and hell contracting to a point and vanishing. Was there any way of getting rid of it for Dolores too?

'What will you do?'

'Wait.'

'How long?'

'Until next month. Then I'll know.'

'You'll be gone next month. Dolores?'

'What?'

'Make him marry you.'

Dolores gave her the glass and closed her eyes. 'Maybe,' she said. 'Turn out the light.'

Ellie got up and turned it out.

'Now lie down with me. No, not on my bed, just on yours.'

'Like this.'

'Yes, that's right. Don't go away for a while.'

'I won't.'

Presently she heard Dolores sleeping. She got up and let herself out of the room and went to dinner.

She still thought stil boestrol had been a good idea.

The best part of living in Brooklyn was travelling to school on the tram. It swayed down out of blue or rainy skies into streets that turned away her loneliness — footpaths full of people and cars with honking horns. Back home her mother tidied the house, moving with exaggerated care while George slept after his late shift. 'Make as much noise as you like,' he told them, 'it takes an earthquake to wake me,' but Mrs Crowther — Mrs Brownlee now — had turned caring for him into a principle and morning silence into an activity. Her fingers stood at her lips, making it hard for Ellie to kiss her goodbye.

She liked her new school, close to the station and the harbour and parliament. The sound of trains shunting and coupling in the railway yards made her think of her father, whom George had not driven out but set more firmly in place. The ships leaving harbour blew rude noises that made the girls in the playground giggle and smirk. They were no different from Willowbank girls, and Ellie made friends with

70

her classmates easily. Give and take, chatter, confession, sharing, sympathy had always been straightforward for her. Her only regret was not having taken Art for School Certificate. The art room was better than the one at Willowbank and the teacher believed in colour as well as pencil lines.

Sometimes in the afternoon she walked up Lambton Quay and Willis Street before catching her tram. She turned down Mercer Street to the library, and read magazines at a table, then borrowed novels and art books to take home. One was about an artist called Modigliani and she kept it in her room so her mother would not see — the nudes were so naked and someone had written alongside one: *Modigliani painted this from the cunt outwards*, which shocked her at first but then grew interesting. She had not known you could think about art like that.

She caught the tram at Perretts Corner, not wanting to walk past the dental nurses' school. Girls she had known stood inside the windows, drilling in children's half-open mouths, and none of them would ever be Dolores. They had hugged each other, stood at arms length, hugged again, and Dolores had patted tears from Ellie's cheeks with a handkerchief. They had promised to keep in touch, meet at weekends, telephone — and after a week Ellie had phoned.

'I'm sorry,' said the woman on the switchboard at Kelburn Hostel, 'Miss Wood doesn't live here any more.'

'Where is she? Where's she gone?'

'We can't give out addresses. She didn't leave one anyway.'

'But, do you mean she's left the dental school?'

'I understand from the other girls she has. Who's speaking please?'

'I'm a friend. Has she gone home?'

'I'm sorry, I don't know. She only stayed here two or three days.'

Ellie waited for a call. It never came, either in her last week at Woburn or in Brooklyn. She found herself trembling at what might have happened to Dolores. She imagined that the Primes had locked her up, or sent her away on a white slave ship, even that they had murdered her — and when she was more sensible, imagined her living alone in a little room, working as a waitress, waiting for her baby to be born. That made Ellie tremble even more, and made her angry with Dolores. They had promised to keep in touch.

Perhaps, she thought, she's run away with Hollis Prime. They might be living in Auckland or in Christchurch. They might be married. Mrs Prime! Hollis would have to learn how to be a Catholic. But why hadn't she written to tell Ellie?

The orange ceiling shone like the sun but the blue and green walls were oppressive. How long did she have to live with her mother and George, who pressed on her and smothered her and already, she was sure, were calculating: where would a new baby sleep? It was not yet *the* new baby, but from the way they kissed hello, goodbye, smiled with complicity, rubbed and touched each other, and the sounds that came from their room, sex was off to a good start and it — *the* — wouldn't be long. Ellie supposed she should be glad for them, for their happiness; but in fact she felt disgusted about a man in his forties and a woman of thirty-five being so eager for all that newly wed stuff. She felt they should be cool with each other and sedate, almost that they should shake hands. How could her mother sit on his knee and rub her palm on his bald head the way she did? Once she had seen her wet a bit of it with her tongue and polish it.

She missed her mother riding in and parking her bike and sitting across from her in their tiny lounge reading from travel books: Canada and Tibet and Brazil. She felt she could not tell her about the girls and teachers at school, and clothes she would like to buy and jobs she would have, and worries about being fat and about her ankles — too thick — and the new cold sore on her lip. Her mother had changed her focus and Ellie had somehow lost her right to speak.

She missed the hostels: the screams and tears and laughing, piano playing, community singing, the practising of dance steps, the hostel dance, the ping-pong tournament, the dining room, women who said grace while others winked, stampeding footsteps on the stairs, girls blowing kisses from bedroom windows, cars full of boys honking by, the exodus in the morning and invasion at night, and running through the rain to the Prince Edward, a dozen of them like a hockey team, and walking back in the dark saying how the picture had been dreamy or scrumptious or a waste of time. She wanted House 4 back, and wondered if she would be allowed to shift to a hostel when the baby was born. It — he, she — would be happy in her room, with the orange ceiling keeping it warm. And she would be away from her mother, whom she loved — whom she *loved* — but who was driving her crazy with George.

She worked hard to get to the top of her class in Social Studies but couldn't beat half a dozen other girls in English. Thank God there's no Divinity, she thought. No one seemed to mind the voice she had learned at Willowbank so she became unconscious of it, until the English teacher complimented her on her vowels. That took a bit of getting over. There was no one at the school like Mrs Nimmo. 'I prefer Charles Dickens to Jane Austen,' Ellie wrote, 'because he was on the side of the common man. The servants in her novels remain invisible.' The teacher wrote: *An original thought* beside it, but did not give her a high mark.

One day she saw Barry Abbot the tennis player crossing Willis Street in his Scots College uniform. She got off the tram and walked back casually to meet him.

'Oh, hello.' Her cold sore was gone. She felt like kissing him from pleasure at seeing a Hutt Valley face.

'Hey, Ellie. How's it going?' he said.

'OK.'

'I heard you'd changed schools.'

'Yes, Wellington Girls' College. I like it there. They don't make us wear gloves.'

'Ha,' Barry said. 'Do you still play tennis?'

'I might start. What about you?' He was thinner, he was losing his fat. She hoped he would ask her to the pictures. They walked down Willis Street to Lambton Quay. She was finding him quick and humorous, and tried to think of funny things to say.

'Is Angela still going out with Rex who loves himself?'

'No,' Barry said, 'she's going out with me.'

'Oh, well,' Ellie said, 'très bon.' Her voice seemed to turn up at the edges. 'Give her my love.'

'She said you used to go out with her brother.'

'Just once. He's a bit of a pill.'

'He's had polio.'

'Yeah,' Ellie said. 'Who needs Limpy?'

She wanted to ask if Hollis lived at home, if he had a girlfriend, but knew it would get back to Angela. The Primes took up a lot a space. They took what they wanted. She said, 'Does Angela wear a proper bra yet or only singlets still?'

'Hey, go easy,' Barry said.

'I thought you'd know.'

'Come off it, Ellie.'

She could see that she had interested him. You could get any boy with a bit of sex. But so what? She would catch the next Brooklyn tram that came along.

'Do you want a milkshake?' he asked.

'No thanks. I've got to go.'

'Things have been pretty grim,' he said.

'With you and her?'

'No, at school. You remember Robert?'

'Who?'

'He was umpire in our tennis match.'

'Oh, him.'

'He hung himself.'

The footpath lurched and she put out a hand to steady herself. Watches in the shop window jerked into a time where she did not want to be.

'Are you all right?'

'What happened?'

'His father found him in the garage. He had some rope tied over a beam.'

'But why?'

'He was shy,' Barry said. 'I think he was mixed up about — stuff. I liked him though.'

'About sex?'

'Yeah, I guess. He couldn't get girls. He couldn't even go to dances. Because — you know.'

'Yes, I know.'

'He quit school. He just used to walk round by himself. I don't know if there'll be a funeral. I hope not.'

'Why?'

'I reckon I might . . .' He might cry.

'I only met him once,' Ellie said.

A Brooklyn tram was swaying up the street. She wanted it to carry her away. Yet she would climb aboard with Robert's death and keep it with her wherever she went because, one afternoon, he had sat on an umpire's stand watching her play. That meant she could not turn away.

'What was his second name?'

'Morton. Robert Morton. We never called him Bob.'

'This is my tram.'

'Can't you come for a milkshake?'

'No, I'm sorry. See you, Barry.' She liked him because he might have cried, but did not like him because it would not last.

The tram took her up the hill to Brooklyn. She got off at her stop and walked towards home, carrying Robert Morton's death. She could not understand such pain: despair so deep you had to throw a rope over a beam . . . Her father's death had been natural, even right compared with this, although it had been an accident. She thought, I've got to laugh, pretty quick, or else I'm going somewhere I can't turn back. She felt in her schoolbag and found a half-eaten sandwich wrapped in greaseproof paper. It was peanut butter and honey, which she'd left after two bites because it made her fat. She took another bite and felt the gluey texture and a lovely sweetness on her tongue. She held it there, crumpled the paper and dropped it by her feet.

'Please don't drop litter in our street,' said a woman walking by. She was small and beaky and carried a knobbled walking stick as thick as her wrist.

'If you don't like it, pick it up yourself,' Ellie said. She sat on the mudguard of a parked car and started to cry.

'What's the matter with you?' the woman said.

Ellie swallowed the bread and honey in her mouth. 'Someone's died, that's all,' she said. She closed her mouth tight and let tears run down her cheeks, then hunted for her hanky to wipe them off.

'I'm sorry,' the woman said.

'That's all right. I didn't mean to be rude to you.'

'That's my husband's car you're sitting on.'

Ellie stood up.

'Do you go to church?' the woman said.

'I used to.'

'I think you should talk to your minister. They're the best when somebody has died.'

'Thank you,' Ellie said. She took a big breath. Crying worked better than ministers. She picked up the piece of paper and wrapped it round the rest of her sandwich. 'It was nice of you to let me sit on your car.'

'I think you're a wee bit brash, my girl,' the woman said.

Ellie shrugged. She walked home, feeling she had taken possession of Robert Morton, swallowed him — but was jolted, almost sickened by the sudden desire she had to draw him hanging on a rope. He was alive like me, she thought, looking at her hand, working her fingers. What might be allowed was to draw his face.

The telephone rang before she could start — rang as she came in the door — and she stopped outside her room, listening to her mother saying, 'Yes . . . Yes, she is. Hold the line, please,' in the switchboard voice she would probably never lose.

'Ellie, it's for you. Someone from school.'

'Hello,' Ellie said.

'Don't say my name. Pretend I'm someone else,' Dolores said.

'OK. How's it going?' She spoke in a calm voice although her heart beat hard and her throat swelled as though there was a breath that would not come out.

'I was holding my nose. Did she know?'

'No.'

'I'm sorry I haven't rung before. I've been away.'

'Where?'

'In Christchurch. I only came back yesterday. Now I've got to go again. It's my last night, Ellie. Can you meet me in town?'

'I suppose I can.'

'It'll only be an hour. Say you're going to the pictures.'

'Yes, I'd like to,' Ellie said, knowing her mother was listening in the kitchen.

'There's a coffee shop called Man Friday in Dixon Street. Meet me there. Half past seven, is that all right?'

'Yes, all right. Thanks for ringing.' She hung up.

'Who was that?' her mother said.

'Gail, from my class. We're going to the pictures. I'm meeting her for some coffee first, is that all right?'

'Coffee will keep you awake.'

'I'm not a kid, Mum. I'm going anyway.'

'I never said you couldn't.' Her mother wanted no trouble. She only wanted harmony, with George, who just lately had a new name, He.

'He'll take you in his taxi when he goes to work.'

'No thanks, I'll go by tram,' Ellie said.

She went to her room. She could not draw Robert Morton any more — she did not understand why she had wanted to.

The Man Friday was crowded so they went to the library and found a seat in the newspaper room.

'Where are you going?' Ellie asked.

Dolores was as slim and sophisticated as ever but Ellie had felt a thickness when they embraced, so the baby was still there. Weight had melted from her face, that was the only obvious change. Lips as red as ever, eyes as bright — an artificial brightness, as though she had squirted drops in them — but a kind of shaving off in diameter. The plumpness that had let her use kind looks wasn't there. Pregnant women, Ellie thought, were supposed to get fatter not thinner in their face. She could see that Dolores had been suffering.

'Where are you *going*?'

'A sea voyage,' Dolores said. 'I'm getting used to them.'

'Where?'

'Sydney. I'm going on the *Wanganella*, leaving in —' she looked at her watch — 'three-quarters of an hour.'

'With Hollis?'

'Who's that? I don't know him,' Dolores said.

'What's happened?'

'I'm three months pregnant, nearly four, that's what. They sent me down to Christchurch on the ferry. There's a chemist down there who does abortions.'

'Who sent you?'

'The bloody Primes. Mr and Mrs, not their son. He's twenty-two and he lets them boss him like a kid. It's a wonder he doesn't go into the bathroom and take down his pants and wait for daddy with his razor strop.'

'You didn't have one though?'

'No, I didn't. I had no intention. But I thought I might as well have a holiday.' Dolores grinned. It was like a display of teeth. 'Then I rang up and told them I wasn't going to do it. I got Mrs. "You're a nasty underhand dishonest girl. We've washed our hands of you." I told her to put on her old man.' Dolores grinned again. 'I could have him if I wanted.'

'Who?'

'Harold Prime. Of Endacott Prime. Have you seen their brass plate in Featherston Street? There's a woman comes out with a rag and shines it every morning.'

Ellie could not keep up with her. As well as her tongue her eyes were darting.

'Mrs knows it too.'

'Knows what?'

'That I could steal her hubby. But all I want is some of his dough. I've got it too.'

Ellie felt so close to her — her face, her smell, her hands twisting one against the other in her lap — and yet so far away from what she said. Dolores had gone years ahead, into something ugly and grown-up, and out to one side of being grown-up.

'How much?'

'Five hundred pounds. Five hundred, Ellie. I'm rich. And my ticket to Sydney. I told him I'd have one over there. Lots of girls do.'

'An abortion?'

'Yes, but I won't. He even found an address for me. And made an appointment. Lawyers can do all sorts of dirty stuff.' Dolores drew her head back as if from something smelly. 'They think they can make me kill my baby.'

'Where will you have it? Over there?'

'Probably. Yes.'

'And then what?'

'I haven't thought that far ahead.'

'If you could get Hollis on his own . . .'

'Shut up about him, Ellie. Just shut up.'

They sat quiet for a moment. People in the reading room sent furtive looks at them. Dolores took Ellie's hand: 'I'm sorry. Let's get out of here before I start bawling.'

They went out into Mercer Street.

'Where shall we go?' Ellie said.

'Down to the ship. I've got to get on board anyway.'

'Where's your luggage?'

'I've only got a suitcase. I took it on before I met you.' She looked at her watch. 'We better get going.'

They walked down to Aotea Quay. People were crossing from the station to Queens Wharf, darting in the traffic as if they were late. Dolores strode like a man, high heels or not, and Ellie had to walk fast to keep up. She did not like the way it made her feel fat. Then Dolores stepped into a doorway out of the wind. She lit a cigarette and came out and strode again.

'There's four girls in my cabin. I bet they're going for the same reason as me.'

Ellie was jealous. She wanted to be in the cabin too, and walking on the deck with Dolores — but not in Sydney, not when the baby was born. What would happen afterwards? She was frightened to ask.

'Will you write to me?'

'Probably.'

'Will you come back to Wellington when it's over?'

'God no. I've had enough of this place.'

'I suppose you'll never be a dental nurse now.'

'I never wanted to be one anyway. Looking in people's mouths.'

Ellie felt herself getting angry. Dolores had asked for her, but was behaving as if she was on the other side.

'Have you told your parents about all this?'

'Are you mad?'

'What do they think, then?'

'They think I'm in Christchurch. We don't write letters very much.' She threw her cigarette into the street. 'Dad would kill me,' she said.

They reached the station and crossed to the wharf. 'Do you want some advice, Ellie?'

'I suppose.'

'Keep your legs crossed. It's only rooting and shagging anyway.'

'I don't believe that,' Ellie said.

'They do. Men do.'

The ship stood as straight as a wall beside the wharf. Up there, high up, passengers leaned smiling, shouting, waving, on the rails. The knots of people looking up — white faces, more serious than the ones on board — seemed to be waiting to be fed.

'I told you once I was a cow,' Dolores said.

'You're not all the time.'

Dolores laughed. 'Well, that's something.' She kissed Ellie. 'I didn't want to go all alone. I wanted to have someone waving to me.'

'I'll use both hands,' Ellie said.

'See those girls up there. One of them's wearing a turban, see? I'll bet she doesn't know what's happening. They're my cabin mates.'

Ellie thought Dolores didn't know what was happening.

'I'll go up there beside them. Will you stay?'

'Yes, I'll be here.'

The *Wanganella* gave a loud blast on its whistle. 'Oh, shut your mouth,' Dolores said. She hugged Ellie. 'Goodbye.'

'Goodbye,' Ellie said.

She watched Dolores walk up the gangplank, neat and brisk and sure of herself. Ellie was the only one who knew it was a lie. In a few moments Dolores came out beside the girl in the turban. Ellie watched her hunt among the faces. She moved away from people and criss-crossed her arms. Dolores smiled and shouted. She was like that actress, Ann Blyth — so beautiful, but with something hidden all the time. Something sad, and cruel as well, waiting to come out. She looked excited, like a girl starting on a world tour — London and the changing of the guard. Not Sydney and a baby. Waitressing.

The gangplank went up. The ship eased out from the wharf as though something huge and silent with no moving parts was pressing inside. Dolores' face blurred in with the others and she was gone, although her arm signalled up and down in a stately way — sophisticated now and not excited. Ellie was choked with feeling but was switched off at the same time. That was that. She waited until she was sure Dolores would not be able to pick her out.

People were turning away, unsteady some of them, a little stunned. They did not look as if they knew what to do. Ellie walked among them, swerving in and out. She passed a shadowy angle at the end of a shed, where someone with a white face spoke to her — pronounced her name softly, as though he was ashamed.

'What do you want?' she said.

'How was she? Was she all right?' Hollis Prime said.

'I don't think that's any of your business.'

Yet her heart was swelling again, the way it had when Dolores telephoned. A minute ago she would have said Hollis was easy to understand — randy and selfish and weak. Now he was a mystery again. She did not believe in him as a mother's boy, with his widow's peak and deep-set eyes and mouth fixed in a painful smile. His crooked teeth. She would have liked to see him walk, see him go up and down on his limpy foot.

'It's your baby. You should have married her,' she said.

'I would have, Ellie. I wanted to at first.'

'So what went wrong? Mummy told you not to, I suppose.'

'Is that what she says?'

Ellie looked at the *Wanganella* turning away. The passengers had gone inside, into cabins somewhere, and the ship seemed bare and cold and set in a direction. Dolores would not write, Ellie knew.

'I don't want to talk about you and her,' she said.

'We gave her plenty of money. She got a lot from Dad.'

'To have an abortion. I suppose you think that's easy?'

He looked at people passing, and wet his lips. 'Ellie,' he whispered, 'what it was, I didn't like her enough.'

'She was just good enough to go to bed with, do you mean?'

'She was the one who started that. I'm not a ratbag, Ellie. I came down to see she got on the ship all right.'

'So you could get rid of her.'

'To see if she was happy, if you want to know.'

'And do you think she is? Why didn't you go and talk to her?'

'You were there. Anyway, she wouldn't want me . . . You don't know how tough she is. Mum thinks she'll keep on asking for more money.'

The harder beating of her heart had stopped. Now she felt only rage. He was so bent and twisted, so shifty in his eyes and mean in his mouth, and ugly inside.

'Ellie, I've got my car. I can give you a ride.'

It should have been him hanging, not Robert Morton, she thought.

'What do you say?'

She turned away, walked away, but spun around, lifting her shoulders, stretching her throat. She shouted at Hollis Prime: 'You should get a girlfriend with a limp to go with yours. Then you could have limpy kids.' She ran across by the front of the station to the tramstop. A Brooklyn tram was leaving and she jumped on board, ignoring the motorman's shout. She walked to the other end and sat down. That's finished Hollis Prime, she thought. But she felt sick and did not know whether it was from anger or from Hollis himself, leaning close to her, or from losing Dolores and knowing all the things she had to go through. Things she had to go through herself? 'No I won't,' she said out loud.

'You stick to that, girlie,' the conductor said.

She bought a ticket. The tram took her up the hill to Brooklyn. She got off before it ran down to the shops, and scrambled up the bank over the road from Central Park. The *Wanganella* was turning out of sight round Point Jerningham. It was the only moving thing. The half moon shone on the water, turning it white.

Ellie saw where she lived — the whole wide high place where she lived: city, harbour, mountains, sky — and suddenly it seemed natural, Dolores going away, and everything that happened, natural, held between water and sky like things in a bowl. People shifted, re-arranged themselves, then changed again, making different patterns and different stories, and everything that happened to them, love and death and babies, was there to be looked at and understood, even if some of it was cruel.

She did not know what she had discovered, it was too quick and went away; but did not leave her empty, just shifting between happy and sad. It was as though she had eaten but was hungry; so she watched a while longer, until the ship was gone.

Waving would be childish. She smiled instead, then pulled her coat around her and started up the hill, trying to remember, then forgetting. She pushed her hands deep into her pockets to keep warm.

With George at work her mother would change into Mrs Crowther when Ellie came in and want to know why she was home before the pictures came out. It would be easy to lie; but why not tell the truth and see what happened?

Ellie missed good talks with her mother.

Between times

1959. ELLIE RETURNS to Wellington Girls' College after passing her School Certificate examination. She welcomes the birth of her half-brother Andrew in mid-year, and surrenders her bedroom gladly for the new sunporch, where she paints the walls yellow to encourage the sun. Her schoolwork fails to improve. There is no Mrs Nimmo to excite her and she decides not to go to university, which relieves her mother, who worries about money more and more. Ellie applies for Teachers' College but is advised to spend another year at school. She is perhaps a little immature, her form mistress says. It annoys Ellie, who believes she knows a good deal more than most of the girls who get in.

1960 is hard and full of quarrels. Mrs Brownlee is pregnant again. Andrew wakes often in the night, and Ellie has to help with him because she has the knack of calming him down. It is not a job she wants, except at times when love for Andrew chokes her. George's Presbyterianism revives and he believes Ellie should be made to go to church, which she argues against and will not do. She leaves school halfway through the year and gets a job in a library, which she comes to enjoy. Her mother refuses to let her go flatting, but Ellie gets her way a month before the baby is born. It's a girl, Heather. Ellie, in a flat in Thorndon with three girls older than her, finds it less easy than living in a hostel. The house clogs up with boys, some of them hers, and everyone seems irresponsible. She sometimes seems to be the most mature one there, although she can be the noisiest.

1961–63. She completes the part-time course at the library school. She has her first successful love affair and completes that too. The man — he's not a boy — does not exactly want to marry her but does not want not to marry her. She knows what she thinks about it: won't be tied down yet. No thank you. His name is Tom and he's good-looking and good in bed — delicious love-making is a phrase Ellie uses — but he's indecisive, the sort of man she will call a wimp later on. Part of the satisfaction in love is falling out of it, almost as good as falling in. She is free again and, not being hurt or disappointed, does not need to throw her diaphragm away. (Had found a broad-minded doctor to fit her with it, an Austrian.) She babysits for her mother now and then. She moves to another flat where the morals are not so loose although the noise is just as bad. One day she sees a newspaper photograph of Harold Prime's yacht — bigger than *Surprise* — preparing for a Wellington–Auckland race. One of the crew members is Hollis Prime, but because the photo cuts him off at the waist Ellie cannot see his crippled leg. The young woman standing by his side doesn't get a name. She's very pretty. Ellie is reminded of Dolores. She writes a card, *Hey, remember me?*, and sends it — *Please forward* — to the Masterton address where Dolores' parents live. There's no reply. Ellie will never see Dolores again. She joins a tramping club: loves fording rivers and reaching mountain tops. Dark valleys and overhanging bush make her uneasy. She does not like the feeling of being locked in.

1964. Ellie takes a job in the Army Department library. She could easily fall for some of the officers who come in but they are married — there's an ease she likes in married men but it has a wall you can't climb at the back of it — so she goes out with a driver for a while but drops him because he's limited, or thick in the head. She learns that good looks are not only not enough but can be used to hide deficiencies. She has not met a man yet who wants to talk to her. Some of them don't even like it when she laughs.

1965. In her summer holidays Ellie and five others complete a tramp from the Lewis Pass to Lake Rotoiti. It's country mapped only round the edges, with no tracks. She has never felt so happy or so free. Keep pointing north. Follow the ridges, trek down tussock hills, cross shingle slides opening into huge wide-open valleys, drink at creeks, climb again. She wants never to do anything else. After ten days they find the Sabine, and Ellie, who has not brought a sketch pad, draws the St Arnaud Range — its bare tops and midnight bush — in the leader's trip book. She washes in the river, where the cold takes her breath away. She cannot understand why she lives in a city. As they walk on the track by the lake and find the lodge she feels something slipping away, some knowledge that was peace and excitement hand in hand. She feels a sob in her breast at the sudden emptiness and knows that she must leave Wellington. The resolution lasts although it puzzles her after a while. She quits the Army Department and takes a job as borough librarian in Taumarunui, where she makes friends. The peace and excitement of her 'long march' fail to return. She does not really expect them (although she does not forget) but believes she has read a signal that sets her in motion after standing still. That is the important thing about 1965. There's a man friend too, whom she enjoys. He is not a nobody but does not need a name, although she remembers it in the list she amuses herself with later in her life. She sees no reason why a woman should not have as many lovers as a man and thinks it might be fun to aim for a hundred (she's had six so far);

but the extravagance of the number causes more distaste than amusement and she decides the right number is one, no matter where he comes in the list. She is not sure she will ever find 'one'.

1966. She leaves her job and joins a small shearing gang as a fleeco. They work on Lands and Survey blocks along the Wanganui River and in Tongariro National Park. There's a gun shearer and his wife (she's cook and rousie), two youngsters aiming for their two hundred, two fleecos and a presser. It's a happy gang. Ellie likes hard work, although she wakes on her first night, sits up in her bunk and throws a fleece, then falls back asleep, and can hardly drag herself to the shed at 5 a.m, she aches so much. She gets a quick crush on the second shearer, a Maori boy who is so handsome she can almost taste him. She would love to wrap him into herself. It's the first time she has gone for someone younger — and he won't look at her, has a girl back home. Soon they're just friends — so Ellie says. She has a sad and happy four months. Draws him but makes him far too pretty. Ends by drawing hills and river instead, sheep and dogs, the men at work, but doesn't much like anything she does. The lanolin in the wool has made her hands as soft as dough. You need hard hands for drawing, she believes. Soft in some way means insensitive.

1967–68. Ellie works at the Chateau in January. It makes her laugh — she's a waitress at last. Then it's back to the gang for second shear. She's been saving hard for an overseas trip although she is not sure why she is going. Everyone does, and she's getting old, twenty-four, and will have to think soon about what she's going to do with her life. She doesn't want to stay a librarian, it's too much indoors. She doesn't particularly want to be married and have children either, especially after helping with her half-siblings. Her mother is pregnant again, unexpectedly, and is frightened of having a baby at her age. Ellie feels bad about going away. All the same, she goes. It's London, where everybody starts. A month is enough. She heads for the country, works in hotels in the Scottish Highlands and on Skye. Winter drives her back to town, and London is better now. She lives in a house in Fulham with seven others — New Zealanders, Australians, a South African — and takes part in demonstrations against the Vietnam war. She tries to get to know some English people. Class makes it easy with some and hard with others. She comes to see class as poisonous and doesn't want to do the Kiwi thing of cutting through — just keep away from it. Ellie oversimplifies and does not get to know as many people as she should. In her second summer she goes north again but it doesn't work this time. These are not her hills. She has a look, moving on, at France and Italy and Spain — hard work backpacking among the hordes of young. She loves what she is seeing but comes to hate the way it must be done. She hates the way money rules everything and how people are always trying to get it out of you. They're lost behind their need and greed for money. It spoils Paris and Rome and Madrid, but cannot spoil everything. Goya, in the Prado, knocks her backwards several steps. She stands there stunned, with her skin stripped off. So that is what painting really is. It is knowledge for her to carry home. She is glad that she has found it at the end of her stay . . .

Good Life

'You've got so thin,' her mother said. 'Ellie, you're not in some sort of trouble?'

'I've never been fitter,' Ellie said.

She would have liked to say 'freer' as well, but landing in New Zealand had squeezed her between two hands — all the things she'd done, and what she might do next — and she couldn't move. Yet she had to and didn't know in which direction. It made her want to put things off, and put them off again, because she might choose a way she couldn't get out of.

'I didn't like it when you got arrested,' Mrs Brownlee said.

'It was only a demonstration. We sat down and wouldn't move, so they threw us in a van and carted us off. There were more than sixty of us in court, so don't worry, Mum. I only got fined one pound.'

'But they might have your name written down. They mightn't ever let you go back in.'

'I don't want to. I'm a New Zealander from now on.' The declaration failed to set her free; she still felt hands shoving and clutching — unbalancing her, constricting her.

'Is there someone you're fond of?'

'A man, do you mean? No there's not. Don't try and make me get married, Mum. I'm not ready yet.'

Nearly twenty-six: she could see her mother about to say it, and did not want it said because it butted blindly, not with her lack of a man — there was no failure there — but with the need somehow to secure herself, hold herself steady, then move on.

'What happened to that one you went to Scotland with? The foreign one?'

'He was a German. He had a girl back home.' All the same, she'd added him to her list. 'We climbed every mountain on Skye. Not that they're real mountains; they're only pimples.' No, she told herself, don't be cheap. They were great hills and good climbs and wonderful days, and dangerous too, with the sort of weather they have there. 'I had a good time in Scotland. And Werner was nice.' But what, she thought, do I do now?

She babysat. She took Andrew and Heather to the pictures and the zoo, went into town on weekdays pushing Derek in his pushchair to give her mother a rest. Sometimes on Lambton Quay she passed people she knew, and twice stopped to chat — a Willowbank girl, an ex-dental nurse. 'No,' she explained, 'he's not mine, he's my brother.' She did not want to have a child like Derek, who had a milk allergy and was raised on soy milk, and who was, putting it plainly, unattractive. He was watchful, slanted, pinched, always damp in his nappies, on his skin. She hated accumulating words like that, impressions like that, for a little boy who was not well, but could not find, when she picked him up and tried to make herself fond of him, any warmth to match the warmth she tried to show — so became attentive, fussy, verbal, diligent, and told herself, It's not for long.

George was kind to her, but with a sadness caused, she supposed, by the things he suspected she'd been up to. He was a storeman not a taxi driver now. The better hours freed him more for his family. He was bone-tired, but also pleased, and would have said if anyone had asked him, 'This is what I wanted. A wife and children.' Ellie tried not to think about it — the price you paid, the things you got, the new lives, the open mouths, the noise and work and anger and the never-failing love. Her mother was almost as good at love as George. Ellie did not want to be locked up with them.

'I think I'll go tomorrow,' she said.

'Where?'

She had not thought about it, but the place had come to her in town when she saw new-season's apples in a greengrocer's shop.

'Down to Nelson for the apple picking.'

'Oh Ellie, that's not a job.'

'It's hard work. I like hard work.'

'But — your future?'

'I don't think in those terms, Mum. Things will look after themselves.' She could not believe she'd said that easy thing, that stupid thing, and she blushed. She was sorry for her mother too — so worn with her own hard life, yet so concerned for her. 'Hey Mum, don't worry. I'll probably get a library job soon. But I want a bit of sun. I've just come out of an English winter.'

'I had you when I was nineteen,' her mother said.

Ellie almost answered, 'Times have changed'; wanted to say, 'Women don't have to have children any more'; yet was confused. She did not want a Derek but remembered the love she'd felt for Andrew ten years before. 'Mmm,' she'd said, nuzzling his downy head, 'mmm, you're mine.'

'Well,' she said, 'we'll see.'

Her mother and George had shifted Derek's cot into their bedroom. Ellie slept her last night in the room with the orange ceiling and the blue and green enclosing walls. Brooklyn thumped its gates and clanged its fences in the wind. She did not feel at home, and she wanted a home, where she would not be buffeted and nudged all the time and made to feel she'd missed a step she should have taken. She wanted to be easy and sure, and then she would find out what came next.

She took the morning ferry across the strait, caught a bus in Picton and slept the night in a youth hostel in Nelson. Backpacking again: in Europe it had seemed natural, but it made her feel out of step here, as though she should hide her nationality. There were Dutch and German travellers in the hostel. She found she did not want them, she wanted New Zealanders, and supposed the orchards would be thick with foreigners. She had chosen wrong and should be back in Wellington, going steady at twenty-five with some steady man — yet when she lay in her bunk in the dark and tried out that future, her mind slid through it and came out the other side. So stop all this head stuff, Ellie said, get out to Motueka and find a job.

She caught a bus in the morning and waited until it ran beside the sea before getting off. There was no hurry; the apples would not fall off the trees. She took off her sandals and walked on the sand and began to feel at home. Cold lapping sea, open water, baches made of corrugated iron and fibrolite, rolling hills, orchards, sheep, mountains in the distance on two sides: although she'd never been here she recognised the place and began to feel a humming in her chest as though a hive of bees was there wanting to get out. She walked into the water up to her thighs, then ploughed back, looked around for people, dropped her clothes beside her pack and ran into the sea. It was like getting baptised, full immersion. She dived and followed her hands down and swam along the sand, where shells slid under her like stars; came up and stripped her hair back behind her ears. Like being saved. She rolled and swam, with salt touching everywhere and changing her flesh — touching in her head with a stinging freshness, turning warm. Ellie floated. Cars went by on the road, too distant to see her pleasure or nakedness. She stayed until the skin on her hands began to wrinkle. It was like growing old in a place where you belonged.

At midday, dried and warm, she shouldered her pack and walked back to a store the bus had passed, and bought a pie.

'Are there orchards round here where I can get a picking job?'

'Are you one of those flower people?' the shopwoman asked.

'God, no. Do I look like one?'

'You can go about a mile along the road. That's where the big orchards start. You should have gone to the Labour Department, though. A bus load from there came out this morning.'

'So I'm too late?'

'There's plenty of work if you're any good. Try Jim Barchard.'

'Where's he?'

'Go back and take the first on your right and keep on walking. He's about two miles.'

She walked into low hills, eating her pie and drinking coke. The sea kept on getting lost and coming into sight, and she hoped she would be able to see it as she worked. The Abel Tasman coast and the Nelson coast made two arms in which she could see muscles work. Everything was warm and alive. The pine trees had a tangy medicinal smell and the blackberry and gorse flowers by the road were honey-sweet, astringent, contradictory in a way that made her feel rounded out.

She passed through farms and orchards, looking for 'Barchard' on a mailbox. Pickers stood on ladders in the trees. The winey smell of apples filled the air. Bins of Coxes Orange waited in crushed grass beside clay roads and open gates. Drunk wasps crawled and hovered. Ellie supposed that getting stung would be part of the job.

She found Jim Barchard's box in a mis-matched pair at the top of a rise. A dirt road ran beside a row of pines to a villa above a paddock where half a dozen black and brown sheep grazed. That must be Anerdi and Webster, the owners of the mailbox with rainbows painted on it. Barchard's was made of creosoted planks and was large enough for a watchdog or a goat. His drive ran down the hill to dark-green hedges encircling a red iron roof. Ellie heard a tractor coughing in the apple trees that dipped and flattened out beyond. She walked down the drive and found a packing shed behind the house. The tractor sped into the yard and speared an empty bin on its front end. The driver saw Ellie and throttled back. He grinned at her.

'Looking for work?'

'Yes. They sent me at the shop. Apple picking.'

'You done it before?'

'No. I've been a fleeco. I can work.'

'A fleeco, eh?' He eyed her. 'I've got a full team. You'll have to do some work in the shed.'

'I don't mind that.'

'Dump your stuff in the hut then. You had your lunch?'

'I had a pie.'

The man laughed. He looked in his sixties and was unshaven, grizzle-haired, with a dirty woollen cap on the back of his head. He got down from the tractor and led her round the side of the shed to the pickers' hut.

'Girls here, blokes over there. I won't have any dope-heads, OK?'

'I don't smoke dope. I don't even smoke cigarettes.'

'There's a fridge in the kitchen. You can bring some beer in, it gets hot work. But no one gets boozed.'

'That's all right with me,' Ellie said. She liked the man. He wasn't being male or trying to make her feel like a girl. Maybe it was because she ate pies.

'Sixty cents an hour. I'll take you down to the gravvies first so you can get the hang. You got other shoes?'

'I've got boots and sandshoes.'

'Sandshoes. You get a wasp in sandals and you'll jump. What's your name?'

'Ellie Crowther.'

'I'm Jim Barchard.' They shook hands. 'No sloping off after a couple of days.'

'I'll stay as long as you like.'

'No promises from my end. We'll see how you go. Bathroom down there, dunny out the back. Grab a bag at the shed when you've unpacked and come on down.'

There were three beds in the room. Ellie put her pack on the one that seemed free. Pressure had glued her shirt to her back. Her feet were dirty and her hair sticky with salt but she felt clean inside from the sea, so she pulled on her sandshoes without socks, found her cloth hat in her pack and went outside.

There were two women grading and packing in the shed. One of them, Jim Barchard's wife, gave her a canvas bag and showed her how to buckle it on. Ellie went into the Gravenstein trees and learned how to pick — palm underneath, lift and twist; how to work a ladder; how to empty her bag into the bin so the apples would not bruise. Branches kept knocking her hat over her eyes. Discovering not to wear it seemed a big step — trade secret perhaps, because the boy in the next tree gave a broken-toothed grin. 'Hats are a pain in the arse. Watch out for wasps.'

'I am.' She did not want to talk, just work, learn what to do. At tea break Jim Barchard transferred her to the packing shed.

'Sore shoulders, eh?'

'Yes.'

'They'll ease up.'

No one was going to treat her gently. Dorrie Barchard was short-tempered, teaching her to pack; and the other woman, Sheila — Sheel — a local, was smug about her own speed and contemptuous of townies.

'It's a piece of cake after the woolshed,' Ellie said.

She picked all next morning, then graded and packed. Dorrie Barchard was grumpy but fair and told her she was learning quick. Sheel offered shallow friendship, which Ellie accepted, so they got on. She was happier in the trees with Jim and Mike and Boggsie and Janice and Fiona. You did not have to talk; you related to your tree, the weight of your bag, the slant of your ladder, and grinned now and then at a face framed in leaves in the parallel row. She ate half a dozen apples a day. It was like eating the sun, eating something alive that didn't object. Holding an apple before biting it, she understood why painters did still life — for the shape, the colour, the connection, for the taste. A jar or bowl might taste in a similar way, even though empty and cool.

'You're a dreamy sort of sheila,' Mike said.

'I pick more than you,' she snapped.

'Got a temper too.'

It was true she picked more. By her second week she was faster than any of them, and just as quick as Sheel in the shed. Dorrie Barchard started smiling at her.

'We got ourselves a cracker,' Jim said.

On one of her trips into Motueka she bought some pencils and a sketch pad. It seemed that when she liked a place she found the need to draw. She sat in the grass by the pine row and drew the orchard leaning down the slope and flattening out, the hills like arms, the sea like a plate, the two coasts and two mountain ranges — all parallel and neat, with too much likeness. She had not let things be themselves. Even the trees, frothing in the hollow, were foam in a bath. She turned the page and started again. It did not work. She could not get her mind, her feelings, her pencil point in tune. She had drawn better at the Woburn Hostels ten years ago when it had only been for fun.

Ellie went back to the kitchen, where Boggsie and Mike were drinking beer.

'Saw you up there,' Boggsie said. 'A bit of an artist, eh?'

He tried to take her pad, but she jerked it away. She did not like Boggsie, who had a handsome upper face, domed forehead and strong nose, but was soft and self-pleased in his mouth. If she was stuck on likenesses, it was curled and wet, like a slug.

'Why don't you draw me? I'll pose.' He rolled his shoulders, swelled his biceps, gave a yellow-toothed smile.

'No thanks,' she said. His name was Helsby not Boggs. The nickname had come from the speed with which he'd dug a longdrop once. 'The Bogdigger' changed to 'Boggsie', which he kept as a compliment to himself — so Mike said.

Ellie liked Mike. She wished he would fix his broken teeth.

'They don't hurt,' he said.

'How did it happen?'

'A friend of mine's starting a commune over in Golden Bay. I was helping him build an A-frame and he got me with a lump of four by two, fair in the mouth. He's accident prone.'

'You sound like the one who's accident prone.'

He had grown up in Christchurch and was twenty-six, not the boy she'd thought him at first sight.

'I've got half a BA,' he said. 'All the dropouts come apple picking.'

'How long have you been doing it?'

'Started at school. Seventeen. I came up with a mate of mine who was on probation. You can do that if you call at the cop shop first. There's lots of guys here on probation, and a hell of a lot of others who don't want the cops knowing where they are. That year the taxi driver got murdered, the orchards just about emptied out overnight.'

He was trying to impress her and she liked him less.

'Come to the pictures in Mot,' he invited.

'Get your teeth fixed first. Is Boggsie on probation?'

'That'd be telling. Hey, I like your drawings. I never knew sheilas could draw.'

'I might do one of you one day.'

'I promise not to smile.'

He sat outside on warm nights and strummed his guitar while Fiona sang. His own husky voice, a little frail, joined in, but he was happier with accompaniment, coming second. Boggsie had a better voice but wanted dirty songs and grew sulky when no one would sing with him.

'I don't like him,' Fiona said. 'He comes out to the dunny when I'm there. He tries to pretend he doesn't know.'

'Tell Jim. He'll fire him,' Ellie said.

'I don't want to get anyone fired.'

Boggsie had a small truck with a rounded aluminium roof over the tray. He called it a housetruck and claimed he lived in it between jobs, but all it contained was a dirty mattress and some apple boxes full of gear. He persuaded Ellie and the two girls to go to Motueka with him for the Saturday night dance. None of them would sit in the cab with him, which he took, after a moment, as a compliment. He had later in the night on his mind.

Janice and Fiona were Christchurch girls earning money in the university holidays. Ellie was amused by their knowingness and innocence — a dangerous combination, she thought. Their jokes about Boggsie's stained mattress could not conceal their curiosity. She thought he would get the plain one, Janice, before long and wondered if it was her place to interfere.

She wanted to leave the dance after only an hour. Every picker in the district seemed to have come and she felt wedged in, unable to free her arms, pressed on by fleshy hands and palpating air.

She danced with a man who tried to talk her outside for a drink, then with one, half drunk, who rubbed his loins on her, and spent the next two dances avoiding them. It was better when the band played music she could twist to. She gyrated in a corner with a tall tattooed self-absorbed boy, not minding him — you could, if you liked, twist with a post — then, hot, sweaty, felt hemmed in again. It was time to go.

She wondered if she could hitch a ride to Ruby Bay and walk the rest of the way to the orchard, and was working her way to the side of the hall where she'd last seen Boggsie when Mike went by with Fiona. She kept on going, annoyed by the jealousy she felt. Mike might not be much but he belonged to her — if she wanted him. Which she did not. So . . .

'Boggsie, I'm going. Tell the others, eh?' She did not wait for him to protest.

The air was warm outside the hall but less oppressive. She walked as far as the main street and saw it stretch away left and right, with empty footpaths and closed shops. Cars were turning down towards the dancehall, where the music lolled out the door like a fat tongue. She was glad to be alone, and going through a change from talk and noise and company. There was nothing to change into, that was the trouble, and no way of seeing ahead; although walking by herself for a while made a choice. Men whistled and invited her, driving by. It might be dangerous hitching. But she wanted to go slowly past the inlet, where the moon would be turning the water silver. Or would it be yellow? She wanted to see.

Ellie walked past the Rothmans clock on to the causeway. The sea was hidden behind the Kina peninsula, and the water in the inlet moved on the rising tide. It was patterned with silver, and the moon was yellow. The orchards on the curving shore were bleached and cold. She listened to their hissing in a breeze she could not feel. The slide of water into the causeway pipes was like a snake. A fish jumped somewhere and a dinghy bumped softly on its mooring post.

Ellie walked as far as Tasman, where she sat on the porch of the darkened store. Now she would have welcomed a ride. After picking all day, another hour of walking was more than she wanted. So, let this car be Mike, she thought. The driver ignored her thumb.

She walked again and had almost reached the bluffs above Ruby Bay when she heard the unmuffled roar of his Holden changing down. He leaned across and opened the door: 'Jump in.'

Ellie climbed up beside him. 'I thought you were in Nelson,' she said.

'There's nothing there. Why'd you walk out?'

'It got too crowded. Too much noise.'

'I just found out from Boggsie you'd shot through. He's not pleased.'

'Too bad about Boggsie. Have you got a beer?'

'There's some bottles on the back seat. We'll stop down here, eh? Could you use a swim?'

'Sure.' It was what she'd like even more than a beer — silver water, deep and cool.

He drove across the grass and stopped by the trees where she'd swum on her first day after getting off the bus. She climbed out and patted the Holden. It was a drifter's car, a hippy car, with its rusty panels and burst upholstery. He opened two bottles of beer on a torn edge of the mudguard and gave her one.

'Cheers,' he said.

She drank half the bottle, thirsty after her walk, then stood it upright in the roots of a tree.

'I'm going in.'

She stepped down to the sand, took off her clothes and ran the few yards to the water, feeling her body gleam in the moonlight. It would arouse Mike, she supposed, which was a pity, but the water would settle him down. She was not doing anything tonight or any night — and she knew that her choice in walking out of the dance and being alone had meant, No Mike, no anyone, until it was more than pleasure or affection, until it fixed something in place. She waded in up to her waist and turned and saw him loping, dark groined, down the sand. She hoped her fondness would be enough for him; he would see swimming naked as a come-on. She sank in the water to her chin and saw him dive, felt him slide along her thigh. He had turned underwater and aimed at her — so she had better make it plain.

'Jeez,' he cried, springing up, 'it's frigid.'

'Mike, let's get it straight, eh. There's no sex.'

'Hey, did I say that?'

'No, but I wouldn't blame you if you thought that's what this was.'

'So it ain't?'

'That's right. I'm off it for a while. Shall we swim?'

She took half a dozen strokes. He was grinning at her. 'I wonder what for a while means.'

'I bet you do.'

They swam out, she faster than him. He stroked awkwardly with his head angled high, which brought her close to pity; and pity could lead to sex, so she turned back and lay in the shallow water, letting small waves run along her back. Mike lay beside her.

'The biggest double bed in the world.'

Ellie splashed him. 'You'd better lay off, Mike. I'm getting my beer.'

She ran up the sand, dried herself with her shirt and pulled it on, pulled on her jeans. She sat on the low bank under the trees and finished the bottle. Mike prowled back and forth in the water. She supposed he had an erection and was letting it go down. Other men might use it to persuade.

'Come on out, Mike. I don't mind.'

He walked up the sand and she saw she had been half right.

'Put your clothes on,' Ellie said. 'I wasn't trying to lead you on.'

He dressed by the car, then sat beside her on the beach with his guitar.

'I'm a sort of an emotional guy, but it doesn't only show in speech,' he said.

Ellie laughed. He could have turned nasty instead of trying to joke.

'It's a compliment in a way. Play me something,' she said.

'I only strum.'

'OK, strum.'

'What I've been doing is writing a song for you.'

'For me?'

'I've only got three lines. Want to hear?'

'Yes, I'd like to.'

He played a dozen soft chords, then sang in his reedy voice:

> 'Ellie, you have bloomed tonight
> Amidst green seedlings
> In the rainbow shadows of my dreams . . .'

He played three more chords and smiled at her. 'It needs a tune.'

'I think it's nice. It's —' She felt soft towards him and could not find a word. 'I like green seedlings.'

'The trouble is, I can't get any more.'

'It'll come. Are you sure it was for me?'

'Cross my heart.'

Now that he had given up he was close to getting her. Ellie did not want him to know. She would lose the new certainty she'd found. She took her watch out of her jeans and strapped it on.

'Twelve o'clock.'

'Do you change into someone different now? What's Ellie short for?'

'Elinor.' She spelled it.

'She's in a poem somewhere. Tennyson?'

She supposed his half degree was in literature. 'Don't know.'

'There's one more beer. Want to share?'

They sat on the bank, passing the bottle back and forth.

'I guess your name got you in some strife?' Ellie said.

'Yeah. Michael Rowe.'

'Halleluja, I'll bet. You can't blame your parents. It probably wasn't around when you were born.'

She told him about travelling in Europe but seemed to be boasting after a while.

'I don't want to go there. I'm happy here,' he said.

'Are you going to shift around like this all your life?'

'Why not? I've got my car. Got lots of friends. Otherwise I'll end up like my my parents, stuck in the same house all my life.'

'Do they know where you are?'

'I go back in the winter sometimes. I've got three sisters. I stay with them. Babysit. You don't stay long.'

'Yeah,' Ellie said, 'I know.'

They watched the sea and saw the tide turn. She felt his thigh warm against her hip and wished that liking could be enough.

'Here another line,' he said, taking his guitar:

> 'Water turns on the sand,
> Turning you to me . . .

'How's that?'

'No good. You can't go from seedlings to the sea. It doesn't follow.'

'Ah,' he said, 'it doesn't follow. Ba-ad.'

'Come on, let's go. I'm getting tired.'

They drove up the hill to the orchard and stopped beside the pickers' hut.

'So?' he said.

'I'm sorry, Mike.' She almost added, 'Thanks for the swim,' but thought he might take it as a rebuff. Sorry meant what it said.

'OK,' he said. 'You can have the bathroom first.'

She showered and went to bed, and was sleeping when Janice and Fiona came in. She woke enough to hear Janice crying, and was pleased when Fiona took her to the bathroom. Mike and Boggsie talked in the kitchen, drinking beer, laughing inanely, and she banged on the wall: 'Shut up in there. I'm trying to sleep.'

'Bitch,' Boggsie yelled, but Mike calmed him down.

Janice and Fiona got into bed, Janice sniffing and making little moans.

'Be quiet, Janice,' Fiona said.

'Yeah, be quiet,' Ellie said.

She turned her face away from the moon and slept again.

Sunday. Ellie wanted books. The only ones in the hut were tattered westerns and spy stories.

'Go and see Audrey. She'll lend you some,' Jim said.

'Which one's she?'

'The big one. Stirling Moss.'

'Is she Webster or Anerdi?' Ellie said.

'Webster. Anerdi is Fan, the little one.'

'In the dresses?'

'Yeah. She reads. Ask her.'

Ellie walked beyond the pine trees into a paddock where Jim ran a dozen sheep. She had seen the two women walking down to collect their mail and speeding by in their Mini, leaving clouds of dust that turned the roadside blackberry bushes white. The big one, Webster, grinned as she drove, changing up and down as though on a race-track. Yet she was slow when she walked, stiff-hipped and beetle backed. She wore tweed skirts and cardigans that merged with the trees. The other one, the little one with the white hair and pink cheeks, dressed in colours, loosely: shawls and scarves, wide-sleeved blouses, long skirts. Everything floated and seemed to shimmer. Ellie thought of her as the butterfly woman.

She had walked in the paddocks several times, and seen their hillside of brown sheep and their witchy villa — probably the farmhouse before the orchards came — with a covered walkway to a long low shed facing the sun. They had half an acre of lawns and fruit trees, and a fenced vegetable garden with a black and tan goat tethered to a spike that the beetle-backed one shifted and hammered into the ground. Ellie thought at first they might be loopy. Then it seemed they might be simply private. All the same, Jim had said they would lend her books.

The small woman was sitting in a deckchair on the lawn, listening to music from the house. The other was busy in the shed. Ellie saw her moving back and forth at some job. She waited a moment to be seen, then climbed the fence and walked across the lawn, keeping clear of the goat. The woman in the chair was lying back with her eyes closed. The upper part of her face was shaded green by a tennis sun visor. She opened her eyes, put her finger to her lips and motioned Ellie to sit on the grass.

The music was not the sort Ellie was used to. The orchestra was pumping and the violin being clever — but it began to interest her, as though through her eyes. If you closed them you started seeing gullies and hills — mostly hills — and rich shifting colours, gold and brown. She was, though, too uncertain, with the woman there, to stay with her eyes closed for long. The goat was nibbling as though obsessed. A tui was feeding at a jar of yellow water in a peach tree. The woman moved her hands minutely to the music. The other, in the shed, was weaving on a frame. She smiled at Ellie and went on with her work.

Ellie closed her eyes again. The music, the orchestra, had a richer brown; the violin stepped out front and then stepped back. Its sound was yellow, orange, red. Ellie smiled. She opened her eyes when it was over and found the woman, Anerdi, watching her.

'Did you like that?'

'Yes, it was good.'

'Do you know what it was?'

Ellie shook her head. 'I don't listen very much.'

'Brahms.'

'Uh huh,' Ellie said. He was a name, like Mozart and Beethoven and the rest.

'Audrey doesn't like music, it upsets her.' She signalled to the woman in the shed. 'Turn it off, Audrey. I've got a visitor.'

Audrey went into the house and stopped the new piece.

'Now, who are you?'

'I'm Ellie Crowther. I'm picking for Jim Barchard, over there.'

'I'm Frances Anerdi. I get called Fan. Audrey, come and say hello. Audrey is a weaver. Have you seen her work?'

'No,' Ellie said. She stood up and shook hands with Audrey, who smiled and blushed. Fan Anerdi, with the pink cheeks, would never blush. She would probably not want to shake hands either. All the same, she smiled at Ellie and said, 'I've seen you sketching.'

'I do it when I'm feeling good,' Ellie said.

'You're not an art student, then?'

'No, I'm a librarian. An apple picker now.' She wondered if Fan would have sent her away if she hadn't sketched. 'What I really came for — Jim told me you might let me borrow some books.'

'What sort?'

Ellie was tempted to say D.H. Lawrence, Virginia Woolf, or Margaret Drabble perhaps — recommend herself. Instead she shrugged: 'Something light. To pass the time.'

Fan Anerdi's smile seemed disdainful and amused, as though she understood Ellie's hesitation while scorning her choice.

'Audrey has plenty of that sort of thing, haven't you, Aud?'

Surprisingly, Audrey laughed. 'Don't be a snob, Fan.' She winked at Ellie. 'She reads romances.'

'I do not. Chase him, Audrey. He's doing it again.'

'Shoo!' Audrey cried, running stiff-hipped on to the lawn, where a tui had swooped from a tree beyond the garden and bullied another away from the jar of yellow water.

'He thinks it all belongs to him. That's honey water. There are five jars out there in the trees, enough for all. But it's his domain. He spends all his energy driving the others away.'

'Can he drink it all?' Ellie said.

'Of course not. He's a capitalist. He's J.P. Morgan.'

Ellie laughed, although she had no idea who J.P. Morgan was. Audrey came back.

'Would you like a cup of tea?'

'Oh, no. I didn't come for —'

'Tea, Audrey, please,' Fan said. 'And you will stay, unless you're bored.'

'No, I'm not bored. You've got a beautiful place. I could live here.'

'It's been hard work. Mostly hers,' Fan said, as Audrey went into the house. 'But I don't like to praise her too much or she gets embarrassed.'

'What sort of weaving does she do?'

'Rugs. Brown rugs. They're comfortable if a little bit the same. She breeds her own sheep for the wool. Audrey is capable. Don't underestimate her.'

'Is she the one who painted rainbows on your letterbox?'

'Well I certainly didn't.'

Ellie wondered if they were lesbians or only friends. The feeling they gave was of a married couple: fondness and spite, service and familiarity. Fan was not necessarily boss.

'Have you lived here long?'

'Twenty-three years. Since the war. It was just a cow paddock when we came.'

'You've made it lovely.'

'Audrey did that. I mostly watched.'

'It's her place, not mine,' Audrey said, coming from the house. 'She's the moneybags. I'm penniless. I do the work.'

'Well,' Ellie said, uncomfortable, 'I suppose that makes it belong to you both.'

'Exactly,' Fan said. 'So pipe down, Audrey. She planted every one of those trees. And she built our two studios there with her own hands. Stop blushing. Make the tea.'

Audrey went back into the house. The tui swooped and drove a smaller one away. 'I'll do it,' Ellie said. She chased the bird, clapping her hands, then walked to the back of the garden, where paddocks dropped away to wattle groves and tea-tree groins. The sea, white in the sun, ended in a horizon so wide Ellie imagined she could see it curve. There were millions of apples hanging on trees along this stretch of coast. They ripened in the sun, enriched their colours, plumped themselves; yet Ellie could not see them — not even Jim Barchard's crop — could only feel, as though a fullness were in reach, as though she had only to stretch out her hands.

She turned and looked at the house. Russet-coloured fowls were advancing on to the lawn, drawn perhaps by the hope of crumbs from afternoon tea. Fan Anerdi and Audrey Webster were like women in one of those garden watercolours Ellie had seen reproduced in books, where everything was colour and light, where the shade was light. They carried a wicker table on to the lawn. Fan wore a dress hanging free, as though it had no one inside it. Green and blue: colours people used to say must never be worn together. Audrey folded out two canvas chairs. She walked up the lawn through the fruit trees.

'Tea,' she said.

'What does she do in her studio?'

'She paints. Fan paints. Nothing else really matters to her.'

You do, Ellie wanted to say, and as if she had picked up the thought, Audrey gave a small embarrassed laugh: 'I just do my weaving so she has company.'

'But people buy your rugs, I suppose.'

'Yes, they do,' Audrey said, sounding surprised.

'Do they buy her paintings?'

'Oh yes. Much more than they used to. She's just put up her prices. She's getting quite pleased with herself. Come and have some tea, Ellie. We'll sort out some books later on.'

Ellie sat on one of the folding chairs, while Audrey set the table with milk, sugar, jam and a bowl of whipped cream. She made a second trip to the house for mugs of tea and a plate of scones.

'A Devonshire tea,' Ellie said, delighted. 'I used to serve them once at a hotel I worked at in Scotland.'

'How old are you?' Fan said.

'Twenty-six.'

'That's older than most pickers.'

'Yes. I'm kind of marking time.' She did not want to explain more than that, or question herself. Working in the orchard had seemed to give her a space where she need not think. 'What sort of painting do you do?'

Fan looked at Audrey. 'Blabbermouth.'

'You love it,' Audrey said.

'I saw your easel through the window,' Ellie said. She had peered in as she and Audrey came down the lawn. 'I've never met a painter before. Can I see inside?'

'I'm not in the mood,' Fan said. 'I want to see some of your drawings first.'

'They're no good,' Ellie said. But the pleasure she had felt in them in the last few days made her add, 'I do them for fun.' There was no fun, she might have gone on, unless she satisfied herself, but that seemed to say they were good in some way after all. Ellie ate a scone. She remembered Mrs Nimmo: If you really want to know something, the best thing is to ask.

'Where does Anerdi come from?' she said.

'Oh, Anerdi,' Fan said, in a tone that meant a person not the name. Audrey laughed.

'He was a young man I met once,' Fan said.

'Once too often,' Audrey said.

'He sat down at my table in a cafe in Nice. Really, Audrey, there's no need to laugh. I was very happy for a time.'

'I just meant the name,' Ellie said. 'It sounds Italian.'

'It's a kind of hybrid, like him. Italian and French. That mix is common all along that coast, with its history. I married Mr Anerdi for a short time. And I liked his name much better than Clark, which I was before. So I kept it.'

'Was that long ago?'

'Do I look so old? It happened before the war. I left him where I found him, in a cafe in Nice, and went to England. I had some trouble with "Anerdi" there. Italian, you see. It was hard to convince people it was French.'

'Did you stay for the war?'

'Oh I'm English, can't you tell? Audrey is the New Zealander, aren't you Aud?'

'We both are now.'

'Nonsense. I'm nothing. I belong to this bit of land.'

'Is that what you paint? This place?'

'No painting. Not today. Audrey will show you how to do weaving if you want. Or how to milk the cow.'

'This cream comes from our cow,' Audrey said. 'Don't worry if Fan seems a bit rude.'

Fan threw half a scone at the hens. They chased it like a football on the lawn. 'I've had enough reminiscing. And my studio is not a gallery. If I ask to see your drawings I'm not just being polite. You sat out there for two hours this morning.'

'I was doing things out of my head.'

'What things?'

'Faces mostly. People I've met.'

'Useless, I'd say,' Fan said.

'Oh Fan, you don't know,' Audrey said.

'Drawing is a trade and you've got to be practical, not play games.'

She got up and went into the house.

Audrey smiled at Ellie. 'She's cross because of Nice. Let her simmer down.'

'I'd better go.'

'Oh no, you need books. Come and see what I do. Bring your tea.

I call it my workroom, not a studio. That's just Fan.'

Ellie admired the rugs, which Fan had described accurately: comfortable. She picked handfuls of raw wool from a box in the corner.

'I was a fleeco once,' she said.

'Were you? I'm a farm girl. Taranaki. It's mostly dairy there. I get Jim Barchard to do my shearing. Do you know how to spin?'

Audrey demonstrated, drawing out fat threads then fine ones, expertly. 'I knit jerseys too, but not for sale. They're for my friends. Ah, there she is. She's changed her hat, that's a good sign. And she's got some books.'

Fan was wearing a straw hat with a floppy brim. It made her less severe.

'Have you ever seen good paintings?' she asked.

'I tried to see the Mona Lisa in the Louvre but people were standing ten deep,' Ellie said.

'What else?'

'I saw the ones by Goya in Madrid. And all the things in Florence. Lots of stuff.'

'Lots of stuff,' Fan said. She raised her eyebrows at Audrey, and Ellie became impatient at being examined and marked.

'I liked Goya. I liked El Greco. What else would you like to know?'

Audrey gave a nervous laugh.

'Nothing, nothing,' Fan said. 'I haven't been to those places for so long. I like to hear. Did you see any modern stuff? "Stuff" is perfectly all right.'

'Some,' Ellie said. 'I can't remember all of it. Picasso. Matisse.'

'Did you like it?'

'Bits. I thought some was just mad.'

'It can seem that way,' Fan said. 'But I'm glad you approved of "bits". Especially Matisse.'

'I liked the colours. And the shapes.'

'I've got a book of drawings by him. Borrow it.'

'Thank you.'

'And here's Cézanne. I think he would have been happy here. In Nelson, I mean. Painting it. Don't read, just look at the pictures.'

'She wanted novels, Fan,' Audrey said.

'Well, she can have them. Go and get some.'

'She might like to choose her own.'

'She can choose next time. Go on. Shoo.'

Audrey went into the house. Ellie laid the books on the lawn by her chair.

'Do you always bully her so much?' she said.

Fan looked startled. 'That's not bullying. We're giving each other friendly little taps. Audrey and I are old friends, dear.'

'Yes. I'm sorry.'

'Tell me about yourself. Apple pickers are usually boys and girls.'

'I'm not old. It's just, I've been away for two years and I don't know if I'm home yet.' She told Fan, and Audrey when she came back, about her time overseas, then about House 4 and working in libraries and the shearing gang. The hens clucked around the table and J.P. Morgan drove his competitors away. Ellie began to enjoy herself. She felt that she was gathering the bits of her life and holding them so the edges joined. She mentioned her men only in passing or not at all. It was interesting how they seemed to pass. Yet she had thought she loved several, and sex with them had been more than just fun. Where were they now? The question pleased her.

'You should smile. It lightens your face,' Fan said. 'If I painted you I'd have lots of light.'

'My mother —' Ellie said, then stopped. 'No, I'd better not talk about her.'

'Why not?'

'She got married again and had more children. I've got a half sister and two half brothers. She wanted to be happy, so did he; but somehow it's turned out sad.'

Fan and Audrey smiled and nodded at her.

'I don't want to end up like that,' Ellie said. It was something she had known, yet it seemed a discovery. 'I suppose I should be back there helping her.' But she knew she should not — and should not be guilty about it either.

She walked down the drive under the trees with her armful of books and turned in at the orchard and sat on her bed reading one of Audrey's novels, which she loved: not a romance after all but a story by someone called Olivia Manning about a couple working for the British Council in Bucharest before the war. How had Audrey chosen so well, after only an hour? Audrey was nicer than Fan.

She glanced at the Matisse book before cooking her tea, and did not like it. Ellie thought she could draw better than that.

They were getting near the end of the Red Delicious when Boggsie told Ellie he was leaving. She had finished tea and was sitting at the table in the kitchen writing to her mother: 'I'm the fastest packer and the best picker too. You get a kind of rhythm going and it starts being automatic, like breathing or the beating of your heart and if you break speed you've got to start all over again and build it up. It's hard work though. I'm getting strong. I'm as brown as a Maori. You wouldn't know me. I like it best getting to the top of a tree. You can stick your head out and look across the orchard at the sea. It's like being a bird that's learning to fly and someone throws you up in the air. I don't mind breaking the rhythm then. Did you get the case of apples I sent . . .'

'I've had enough of this shit, I think I'll shoot through,' Boggsie said. He sat down over the table from her and ran his tongue over his pink lips. 'Want to come?'

'What?'

'I'm quitting.'

'Goodbye.'

Boggsie leaned forward. 'This guy's making money out of us. We could be in business on our own.'

'What, plant an orchard?'

'I've got something in mind. It's easier than that.'

She supposed he meant peddling dope. He drummed his fingers on the table, then slapped his hands down two or three times.

'Yeah,' he said.

'Yeah what?'

'You're not like these university sheilas. You've been around.'

'What's that supposed to mean?'

'We could set something up, you and me.'

'I don't do dope.'

Boggsie grinned. His lips had a way of spreading flat when he was pleased. 'It's easier than that. We could make maybe a hundred bucks a night. Even splits.'

She knew what he was going to say, yet could not stop him. The muscles in her throat had paralysed.

'See, I'd park down the road from the hall. Some weeknights we could do the big orchards. These guys don't want much, it's quick and easy. Fifteen bucks. You could get twenty. I wouldn't send any rough buggers out. It's not like you'd be a pro, Ellie. It's just for the season. We should've done it sooner, eh?'

She leaned across the table and punched him in the mouth. It was soft and slippery, with hard teeth inside. He spun backwards, lurching from his chair, which fell with a clatter on the floor.

'Bitch,' he said, 'I'll rip your head off.' He came around the table, bloody mouthed.

Ellie threw a sauce bottle at him, splashing more red on his shirt.

'Get away from me,' she screamed.

'I'll kill you, cunt,' Boggsie said.

She tried to keep the table between them but he rammed it hard and caught her at thigh level against the sink. She scrabbled among the dirty knives but found that she'd picked up a spoon. He leaned across for her as Jim and Mike ran into the room.

'Stop,' Jim bellowed.

Boggsie caught her arm and tried to drag her over the table. Her shirt ripped at the shoulder. Then Jim had his arm round Boggsie's throat and was bending him back. He flung him sideways, and Boggsie fell on hands and knees by the wall.

'Stay there,' Jim said. 'You all right, Ellie?'

'Yes,' she said. Her throat was thick. She felt blind.

'So what's going on?'

'Bitch hit me. Cut my lip,' Boggsie slurred.

'He . . .'

'Take your time.'

Ellie swallowed. She pushed the table out and breathed deeply. 'He wanted to put me in his truck and park outside the orchards and send men out.'

'You prick, Boggsie,' Mike said, moving at him.

'Keep back,' Jim said.

'Bitch is making it up,' Boggsie said.

'No she's not. He tried the same with me,' Janice said from the door.

'I knew he was bloody rubbish,' Jim said. 'Get your things together and get out.'

'Go fuck yourself,' Boggsie said, standing up and feeling his mouth.

'You want the cops?' Jim turned to Ellie. 'You want to charge him?'

'No,' she said, 'just get him out.'

'I could charge her,' Boggsie said.

'Don't be bloody wet,' Jim said. 'You think I don't know you're smoking dope out in your truck? I'll put your weights up, boy, quick as bloody looking.'

Boggsie wiped his mouth, leaving a smear of blood on his arm. 'You owe me wages.'

'You get in your truck, and fast. I'll bring out what I owe. It's more than you're worth.'

Boggsie looked around — Mike, Janice, Fiona — then moved his head jerkily, avoiding eyes. 'I'll get you,' he said to Ellie. He went into the men's bunk room for his sleeping bag.

'Ellie, hey-ey, come here,' Mike said. He tried to put his arms around her.

She jerked away: 'Don't touch me.'

She went into the yard, shied away from Boggsie's truck as though it was a person, and went up the drive beside the hedge. She wanted to follow the road, walk hard and far, but did not know which direction Boggsie would take. She half-ran under the pines towards Fan and Audrey's house.

The truck came up Jim's drive, bouncing as Boggsie picked up speed. He blared his horn at Dorrie Barchard standing by the hedge, turned his lights on at the road and drove away, slamming through the gears, towards Mapua. Ellie could have turned back then and taken the road herself but wanted to follow the path beneath the pines and make it go on and on until she grew calm.

Fan and Audrey's gate turned her aside. She climbed the fence into the sheep paddock and walked down to a patch of dried-out swamp. The sheep galloped twenty yards and stopped, almost invisible in the dusk. Black muzzles, glinting nostrils, glinting eyes: more wild-seeming than white sheep. She walked through rushes, climbed a hill, then a barred gate, and swished through long grass as dry and light as feathers. She came to the fence at the back of Audrey's garden. Far away, Mike called 'Ellie' three times. She found it a strange name, coming so distantly: a primitive sound. She lay down in the grass, watched the sky darken and the stars come out. They multiplied, and she forgot Boggsie; eliminated him when he came back; lost Mike and the orchard in the immensities that opened up. She felt her heartbeat slow and her breathing almost stop. Boggsie doesn't matter, she thought. She could scarcely remember who he was.

Later she slid through bottom wires into the garden. The goat stood up and rattled his chain. Ellie smelt his rancid stink. She sat on the lawn cross-legged, out of his reach, and folded her hands. Her knuckles stung where Boggsie's teeth had torn them. She ignored them and watched the house as though it were as distant as the stars. Light spread from open windows across the veranda and faded among the nearer trees. Ellie felt she was breathing cold black air, clean in spite of the goat, that came from the ground the way light came from the stars. She almost laughed: such a physical thing, touching air. It made her feel that Boggsie was some dirty bit of phlegm you could cough up and spit out.

Audrey worked in the kitchen, drying dishes, stacking them. Fan seemed to be watching television. Ellie heard her call, 'Aud, come and see.' Audrey left the kitchen for the lounge. A window framed her leaning sideways to the screen. She laughed and said something to Fan, then went back to her work. Fan crossed in front of the window and switched off the set. She put her hands on the bunched curtains and looked outside, halved by a silhouetted branch, then slid left from the frame in her multi-coloured dress. Ellie thought she would not care to be like these women. They seemed to be merely going on. It was as if nothing lay behind the plane she saw them on.

The chooks in the fowlhouse exploded, beating their wings, then subsided. Audrey opened the back door and peered out.

'No one there.' She closed the door.

Ellie stood up quietly and walked down the lawn and around the side of the house. She opened the front gate and went under the pine trees to the road, then down Jim's drive to the pickers' hut.

I don't need people, she thought; and the next moment, I need them, I do. Like breathing the black air, it made her want to laugh.

Mike was playing Patience at the table.

'Hey Ellie, where'd you get to? I was calling,' he said.

'I went for a walk.'

'Boggsie's gone. What a bastard he turned into, eh?'

Ellie went to the sink and washed her hand, wincing as the water stung.

'Let me,' Mike said.

'I can do it.' She dried her hand, found bandaids in the cupboard and stuck them on.

'You could get rabies,' Mike said.

'Yeah,' she said.

'Mad dog.'

'I don't want to talk about him.'

'Sure. I understand. There's room in with me if you get nervous. Ellie? Eh?'

Ellie drank some water.

'Give it up, Mike. I'm not interested.'

Yet she felt sorry for him and touched his shoulder lightly as she went to her room: 'Another time.'

She meant another life, and hoped he had understood.

She heard him strumming softly through the wall as she went to sleep, a soothing invasive patient sound that settled her and helped her drift away. She had thought she would not trust the hut any more, but it was safe.

Jim took on a Dutch backpacker in Boggsie's place. He was a morose boy who tried to live off apples to save money. He got diarrhoea and left after a week, but the Reds and the Goldens were almost done. Janice and Fiona left soon after, with more pledges of friendship than Ellie thought were called for. She and Mike stayed on for the Sturmers and Granny Smiths.

They took turns cooking. Mike, who had been happy frying chops and sausages, bought a wok. He cooked meals of rice and vegetables with diced lamb and pork and soy sauce, playing Chinaman at the stove, a French waiter serving, then Harold Steptoe pouring wine into beer glasses. Ellie had never known a man work so hard at seduction.

She did not enjoy picking the Granny Smiths as much as the Red and Golden Delicious. She thought of them as apples that had missed a step somewhere and not grown up. Their green made the orchard monotonous. Ellie wondered what job she would do when they were picked. She didn't want library work. Books on shelves were like apples on trees, not something you could work at all your life.

Helping Mike wash up, she began to wonder if sharing with a man — not necessarily marrying him — might provide a way of finding things. That was what she was after. She had no idea what they might be. And why should she have to have a man around for that? For something that would — Ellie struggled — open her up? To some sort of danger, perhaps? To getting something done, some sort of work? Mike would be no good; he would be in the way, if she ever found out where she wanted to go. He opened a bottle of beer from the fridge. Inadequate, superfluous: words she hated using for someone she felt so friendly towards; and she had to stop herself from touching his hand as she took her glass. Sex with him would be like sex with a teenager. There would be nothing to talk about afterwards.

One drizzly morning when they could not pick he went into Nelson without inviting her.

'Well thanks for nothing,' Ellie said as he drove away. She put on her parka and walked down the road to Ruby Bay. The tide was out and little ruined castles of sand stood on the stretch between the water and the shore. Were they made by some creature in the sand or by the action of the tide? She wished she had her pad with her to make an illustration. She walked past the camping ground, where housetrucks reminded her of Boggsie. What would it be like with a mind like his — living in that sort of ugliness? And what would it be like being Mike — simple, suggestible, hungry, generous? She found it hard to believe that he couldn't see further than he seemed to, and felt a kind of bitter frustration that she too could not see into a place that opened out.

She walked beneath the cliffs for half an hour, then turned back. The ragged little castles were drying out. She broke one open but could not find anything inside — no living creature. The drizzle started again, making the bay ghostly and the pine island lying across the inlet insubstantial. It turned from black to grey, then almost vanished, and she found herself thinking of her father. Who was keeping him alive? She might be the only one. He must be changed utterly for her mother, with George and three children in between; he might be no more real than a man she had shared a seat with on a bus or train. Only Ellie kept him unchanged, from sitting on his shoulders and holding his head. Amazingly she felt the warmth of his brow in her palms, the warmth of his neck between her thighs. She held up her hands, stared at them, and was connected with her mother as well, scolding her to hang on tight or she would fall off. Impossible to know how they had arrived. From hands warmed in her parka pockets?

It did not matter. She had looked through a door and found her parents, and she wondered if other moments could be recaptured like this; if she could make her life and carry it, study it whenever she chose. Would it help her look ahead and know which way to go? The next step might be natural and plain.

Her elation lasted as she walked up the hill. Audrey and Fan stopped their car and offered her a ride.

'I'm out for a walk,' she cried.

'Come for some more books when you want to,' Audrey said.

They drove on. No dust today. There was a rainbow in the sky.

She wrote to her mother, promising to visit her when picking finished.

Mike came back late in the afternoon, bringing a jar of purple wine. He frowned and pursed his lips, then turned away, starting to grin.

'I'm no bloody good at pretending. Are you ready?'

'What for?'

He spun back, spreading his arms, baring his teeth. 'Da da!'

'My God, you had them done,' Ellie said.

'These are only temporary. I go back for the real ones next week.'

'What is it? A plate?'

'Nope. They're capped. They won't fall out.'

Ellie hugged him. She kissed his mouth, which tasted of dentist and beer.

'So, do I get my picture drawn?'

'I hope you did it for more than that.'

'Yeah, I did.'

She felt him getting hard so she broke away and uncapped the wine. They toasted his new teeth, then she got her pad and tried to draw him; and when it wouldn't work — his features flattened instead of taking shape — turned it into a caricature, gave him rabbit teeth.

'I reckon I'm better-looking than that. Sign it, eh?'

She signed: *Ellie Crowther*. It made her serious. Ellie was her, taking easy steps that might be hard to retrace.

'I'll cook,' she said, although it was his turn.

She made spaghetti and they drank wine. She found herself thinking almost hungrily of sex — remembered her old phrase, delicious love-making. From several of her men she had learned to call it fucking but kept her own description for private use, which surely was illogical. Ellie was confused. She did not know what it would be with Mike. Perhaps whether they washed up first, and showered, and started slowly would decide.

She put the plates on the bench, languid with indecision, then washed her hands under the cold tap and was brisk and sure.

'All right, come on.'

She chose her own room — would never go in with him where Boggsie had been.

'Have you got any condoms?'

'Yeah, sure.' He had them in his pocket.

'God Mike, they're old. They look perished.'

'No, they're not. Hold on, I've got some more.' He ran to his room and back. 'These are OK. I had a girlfriend once who put pinholes in all my frenchies when she left.'

'Shut up, Mike. Just get in bed.'

So it was fucking; but later in the night it became love-making, almost; and was almost delicious too. It was a pity he stayed so eager when he should slow down; but she said, 'Slow, slower, Mike, it's not a race,' and it worked quite well: a pity he *would* talk but could not *talk*. He wanted to boast and be told how good he was. She liked to have men look in her eyes, and he could not but turned away and clenched his jaw and then collapsed. Knowing him would be easy, like peeling a mandarin. It might be just as well to leave it fucking most of the time.

'Most of the time' made her think again. She could if she wanted make it only one night — for his teeth. Ellie sniggered.

'What?' he said. 'What's wrong?'

'Nothing.'

'If you think I can't get it up again I can.'

'Oh, I'm sure you can. Let me help . . . Now do that to me. The same for me.'

He didn't know a lot about giving pleasure but provided it by accident.

'Slow down now. We can go a long time.'

'Tell me what the record is. I'll break it.'

'Shut up, Mike. Don't talk.'

He told her that she made a lot of noise when she came.

'Don't you like it?'

'Sure I do. Most sheilas don't is all I mean.'

'What's this "most sheilas"? I'm Ellie. I'm me.'

'Yeah, I'm sorry.'

She forgave him because he had understood. But later on she said, 'I'm not sleeping two in this sort of bed. You can get in one of the others or go back to your own.'

'Which one was Fiona's? That'll bring me on.'

He thought this sort of remark was intimate. Amazement stopped her from being angry. All the same she made him go back to his own room.

'Mike,' she said as he went out the door, 'you needn't think you can come in here every night. OK?'

'I bet you can't stop yourself. Hey, hey, joke. I love you, Ellie.'

So she saw no reason not to spend her time making love — every night, fucking, making love. They did it in the apple trees once while Jim was at the shed. His virility delighted her, but his eagerness was boyish and pleased her less. She felt that she owed it to good sense to stop soon and was happy that the season was almost finished. He did not say he loved her again but she waited for it, waiting to say, No, Mike, no.

When there were only two days left Jim gave them Wednesday as a bonus. They set off early to drive to Golden Bay. They might go up Farewell Spit, Mike said, since she was talking about farewell.

'No I'm not. But I've got to do something. We'll have the Sturmers done by Friday lunch time.'

'Come with me. We'll hit the road.'

'I don't want to hit the road.'

'Have you ever read Kerouac?'

'I thought he was a silly little boy.'

She could have said the same about Mike: lovely body, slab sided, with joints that intrigued her, working parts running as though on oil, and washboard ribs where her knuckles played, and tight snaky skin, dark in the hollows and pale across the bone — but the clever head of a silly boy. She wanted to make their difference plain, if she could find a way that wouldn't hurt him — and make it plainer to herself, otherwise she might stay drunk on sex and not have any other life. She must get back in control.

They stopped at the lookout on the Takaka side of the hill. The drop into the valley hollowed her — sudden, deep, arbitrary. There was no reason for this place, but a kind of recognition in her fingertips, which wanted to slide on it and feel the shape. It was full of sunlight, brimming with sun, and smooth with paddocks, but the hills were raw, their folding unfinished. She remembered that someone had painted the Takaka valley, perhaps from where she was standing: put day on one side and night on the other, and got — she remembered — the moulding and the folds and, somehow, fear. She could understand fear; she felt it herself.

'Good place, eh?' Mike said.

'Yes.'

'We go through Takaka, then along the coast. We'll drop in on some mates of mine, down past Collingwood.'

'I thought you said Farewell Spit.'

'Too far.'

They drove down the valley, through the busy town, over the river and along a dipping road half a mile from the sea. Ellie found the countryside scrubby and dull after the deep indented valley back there. She did not want to meet Mike's friends. He would try to show her off.

At Collingwood they turned south down the Aorere. More scrubby farms, but the hills were closing in and the bush crept low. It was another valley where you might be afraid. They went through Bainham, a hall and a church and a post office store, and down towards the Heaphy Track. The road was metalled. Hot dust smoked behind them, dirtying the blackberry and gorse. She wondered what sort of friends Mike would have down here — Black Mountain people, Sawney Bean in his cave?

He turned off the road. 'Open the gate.'

She jumped out, unhooked it and swung it back, seeing green paddocks through a fringe of trees. Mike drove inside and she climbed back in. The paddock opened out like a lake. They drove across it on a rutted road, through another wall of trees to a second paddock enclosed like the first. It seemed to Ellie secret and removed, as if her coming on it made it hers.

'I built that,' Mike said, pointing at an A-frame house.

A man and a woman were sitting on the porch, brown torsos gleaming in the sun. A child crawled on the grass away from them, as if setting out across the paddock. Mike blew his horn. The man raised his hand in a slow salute.

'That's Terry and Glenys and their sprog,' Mike said. 'See the old farmhouse over there? There's two more couples.'

'What are they, hippies?'

'I dunno. Does it matter?'

'Is it a commune?'

'Ask Terry. He's the boss.' He stopped the car. 'Gidday, Terry. Gidday, Glen. Like my teeth?'

The woman gave an unfocused smile. She hitched her hibiscus-flowered sarong further up her thighs. Terry raised his hand again, like a Red Indian. Ellie almost expected him to greet them with 'How!' He was a small, bushy-bearded man, muscular in his chest and arms, which were tanned as though with nugget and smeared with paint from the child, who was sitting naked on the grass, bull's-eyed in yellow round her navel and striped with red across her chest.

Mike picked her up and held her at arm's length. 'Pow!' he said and put her down. 'This is Ellie. She's my apple-picking mate. Hey, we should have brought some apples, eh?'

'Sit in the sun,' Terry said.

'Not with spray on them,' Glenys said. She lifted her breasts on her palms as though they were fruit. Milk seeped from the nipples and dropped on her sarong. She got up and fetched the child, who fastened on rapaciously. Glenys was a pretty girl with a sulky face that might be adaptable. Put make-up on, arrange her hair, it could be a Lambton Quay chemist-shop face. She was, Ellie guessed, about nineteen.

Ellie sat on the porch. 'What's the baby's name?'

'Terra,' Glenys said.

Ellie laughed. 'I can see she's a handful.'

'No. Terra. The earth.'

'Oh, sorry. It goes with Terry, I suppose.' She did not want to sit with these people; she wanted to walk, explore the place.

'I'm not Glenys any more, either,' Glenys told Mike. 'I've changed to Rain.'

'Whatever makes you feel good,' Mike said. 'Who are you?'

'I'm Terry still,' Terry said. 'A name has got to kind of settle on you. I'm still waiting. Glen — sorry, Rain — was kind of chosen, I guess.'

He was mild but his uncertainty might be 'a kind of' strength — he would say 'kind of' frequently, trying to understand. Ellie liked him better than Rain, who was overdoing dreaminess as she fed her child. She might be as bogus as her name. Terry, on the other hand, might be genuine.

'It was soft Rain,' Rain said, looking as if it was falling now.

'How many people here?' Ellie said.

'Six adults, three kids. There used to be eight adults but two shot through,' Terry said.

'And what do you do? How do you make money?'

'Money is dross,' Rain murmured dreamily.

'We go out and work when we need to buy something. Mostly on farms,' Terry said. 'Mark and Shawn are working now. We try to be self-sufficient, though.'

'Do you have gardens?'

'Sure. Down the path behind the house. Have a look.'

'Base metal,' Rain said.

Ellie wondered if she meant money or her. Rain might be stoned, but wouldn't that make Terra stoned too, with all that milk?

'No, stay and talk,' she said as Mike stood up. She walked across the paddock to the two-storeyed farmhouse. Its veranda roof sagged parallel with the decking — nice lines. She peered through the front door and saw a wooden table with bench seats. A Shacklock stove was set in an alcove beyond. Stairs like an upward-slanting cave went into the dark. Ellie walked around to the back. A shed stacked with tea-tree firewood leaned off the wall, with a broken-backed canoe, a bath, a motorbike with no tyres piled on one side. Blankets aired on a rope line running from a tank-stand to a nearby tree. The tanks were made of corrugated iron, painted green. She tapped one and heard it drum: less than a quarter full. A set of wooden tubs was fixed on a free-standing frame, with an iron wringer clamped between.

'Ha,' Ellie said, half scornful, half intrigued. She had no idea people lived — chose to live — like this. She went along a wide straight path through fern and scrub and cutty grass and found the garden in a clearing. It was fenced with head-high wire-netting, to keep out possums, she supposed. A woman stood with a wheelbarrow tilted up, while another forked compost from it into a trench. Behind the wire they seemed like workers on a prison farm. Ellie walked around the outside.

'Hi there,' said the woman with the barrow: American.

'Hello.'

'You visiting?'

'Yes. With Mike. Mike Rowe.'

'Ah, Mikey. He's turned up.'

'If you want to do some work there's spades in the shed,' said the other woman.

'That way you earn lunch,' the American said. 'I'm Lee. She's Annie.'

'I'm just having a look,' Ellie said. She did not like the challenge Annie had made, or the look of her: a long-bodied woman with a contorted jaw and eyes out of balance with each other. Lee was stringy, muscly, like a whippet, with a plump face and curly hair — most Americans managed a bit of the film star look. Ellie went to the shed, a railway carriage with its wheels taken off. Someone had built a hut to one side and installed an iron stove and a copper. A bath stood in the open with its claw feet curled on blocks of wood. So the carriage had been a house before it was a shed. Some of the windows still had curtains hanging on string. She did not look inside, in case Annie thought she was getting a spade. Who said I wanted lunch? she thought. They took her for a townie but she would back herself to work as well as either of them after three months with a forty-pound bag of apples round her shoulders.

Pale light showed through trees beyond the garden as though the river generated it. Water sliding over stone made a hissing sound. Ellie followed a path over hump-backed roots, down rocks with their edges hammered off. She found a beach of gravelly sand where a clinker-built dinghy was tied to a tree. There were no oars. It made her impatient. She wanted to cross the river and walk on the rocks on the other side. They were glistening in the sun, baking in the sun, around the mouth of a side-creek where a thin waterfall splashed into a pool.

She edged around the rocks on the downriver side and climbed the bank, using trees as hand-holds, until she came to a rock jutting over the river, as broad as a table. She lay on it, warming herself, then crawled to the edge and looked in the water, where pebbles lay deep down, as white as if she held them in her hands. A world needing nothing from her: Ellie felt drawn into it as though clean and cold were all she had ever wished to be. She saw a fish, a trout she guessed, resting down there, *living* down there, holding its place with tiny movements of its tail. She watched until it tipped her and almost slid her in, then edged back to the centre of the rock, took off her shirt and bra and baked in the sun. I could live here, she thought.

The wheelbarrow squeaked, a spade thumped in hard earth, sounds that came more clearly than the voices of the women. She could live with them too, if she had to, even with Rain, if there was work to do and places where she could be alone. She wondered if anyone else had found this rock, from which she could see, down-river, a bending water-chute, as smooth as oil. Blocks of stone like derailed freight cars lay upriver. The waterfall was opposite, with hills rising behind in humps and platforms. Crooked gullies, filled with bush, cut into uplands bare as skin. Poor land, but poor for what? She felt rich with everything around her.

But there was Mike. If she stayed he would want to stay, and was he good for anything but sex? She heard him calling her. On this bed-shaped rock he'd want one thing, no stopping him. After a while she'd want it too, with his cock standing up so importantly. Ellie shivered and put on her bra, pulled on her shirt, then struggled through the bushes to the garden.

He was talking to the women inside the wire. Mikey, the American had called him, with a mixture of knowledge and contempt. What knowledge could she have? And why contempt, unless she had discovered him as Ellie had done? She felt a surge of anger, compassionate and possessive at once, and a sour little pricking of jealousy. She walked around the outside fence, ignoring him, and looked inside the railway carriage. Beyond the tools and sacks was a timber-framed bed with seed potatoes spread on the wire mattress. She edged her way to it and pushed it with her foot: built in.

'Move them spuds,' Mike said from the door.

'Someone lived here once,' she said.

'Sure, Mack and Jenny. They were Christians. Couldn't take old Terry's guff. They've gone to Riverside.'

'Where do those two out there live?'

'In the farmhouse. Where'd you get to? I was calling.'

'I wanted to have a look at the river. Do they have cows? All that stuff?'

'They did when I was here. Two cows. They're in another paddock probably. There's a whole string of clearings in the scrub. It was rough grazing for some cocky once.'

'Did Terry buy it?'

'Yep. Thirty acres. The rest sort of buy in. Buy shares. You'd better come. Glen's made some lunch.'

'I hope she didn't drip milk into it. Do you think this roof leaks?'

'Yeah, it does. Mack gave up on it. He built a sleepout back in the bush. Come on, I'm hungry.'

They walked to the A-frame, past Lee and Annie washing their hands at the tubs. Rain had spread a cloth on the porch and laid out tomatoes, cucumbers, pickle, butter, bread. She carried out a bowl of salad. Terry followed with a pot of steaming corncobs.

'So,' Terry said, 'it's welcome to our guests.' The others took no notice but Ellie liked him more for attempting ceremony.

Rain had pinned a napkin around her breasts. She stripped corncobs with her small white teeth, moving up and down the rows like a tractor. Lee and Annie ate hungrily, while Terry told Ellie about working as a teacher in Christchurch and how keeping discipline had been his problem, how it had made him sick the time he'd had to cane a boy — 'Literally. I ran into the storeroom and threw up. Then I went back and apologised.'

'The kids really paid attention after that,' Annie said.

'Well, Annie,' Terry said mildly, 'you've heard all this. So laugh, OK? I don't mind. I knew I couldn't live in that kind of world, that's all.'

'That and materialism,' Rain said.

'We're happy here. We're trying new things.'

'And it's bloody hard work,' Annie said.

'What did you do?' Ellie asked.

'Lab technician. Mark worked in a bank. Does all this tempt you?'

'Me? No. It's interesting.'

'What we could do with is a physiotherapist.'

'And some more manpower,' Lee said.

'Don't look at me,' Mike said.

'She was looking at Terry,' Annie said.

'How old are your children?'

'Six and eight. Carla's six, Sandy's eight.' Annie smiled for the first time. It put her face in balance, although her twisted jaw and offset eyes remained. 'They go to school in Bainham. There's a school bus.'

'I'm going to teach Terra myself,' Rain said. 'I don't want her corrupted by false ideas.'

'Like one and one are two?' Annie said.

'Like money is the most important thing.'

'I'd sock any teacher who said that to my kids.'

The place is what I like, not the people, Ellie thought — although she might come to like Annie. They would knock against each other for a while, but she could see them working in the garden side by side.

She and Mike left in mid-afternoon: down one valley and up the other. She sat quiet and still, as though somewhere within her a tuning fork was humming.

'Poor old Glen,' Mike said. 'She was top of her form at Christchurch Girls' High. Scholarship class. Then old Terry came along and lay down and waved his feet in the air. If she's Rain, I guess he must be Puddle.' He laughed. 'If they'd had twins the second one could have been Firma.'

'I think I want to live there,' Ellie said.

'You're joking.'

'In the railway carriage. We could fix it. There must be stuff you can put on the roof.'

'Sure, malthoid. Fixing's easy. But Terry and Glen are off their bikes. You don't go for all that stuff?'

'No, I don't. But nor do the others. Annie doesn't. We could . . .'

It was the river, the warm rocks, the water-chute, the trout holding its place with a trembling of its tail — and the secret paddocks ringed with bush, the possum-fenced garden, the railway carriage unattended by the trees.

'What do they call it?'

'Yeah, I asked. It's Good Life. They're waiting for the proper name to "settle". But listen, Ellie —'

'You have to buy in, you said.'

'Yeah.'

'How much?'

'Three fifty.'

'I've got six hundred saved.'

'I'm pretty broke, Ellie. My teeth cost a lot.'

'You could go out to work. The other men do.' She wanted him to go out.

'Terry stays home. He sits there waiting for enlightenment.'

She did not care about Terry, or Rain. They could be what they liked. The land and the river and the work were what she was after.

They drove up the hill and across the tops.

'I suppose I could give it a go,' Mike said. He smiled with his temporary teeth and her tolerance of him almost turned to love. It was as if he'd touched her and they'd joined. She did not try to stop him when he turned into the Canaan road. He pulled up on the grass half a mile along. The dust settled. Silence came out of the ground and piled up in the air. She led him with a finger in his belt. They lay down behind a marble outcrop as sharp as dog's teeth, where she unzipped him and herself. The horizontal answer to the vertical proposition: his joke, which she enjoyed, although he'd stolen it from somewhere.

It became love-making. It seemed almost like love.

Ellie returned Audrey and Fan's books on her last night. She refused Audrey's invitation to stay for tea.

'We're leaving early. Thanks for everything.'

'Did you look at them?' Fan said.

'I didn't have time. Well, the Matisse. Not the other one.'

'And?'

'It's sort of clever stuff. It's like he's playing games.'

'You don't like games?'

Ellie became impatient: examinations again. 'I just like to look at things and draw them.'

'And you think Matisse didn't do that?'

'I don't know. Well, I've got to go. Thanks again.'

She walked back, glad she had escaped them — escaped the bossy one at least. She could sit in her castle and bully her servant or her mate, whichever it was. Their place, their lives, were artificial alongside Good Life — which Ellie had changed to 'good life'. She was going just to try it and would keep her expectations lower case.

Wellington depressed her. The hills stood too close. Down in the gullied streets the buildings seemed top-heavy. People walked by in multiples. Ellie looked for faces she knew, but everyone hurried past — on business, to some meeting or conclave — and she felt like the wrong sort of insect in a hive.

At home her mother seemed shrunken, as though the children had sucked her dry. Ellie slept on the fold-out sofa in the lounge and felt in the way — and felt guilty too at not staying for more than a week. George watched her sadly, judging her.

Her optimism did not return until she was on the ferry, in the strait.

Mike met her in Picton and they drove to Collingwood, where they filled a box with groceries and set off for Good Life. Mike had spent the week working on the railway carriage — which had been shipped from Nelson on a barge and used as a holiday bach in Collingwood for ten years. Then Terry had bought it — for a crate of beer, Mike said — and trucked it in halves to Good Life, where

Mack put it together and used it as a house. He had moved to a new sleepout by the time the County Council inspector turned up and condemned it.

'Can we live in it if it's condemned?'

'They haven't been back. We just keep quiet. Wait until you see what I've done.'

'The roof?'

'I've tied some plastic over that. I concentrated on doing the inside.'

She went in through the veranda and found the interior scrubbed and painted. He had borrowed Terry's trailer and gone around second-hand shops for a kitchen table and wooden chairs, a chest of drawers, a tin trunk, shelving, a mattress and pillows, a box of assorted crockery, and bundles of knives and forks and spoons.

'That's too much.'

'Don't you like it?'

'Yes, I do. I love it, Mike.'

He had bought a picture — the twin of the one George had bought for the Brooklyn house. It moved her in a strange way, as though a path had opened between what she had been then and what she was now.

'That was five dollars. I knocked him down.'

'Where'd you get all the money, Mike?'

'I phoned my old man. I told him I was thinking of getting married. He sent me two hundred bucks.'

'We're not getting married, are we?'

'I reckon we are already. We don't need any legal stuff.'

Ellie was relieved. He was moving across her like something in the sky — must be getting close to midway now. She would live with him in the carriage until he was gone. What would happen then? Was there any need to ask? She took clothes, her dozen books, some blankets and sheets from her pack and suitcase.

'The only thing is,' Mike said, 'they still need somewhere for the tools and gear and stuff. So we're putting a partition up with some demo timber. You and me'll still have thirty feet. Thirty by eight. I'll make a sort of wardrobe across the end. Is that OK?'

'Yes.' It halved her pleasure, even though she saw how empty the whole carriage might have been. 'We'll have to get an eiderdown for winter. Is there a heater?'

'There's plenty of kerosene ones in the junk shops.'

'What about lamps?'

'Terry's got a Tilley we can use.'

'Water?' She had not thought about these things. The carriage and the river and the land had made her irrational. It had been a seduction. She looked out the windows — Mike had cleaned them — and saw the last sunlight washing the garden with yellow and green.

'Mack put a tank in at the sleepout. It's got a spring feed. I'm running a hose down from there,' Mike said. 'The only thing that pisses me, Rain wants us all to eat at the house. They're building a community room. It's all part of mutual help and harmony and all that.'

'I'm not going.'

'Me neither. Hey, relax. I'm going to light the stove, eh? We'll cook some sausages.'

'Visitors,' Ellie said.

They were coming round the top end of the garden: Terry and Rain, with Terra swinging between them like a shopping bag; Lee and Shawn; Annie and Mark, with two small girls playing tag behind.

'Welcome,' Terry shouted.

They were all grinning — even Annie grinned. Ellie and Mike went out to meet them, and Ellie felt herself growing pleased. They made a wall around her, an encircling arm, taking her uncertainty away. She had always been comfortable with people — the touch of hips and elbows, the easy crowding in — since her days in House 4. Being alone was no more than a story she wrote for herself now and then.

'I think we should hold hands,' Terry said.

They stood in a circle. Mark, a thickset balding man with a face as round and amiable as Annie's was forbidding, was on one side of Ellie; the older child, Sandy, on the other.

'Let's all be still,' Rain said.

Ellie supposed something was meant to settle on them. She did not mind.

'Shawn and I dug a longdrop for you back in the bush,' Mark whispered.

'Thanks.'

'There's only a seat so far. We'll get it closed in. You can grow roses.'

'Hush,' Rain said.

Terra crawled into the middle of the circle. It almost seemed they were worshipping her.

I'll start laughing if this goes on too long, Ellie thought. She also needed to use the longdrop. It was something she looked forward to.

'No words. There's too many words,' Terry said.

'A new philosophy,' Annie said.

'Hush.'

They stood quietly for a moment. The smell of compost and river and trees moved through the group on the shifting air. The afterglow intensified then faded in the garden.

I can stay here if these people will be quiet, Ellie thought.

They dropped hands and smiled as though meeting after an absence. The Americans, Lee and Shawn, drifted away hand in hand.

'Bring your guitar up, Mikey,' Lee called.

Ellie went back to the carriage. She found a toilet roll on the shelves.

'Where?'

'Turn right, follow the path. Don't fall in,' Mike said.

The others had gone when she came back. Mike was sitting on the steps, smoking a joint. He offered it.

'Where'd you get these, Mike?'

'Wedding present from my old man. Not that he knows.'

Ellie took a drag, then handed it back. It would relax and lift her, a curious combination, then make her droop. 'Do they have much of this stuff here?'

'None. They don't use it. So we'll have to do it down here on our own.'

'I don't like it much, Mike. It puts me to sleep.'

'You'll learn.'

'I tried to learn in London. I'd sooner have beer.'

'They don't have that either. Just greens. It's a pretty pure outfit here, I should have told you.'

'That suits me. I didn't come to smoke pot anyway.'

'Being free, that's why we came. Hey, relax.'

They walked up to the A-frame, where Rain had made a banquet of rice and curried vegetables. Ellie wondered who made the rules, and how they were made. Would she be allowed to cook the sausages she had bought? She imagined the smell drifting from her stove across the paddocks and Terry and Rain clutching their throats.

'Joke, Ellie? Share it,' Terry said.

'I was just feeling good. I like it here. But . . .'

'Ho,' Annie said.

'Who makes the rules? I mean, who does what jobs and what do you plant and what do you buy — all that stuff.'

'It's fairly simple,' Terry said.

'Do you have something we're all supposed to believe in? Are we all vegetarians?'

'Ah, beliefs,' Terry said.

'Can we drink if we want to? Have beer?'

'I make home brew,' Mark said. 'I'll bring you some.'

'But this is Terry and Rain's house. So when we come up here it's what they say,' Lee said.

'I thought I'd better find out,' Ellie said. 'I like the curry, Rain. It's great.'

Rain smiled. She had her dreamy look. It seemed to come from a kind of intoxication, perhaps from warmth or from situations. It was possible she wasn't bogus after all. 'The gardens are organic. That's a rule but we didn't make it,' she said.

'Who did?' Ellie said, then felt foolish.

Rain smiled at her, with a mild encompassing movement of her hands.

Oh God, Ellie thought, I'll have to stay alert.

'I say what gets planted,' Annie said. 'Don't let anyone tell you different.'

'She's a slave-driver,' Lee said. 'Say Ellie, will you take my place in the garden? Shawn and I are heading out for a while. We want to earn some money over in Nelson.' She grinned. 'It gets cold here in winter.'

'She's got me to keep her warm,' Mike said.

'Sure, Mikey. Play us a toon.'

He strummed his guitar and they sang old songs, then country ones Ellie had never heard.

'How long have you been playing that thing?' Annie asked.

'Since I was sixteen.'

'Is bloop bloop all you can do? Can't you pick or something?'

'Never learned.'

'I sang in a choir. I miss that,' Rain said. She raised her voice and sang: 'Panis angelicus fit panis hominum, Dat panis coelicus figu risterminum . . .' Her voice was pure and natural, rising in a lovely thread, then falling like water, and Ellie felt her eyes fill with tears. Shawn, sitting by her, took her hand. That was natural too, without intent.

It's going to be good here, she thought. She smiled at Shawn — a dark man, quiet, deep set, whom she hadn't said a word to yet.

She and Mike walked back through the paddocks, holding hands. She carried his guitar while he shone a pocket torch.

'We didn't get the Tilley,' she said.

'We'll light a candle.'

'Stop, Mike. Hear the river?'

'Yeah, it scares me.'

'How?'

'I lie awake and hear it like a snake. It kind of slithers.'

'Can we swim?'

'You'd die. Let's go to bed.'

They went by the gardens, chasing a possum away from the fence.

'Can't keep 'em out,' Mike said. 'Possums are the winners.'

'Why are Lee and Shawn going?'

'Like she said, to make some money. They'll come back.'

'You had something going with her, didn't you?'

He was quiet for a moment, then he shrugged. 'Not much.'

'What about him?'

'He looked the other way. It's Freedom Hall, Ellie. When the spirit moves. It didn't last long. Just a couple of times.'

'You don't have to explain.'

'Rain doesn't share it round. Nor does Annie. Lee likes to work in the nuddy, that's all. Have you ever seen a naked sheila digging?'

'What did you do, go in the bushes?'

'Yeah, I guess. It might be why old Shawn's making a move.'

'On me? A quid pro quo?'

'Take it easy, Ellie.'

'I didn't come here for screwing round. Or for smoking pot. OK?'

'Sure. OK.'

'You can do what you like.'

'Hey Ellie, I love you, don't you know that?'

'Well I don't love you.'

'But you like me OK?'

Ellie laughed: a single sound, frustrated, like a cough. 'I don't know how anyone couldn't.'

'And you'll come to bed?'

'I'll consider it. But I want to see the river first. By myself.'

She took the torch and picked her way through trees to the table rock. The river was black, with glimmers on its surface coming out and turning off. It smelled part clean and part corrupt, a smell like eels. She heard the muffled boom where it undercut the bank by the water-chute and saw how it would frighten her if she allowed — but she was Ellie and in control. And the river was the river, not a snake, whatever Mike said. It annoyed her that he was twitching her around, making her see things in a way that wasn't hers. Already he had managed to spoil Shawn.

He wasn't enough. Not complete. And Annie was right: after ten years he should be able to do more than strum. The only thing Ellie could do was enjoy him.

She left the cold rock, went by the garden into the carriage, where she found him in candlelight, trying to make the bed.

'Here Mikey, let me do that.'

In the warm blankets they made love. Yes, delicious. She lay awake listening to his breathing and the night. 'Take it step by step,' she whispered.

A breeze came up and woke her before dawn. The plastic cover on the roof popped and subsided. She listened to it, smiling. Today we'll start on the roof, she thought.

Good Life was made up of six clearings, some in the scrub, some in the bush. Annie and Mark had planted fruit and nut trees in two, and fenced the largest for the cows. They kept pigs and goats, a doe and a buck; and were the brains, and the bone and muscle, of Good Life. Terry had income from some source Ellie never found out. He worked in fits and starts, for half an hour, for half a day, while Rain's way of working was long and slow and semi-conscious. She liked to wash clothes and knit and sew and clean out sheds and paint walls. She milked the cows and hunted for eggs the fowls had laid in the scrub.

'Everyone finds his own way,' Terry said. All the same he knew the way he wanted the community to go and kept up a wordless pressure for more simplicity. He did not like Annie and Mark keeping pigs, and took Rain and Terra to Takaka on the day they slaughtered one. Ellie watched — the knife thrust in, the twist to cut aorta and heart, the hanging and scalding and scraping and gutting, and next day the butchering. It made her sick and excited, which she did not like, and she told herself, Get practical, just do it one two three if you're staying here.

Terry would not allow the possums to be trapped. He would leave the day a gin trap came through the gate — and no poison either, not on Good Life. So Mark went out at night with an old single-shot .22 and Annie with a torch, and they pinned possums in the trees with a beam of light and shot them down. It was necessary. There would be no garden and no orchard if they were allowed to breed. Ellie learned to make possum stew.

She learned to drive the Holden. She and Annie collected trailer loads of cow and horse and pig manure from farms. Annie and Lee had double-dug the garden, trenched and composted and manured, and turned the thin soil into rich.

'I learned it all from books,' Annie said when Ellie asked. 'A lot of it is common sense anyway.'

'Whoever put the carriage there didn't have much sense.'

'Why?'

'Look at where the sun is. It should have gone on the south side, not the north.'

She was no longer pleased with her choice of the carriage and would have moved to the farmhouse if two American women, sent by Lee, had not got in first. (She hoped they would not distract Mike.) By mid-June the sun barely touched the carriage, and rain leaked through the joins in the new malthoid roof. She looked at the sign painted on the door: *Second Class*; and thought, That's right.

'If I paint it with tar?' Mike said. 'And dress it with sand? Next summer, OK?' He tied the plastic cover back on. For two weeks he helped Terry dig foundations for a community room beside the A-frame. The trenches filled with water in storms, so Terry put the project aside until spring and Mike found a job in the cement works at Tarakohe. Ellie worked with Annie and the two Americans, Bella and Tully, planting cabbages and leeks and cauliflowers. They built a hot-house and a seedling shed and a bean and cucumber fence and potato trays and ran a new hose down from the spring and put in taps for summer irrigation.

Bella and Tully left and a couple from Auckland, Tom and Carrie, moved into the farmhouse. Ellie did not mind. By that time she had grown used to the carriage, its narrowness, the smell of kerosene, the flapping of the plastic on the roof. Mike had built a brick platform for the bath beside the stove-shelter. They boiled water in the copper and carried it to the bath in preserving pans and sat washing each other, sometimes with a storm howling round. Ellie loved it: slippery sex, soapy sex, in warm water in the dark, with rain driving in and slicing their backs. She took risks she never had before. Her supply of Anovlar had run out.

They bought rolls of second-hand lino and covered the floor. Ellie sewed new curtains on Rain's treadle machine. She dug a flowerbed along the front wall and bought seeds, waiting for spring. Mike brought home another load of demolition bricks and made a hearth for the pot-bellied stove. When their firewood ran low they cut manuka around the clearings and hauled it home and sawed it, two-handed, by the carriage. Looking at her callouses, Ellie remembered the gloves she'd worn as part of the uniform at Willowbank School. They would never fit now. Work had made her hands several sizes larger.

September the first. The weather agreed with the calendar; it was spring. Mike walked about doing high kicks. He spent half a day long-jumping into the sand Terry had bought for the hall foundations — trying to break the record he had set at school. He had left his job at Tarakohe, ready for carpentry again. 'Jack, Jack, the ladies' man, He can make love like no man can,' he sang, walking through the paths. The next morning, naked from bed, he slammed up a window to breathe the air and it rushed down as smoothly as a guillotine blade and broke his thumb and index finger. Ellie dressed him. She bound his arm across his chest, gave him Panadeine and drove him to the doctor in Takaka, then across to Nelson to have the bones set. She sat in the waiting room, half loving him and half disgusted. Mike invited accidents, she was sure. He used them as a way of taking a rest.

She drove home — nervous because she had no licence — while he sat beside her, hand in his lap, humming now and then as though pleased with himself.

'What fucking bad luck. Just when things were getting sweet.'

They reached the top of the hill and plunged into the valley.

'I've got the tar and sand all ready to go. Someone up there doesn't like me, eh?'

'I'd say you're pretty popular.'

'It's not my fault, Ellie. And this thing hurts. I don't like putting all the work on you.'

'There's still some things you can do with one hand.'

'Yeah, like what?' he leered.

Oh Mike, grow up, Ellie wanted to say. She saw how things would be 'sweet' for him now — how his broken fingers were a sign that he had done enough.

The next day she climbed a ladder on to the roof and started painting it with tar and dressing it with sand.

'You'll need two coats,' Mike said.

'I know. Why don't you plant the flowerbeds?'

He knelt and planted half a row. 'It's like having only one ball.' He sat in the sun and smoked a joint. 'Come on down.'

The tar — gasworks tar — was hard to spread and the smell made her feel sick. She knew that if he sat there inhaling his weed she would tip the bucket over him.

'Can you drive with one hand?'

'Sure. I s'pose.'

'Well go into town and see about going on compo then.'

'Yeah, good idea. Tomorrow, eh? Hey, I know what I'll do.'

He went through the path to the farmhouse. She watched him amble away and thought it was like having a child. He had been a grown-up for three months — a husband almost. Did she want one of those? Not if he was Mike. All through winter she had enjoyed him,

143

needed him to make herself feel joined with Good Life. Now she was aware of spaces opening up, and wanted to go there and see what she could find. Did not need companions for that, although Annie might be one, and Rain too in her way. Both had found what they needed at Good Life — Annie plain connections with her family, and Rain the soft acceptance that settled on her in the paddocks and bush, curing her of sulkiness and calming her down.

Ellie stood on her rounded platform with her tar brush in her hand. Far away, Rain, naked to the waist, was gathering eggs along the fringes of the scrub. Terry sat reading on the porch: he had discovered someone called Carlos Castaneda and was preparing new philosophies. A smell of spices and vinegar drifted down from the farmhouse where Annie and Carrie were making sauerkraut from left-over cabbages. Ellie turned the other way. She could not see the river but traced the narrow gorge bringing one of its tributaries from the uplands. She had rowed the dinghy across to the mouth of Salisbury Creek several times but not explored beyond the waterfall. Winter seemed to forbid it with shadows and wetness and heaviness. Now the land on the other side invited her. The gorge was like a pathway into the hills.

She bent and made three lines with tar on the malthoid roof: a rounded hill, a broken one, the gorge jagging down. They were beautiful and Ellie was thrilled. She had never drawn anything so simple. It was as if the hills said, This is me.

She was dizzy with the knowledge she had gained, and she steadied her feet on the curve of the roof. White soapy clouds came up, making blue shadows: she marked them in with tar — brown tar — on the grey roof. 'That's enough, no more,' she said.

It was her best picture yet. She wanted no one to see it, wanted it for herself; so, after a moment, painted it out, but kept a copy in her head.

Mike came back through the path with a tin basin. She sat down and watched him, still simmering with excitement at what she had done.

'What's that for?'

He grinned at her, went into the toolshed end of the carriage and came out with a shovel, holding the basin under his arm.

'What are you doing?'

'There's gold in them thar hills.'

'You can't, Mike, with your hand.'

'You watch me. This is a proper pan, for panning gold. I'm going up past the waterfall. Want to come?'

'No I don't. And you can't row.'

'I'll jigger across. If I find gold up there I'm going to build a sluice.'

'You don't know how.'

'I'll read a book.'

She watched him go, and later saw him come out at the top of the waterfall. He waved to her and was so carefree and somehow so defenceless that she waved back. It was better to have him doing something, anything, up the creek than sitting on the doorstep, smoking pot.

When he came back late in the afternoon he had three tiny flakes of gold in the bottom of a corked test tube.

'Not bad,' he said. 'I reckon it's been worked pretty hard, but there's still some there.'

'How much is that worth?'

'Yeah, ten cents. But if I make a sluice? Hey, I can build a suction dredge, two-stroke motor on a little raft — I've heard of those. There's a hell of a lot of gravel, they can't have gone through it all. Anyway, it changes every year.'

'Good luck, Mike.'

He panned until his fingers were healed, then he built a sluice. Ellie helped Annie plant the garden with corn, potatoes, tomatoes, beans, cucumbers, everything.

By the time the first shoots broke through she knew that she was pregnant, and she kept it as hidden as her painting on the roof. Mike had his half centimetre of gold and she had something in her not much larger, causing both fear and delight. She kept it sheltered, locked away, her best thing yet, filling the space she had made — a creature you might warm in your palm, as small as that; and she did not know what to do except grow it, grow herself, or what it — he, she — might mean other than trouble: love and trouble. She was determined Mike would never find out. At times pleasure, then terror, came on her so suddenly she almost cried out, almost rushed to Annie, rushed to Mike. Then she was calm, as though a hand, perhaps the thing that settled on Rain, touched her on head and shoulders, belly and breasts, and she slowed down all her actions and thoughts, and although she kept on moving was in a kind of sleep.

'Wake up, dopey,' Mike said.

She let him think she still had pills and was taking them. Her fondness went as far as touching him and patting him, sometimes with words, and fucking for their pleasure in bed, but no space in her mind opened where he might take a permanent place. It was as if he moved towards a horizon and would sink below it before long and be somewhere else and out of her life. It caused her no fear and no regret. Mike had been, what? Fun? He had been useful — a word that made Ellie laugh.

He came to her one day, holding a tooth on his palm.

'One of these sods has fallen off.'

A brown stump as small as a milk tooth stood in the place where it had been.

'You'll have to go back to your dentist. Go tomorrow.' She would enjoy not having him for a day.

'Can't,' he said.

'Why not?'

'Shifting my sluice.'

'You haven't been going up there. I thought you'd given up.'

'Going tomorrow. Anyway . . .' He grinned.

'What, Mike?'

'These are still the temporary ones. I never got the good ones put in.'

Ellie felt her fondness for him die. 'What did you spend the money on? Pot?'

'Stuff for in the carriage, Ellie. Pictures and stuff. I'll go to another dentist, get them fixed. Next year, eh?'

'Do what you like.' She turned towards the garden, where Annie was listening, then turned back. 'You're not doing any work here, Mike. Why don't you leave?'

'We will. End of summer.'

'Not me. I'm staying here. You should go by yourself. Hit the road.'

'Hey, Ellie.' His eyes filled with tears. It astonished her, made her want to comfort him; but she stepped away.

'This place isn't right for you, but it's right for me. I like it here.'

'So do I.'

'No you don't. It's just an easy ride. You're bludging now. That's not fair.'

'You'd be surprised what I'm doing.'

'Gold? Grow up.' She moved towards the garden, turned again. 'You can stay or go, whatever you like, it's not up to me. But find yourself another bed, Mike, eh?'

She joined Annie in the garden, and felt something strike her on the leg.

'You can keep that for a souvenir,' he yelled. 'It's more than you're worth.'

'What is it?' Annie said.

'His tooth.' Ellie pushed it into the soil with her boot. 'Sorry about all that.'

'You still don't know what he's doing, do you?'

'What?'

'He's growing marijuana. Me and Mark baled him up about it. He grew some seedlings down in Mack's old sleepout and he's got them planted somewhere over there on the other side. Gold sluicing is just a kind of cover.'

'What did you and Mark say?'

'We should have dumped his trays in the river, but we just told him to get them out. The plants were ready anyhow when we found them. So he took them over. It'll be a fair-sized plot, Ellie. Maybe a couple of hundred plants.'

'If the cops find out . . . Are you sure he hasn't got some planted here?'

'Mark and me searched. There's none. What we told him, he could do what he liked over the river but he's got to keep his tools over there, and when he harvests it he gets it out some other way, not through Good Life. We'd all get done, Ellie, the lot of us.'

'I know.'

'We told him he could stay and do this crop, and then he's out, he doesn't come back.'

'Have you told Terry?'

'Not yet. You know what he'd say: everyone's free. But me and Mark, we're drawing up some rules. And Tom and Carrie. We're going to put this place on a proper footing. I want to bring my kids up here. We don't need . . . Listen Ellie, it's not you. We don't want him, but we want you.'

Ellie watched Mike drive away in his car. He was probably heading to the pub in Collingwood. She could not feel anger, although he put them all at risk, but only contempt and sadness at his inadequacy. He could learn, she knew he could learn; but he refused — and she could not be with him any more or he might stop her going where she was going, finding out. She was jolted with fear for her baby. The child might be like his father, half-formed.

Annie said, 'You needn't tell me because I know.'

'What?'

'You're pregnant.'

'It's only two months. It doesn't show.'

'It does, though, the way you behave.'

'What do I do?'

'Stop and kind of say hello to it. You're all slowed down.'

'Am I? Annie, I don't want Mike to know.'

'I won't tell him.'

'I mean ever. I don't want him having any say.'

'He'll be gone. March, I heard him say. He'll have to get the stuff away and sell it. Then we won't let him come back in.'

'I'll be five months.'

'Yeah, well, keep him out of bed with you. He's not the most observant guy.'

He was hang-dog, apologetic, when he came back. She let him sleep alongside her but wondered how she would get on in the next three months. Being pregnant made her randy, which would be a problem if it went on. She shifted to touch him but stopped herself. Words were circling, dancing on the other side of the sexual warmth that flowed in her; and how could they describe him, 'pale', 'cold', 'thin', who was tanned like leather and thick with muscle and as horny as a bull, unless some more essential part called them up and warned her off? Morally weak? Morally thin? Again she was frightened for her baby. This man who lay here snoring, smelling of beer, dreaming of good times with his drug money, *easy* times, was father of her child.

Ellie drew away and curled up, sheltering it. Nothing could be changed — except for circumstances. Except for example and quantities of love. She did not want him at Good Life where he might work in close and influence her, get words and thoughts into the secret room where the child was growing. If he even touched her any more — leave out sex — it would be a betrayal of the child.

Tomorrow she would talk to Annie, and to Terry as well, make them see that Mike must not be allowed to stay and harvest his crop. He must be got rid of now.

She made breakfast early and half-listened to his promises to get his teeth fixed. He seemed to believe it would end the trouble between them.

'Missed you last night,' he said, patting his crotch. 'I guess I must love you, Ellie, eh?'

'Why didn't you tell me you were growing marijuana?'

'Well, I thought you probably knew. It's a kind of present anyway. We can make some real dough out of this.'

'You can. I'm staying here. And I want you out today.'

'Hey, you're not boss.'

'Does it strike you that pot is against the law? If the cops come —'

'They won't.'

'— we're all in trouble. They'll close this place. And marijuana mucks people up. Who'll you be selling it to? Kids?'

'It doesn't hurt them. That's all bullshit.'

'You think so? Try talking to yourself when you're stoned. You're a fucking zombie. You think you're full of — wisdom, I don't know. And you can't even say your own name.'

'Bullshit.'

'It's true. But I'm not going to argue. Pack your stuff, Mike. You're not spending another night in here.'

'It's my place as much as yours. Who bought the furniture, eh? Who bought the bed?'

'Take it, then. Do what you like, as long as you don't come near me.'

She walked past the gardens and across the paddock to the A-frame. Rain was feeding Terra, breastfeeding still, and Terry was writing in a notebook.

'You know about the marijuana, don't you?' Ellie said.

Terry closed his book. 'Annie told us. It's all right, Ellie. As long as it's on the other side we don't mind.'

'Even if it is against the law? You know this whole place could get closed down?'

'Mike promised he'd be careful. We trust Mike.'

'We thought you were in it too,' Rain said.

'Is that what he said? For God's sake, Rain, don't you see it'll ruin Good Life.'

'Please Ellie, no angry voices. Not in front of Terra.'

'All right. But I want Mike turned out of here. I want it today.'

'I'm not getting mixed up in any fights,' Terry said. 'And we need more people, not less. We'll be starting on the community room next week. Mike is going to help with that.'

'So, he stays?'

'You both stay, Ellie. We need you both. But what we need most is harmony or else we can't begin to know ourselves. And drugs, if they're natural, needn't be bad. Anything that opens up new channels. Anything that gives us more of ourselves. I'll lend you Castaneda if you like. You should read him.'

'No thanks.'

Mike drove by, heading for the gate. He tooted his horn and Terry waved, giving his beatific smile.

'He's not staying in the carriage,' Ellie said. 'That's mine. He can shift to the sleepout.'

'Nothing belongs to anyone, Ellie. You know that. It's why we came here.'

'Ellie, go away,' Rain said. 'You're upsetting Terra.'

'I'm sorry. But I mean it. The carriage is my home. It's where I'm staying. Maybe you don't know it but Mike is only passing through.'

'You must both do what is right for yourselves,' Terry said. 'But Ellie, please, no bad vibes. Good Life is about harmony.'

Ellie went back to the carriage and tidied it. She folded Mike's clothes and stuffed them in his pack, which she put by the door. Annie came down to the garden with her daughters. She pulled radishes, nipped off their tops and rolled them in her palms.

'What's happening, Ellie?'

'I don't know yet. Terry won't help.'

Annie put the radishes in the girls' schoolbags. She kissed them and sent them off to catch the school bus.

'Mark had a look at Mike's plantation, did I tell you? He's got a little micro-climate down there. Mark reckons he'll harvest in March all right. He'll be gone then, Ellie. We'll set up a constitution for this place. I'll ram it down Terry's throat if I have to.'

Ellie nodded. She had turned a corner in the night and left Mike somewhere else. If she had to, she would leave Terry too.

'I'm not coming to work this morning. I'm going across there.' She waved at the river.

'You're not looking for his garden?' Annie said.

'No. Up in the hills.' Seeing Good Life from the other side might be a way of putting more space between her and Mike.

She rowed across and pulled the dinghy on to the shingle fan above the creek. She might have been in a wilderness with nothing man-made visible. When she reached the top of the waterfall the roofs of Good Life came into view. They seemed too cosy for her liking, and she walked, stepping upwards, for half an hour before looking back. The longer view made Good Life small and lonely, which suited her better, reinforced her independence and the strength she felt. The valley was crescent shaped, enclosed, held still by the weight of hills leaning on it. She climbed again, through rocks and stunted scrub and gravelly soil, moving in a straight line and meeting the gorge as it twisted. The creek ran in shingly banks, then slipped to lower levels on slides of stone. She saw Mike's sluice dug in and fixed with stakes, and was impressed by how far he had carried it. For a while he had been serious about his gold prospecting. For a while: that was Mike. It put another step between them and made her tolerant.

The gorge cut through reddish-brown rock, part of a mineral belt. Bush grew at a distance on both sides, thicker and blacker to the north. Somewhere down there Mike's plantation lay. Green seedlings, she thought. Green plants by now. His dreams would be of money instead of rainbow shadows. Ellie grinned, then was angry and sour. Letting him get away with his crop seemed like complicity. He put a stain on Good Life and on her.

She ate the cheese and tomato sandwich she had brought, then climbed down to the creek and drank from a pool. She lay on a patch of grass and stared into the sky, tried to see deep into it. There was no way of telling how far the eye travelled out, how far it would penetrate, at its speed of light. If she blinked, did the journey start again?

She closed her eyes. She tried to sleep, but the grass pricked through her shirt and the ground made her hips ache — and perhaps made her baby uncomfortable. She wondered about that. Could it feel yet? She could not imagine it without responses, or that they were simply physical. Her ignorance made her ashamed. She would have to get books and read — must not go through pregnancy without *knowing*. She wanted to know everything the baby knew.

She stood up and climbed again, and each level sank Good Life deeper into the valley. There were goat droppings on the ground and it pleased her that something lived up here. Goats on the high hills. Trout and eels in the river. People at Good Life. It all seemed linked. She rested again, then wound her way through clumps of nibbled tussock grass to the bush. Some of the trees she could name, others not, but she knew their shapes and would be able to draw them, leaf and trunk and tree-head, if she chose. It was as if they gave themselves to her and she might carry them away.

Her watch said midday. She walked down slowly, angling back and forth. Pieces of the river shone, trailing like snail slime. She saw her table rock, its surface white in the sun. She had stood there in mid-winter with the river boiling less than a yard below, hammering in the undercut above the water-chute, which had turned into a rolling coil. The wind had torn her hat off and boated it halfway across before the water sucked it down. Ellie shivered. It had been her lesson in smallness: was today her lesson in her true place? She wondered about it. The valley was here when she was not. The hills sat still, the river ran. So what was she, moving through it, seeing?

She stood on the lip of the waterfall. The pool at its base was less clear than the river. An eel pool, not a trout pool: green glass. Mike had trapped eels and tried to smoke them. He talked about setting up a business, then forgot. Poor Mike. He was strictly short term. He should forget his marijuana garden and move on.

Something was flashing in the sun through the trees. It moved slowly: Annie shifting sheets of tin in the garden, perhaps, strengthening her possum fence. Ellie rowed across the river, hauled the dinghy up and fastened it. She heard a car door slam and Mike's voice cry, 'That'll do. Leave her there. What do you think?'

The river, lying still, transmitted voices.

'Yeah, some place,' Boggsie said.

Ellie's stomach heaved. She thought she was going to vomit, and she stood for a moment with her hand pressed to her mouth. Then she climbed the bank and broke through the trees.

His truck was pulled up beside the stove shed. He and Mike stood at the edge of the garden, talking to Annie, while a woman wearing cut-off jeans rolled a cigarette on the carriage steps.

'Hey Ellie, look who's here,' Mike called.

She was dizzy and could not see properly. Mike and Boggsie were flat as though pasted on a wall. She stopped short of them.

'Get him out of here.'

'Take it easy, Ellie. Hear what he's got to say.'

'I'm not interested. Get him out.'

But it was too late. Boggsie had set foot on Good Life and that was enough.

'All it is, Ellie, I was out of line back on the orchard,' Boggsie said. 'So we'll shake hands, eh, and start again?'

'No,' Ellie said.

The woman by the carriage laughed and lit her cigarette.

'Listen, Ellie,' Mike said, 'and get it straight. You don't run this place. I've already talked to Terry, and he says Boggsie and Tina can stay. OK? Boggsie's going to help with the community room. Ellie, he was a plumber. We can use a plumber here.'

Boggsie spread his mouth in its pasted-on smile. 'I'm a tradesman,' he said. The woman laughed again.

'You know what he did to me, and you asked him here?'

'Ellie —'

'It's your marijuana, isn't it? You need him to help sell it.'

'You better shut up about that.'

'You can get in trouble,' Boggsie said.

'Hey, just a minute,' Annie said.

'Keep out of it, Annie. This is Ellie and me,' Mike said.

'Not any more. No more, Mike. We're finished now,' Ellie said. She turned and walked to the carriage. 'Get out of my way.'

The woman, Tina, stepped aside. 'Take it easy, chickie. It's a long life,' she said.

Ellie lay on the bed, shivering. Then she jumped up. She wanted to wash. It was as though Mike had lifted his leg on her. She went into the garden and turned on the tap; gathered water in her palms, splashed it on her eyes, her cheeks, her throat.

'What are you going to do, Ellie?' Annie said.

'I don't know.'

'Please don't leave.'

Ellie had not thought of it, but Annie compacted Good Life with those words and put it aside.

All I have to do is pack and go, Ellie thought. It's not running away, it's finishing. She felt it like an instruction. Good Life was bundled up; it was property, which she took away as well as left behind. She felt as if the child inside her had said yes.

'Annie, don't let him stay too long or he'll ruin this place.'

She walked as far as the wire. 'Keep him away from your girls.'

'Shit!' Annie said.

Tina was leaning on the truck, rolling another cigarette. She winked at Ellie. The mattress was rolled up in the tray, tied with twine, and Ellie wondered if Boggsie had managed to put this woman to work.

'Where have they gone?'

'In a boat somewhere. Relax, kiddo. Boggsie never stays anywhere long.'

'Five minutes is enough,' Ellie said.

She put everything she wanted to take in her pack. Annie came in.

'You're going?'

'Yes.'

'What did you mean, the girls?'

'Nothing. It's just, he's low-grade shit. Anything he thinks he can get, he'll take. I'm sorry, Annie. This woman he's got probably keeps him happy.'

'She'd better. Don't worry, I'll watch. Mark will have him out if he puts a finger wrong. Ellie, please stay.'

Ellie shook her head. 'It's spoiled now. It's finished for me.'

'They'll be gone soon.'

'He came here once. That's enough. I know it sounds hysterical, but — I've got to go.'

'It's because you're pregnant.'

'Not only that. Don't tell Mike. I don't want him hanging round.'

'He'd probably head the other way.'

'Yes, he would. But I don't want him turning up years from now. That'd be his style.'

She looked around the carriage. Boggsie and Tina would commandeer the bed and put Mike, with his brown baby tooth, into the truck — unless they invited him for threesomes. Ellie was tempted to slash the mattress and put her fist through the stupid picture he had bought. Instead she lugged her pack outside. Her rage subsided and her clear sight came back. The sky was enamelled, blue and hard, the plants in the garden enamelled too. Everything was picked out, lifted off a surface. She wondered if it was some sort of marking of things in herself, a way of possessing.

Annie's face was lopsided, tragic. Ellie hugged her.

'You'll come and see us?' Annie said.

'Probably not.'

'We'll make this a good place, wait and see.'

'I know you will.' She threw her pack on the back seat of Mike's car.

'Hey, you can't take that,' Tina said.

'Try and stop me.' The keys were in the ignition. 'Tell him I'll leave it in Collingwood,' she said to Annie. 'And give my love to Mark and the girls.'

She backed out past Boggsie's truck and drove through the paddocks. Terry and Rain were cleaning demolition timber beside the

A-frame. She tooted her horn and left them staring. Opened the gate, closed it, and drove, leaving a trail of dust, up the Bainham road to Collingwood.

Ellie spent a week with her mother, then telephoned Jim Barchard. Two days later she was thinning Golden Delicious on the orchard.

'Where's your boyfriend?' Jim said.

'Dumped him,' Ellie grinned. 'If he turns up for a job here, I'm leaving.'

'You've got some sense,' Jim said.

Ellie drew back from the exchange. That's my baby's father we're talking about. Confusion of this sort might last for the rest of her life. Her feeling of loss for Good Life might last too. For a while it had provided a perfect mixing of time and place. As well, it had shifted something in her, more than a point of view: some method of touching and accepting. She had found a way of seeing that was different from simply letting things happen and looking at them.

Ellie smiled when she reasoned like this. The lessons she had come away with: work was good and people difficult and she could not get by without both of them. But she also began to feel that she had locked herself up. There had been no newspapers or radio at Good Life. She had had little idea what was happening in the world. An election had come and gone: she had picked up that. The party she would have voted for had lost. It had not seemed important at the time. Now it displeased her. She wanted her chance to say no to the right-wing lot, who kept on supporting the Vietnam war.

She had not heard of Charles Manson and his murders. Seven people butchered, one of them a woman eight months pregnant. Ellie wondered if the baby had been stabbed. Her mouth stretched wide with shock as she thought of it. Her own child, although not quickened yet, seemed to shrink, and she clamped her hands low, protecting it. Boggsie might be Manson, although his pan-faced look was nothing like. He had the same savagery.

She asked Jim for a key and kept the pickers' hut locked at night. Walking on the roads, she stepped away and sometimes hid when cars approached.

Audrey stopped one day in her Mini.

'You're back?'

'Yes. Hello.'

'What's the matter, dear. You look evasive.'

'No, I'm not. I don't like the dust.'

'Do you want a ride?'

'No thank you. I'll walk.'

'Well — if you want some books to borrow, come on up.'

Ellie watched regretfully as the car moved off. She had been working all day and would have welcomed a ride. She would have liked to talk as well, and borrow books and be less solitary. She was missing Good Life, and Annie and Mark, Rain and Terry too — and Mike, sometimes in a way that made her breathless and greedy, and at other times ashamed. Mike was gone. They were not connected any more. But oh if she could just have him in bed for half an hour.

It was in this state that she walked out to the road one night and instead of heading down towards Ruby Bay turned into Fan and Audrey's driveway. It was ten to eight, visiting time. If Fan was unwelcoming she would turn round and go away.

She stopped under the pine trees and heard them sigh. That was simple. That, tonight, was their sound. Their branches closed the sky which, low above the paddocks, was darkening and pricking with stars. She remembered her painting in tar on the carriage roof. The truth of it was in the lines: lines making shapes and the shapes balancing. How had she seen that, looking at the hills? Nothing had been balanced there. She had simplified.

Ellie hummed with pleasure at the memory. She went along the side of the house and knocked on the back door.

Audrey came, like the maid, while Fan, presumably, waited in her chair.

'Ah Ellie, come in, come in,' Audrey said in a voice meant to warn

Fan as well as welcome Ellie.

'I thought I'd take you up on borrowing books,' Ellie said.

'Of course. Fan, look who's here.'

'Ellie Crowther,' Ellie said.

'I don't need to be told. The girl from the orchard. I thought you'd given us up,' Fan said.

She was sitting in an armchair, listening to music, with only the table lamp switched on. A cave, Ellie thought, with humpbacked Audrey and little Fan, still as a cat and ready to spit, the inhabitants. Above the shadow-line the walls were jewelled with colour that advanced and then retreated, disturbing Ellie as though with an illusion.

'Turn off the record, Audrey. Turn on the light,' Fan said. 'Sit down and let me look at you.'

Ellie sat. 'I'm sorry if I left in a hurry last time,' she said.

'Where've you been?'

'On a commune over in Golden Bay.'

'Flower power, all that stuff?' Fan said.

'No. Growing vegetables. Hard work.'

'Back to the soil?'

'Not at all,' Ellie said. She could not work out whether this woman meant to annoy her.

'The simple life?'

'Do you always want to quarrel? All I came for was some books.'

'You took some last time and never read them.'

'Give over, Fan. Let the girl catch her breath,' Audrey said. She had stopped the record. Now she turned on the ceiling light.

'Ah, pictures,' Ellie said. 'I couldn't work it out.'

'Why not?'

'They were in the shadows.' She wanted to say that they had been like eyes watching her but thought it might sound stupid. Red eyes, blue eyes, green and yellow eyes turning into fruit and jugs and violins and a woman with black hair sitting on a sofa: half a dozen paintings with objects so sharp and colours so bright her eyes contracted. 'Are they yours?'

'If you mean did I paint them, yes I did.'

'So,' Ellie said. She did not know how to go on: felt assaulted and occupied and pleased.

'So,' she repeated.

Fan laughed. Audrey said, 'I'll make some tea.'

Ellie turned in her chair. Further along the wall were darker paintings, brown and green, of trees and foliage and hills. She stood up and looked at them; and felt hollowness inside her, something like hunger, and a prickling of hair on the back of her neck. Trees that were not like trees but were trees. And hills with the roundness and fullness of hills — again not like.

'I didn't know you did this sort of thing,' she said.

'You thought I was a lady painter? Pretty pictures?' Fan said.

'I didn't think about it at all. Have you been doing it all your life?'

'All my life,' Fan said.

'Can you make enough to live off? Doing this?'

'I couldn't always. Now I can, just about.'

Ellie remembered that Audrey had called her a moneybags.

'I've got a dealer in Wellington. He sells one or two.'

'I suppose I should have heard of you?' Ellie said.

'Don't look any more. Come back in the daytime when there's proper light. In fact, let's give our eyes a bit of peace.' She got up and switched off the ceiling light, leaving only the table lamp. Audrey came back.

'Ah, so it's going to be gloom.'

'Not at all,' Fan said. 'We thought we'd talk.'

'This is my spiced apple cake,' Audrey said. 'You eat it with cream. I hope you like cream.'

'Yes, I do. And that's one of your rugs on the floor,' Ellie said.

'That's right. It's just as well you've turned off the light or you'd see my mistakes. I sell my good ones and keep my bad. She keeps all her best things, silly girl.'

'You've no idea what's best, so pipe down,' Fan said.

Bickering was a game they played. It disguised affection, although better on Fan's part than on Audrey's.

'We didn't expect you'd come back here. Pickers usually turn up only once,' Fan said.

'I just thought I'd like a familiar place,' Ellie said.

'Why did you leave your commune?'

'They started growing marijuana. Besides, I'd come to the end of it. I think.'

'You're not sure?'

'I went there so I could stop going forward for a while — and let myself settle. Things were pretty basic. I didn't need to worry about myself. I loved it for a month or two. There just seemed to be no uncertainties. No holes you kept falling into all the time. But then it all began to get too static. It started to seem we'd built a wall around us. And I had to come back and start moving again. There were other reasons too.'

'Men,' Fan said.

Ellie laughed distractedly. She was interested in her explanation for leaving Good Life. She had found it as if by chance but it seemed to be true, at least in part.

'I'm pregnant,' she said. 'But don't tell Jim or he might try and stop me climbing ladders.'

'You don't look it,' Fan said.

'Nearly four months.'

'So you're having it, then?'

'Fan, what a terrible question. Of course she's having it,' Audrey said.

'Some girls don't.'

'Be quiet. Take no notice, Ellie. We're just two childless old women. There are all sorts of things we don't understand.'

'And a hell of a lot of others we do. Does the father know?'

'No. And I don't want him to.'

'There are good reasons for keeping them around for a while. But on the whole I think you're right. They usually cause trouble. If

161

you're having it you're keeping it, of course?'

'Yes, of course.'

'It won't be easy.'

'I know,' Ellie said.

She did not, in any detail. And did not want to think about difficulties yet. She would face them when the time came, and find her way round or through or over. She ate her apple cake and complimented Audrey, who said, 'Have another piece. You're eating for two.'

'Does being pregnant make you want to draw?' Fan said.

'Not really. Should it?'

'I don't know. I'm curious. I thought there might be a connection.'

'If there is I don't feel it.' She needed nothing like that, no extras, only the baby. 'But I'd like to borrow that book again. Matisse.'

'Why?'

Ellie thought. What she wanted to say might sound stupid to Fan, but she would say it. 'I want to see how he draws his lines.'

'Ha! It's easy to see but hard to do.'

'I did a picture once,' Ellie said, and stopped.

'Yes? Have you got it?'

'It was in tar, on a roof. It got painted over.'

'It must have been a good one, though, if you remember it.'

'It was just half a dozen lines. But . . .' She could not say why it had pleased her.

'Do it again,' Fan said.

'I don't want to.'

'Why not? Do you know how many times Cézanne painted Mont St Victoire?'

'He was in that other book you lent me. Can I take it as well?'

'If you like living in Nelson I think you'll like Cézanne.'

'She always says she's broken in two parts, Matisse, Cézanne,' Audrey said. 'But listen, dear, you really must be careful climbing ladders.'

'Yes, I will be.'

'And you must let me drive you wherever you want to go. Have you seen your doctor?'

'I haven't got one.'

'But Ellie, you must —'

'Don't nag the girl, Audrey, or she won't come back. If you want some paper and pencils, Ellie, I can let you have some.'

'No. Just books. And could I have another piece of apple cake, please?'

She was happy but wanted things kept equal, between them and between her and them. She would not be pushed where she did not want to go.

Later on, walking back to the orchard with her arms full of books, tears came into her eyes at the loss of Good Life; and then she let her mind go around and over it, and would not have to think of it again as snatched away. Audrey and Fan had shown her how to bundle it up, encompass it. She wanted to know that pair, but not too well. She did not want to go with them too far.

Ellie put the books down and stood with her back against a tree. She listened and waited. Was that a movement inside her? Was it too soon? She must get other books, pregnancy books from the library. She needed to know. Audrey could drive her. She would ask Jim for time off and they would go tomorrow.

The baby was her company. There was a movement there, so tiny she almost could not feel it; and she said, 'Yes, it's you, you're saying hello. Who are you down there? If you tell me, I'll give you a name.'

Between times

1970. AFTER THE Gravenstein pick Ellie shifts to the packing shed. She would rather be out in the sun — and climbing ladders — but the laden bags sit awkwardly and she is frightened of hurting her baby. She tries out names for it, and chooses Roland for a boy because of a poem Mrs Nimmo had read to her class at Willowbank school: *Childe Roland to the Dark Tower Came*. Robert Browning wrote it. Mrs Nimmo had not said what might emerge from the tower when Roland blew his horn. They must work that out for themselves. Ellie isn't sure she should condemn her child (her Childe) to a life of struggle. She borrows a Browning collection from Fan and reads the poem (it's longer than she remembers) and thinks: Yes, Roland, but he can choose what he wants to be. A girl's name is harder to find. Melanie, Jane, Annette? What about Dolores? In the meantime, when she talks to the baby she calls it You: 'Hey, you in there, how are you getting on?'

She doesn't read much. She doesn't draw. She looks at Matisse's drawings and they don't work for her. Fan is disappointed, but paints Ellie, both clothed and naked. Ellie is too polite to say, I don't think it's me.

She moves into Fan and Audrey's spare room in her seventh month. The baby is born in June. Ellie doesn't say, 'Roland.' She holds her child's damp head in her palm and feels it throb and she says, 'John' — her father's name. John Crowther. (Mike is even further away than Roland. Mike is gone.) She telephones her mother and cannot tell if the sound she hears is weeping or laughter, then if the weeping is happy or sad. Cannot answer questions: doesn't know. All she wants is love, a welcome to pass on to John through a whisper in his ear, through the touch of her hands, although her own love is enough, Ellie knows that.

Audrey offers love. There is a danger it will be too much. A baby in the house will get on Fan's nerves, so Ellie turns down an offer to stay for a while. She shares a house in Nelson with two other solo mothers, which isn't easy. Both are younger than her and need more fun. She seems to be back in her first flat, with children added. She tries to like Glenda and Nettie's two boys, who are older than John, but finds it hard. There are arguments and fights — some pushing, no blows — which interfere with Ellie's flow of milk. It is lucky that John is an easy baby. He eats and sleeps, he grins and cries, reminding Ellie of Mike, which is a worry. She does some house-cleaning, taking John along in his pram. Noisy vacuum cleaners frighten him. She shifts the pram continuously, keeping it one room ahead, then a room behind. Her wealthiest employers — her easiest house — fire her on her second visit: 'We don't like your sort coming here.' Ellie walks home numbed, then the insult works her into a rage. She goes back in the night and hurls a river stone through their picture window. (In her apple fights with Mike in the orchard she has learned to throw as accurately as a cricket outfielder.) The noise of glass breaking fills her with elation, which does not last. 'Your sort.' It seems that Mrs Prime has come back to haunt her.

She goes to her mother for Christmas and that's a hard time. Mrs Brownlee — Ellie names her Brownlee with relief — feels that Ellie has spoiled her life. Ellie stays pacific, then is sharp. She thinks of how much money she has wasted on this trip, how many hours of mopping floors. Mopping floors — like waitressing — doesn't mean 'ending up'.

1971. She meets a woman with two children, the younger John's age, and accepts an offer to move in with her and share the rent. Carol's husband, a fisherman, is away at sea most of the time. Carol is plain in looks and behaviour and has a strange speech impediment: before starting she must work her jaw as though freeing toffee stuck in her molars. Yet when she speaks her voice is soft and clear, and somehow endearing. Her opinions are sensible. Ellie soon likes her as much as any woman she has known. She grows fond of Carol's children, and likes Denis well enough when he comes home from sea. She enjoys the supply of fresh fish and starts John eating it quite early. What she would like for herself is a share of the love-making Carol and Denis enjoy on the other side of the uninsulated wall. Not *their* love-making — Denis doesn't attract her in that way. She denies that she is looking for a man. She would just like to have one now and then.

Carol weans her daughter at ten months. Ellie follows reluctantly at twelve. She wants to go out and work, and knows she can trust Carol with John. With apologies, contrition, lots of extra cuddles for her boy, she takes a part-time job in the public library. Is anxious away from him but likes the work and enjoys meeting people. Money is still her greatest worry. She paints watercolours of local scenes to sell in gift shops. Fifeshire Rock. The Boulder Bank. Yachts sailing through The Cut. No one will buy and she doesn't blame them. There is no pleasure in doing it. She cannot see the things she tries to paint or paint things she cannot see.

1972. Money. Money. The child allowance is $1.50 a week. Ellie asks for more hours at the library but is told she will have to work full time. She delivers advertising circulars in the afternoons, with John in a carrier on her back. Enjoys it over summer but has to give up when bad weather comes. She paints birds and flowers on plywood for a woman who makes mobiles; learns to paint on glass for another; weaves tiny pretty flowery raffia baskets, hating it. Joins a women's liberation group, which Carol won't go along to, frightened it will spoil her happiness with Denis.

1973. Ellie looks after Fan and Audrey's house while they holiday in Sydney. It's only for a week but she wants it to be forever — not for the money (they insist on paying her a hundred dollars) but for John. He runs on the lawn and she chases him with a hose, even though the water tanks are low and Audrey has asked her not to flush the loo except for big ones. Still without a licence, she takes him in the Mini to the beach and smears him all over with muddy sand and washes him clean. He has Mike's colouring — lucky boy — but everything else, Ellie insists, comes from her. She carries him on her shoulders through Jim's orchard and lets him pull fat apples two-handed from the trees. At night when he's asleep she watches TV and listens to music, surrounded by Fan's paintings advancing and retreating in the shadows. She can't explore the studio — Fan has locked it and closed the curtains — but she looks at art books from Fan's collection (thousands of dollars' worth of books): Matisse, Cézanne, who puzzle her and begin, just begin, to stir in her blood, and *everyone* else. She's alarmed at her ignorance. How is it she has never heard of half these people? Goya she has heard of, and seen. He strips off her skin again, and when it gets too painful she snaps the book shut and puts it away.

In 1974 Ellie turns thirty. Where have I got to? she thinks. John is part of the answer but cannot be all. Another question, mingling with the first, is how is she going to see he gets a proper chance? Doesn't a boy need a man? And doesn't she? She realises that she has never been in love — not in the way people are in books, enough to make them jump under trains. She's been infatuated; she's had crushes; but her better affairs have been for pleasure and affection. Mike had been like that. Love had been missing, and respect. She reads Jane Austen again (forgets the servants overlooked) and enjoys the progress, the orderly complications, of the love her young women feel. Perhaps, though, you need money and leisure for that sort of thing. Would it be worth sitting in parlours and sewing ribbons on bonnets for? Ellie doesn't think so.

As much as a man she wants a satisfying job, something to fill the empty parts of herself. She is fretful by mid-year. She turns about, looking for somewhere to go. Then Denis is drowned in a winter storm. Pieces of his boat wash up on a West Coast beach but his body is never found. Carol weeps week after week. Ellie has never seen this sort of grief. Did her mother feel it for her father? She finds herself recreating him: riding on the footplate, coming home from work, leaning over her cot. She holds his forehead in her palms. It's sad and supportable and sometimes makes her smile. Carol's grief is insupportable. Ellie is afraid she will die. She gives up her library job and looks after her. Late in the year she sends her to stay with her married sister in Murchison.

Ellie is alone. And she has no money. (Fan gives her a painting but she'd sooner have cash.) She takes in boarders, two young men who work in the bank; but it doesn't last. One of them thinks she must be easy. He turns nasty when she tells him no. The other has an allergy to cats (Ellie has adopted a stray tom) and thinks it might extend to John. He draws away as though he'll get a rash. She sends them packing and takes in two girls, who ask to have their boyfriends stay all night. Two couples in one room: Ellie says no. They get nasty like the man from the bank. She turns them out and telephones Carol: Please, is there any chance of her coming back? Carol says she has been going to write. She is teaming up with a sharemilker whose wife has left him. She had never thought she could be happy again, but he's such a good man and so good with the children. Ellie understands: you've got to keep going. She puts the phone down and weeps.

1975. Her luck changes. Fan and Audrey are going to Europe for three months. They ask her to mind the house from April to June. (They want to be back before the Mediterranean tourist season starts.) Ellie settles in, then gets her driver's licence. House and car and money (just enough). She wants to sing like Mary Poppins. She wants to throw John in the air and catch him coming down — but he's too big. 'School in three months and holidays till then.'

The dry summer has left the tanks even lower, washing-up water must be saved for the plants, so she doesn't chase him with the hose. She takes him to beaches and playgrounds, helps him climb trees, feed the goat and feed the fowls, chase J.P. Morgan (or one of his descendants) away from the jars of honey water. She teaches him to swim so that he will never drown. His piping, inquiring four-year-old voice makes her delirious with love. She hugs him so hard it frightens him, and frightens her. She's hungry, she's desperate for another kind of love.

There's a Swedish boy picking the last Grannies in Jim's orchard. She invites him in to watch TV. They drink a bottle of Fan's Australian wine. 'Ellie,' he says, 'as well as myself I have brought these.' Contraceptives. She feels that making love in the house will betray Audrey (not Fan) and change her luck, so they spread an eiderdown on the lawn, in the warm night. She leaves the door open to hear John if he should wake. It's inhibiting, and Lars is too quick, but is eager to try again. She's half satisfied. Won't let him come into the house and stay all night; sends him away frowning the next time he calls. He looks like Werner, her boy on Skye, but he isn't half as nice. And this is not the way to find love. She won't be the sort of woman men visit with condoms ready to put on. She has the eiderdown drycleaned.

1976–79. John is happy at the school in Tasman Street and later on at Nelson Central. Ellie works full time in the library. She wants to buy a house but the bank won't give her a mortgage. She'd throw a stone through its plate-glass window if Trafalgar Street wasn't so well lit.

She rents, and rents again, but cannot save. Drives a Datsun Bluebird that is always breaking down. Has a man friend. Has another. (No names.) They don't stay all night. She is determined that John will not find an uncle in the house on Sunday mornings; and to keep her resolution keeps her single bed.

She joins a group trying to stop Council from planting a pine forest on a public reserve. Looks up the river valley from the library steps, sees the hills golden in the afternoon sun and cannot understand how people can uncolour them, geometrise them with foreign trees. It's just for money, the filthy stuff. Ellie becomes secretary. She writes to the *Mail*; she heckles at Council meetings. The mayor threatens to have her put out but she's unafraid. Marches up and thrusts her manifesto in his hands. She distributes leaflets written by herself, one in every letterbox in town, but it's all for nothing. Teams of forestry workers plant the hills, put ink dots all over the golden slopes. One Sunday morning Ellie can stand it no longer. She sends John to a friend's house and walks along a face above the river, pulling out seedlings as she goes. The spread-out town unnerves her. There might be a hundred pairs of binoculars trained on her. She cannot afford to pay a fine so she comes down, digs out her watercolours, tries to paint the hills the way they were, keeping the lines as simple as in her painting on the carriage roof. It doesn't work. Watery, slack, insipid. She's upset. How can what her hands do be so weak when she feels so strongly?

1980 is a year for joining. NFAC. The Values Party. She hates Muldoon. *Hates* him. Believes he'd get rid of parliament and run the country as a fascist state if he could. She knows people who have emigrated because of Muldoon. Tries cartooning in broadsheets — Piggy as pig, as crocodile, as Uncle Sam's rat on a leash — but fails again. There's too much anger and too little wit. She gives it up. Tries to calm down, knowing the damage she does to herself. 'Fan,' she says, 'next summer will you teach me to paint?' 'We'll see. You'll probably go shooting off in some other direction before then,' Fan replies.

The prophecy comes true. In mid-winter Ellie meets Neil Higgs. Another group she's attached to — as library representative — is Coffee and Books. She goes along to listen to him talk about his novels. After ten minutes she thinks, What a delicious man. In looks he's not bad, he's average — large ears, long nose, mouth that twists left when he smiles and pouts when he's serious. He has a way of crinkling his eyes that's perhaps over-sweet. All the same, he's masculine — good shoulders, wide throat, square hands. His mind is a nice mix — sensitive and tough. He can laugh at himself. Tells a story about going to the landfill with a trailer load of rubbish and trying time after time to back it to the tip-face. He slews left, he slews right — until a little old lady jumps out of the cab of a truck and parks it for him with a single twist of the steering wheel. All the ladies laugh. Ellie laughs, wondering if it's true. She wishes she had read one of Neil Higgs's novels. So far he has written three. How old is he? She works it out from a dust jacket. Forty-two.

Ellie interviews him for the library newsletter. She tells him that she paints and mentions that she knows Fan Anerdi. His eyes light up: he'd love to meet her. Ellie telephones Fan, who shrugs along the wire — 'Why not?' They drive in Ellie's unwashed Bluebird to Ruby Bay. Fan is polite (while Audrey only wants to hear about John). Neil Higgs walks along Fan's paintings. He murmurs, he exclaims, and Ellie cannot tell whether it's from pleasure or greed. How are his eyes? They shine. Is it calculation? Fan doesn't invite him into her studio. Audrey makes tea while Neil mentions painters he knows. 'Oh yes,' Fan says. She does not say whether she knows them or not. 'I suppose none of these are for sale?' Neil asks. 'No. Talk to Ellie about her one. She might sell it.' It's more than a rebuke for turning up with a man Fan dislikes; it seems like a severing of friendship. Ellie drives Neil back to Nelson. She has time to show him her Anerdi painting — which is not for sale — before taking him to catch his plane. They shake hands, he crinkles his eyes and flies away. Why does Fan dislike him? It's far too quick, must be shallow. Fan is jealous perhaps.

Ellie sets her course away from Fan towards Neil Higgs. She buys his latest novel and is cross when two days later an inscribed copy arrives in the post. The hero is a wimp, which is disappointing. He's meant to be deep and sensitive but is shifty and hysterical. The women — there are several — are simply decorative. Ellie knows that Neil Higgs can do better than this — and she's right. In October he invites her to the launching of *The Dark Before the Light*. She leaves John with friends and crosses on the ferry to Wellington. Is this her crossing? Ellie is nervous. She sits on the open deck, reading the advance copy of his novel Neil has sent, and is caught up in it. The old clergyman is brave and unlikable, his wife patient and loving and strong, his children — so many of them! She loses count. Searches for a word she might offer the author. Olympian? After the launching there's a party at his house. Ellie stays all night. They make love in a huge bed made for love. Talk. Make love. Talk again. He's separated from his wife. He has a son John's age and a daughter two years younger. They live in Auckland with Betty — a name Neil utters with dislike. He's a socialist. It's in his blood, no matter all the stupid things they do. His hand would shrivel and turn to dust if he tried to vote National. 'Me too,' Ellie says, concealing that she's in the Values Party. 'Why don't you shift to Wellington?' Neil says. 'Do you mean it?' 'It's a big house. I'd like your little boy, I promise I would.' 'He's quite big now.' 'I like you,' he says. 'You make me laugh. You're beautiful.'

Glenmore Street

ELLIE COULD walk to Lambton Quay in ten minutes. Her favourite way was through the gardens and the cemetery: fountains and roses and cricket players, then names and dates and family tragedies. Children died and wives died young — and, to be fair, husbands too. Diphtheria, Ellie wondered, scarlet fever, whooping cough? Childbirth for the women, and perhaps anaemia; and, for the men — she did not know. TB? Drink? Disappointment? Drowning? The 1800s had been dangerous times. Her greatest danger was that she might walk up Lambton Quay behind Muldoon and find him just a little man in a baggy suit. Perhaps someone like him had stepped out when Childe Roland reached the Dark Tower and blew his horn. The ruined landscape Roland had ridden through was a psychic portrait of New Zealand.

Ellie liked that idea — she thought it was clever — and tried it out on Neil, but he didn't read Victorian poetry, he said. Or novels either: they were spoiled by what they were not able to say. If Dickens had been allowed to write about sex . . .

She found out almost straight away that Neil had an ordinary mind. In some ways it was a relief. On the other hand, it made him mysterious. Where did his books come from? There were so many smarter people than Neil around. Some of them even tried to write, but they could not. It made Ellie suspect something deep and broad in him, but parallel, out of the usual way of intelligence. I'm in love with someone I don't know, she thought; and set herself to find out who he was, with anticipation, with enjoyment, and a small amount of anxiety that she had perhaps committed herself on insufficient grounds.

She liked the house in Glenmore Street, although it needed doing up. She liked Neil's behaviour with John most of the time. He had a way of withdrawing with a sigh when the child became boisterous. Ellie supposed he was missing his own son, Kevin. She did not expect John to replace Kevin or even make up for him but she wanted Neil to behave, in all the ways open to him, as her son's father. Some things might be impossible, but she could not see that Neil should find it necessary to step back when John became a rowdy small boy. 'Maybe we could tone him down a bit,' Neil said. Ellie had heard 'tone down' before. She did not like it. But then she saw that noise was painful to Neil, disturbing an equilibrium. She made allowances, diverted John. She let him watch more TV — down at the other end of the house — than she thought was good for him. They all had to make small shifts, give something away.

She enrolled John at Thorndon School, next door to Wellington Girls' College where she had gone. A circle seemed to close — she hoped she had finished with perimeters and could occupy the centre. She strode across the playground with her son, feeling confident, feeling big. Being looked at twice was new to Ellie but people had started doing it, men especially. She was thirty-six, lean bodied, big breasted, dark blonde, strong in her features: she was handsome. She should perhaps take more care with her clothes, but that was a small thing. Her colour sense never let her down.

She filled in a form in the principal's office and stopped when she came to *Father's name*. 'I live with my partner,' she said, overloud. Partner was a new word and she had not got it right; but she gave a smile that might be seen as bold. 'Not applicable, I'll put that.'

'Perhaps we could have your partner's name? In case of emergencies,' the principal said.

'Neil Higgs.'

'Ah. The author?'

Neil Higgs the truckdriver, Ellie wanted to say. 'Yes,' she said.

'We had his children here.'

'He told me.'

'Well. We're pleased to have John. He looks like a bright boy.'

'He is.'

She went away feeling that the man had made her up — put her in one place, then shifted her to another without seeing her properly either time. She might have settled him down if Neil had not got in the way. How could she stop that happening, stop him from intruding on her? It wasn't his fault, she saw that. It was the silliness of other people.

She walked up Glenmore Street and looked at the house — her house and Neil's — and saw, not for the first time, that it needed a coat of paint. She would choose off-white, with a stone-grey roof and orange trim. That would fold it better into the hill. Blue roofs, she believed, were against nature. Sky and sea should not be mimicked where land mammals lived. Ellie smiled: she would try that out on Neil, get him to agree. She wondered how he would feel if she did the painting herself. She could tell him that she had experience.

Ellie crossed the road and climbed the steps, passing below the high front wall. It was like a cliff, with Neil in a cave at the foot. He had a four-paned window with a roller blind that he kept down so the outside world would not distract him, and a door — painted blue, like the roof — with a screwed-on panel reading: *Visitors proceed to upper level*. That was OK. Ellie accepted it; she even approved, except for the blue; and accepted that during working hours she was a visitor and must climb past. She had hoped she might be admitted now and then, to see how he was getting on, even perhaps to hear what he had written. She had hoped he would call her down to try out sentences on, or for a quick one if he got randy writing sex scenes (although he did not put in many of those); and had expected to call him upstairs if she needed him, and had made what she called a Stamp Chart: *Visitors, one stamp. Important mail, two stamps. Phone call, three stamps. Emergency, running on the spot.* She worked out the place in the bedroom exactly above his head: 'Go down now. We'll try it out.'

Ellie blushed, recalling it. How could she have been so stupid? Neil had explained that he went to work. 'It's my job, Ellie, it's not a game. What this is — it's like asking a mathematician to stop halfway through a calculation. Or a brain surgeon in an operation.' He had gone on to say that being interrupted actually hurt him. It was like being punched between the eyes. 'I'm sure I lose a whole bunch of brain cells. Listen love, if anyone can interrupt me you can. But please don't unless the house is burning down, OK?'

OK, OK. She'd acted like a girl instead of a woman. Instead of a wife. Living with someone, loving someone, lowered her guard and made her — gush? Made her callow, made her green, when what she had been hoping for was purity. And trust. And a kind of happy thoughtlessness. All day long, including working hours? She blushed again, stepping carefully past the door. But she hated that blue. It had to go.

She went inside and washed the breakfast dishes. The kitchen faced uphill, where a tangle of ngaio bushes rose to the skyline. In mid-winter the room would get no sun. And Glenmore Street was a wind tunnel with storms blowing up and down. The house needed better heating than the single Nitestor in the hall. She would talk to Neil about a spaceheater for the living room, and get a part-time job to pay for it if it cost too much. He made almost nothing from his books and had to write for television — was writing an episode for a cop show in his den right now. Let me bring some money in, she would say, then you can do your proper work. Betty had left because he was poor — which was a good reason for being poor, he said. But no reason for me to be, Ellie thought.

She went to the bedroom and made the bed, smiling at him working out plots beneath her feet. He had written four episodes of the cop show so far, all with a dark edge and plenty of suspense. He was clever with twisted motives — surprising, really, considering how much he needed to have explained in real life. Maybe keeping things shallow built up a store of energy for diving deep. But you had to recognise what you found down there. He seemed to manage better in his TV scripts than his novels. Neil was a confusing man, which kept her busy and alert.

The bed that had pleased her so much on the night they first made love annoyed her now, because of the huge blankets and sheets. They were part of Neil's old-fashionedness. 'I hate those new-fangled duvets,' he said. 'They've been in for years,' Ellie protested. 'It's much easier making the bed. And more fun when you're under them. Let's get some, Neil.' 'I like blankets,' he said.

'Stupid bugger,' Ellie said, grinning down at him.

Back in the kitchen, she made his morning coffee, wrapped the pot in a teatowel to keep it warm, put three mallowpuffs on a plate — his greediness for mallowpuffs had charmed her — and took the tray outside and down the steps. She placed it, dead on time, 10.15, on the wooden ledge built waist high by the door. Ellie did not like this chore. It seemed reasonable when she thought of it — taking someone (her husband for want of a word) his morning coffee the way women through the centuries had taken lunch to their men working in the fields — but somehow it demeaned her. She wanted to open the door, put the tray on his desk, and say, 'Don't let it go cold or I'll screw your neck' — something like that, instead of creeping away making no sound. As often as not the coffee went cold. Why couldn't he bang on the ceiling when he was ready? It would make more sense than 10.15, although sometimes he reached out on the dot — an extendable arm — and lifted the tray inside. It was going to be interesting to see what would happen in the winter. I'll be buggered if I'm taking it down in the rain, Ellie thought.

Now she had two hours to herself and could go into the garden — Betty's weed-patch, Neil called it, which put Ellie off, although she would make it her own with flowers and herbs and vegetables very soon — or paint the roof or paint a picture or walk through the gardens and have her own coffee break downtown. It's early days, she thought, and chose for pleasure: Lambton Quay and Taste of France. Walking through the cemetery, she remembered her promise to visit her mother. Their conversations went round and round: the children, George, the need for this and that in the house, the shortage of money, the greediness and selfishness of people, the stupidity of politicians; and Ellie was left thinking, Why can't we sit and hold hands? She would like to be with her mother and not talk. It made her guilty that she did not want her visiting Glenmore Street — not, she said quickly to herself, until Neil and I are a bit more settled.

She ordered coffee and a Danish and sat at a table with a view of the street. Coffee black, unsugared; Danish sweet. She became both sharp and melting too. At lunch time we'll go to bed, she thought. What was the use of having your man at home if you couldn't do that? He had a puritan disapproval of daytime sex, at war with his appetite for lots of it. Neil most certainly needed her help. Ellie smiled.

'Ellie, I thought it was you,' a woman said. She got up from a nearby table and approached. 'How lovely.'

Ellie took a moment to find someone she knew: a girl's face inside the plumped-out one. 'Angela,' she said, and wanted to gesture casually, Have a seat, but knew she must get up and embrace. They stood off and studied each other and laughed. A scented sophisticated creature: she's no surprise, Ellie thought. And I've become a country girl — although I can drink coffee and eat Danish with the best.

'Sit down. Let's talk.'

'Oh no, I can't, I've got my daughter' — a girl in a Marsden uniform eating chocolate cake. 'She's just had her braces off, poor lamb, so I'm treating her. Ellie, it's twenty years. Tell me — oh I wish we had time. Are you married? Have you got children?'

'I've got a son,' Ellie said. 'He's ten years old. We've been living in Nelson but we've just come over here.'

'I've got three. Three girls.'

'So you never got to be a ballet dancer?'

'Oh, that was just one of my silly fads. And you wanted to draw cartoons, I remember. I suppose we were both a bit unreal. Look, telephone me. We'll meet and have a proper talk. Here, I'll give you one of Barry's cards. It's got our home number for after hours.'

Barry Abbot. Real Estate.

'You married Barry?'

'Yes, I did.'

'I went out with him a couple of times.'

'Well, we were young. He's standing for parliament, did you know?'

'What party?'

'Oh, Ellie.' Angela was not pleased.

'National, eh?' Ellie grinned. 'I suppose I could give him my vote for old time's sake. What electorate?'

'Here. Wellington Central. Now I must get this one back to school. You will ring me, won't you?'

'Sure,' Ellie said, not meaning it. She meant her smile. Although Angela had not been missing from her life, it was pleasant to fill her in. And Barry Abbot — fat tennis player, prim-kissing date. Her memory of him had always been shadowed by the boy who had killed himself. Barry was looped inside the noose. Now he was a man with daughters, selling real estate and standing for parliament over on the right. The line seemed straight enough from the Primes' tennis court to this comfortable state — except for Barry's admission that he had been afraid he might cry for Robert Morton. Ellie hoped he had stayed sensitive, although it would not be enough to make her vote for him: Wrong party, buster. Then she remembered, with annoyance, that she had not asked Angela about Hollis. Where had he gone, with his limpy foot? Dolores might have turned up in his life again. The baby might have turned up. Was it malicious to hope it had?

Back in her kitchen Ellie made macaroni cheese, which Neil would eat every day if she offered it. He had plain tastes, a working-class boy, and Ellie liked that, even though the sauce he splashed on made her think of murder.

'Watties,' he said, banging the bottle with the heel of his palm, 'our life's blood.' It was a joke he repeated superstitiously. *The Dark Before the Light* was entered for the Wattie Award.

Ellie let it pass.

'I started John at Thorndon. You didn't tell me Kevin and Siobhan went there.'

'It's the local school,' Neil said.

'Yes. How did you get on?'

'What with?'

'Sergeant Padget and the murdered chicken farmer?'

'He's just gone into one of the sheds and found three hundred chickens dead.'

'How? Wouldn't they squawk?'

'I haven't worked it out yet. Gas maybe.'

Ellie laughed. He would not discuss his novels, as though hearing praise might damage them, but enjoyed throwing out script ideas and having her ridicule them.

'That's not spooky enough.'

'Yeah, you're right. I'd like them all beheaded like Giltrap.'

'Who's he?'

'The chicken farmer. I've changed his name. I might make him castrated too.'

'They'll have to buy whole cartons of tomato sauce. You could tell Watties. Make sure of the prize.'

'That's not a joke, Ellie. Just shut up about that.'

'Sorry. Who's the murderer? Is it the wife?'

'Too obvious.'

'How about a nun? You could have a convent next door.'

'Maybe a man dressed as a nun.'

'Or a nun dressed as a man.'

'Hey Ellie, that's good. A nun dressed as a priest.'

'Or as the pope.'

'The pope disguised as a rooster. We're getting somewhere. Celestial rooster. The feathered hand of God.'

'This will be a good episode,' Ellie said. She wished she could keep him writing scripts. Lunches would be no fun when he went back to novels.

She took him to bed — 'Can you spare an hour?' — but made him scrub his teeth first: macaroni. There's nothing like living together to take the romance out of an affair, Ellie thought. Reality had a longer life and was more fun in the end. Reality was an aid to sex. But love was the best aid — love was best.

She did not know why she loved Neil, or even how; had learned it quickly, as a fact, and was finding that it survived later discoveries: his selfishness, obtuseness, snobbery, silliness. She did not like his way of driving the car, impatient and dreamy by turns, and thought she might have to leave him to save her life. When John was a passenger she drove. Nor did she like his dislike of climbing hills and getting views: 'Come on, Ellie, people are what matter, not all this clouds and rainbows junk.' His ignorance: of politics, religion, medicine; of architecture and music (he knew even less than her), and native trees, gardening, astronomy, law; of sex and childbirth, childcare, education; of how the world worked and much more. She had never met a person who knew so little and made so many mistakes. 'Well, Ellie,' he said; and confessed that until his late teens he had not known babies were born through the vagina. He had thought the woman's abdomen split to let the baby out. 'It seemed logical. A baby's so big.' 'Oh, Neil. Oh, Neil.' She was close to tears, and yet such huge ignorance meant failure; it was sick. She would have hated him if she'd met him then. Yet she had to admire the way he had put himself together. Neil was a self-made man. And somehow, for some reason, she loved him, even though she was not sure he knew about love.

'I get things right in my novels,' he said.

Ellie was uncertain about that. Sometimes she wondered if they worked by cunning placement or a trick of words or his cleverness in pushing the story on.

'I do research. Afterwards, though, not before, unless I have to.'

But the things that made her shiver, sometimes with fear, then with delight, in what he wrote, did not come from research. Or from normal intelligence . . .

All this Ellie turned over while he snoozed post-coitally beside her. His energy wore him out. She loved his enthusiasm, once he had got his puritan hang-up out of the way (closing the curtains to keep out the light), but wished he had less of it when, as usually happened, they carried on. She liked long close love-making, deeply involved and slowly building, but he had no patience, preferred athletics: a great pity. She was trying to teach him. But lunch hours were not the best time.

She got up and dressed, then sat on the bed and kissed him on the mouth. He woke and blinked at her. 'Hey, you've got your clothes on.'

'It's time you got back to your chicken farmer. Listen, Neil.'

'Ah, no —'

'I want to get a job. Part time. I had a job when we met and it wasn't part of the deal for me to stay home. I either start applying next week or I paint the roof. I'm good at painting roofs.'

'Have you seen the height? It's a bloody cliff.'

'Neil, listen —'

'You'll fall off.'

'No I won't. I'm serious, Neil. A job or the roof, or we start a baby.'

'Jesus, that's new. You never said babies.'

'I am now.' She had thought of it suddenly. It was seeing him on his elbow, blinking in the gloom. She had felt a sharp kick, the twist of a muscle inside her, and along with it a wave of love that washed further on to take in a child. It was Neil and Ellie and what, between them, they might make. She had cleared a space.

'Ellie, we've got children,' he said.

'Not yours and mine.'

He wet his mouth and swallowed. 'I don't want any more. I'm forty-two.'

'That's not old. I'm serious, Neil. We're not just going to put this aside.'

He hung his head for a moment, then looked up and sighed. 'I'm sorry, Ellie, you're out of luck.'

'What do you mean?'

'There's no babies.' He pulled the sheet off his loins. 'Give me your hand.'

'Neil, I'm talking to you. I don't want that.'

'Just give it to me.' He guided her fingers. 'Feel that lump?'

It rolled inside the crinkled skin, as hard as a knot in a piece of string.

'That's where they tied me. I've had a vasectomy.'

Ellie withdrew her hand. She sat still.

'When?'

'About five years ago. Betty was scared of having more kids. So was I.'

'Scared?'

'I didn't want them, I mean. And now I can't. So —' he spread his hands — 'I'm sorry, Ellie.'

'You should have told me.'

'I would have. When I got the chance.'

'You let me go on taking my pill.' Her mouth was wooden, as though she was drunk.

She stood up and went outside and sat on a bench with her back to the kitchen wall. So, she said to the baby, you only had five minutes. Goodbye. She closed her hands across her abdomen and rocked herself, but stopped when she heard Neil coming through the kitchen.

'You OK?'

'Yes. I'm not going to paint the roof.'

'That's good. I don't want to lose you, Ellie. It's a long way down.'

'I'm getting a job. But I'm going to do the garden first.' That was for herself. It would also be, in some way, for the baby.

'I hoped you would. Ellie, we're still all right? You and me?'

'Yes.'

I suppose we are, she thought, but how much is lost?

'I didn't mean to hurt you,' he said.

'Go back to your chickens.'

'Yeah.'

She could see him thinking that if she could joke she had forgiven him.

'Ellie, one more thing.'

'What?'

'There's a board that creaks in the bedroom over my head and it goes right through me. So, if you could make the bed in the morning before I go down? Or lunch time, eh?'

'I'm getting duvets.'

'Ah. They're expensive.'

'I'll use what I save on contraceptives.'

He took it as another joke. 'I don't mind how much we creak the bed. Can I ask you something?'

'Of course, Neil. Ask away.'

'Some women think if a man's had a vasectomy he's sort of not complete . . .?'

Ellie looked at him seriously. This was some new sort of man, a new sort of being. She wondered if she loved him still.

'Oh, you're complete, Neil. Don't worry,' she said.

Ellie attacked the slope at the back of the house with spade and saw and clippers and secateurs. She cut out stunted trees, lopped branches off others, tidied up flax bushes, opening the ground to the light. There were seedling kowhai trees in there. She might have her own band of tuis. She could make a bower halfway up and sit listening to them while she sketched the ponds and paths in the Botanical Gardens across the top of her sky-blue roof.

In the weekend she and Neil dragged the rubbish down the steps into a skip. John helped, hauling branches manfully. On Monday Ellie cleared the weeds in the vegetable garden and discovered an infestation of onionweed bulbs in the topsoil. She scraped it off and added it to the skip. 'Sorry, Neil,' she explained when he flung open his door, 'it's an emergency. If we don't get rid of these things they'll take us over.' She dug the garden, fertilised and limed the clayey soil, planted seeds and seedlings, thanking Annie for her training at Good Life. Made a bin for compost. Cut the patch of rank grass passing for a lawn, first on her knees with clippers, then with an old hand mower she'd uncovered in the basement. If she had not come to live with Neil, weeds would have trapped him by his ankles one day. Overgrown him. Taken him down into the soil. Who would he have called for? Betty perhaps.

Ellie made a herb garden by the kitchen door. She planted flowers alongside the steps leading down to the road, then studied the near-impossible slope outside the blue door. Some sort of groundcover, she decided.

'Ellie, you can't work there while I'm writing,' Neil complained.

'All right,' she said, 'we'll do it in the weekends. You can help. This summer we're getting the section right. And next summer the house gets painted, OK?'

She saw annoyance — or was it fright? — in his face, and expected him to say, I don't need this; but instead he suffered the curious inner collapse she was getting used to, and said, 'I guess I need someone to tell me what to do. I'd be lost otherwise.'

I should buy a whip and some leather boots, Ellie thought, and practise saying, Kneel, Higgs!

He was working nine hours a day. His typewriter never seemed to stop. 'I can be your researcher,' she offered.

'No, it's too hard . . .'

'How, hard?'

'Explaining what I want.' But the next day he said, 'Can you find out about the brain for me? You know, the part that's called the reptile brain. I need the scientific terms.'

She went along to the library and wrote down the names of all the parts. She made a diagram, and then another, top view and cross-section.

'Wow,' he said, and grinned and kissed her.

'Any time.'

'Well, it just so happens I've got some more.' Factory farming, mortgage law, neo-Nazi groups, artificial insemination (of animals not people), the shapes of the different sorts of pasta. Ellie enjoyed being used in this way. It seemed both familiar and dangerous. She was interested to know if some of the material she found might spoil his story, but he explained he threw away what he couldn't use, and other things were simply for metaphors.

'Oh,' she said, not understanding. It made her want to paint — learn to paint — so that she might use things: find out ways to use them. She looked at Neil with a new respect. Whatever his faults, he was serious. He was prepared to face one way and make his life in that direction, turning his back on the rewards and comforts he might have found by taking another.

She tried to explain it to her mother, drinking tea in the Brooklyn house, while a northerly gale blasted down Ohiro Road and rattled the painting over the fireplace.

'You're making a religion out of this man,' Mrs Brownlee said.

'God no. He's a kind of job. Getting to know him is a job. I've hardly started.'

Her mother had been tough and humorous once but had lost those defences — ways of attack, they had sometimes been — and often seemed close to tears. She was disappointed in Ellie and frightened that her other three would disappoint her too: would 'go to the bad' — an expression she used about Ellie more than once. She and George had left the Presbyterians and joined the Elim Church, where people spoke in tongues as far as Ellie could make out and baptised newcomers by holding them under in a bath. To Ellie it seemed outlandish and sad. She had trouble locating any remnant of her hostel mother, who had laughed and sung with the nurses and dosed them with ginger water and left them plates of broken biscuits for a treat and bullied them into doing their prep, then sat with her feet up by the heater, reading books on Tibet and Peru. Was she still there in this anxious woman sweeping cake crumbs into her hand with a little broom? It was worry not religion that had brought her to this state: worry about George, back at driving taxis although it exhausted him; and Andrew gone to Auckland (to escape, Ellie thought) and writing letters home that George suspected were full of lies about what he was doing and who he was seeing; and Heather sulky and rebellious and *intense*; and Derek, the youngest, lonely and *strange*; and money always short and the house needing repairs.

'I'll paint it for you,' Ellie said. 'If I can choose the paint.'

'No, Ellie. You've got your own life. There's John and Neil to worry about.' 'Neil' was hard for her to say.

'I don't worry,' Ellie said, getting ready to go. Her mother was being precautionary rather than generous. Her daughter who had borne an illegitimate child, who lived with a man she wasn't married to, must not be allowed to come too close to the other children.

'It would do Derek good to splash a bit of paint around,' Ellie said.

'He's too young,' Mrs Brownlee said.

'Nonsense. Thirteen. I'll bring John next time. They should get to know each other.'

'No, Ellie. George . . .'

'George what?'

'He doesn't think you should come when Derek's at home.'

'Shit, he's my brother.'

'Half-brother. Don't swear. And you've never shown any interest before.'

'I used to take him out in his pushchair,' Ellie said.

'That was a long time ago. Ellie, please, you've got to understand we're different now.'

'Do you still want me to visit, Mum?'

'Yes. Yes. I love you, Ellie. You'll never understand how much.'

Ellie held her as she cried. She was almost crying herself. I could dong that fucking George, she thought. Yet, going home, she remembered how kind he had been to her as a girl. How do things get so ballsed up? she wondered. It chilled her when she remembered that her mother believed in hell and that Ellie was going there.

'How can someone live with all that ugly stuff inside them? Especially when they believe in love?' she said to Neil.

'Don't ask me.'

'I am asking you. You've written a book about a Presbyterian minister.'

'I only found out as much as I needed. I'm on something else.'

'Chicken farming. Useless.'

'That's finished too. I think I've got a new novel. I'm pregnant, that's me.'

'Congratulations.'

'Ellie, cook some steak tonight. We'll buy a bottle of wine.'

The working-class boy. Steak and wine was his idea of high living. Sure, she thought, why not? It would get the taste of her mother's religion out of her mouth. As for her sadness and her love — Ellie knew she had to live with those.

One afternoon, driving home from Brooklyn, she passed Derek walking up the hill by the tennis centre. She stopped and opened the passenger window.

'Hey, Derek.'

He bent and peered at her. 'Hello.'

'Jump in. I'll drive you home.'

He opened the door. 'Getting in a car with strangers, eh?'

'I'm not a stranger, I'm your sister.'

'It was a joke.'

'Ah.'

'No one gets my jokes.'

'OK. Ha ha. Why don't you walk through Central Park? It's shorter that way.'

Derek settled himself. He buckled his seat belt. 'Guys in there hassle me. It's better if I stay on the road.'

She was surprised to find him so direct, and realised that this was the first time they'd spoken alone.

'Guys from school?'

'Yeah. Fourth formers. They go in there and smoke.'

'You ought to start a third form gang. Take them on.'

He looked at her flatly. 'Sure,' he said.

'I was joking too,' she said, trying to excuse herself for being — what? Unreal. She made a U-turn and drove up the hill to the village.

'This'll do,' he said.

'How's it going at school, anyhow?'

'All right.'

'Have you got some friends?'

He gave a small grin, humouring her. 'Lots,' he said.

He got out of the car.

'Derek, do you know my address?'

'No.'

She told him. 'Come and see me, eh? Any time.'

'Thanks.'

'Has your father told you not to?'

'He hasn't said anything. So long.' He put his schoolbag on one shoulder and walked away.

Ellie was annoyed with herself — a meeting with her brother, so bare. Then she realised it had not been bare. He had made a joke. Had been both direct and indirect, and had told her that he was alone. She was left with a strong impression, from five minutes and a dozen words, of his curious mixture of honesty and tolerance; and a physical impression of bone inside his flesh, as though he might be weak and enduring at the same time. If he did not visit her, she would wait for him again on Brooklyn hill.

The next day she went into the yard to throw bread crusts to the birds and found him sitting on the bench under the window, with his eyes closed and the sun warming his face.

'How long have you been here?'

He smiled at her. 'I thought I'd wait until you finished lunch. Has he gone?'

'Do you always move as quietly as that?'

'When I want to. You said to come.'

'I'm glad you did. Are you wagging school?'

He nodded. 'I often do.'

'Don't they find out?'

'They just think I've gone home sick. I get lots of flu and stuff. It helps.'

'Does Mum know you do this?'

'No. Can I sit here for a while?'

'Sure. Help yourself.'

'It's nice.'

'Have you had your lunch?'

'I ate my sandwiches. Maybe I could have a glass of milk?'

'Aren't you allergic to it?'

'Not now. I'll have water if you like.'

She made him Bournvita and brought it to him with a plate of biscuits, which he broke and threw to sparrows on the lawn.

'They're like school,' he said.

'Fighting in the playground?'

'Shags are the best birds.'

Because they're alone? Ellie wondered.

'I like the way they sit on piles and dry their wings.'

'Like black crosses,' she said.

'Yeah. I saw two seagulls chasing one. I go down on the wharves.'

'Did it get away?'

'It went underwater. That fooled them. Does your husband write books?'

'He's not my husband.'

'I know. I was being polite.' He grinned with crooked teeth — Hollis Prime teeth. He should have braces, Ellie thought.

'He writes novels and TV scripts. *Padget's Casebook*. Have you seen that?'

'Dad doesn't believe in TV.'

'I meant at other people's places.'

'I don't go there. Can I use the toilet?'

She suspected that Neil had been like Derek as a boy — lonely and intelligent and awkward. He had come from a similar puritan background, although his had been secular, and had suffered similar mental deprivations. She could not see him as so watchful and amused, or so sickly (colds and flu); but he had had Derek's lankiness and knobbliness and skinny buttocks and pointed Adam's apple (judging from photographs Ellie had seen), and had probably outgrown his strength in the same way. Neil had thickened later on; he had grown muscles and got his mind in order, up to a point — had created Neil Higgs. She wanted to imagine this boy reaching a similar place.

This boy? He's my brother, she protested.

'I like your house,' he said when he came back.

'What, all the books?'

'Yeah. But I meant those ceilings and the fancy wood. You've got a good fireplace too. Our one has got fake logs. Did you know I've got your old bedroom? Where you painted the walls?'

'I hope you like it.'

'It's still pretty bright but it's got mould.'

'Wash it. Soap and water. Or try Janola.'

'Sure. I like that painting inside. Over the fireplace.'

'That was done by a friend of mine. Fan Anerdi. Have you heard of her?'

'I don't know painters.'

'She's quite famous. What do you like about it?'

'It's got good colours. I don't know what it's meant to be, though.'

'One end of a room. That's her friend Audrey sitting by the window. The garden's outside.'

'It's cool the way it's all sort of broken up and everything's flat.'

'Fan paints that way.'

'The basin looks as if it's sliding off the table. She kind of does things that should be wrong. Mum said you paint.'

'Not very much. I should do more.'

'You paint good walls.' He grinned at her. 'What's the time?'

'Ten past two.'

'Phys. ed. I reckon it's better sitting here. Getting vitamin D.'

Ellie laughed, but he puzzled her: a lonely boy who was a chatterer, and chatter that somehow angled away, passing little windows and half-open doors. She said, 'Do you go to church with Mum and George?'

'It sounds funny you calling her Mum.'

'Well, she is. And my son John is your nephew.'

'Half-nephew. Mum says half. There's probably a special word, though.'

'I don't think so. Neil's got all the dictionaries.'

'I'll go in the library and look. We've only got the bible in our house.'

'Does your father let you go to the library?'

'He doesn't know. I only go when I'm wagging school. Mostly I go down on the wharf.'

'What about church?'

'Sure, all the time.'

'Do you believe in what they say?'

Derek looked at her sideways. He smiled at something private and turned away. 'Did you know Mum and Dad pray for you?'

'I thought they might. What do you do?'

'I just sort of close my eyes and wonder who they're talking to.'

'You're supposed to know.'

'I know who I'd talk to if I talked.'

'Who?'

'The one who made all this. The world. That's God.'

'You sound very sure.'

'I am. Someone had to make it, didn't they?'

'Who made God?'

Derek smiled. 'Yeah, I've heard that one. You keep on going back forever. It's pretty neat. But you've got to stop somewhere or else there's no sense. And that's where God is. I don't believe he made us, though.'

'You don't?'

'I don't know how we started. It might have been when he wasn't looking. Son of God. Jesus Christ. I don't believe that.'

'Don't you?'

'Or maybe he just kind of started us off. Gave us a push and said Good luck. We haven't had much.'

'So what about sin and salvation and all that?'

'I can see why they got invented. There's some pretty nasty stuff.'

'Nasty people.'

Derek pulled a face. 'I like people, don't you?'

She went inside for her pad, and drew him as he leaned against the wall — torn shirt, tumble-down socks, elongated face. He had black wiry hair — hiding, she supposed, a ridged scalp, George's scalp — and large thin ears, Neil Higgs ears, one of them bent forward in a listening way. A plain boy with an interesting mind. She began to be angry with her mother and George for not encouraging him to use it; and let her aggression show on the page: boy and shadow boy and shadow boy, progressively more lumpy and belligerent.

'Can I keep these?'

'They're no good.'

'They're not really like me, I know that. But you're sort of drawing an idea. That woman in the painting inside — does she knit?'

'Audrey? Why?'

'There's a couple of things like needles up in the corner, in the dark. And some unravelled stuff that looks like knitting. They're not near where her hands should be.'

'Fancy seeing that. Audrey knits to express herself. When she's feeling cross, and other things. But paintings get spoiled by stuff coming from outside. That's why Fan gave it to me. It's no good.'

'I like it, though.'

'So do I. I like ideas' — although she could see, as Fan had meant her to, how they damaged paintings when they were put in instead of finding their way out.

Derek fitted the drawings into his schoolbag. 'I reckon you could be pretty good. I can't draw.'

'What are you good at?'

'Nothing much. I like watching things. I'd better go. I've got to use the back streets so I don't pass taxi ranks.'

'Go through the gardens.'

'Yeah, I might.'

'Past the university, then down the back way to Aro Street and you're nearly there.'

'Do you talk the way you do because you went to a private school?'

Ellie laughed. 'Does it upset you?'

'It's interesting.' He put his bag on his shoulder and smiled at her. 'People don't upset me very much. Thanks for the Bournvita.'

Ellie watched him go down the steps and cross the road into the gardens, moving with a dislocated step as though some left-side weight drew him off-centre and after a dozen paces he had to right himself. She remembered how his pallidness and dampness had put her off when he was small, and was ashamed. Babies could pick up dislike. She might have helped turn him into this lonely thirteen-year-old. There was nothing damp and pallid in him now — a dry sweetness rather, an indrawn strength, a largeness that he kept rolled into a ball.

She was pleased at how normal John seemed and praised herself for making him that way. She walked down Tinakori Road and saw him approaching in a group of boys, so kept clear. She knew how mothers embarrassed their sons — and wondered if there were things that might embarrass Derek. Wouldn't he look at them and simply smile? It seemed to make him wiser, brighter, larger than her son. She grew jealous for John, but shook it off: he was friendly and clever and had the chance of a happy life. Derek would travel by ways where happiness might be hard to find — yet she imagined he would smile.

John's friends dropped off, and she waited for him at the Bowen Street corner.

'How was school?'

'Good.'

'Anything interesting?'

'No.'

'Did you eat your orange?'

'Yep.'

So complete in himself. Yet she knew he would wrap himself around her at home as if trying to fuse himself with her, and she was overcome with love. How could she have thought him less than Derek?

'Sit still,' she said as he ate biscuits and drank milk, 'I want to draw you.'

'Come off it, Mum.'

'Just for five minutes. I haven't drawn you since you were a baby.'

'Take a photo.'

'Please, Johnnie. For me. I want . . .'

'What?'

'Nothing.'

She had seen again what she'd hoped not to see: Mike in his jawline, in his mouth (when satisfied), but especially in his eyes: generous and thoughtless, if eyes were the feature that signalled thought. That did not mean he wasn't sensible. He was good at school, practical and inventive round the house, easy with people. But Mike was starting to emerge in easiness that was excessive, perhaps — how could one judge? — and energy in search of what was new, and quick boredom, laziness. She told herself that boys were like that — small boys — but suspected it wasn't universal. She hated seeing Mike in his face.

He sat still. He let her turn his head, raise his chin. She asked him for a serious expression and he obliged with a solemn one.

'Mum?'

'Mm?'

'How long are we staying here?'

'In Wellington?'

'In this house?'

'You like it, don't you?'

'It's all right. It's a bit funny with him sitting under there all day.'

'It's his work, Johnnie. He's writing. That's his job.'

'A funny job. He doesn't make much money at it, does he?'

'Who told you that?'

'I heard you talking. There's a kid at school says his father's a millionaire.'

'I'll bet he's lying. You like Neil, don't you? He's kind to you?'

'He's not bad. He's a bit creepy sometimes.'

'Creepy?'

'When he pretends he's looking at you but he's not. It's like he thinks of something else all the time.'

'He's dreamy, Johnnie. He doesn't mean it.'

'No, I guess. I'm meeting some kids down the cricket ground. Can I go?'

'Use the pedestrian crossing,' she said.

He walked in a straight line, unlike Derek — and not by back ways to a home full of prohibitions, where he would have to grow his mind secretly. She wondered what her mother would say if she offered to have Derek. What would Neil say? Ellie shivered. It worried her that John found Neil creepy, although it must mean preoccupied. He was starting his new novel — another old man, a rationalist, unlike the Presbyterian parson in his earlier book, and without a wife and children orbiting him. There were enormous problems finding the voice, finding the tone — and no, it would not help to talk about them with her. She wondered where he went, so deep inside.

Neil and John; and Derek now. Soon she must start living for herself.

Ellie found a morning job in the National Library. It helped keep the household finances in the black. Then Neil won an Arts Council scholarship and wanted her to stay at home.

'No,' she said. 'If it's just for coffee you can use some of your money for a machine.'

'It's more than that. I like having you around.'

'Even if I make the floorboards creak?'

She told him she might leave her job next year and do a painting course at the polytech. 'That way you needn't be scared I'll fall off the roof.'

'Yeah,' he said. 'You could be quite good.'

'Thank you, Neil.'

'In a sort of decorative way.'

'Shit,' she said.

'No, wait on, you've got a nice eye. And a good sense of colour.'

'Go back to work.'

'All I'm saying is, you don't want to get ahead of yourself.'

'Go back to work.'

'I can't work when you upset me. Jesus, Ellie.'

'Calm down. Breathe deep. OK?'

'Stay with me. Don't go away.'

'I won't . . .' She kissed him. 'All right now?'

'Yes, I'm all right.'

'Off you go, then. A thousand words.'

But when she was alone, 'decorative' angered her again. He'd insulted her. And then had asked to be comforted. She was like the woman who had parked his trailer for him. How did he pull that trick? How had she let it happen?

The phone rang. 'Ellie? It's Angela. Angela Abbot.'

'Ah, how are you? How did you get my number?'

'I remembered you went to Brooklyn and your mother married someone called Brownlee. So I tried a Brownlee up there. She gave it to me. I thought you were going to ring me, Ellie.'

'Yes, I would have. I've been busy. I've got a job.'

'Oh, what a pity. I was going to say morning coffee, perhaps. Somewhere downtown. I'd love to talk. What about lunch?'

'Well, all right. I can do that. But nowhere flash. Just a roll and coffee, that sort of thing.' She concealed that she did not work afternoons.

'Bugger,' she said as she put the phone down. She did not want talking, looking back; was more concerned with trying to see what was up ahead — which disturbed her when she thought about it. Where was *now*? When she'd come to live with Neil she had expected it; *now* she could be happy. Where had that consummation gone? There seemed to be no place to stand. Things fell away behind her the instant they were done. She had to keep on stepping, and adjusting her step, and looking round to see in which direction to go. She tried standing off to see the figure she made — this woman on the move — but could not make out stance or gait or even face.

Stop it, this is neurotic, she thought.

She looked out into the drizzling rain; wished it would go away so she could work in the garden. Derek passed the window and tapped on the door.

'You're wet,' she said. 'Don't you have a coat?'

'It was fine this morning. I think all I am is John's uncle. Just half.'

'Yes, of course.' She could not understand whether she had failed to see him in that role because he did not seem old enough or because she did not want him moving close. 'Take off your shirt. I'll get something dry.'

'No, I'm all right.'

'Take it off. Mum will kill me if I send you home with pneumonia.'

She gave him one of Neil's flannel shirts and hung his on the inside of the airing-cabinet door.

'Bournvita? It's turned into a southerly out there.'

'Bournvita, great. You'd better not tell Mum I come here.'

'What would she do? Does your father give you hidings?'

'No. He wants to, but I think he's too soft hearted. Don't get me wrong, I like Mum and Dad.'

'So would I if they'd let me. I can't believe it, Derek; they think I'm going to hell.'

'Yeah. I suppose.'

'I mean, real hell. Flames and stuff. Eternally.'

'Don't worry, it'll be different from that.'

'I'm not worried. It's just the thought of them having muck like that in their heads.'

'It's all just part of . . .' Derek shrugged. 'People are like that.'

'Not Mum. She used to enjoy life. You'd have loved her then.'

'I love her now.'

'She followed your father. I used to get on well with him and he liked me.'

'They both still like you. Hey, they love you. But unless you accept Christ and He's your Saviour and all that . . .'

'Yes, I know.'

'The milk's boiling over.'

He talked about Heather and Andrew while he drank: Andrew in Auckland and not going to church, although elders kept turning up to save him. 'His flatmates have to tell them he's out.' Derek grinned. 'He'll be company for you down there.'

'What about Heather?'

'She's got a boyfriend. He's not in the church. She stays nights with him, so she's a goner. You see why I've got to stay? I've got to keep pretending.'

'You can't keep that up all your life.'

'We'll see. Mum says you used to live in a commune.'

She told him about it: told him about her life, talking as though to an old friend, wondering, as she paused, about the agelessness of his demeanour, about his receptiveness that made her talk on, his sympathy, never expressed but palpable. She wondered if in some strange way he was a neuter and so able to take in everything. It seemed impossible, yet she described her life and found herself — under his influence? — moving it from sad to happy. It was not, she was not, sad. When she reached Neil she stopped: would not go there.

'If you want to paint that much, why don't you?' he said.

'I don't know how. It's not something you can just take up. There's all sorts of things, technical things, you've got to learn. It's like an apprenticeship. Anyhow . . .'

'Yeah?'

'I'm waiting. It hasn't happened. There's a kind of button I've got to push.'

'OK,' he said.

'OK what?'

'Find the button. Push it. Is there any hurry?'

'I'm thirty-six.'

'Yep, that's old.'

She thought he was joking, then saw he meant it, and he became thirteen again. She was astounded at the way she'd spoken to him, all the secrets she'd given up. How could she burden him with them? — except, she realised as she saw him yawning and laying his head on the table, it hadn't been a burden, had just made him tired. It was as if he'd recognised that her talking was the important thing and his listening simply a window she looked through. There had been no sense in which she had asked him for help.

He went to sleep with his cheek on the tablecloth. School must exhaust him — 'hassles', which meant bullying, she supposed, and lessons that bored him and teachers who probably had no time. Home, when he reached it through the streets, would provide little rest, with precepts and restrictions hedging him around. She could not see where on earth he might go or what he might do. The best she could offer was to let him sleep at her table — although there was a sofa, and she woke him and led him there and settled a blanket on him — let him sleep, make him Bournvita, send him home in a dry shirt, and say, Come again, Derek, as often as you like. She must provide a place where he could talk and relax and yawn and sleep.

The next day she went to the lunch place Angela had chosen, and found a restaurant with white cloths and wine glasses on the tables and a waiter who looked sideways at the daypack of books slung on her shoulder. She should have known Angela would not be happy with coffee and rolls. The table was set for four. She sat and waited, refusing a drink and growing angry. Angela was probably bringing Willowbank girls and that meant gossip, questions, comparisons. Judgements too. Stuff it, Ellie thought, I don't need this. She recalled that Angela had described her ambition to be a cartoonist as unreal. It had been nagging at her ever since. Why unreal? Was it something girls were not supposed to do? Or Woburn Hostel girls? Or was it deeper? Was she saying that Ellie did not have the ability? I'll give her one more minute, Ellie thought.

A man came in the door, waved away the waiter and approached. 'Ellie.'

Bald as an egg. 'Barry Abbot?' She had not known hair played such a part in identification.

'We haven't kept you waiting long, have we?'

'No. I'm all right.'

'Arriving late is an art form with Angela. How are you, Ellie? You're looking great.'

There was no noose around him but an aura of cheerfulness. He shone with well-being; was fitted, scented, groomed with it. Ellie smiled as though at an artefact.

'You too,' she said. 'You look — contented.'

'Yes, I am.'

'And prosperous.'

'Don't know about that. 1958, Ellie.' He sat down, signalled for the waiter. 'That was the last time we met. I think I tried to proposition you, and you bolted.'

'You told me about your friend who killed himself.'

'Hell, did I do that?' He ordered a bottle of wine. 'Pretty morbid, I'd say. Not a good line.'

She was sorry to be talking so glibly about a death that stayed new, and she said, 'You told me you were going out with Angela. Not many teenage romances make it through to marriage.'

'We did. We were pretty solid from the start.'

She wondered if he'd ever fucked anyone but Angela, and thought not. He was a simple person with a gift for contentment, and she smiled at him with liking but somehow not approval. There did not seem enough of him to grasp for an assessment.

'Three daughters. Congratulations,' she said.

'Thanks. But what about you, Ellie? Married? Kids? All that?'

'I've had what they call a chequered career. Here's Angela. Who's she got?'

Hollis Prime, with still face and widow's peak and walking stick.

Damn, Ellie thought. A burning, as though of sickness, rose in her throat.

Angela, pumped-up in her cheeks, coloured that glorious violet in her eyes, cried as though triumphant, 'Ellie, I'm sorry we're late but I knew Barry would look after you. You remember Hollis?'

'How are you, Hollis?'

'I'm well, thanks. It's good to see you, Ellie.'

He and Angela sat down. He leaned his stick against the wall. The waiter arrived with wine and filled their glasses, which gave Ellie time to calm her anger at Angela and her dislike of this man and make herself social. She would say nothing more than she had to. But she found herself the focus, with Barry and Angela leaning at her and Hollis leaning back with his arm stretched out to his glass on the table edge. He looked as if he was measuring her.

'Your mother wouldn't give me any news about you, Ellie. I asked your married name, all that. I wasn't being nosey,' Angela said.

'Mum gets embarrassed. I haven't got a married name.'

'But you've got a son. You told me.'

'I've got John. He's ten years old. The man I live with isn't his father.'

Let's see how they handle that, she thought.

'So, you were married to John's father?' Angela said.

'It's none of our business, Angie,' Hollis said.

'I don't mind,' Ellie said. 'No, I wasn't. He was a guy I lived with on a commune.' She felt she was throwing facts, hard, like cricket balls, at Hollis Prime.

He took a sip of his wine and gave a smile of apology.

'Where was that?' Angela said.

'In Golden Bay.'

The waiter came for their orders. Ellie chose chicken salad, the cheapest thing. She was determined to pay for herself. Angela dithered, which was interesting. She had always been decisive, but now, had she settled into a part? Did she bolster Barry, try to make him substantial, by playing the little woman and letting him decide? Ellie would be willing to bet they didn't go on like that at home.

She glanced at Hollis and found him with his eyes closed as though he was bored. Her antagonism increased. I didn't want to meet you either, buster, she thought.

He opened his eyes and smiled at her.

'You look as if you're doing sums,' she said.

'Just calculating how long since we met.'

'Twenty-two years,' Barry said. 'I already worked that out.' He rolled his lips together as if he had fed on the years and was satisfied. Angela had developed a matching, a connubial fulness in her face. Hollis Prime, on the other hand, looked as if he fed on scraps. In spite of his tie, his suit, his immaculate cuffs, he had crouched beside a fire, gnawing on bones, while eyes watched from the darkness all around. She found herself glad that his life had not been easy; and was disturbed that she should find him wolfish still.

'That's more than half our lives,' Angela said. 'Ellie, I was devastated when you left Willowbank. You were the only one there I wanted as my friend.'

'Me?'

'I just wanted to be like you. You seemed so free. I fantasised about living in a hostel.'

'I don't think you'd have liked it.'

'I used to ride past on my bicycle and see all the girls going in and out, and hear the piano playing and the singing, and all the boyfriends in their cars waiting outside. It was another world. I used to think you were a kind of princess in there, with all sorts of magical things going on.'

'I remember you asked me about it,' Ellie said. She did not believe Angela. It was embroidery. Yet that mother, that self-communing father and crippled brother . . .? She looked at him and found him impassive. He sipped his wine.

'We had jokes about the Y-dub,' Barry said. 'Sorry, Ellie, but you know boys. One of my cobbers reckoned he went panty-raiding there.'

'Well, they did go missing from the line,' Ellie said.

'You know, it makes me mad,' Angela said, 'the way people sling off about the 1950s, as though we were deprived or something. As though life didn't start until the 1960s.'

'The fifties were a great time,' Barry said.

'Because that's when we were young,' Angela said.

'There were all sorts of extras,' Hollis said.

'What do you mean?'

'Guilt and prohibitions and ignorance. It certainly made life interesting.'

'And fear of pregnancy,' Ellie said.

'Oh yes, no pill.' Angela snapped her jaws shut. The subject had gone far enough. 'Ellie, what's the thing you remember best about Willowbank?'

'That's easy. Mrs Nimmo.'

'Her? But I hated her.'

'She was a great teacher. She started me off on all sorts of things.'

'You knew she was a communist?'

'Not after 1956.'

'What happened then?' Barry said.

Angela ignored him. 'She was a socialist at least. She tried indoctrinating us.'

'It didn't bother me. My mother was Labour. And I still am. Sorry, Barry, no vote.' She grinned at him, then returned to Angela.

'Mrs Nimmo proved that Willowbank wasn't the whole world. Every time she opened her mouth she blew the place away. Didn't you feel it?'

'No, not really. I thought she was play-acting. Setting herself up as a character. You can still see her, you know, shuffling round Wellington. She wears an old overcoat and walks with a stick. She's got a dog almost as old as her. I stopped and said hello one day, and do you know what she said? "Go away, whoever you are. I've had enough of girls."'

Ellie smiled and ate her salad, confident that Mrs Nimmo had not forgotten her. She had probably finished herself with Angela and Barry by confessing to Labour. But it had been more a declaration: a challenge in defence of Mrs Nimmo. She was not going to have her favourite teacher spoiled.

Barry ordered more wine, then asked Ellie if she still played tennis. 'We've got a court. You can come on over.'

'That year was my last,' Ellie said. 'I took up tramping.'

'One of my daughters is going to be good at tennis,' Angela said. 'One of your boys too, Hollis. It runs in the family.'

'Don't I get any credit?' Barry said.

'The tennis genes are ours. Yours are all political,' Angela said.

Ellie turned to Hollis. 'How many children have you got?'

'Two boys.'

'Do you still live out in the Hutt?'

'No, I shifted from there. I'm in Auckland.'

She wondered why he said 'I' not 'we'. 'And you're a lawyer?'

'Yes.' He seemed evasive.

'What sort?'

'Tax mainly. Financial law. Property law.'

'Ah' — which let him go. She could not connect him with the surly randy boy in the pink Morris Minor. Only his widow's peak was the same: it still had the appearance of digging into him. His eyes were less glittery, less fixed on himself. Life had taught him something — inevitably. You might get your teeth straightened — somewhere along the line he'd done that — but you could not get away from a crippled leg. Could get away from a pregnant girlfriend, though. She wondered how well he remembered Dolores, and if it was that near-escape that had turned him away from — that fifties word — delinquency. He had been, hadn't he, a near delinquent? But he'd had his family to fall back on — fall into softly when his damage was done.

She put her hand over her glass as Barry tried to pour more wine. 'I've got to go. I've got some books Neil needs.'

'Is Neil your . . .?' Angela said.

'The man I live with. It's my job to keep him supplied with facts. I'd better make a note of this wine. He needs things like that.'

'What does he do?'

'He's a writer.'

'Do we know him?'

'Neil Higgs.'

'Oh, but I've read one of his novels. About the minister who loses his faith. Is he religious?'

'Neil? Not a bit. His grandfather was, but then he became an evolutionist —'

'Like in the book.'

'— so Neil's mother had no religion. She stayed a puritan though. My God, it was ruinous . . .' Stop, this is none of their business, she thought. She recognised too, with some confusion, that she was trying to make herself interesting to Hollis. 'Anyway,' she said, 'I've got to get home. I've enjoyed my lunch. I think my salad was twelve dollars.'

'No, no, my shout,' Barry said.

'Yes, I invited you,' Angela said.

Ellie decided not to argue. She would have had to dig for coins in the bottom of her pack. Her clean exit would be spoiled. 'All right. Thank you very much.'

'Ellie,' Hollis said, 'I've got to go too. Can I walk a little way?'

'I'm going up to Tinakori Road.'

'I've got a meeting on The Terrace.'

He had his stick, was making quick goodbyes to Angela and Barry. She waited at the door and watched him limp towards her: a thin man, thin faced, dark haired, in a lawyer's suit — National Party suit — with his bone-handled stick held like a baton as he angled his way past the backs of chairs, as far removed from Hollis Prime, pale and bitter faced, as it was possible to be. She could not fill in the years of his life that had worked the change, except by seeing family there, comfort, the soft fall, the spending of money, the retreat from responsibility; but supposed, all the same, that he had worked hard to get his degree and his position, whatever it was, get his lawyer's manners and lawyer's suit.

'I like your stick. Do you have to use it all the time?'

He banged its rubber tip on the pavement. 'This is my favourite. I've got a couple of dozen. It's a hobby. As for using it — it's mainly a prop.'

They walked down Lambton Quay.

'How are your parents?' Ellie said.

'Oh, fine. Dad's retired. He's got a little place in the Sounds and he lives there most of the year. Catching fish. Mum — she went to England. It's her spiritual home, she says. She lives in Cheltenham. Ellie, do you mind me asking if you ever heard from Dolores again?'

'No,' Ellie said. 'I wrote a card and I got no answer. Did you try?'

They stopped at the Bowen Street corner. He shook his head. 'No.'

'I thought you might have. You were happy just to leave it the way it was?'

'I, ah, I couldn't see what else I could do.'

'Did the people in Sydney who handled things for you tell you how it went?'

She saw his pupils dilate. 'There was no one in Sydney handling things.'

'You just gave her the address? And the money?'

'My father did. He did it all.'

'And no inquiries about her health? You didn't want to know if she'd died or something?'

'She wouldn't die, Ellie. Look, I understand the way you feel and I'm not making excuses for myself — but I do think about it. I think about it all the time.'

'Good on you.'

'Yes, all right. But I'd just like to know that she — I don't know, managed all right.'

'Didn't go on the streets, eh? Married some nice man? I thought you lawyers could track people down.'

He stepped back a little. The handle of his stick rang on a shop window. 'All right. I understand. I'm sorry I've troubled you, Ellie.'

'Do you know what having abortions was like back then? It was no picnic, even in Sydney. Didn't you even want to know she got through it all right?'

'That's why I'm asking you now.'

'Twenty years too late.'

It would have been easy to tell him that Dolores had no intention of going through with it, that he had a child somewhere in Sydney — just to see his eyes dilate again, to slap him into some sort of knowledge. She was on the point of it, but bit the words back.

'Dolores was a Catholic,' she said.

'Yes, I know.'

'You know what they think about abortion?'

'Ellie, you can't say anything I haven't thought a thousand times myself. I wouldn't have troubled you except I thought you might know something. But you don't.'

'No, I don't. I'd give up on it, Hollis. There's no point now.' She grew sorry for him: such a sideways-bent, worried-looking man. 'I imagine Dolores got on with her life.'

'I suppose she did.'

'So, I'm crossing here. Be seeing you.'

'Yes. Goodbye.'

She crossed on the lights to the memorial, then walked up Bowen Street alongside the Beehive. Hollis was ahead of her, on the other side, making a dipping stick-assisted progress. She wondered if it hurt, each step, or if it was more like carrying a weight, lumping something dead along. She felt a rush of sympathy that made her eyes sting, and was sorry she had been so hard with him. She wanted him to look across so she could raise her hand — not in apology, for they had behaved badly, the Primes, like barons in a castle, but in solidarity, acknowledging that, separately, they had lived their way through a length of time. It must be hard work with his added burden. And hard, too, asking about Dolores, remembering what Ellie had shouted the last time they had met.

At the last moment he looked at her and made a formal nod, then turned into The Terrace before she could respond. That's that, she thought; but wondered at his talent for getting into her mind. After twenty years he might not have been away, yet she found no continuity between his former and his present selves. She wanted to fill in the years — wife, children, job, home, failure (there was failure, his behaviour made it plain), success. Disease — his foot. In a way he belonged to her, as surely as her past belonged, and she needed more substance in him before letting him go.

She walked through the cemetery, then climbed again on winding paths above the rose garden. The roof of her house — Neil's house — glared between the tops of trees. I have to change that colour, she thought. The basement door opened and Neil came out, arching his back and stretching his arms. He put his hands on his hips and swivelled left and right — his idea of exercising. Sitting hunched nine hours a day was giving him curvature of the spine. He would be a little bent old man. Ellie felt a rush of tenderness for him. She wanted to lay him on the mat and knead his muscles, play her knuckles on his vertebrae and make them click. Yet she wondered if she would stay with him. There was no *need*. Although she could not see it clearly, there might be a need to go. They gave each other company, not love. They were only half full of each other. Yet she wanted more, and would not give up hope of releasing the love she'd sensed in him, trapped in him, in their first few meetings. She knew it was there. And her own was trapped. They just needed to stand differently, adjust their angle, and they might see into each other.

She felt like a girl outside a window with her mirrored face hiding the room inside.

The Dark Before the Light was shortlisted for the Wattie Award but failed to win a prize.

'I need to be a woman or a Maori,' Neil said.

Ellie could not tell how deep his disappointment went. His new novel was going well and all his moods came easy. He had Ellie search the files of farming magazines for information about trace elements, swamp drainage, pakihi land, top-dressing. The old man in his novel was a soil scientist.

'Neil, you don't know anything about that.'

'I will by the time I finish. I like to make things hard for myself.'

She asked to read the manuscript as he went along but he refused. 'When it's finished you can read it. You'll be first. I want to dedicate it to you.'

The only thing that made him take time off was the Springbok tour. They watched the occupation of the ground in Hamilton. 'We won,' Neil cried when the game was called off.

Then the assaults on the protesters began: 'Jesus, look at those fucking rugby morons. I should be there.'

Later in the week he and Ellie joined the demonstration in Molesworth Street. The cheering and the surging elated Ellie. She locked arms with Neil and strode unafraid at the police. Everything was plain, the smell of the crowd an elixir, thought the incessant slogan, the orchestrated chant. Movement stopped. They faced drawn-up ranks of police and she saw them as a different species, beetle shelled.

'You should be ashamed,' she cried. She wanted to put her face up close, look into these young men and say the word that would turn them round.

Feet clattered and a huge breath blew out. The crowd contracted, lurched a dozen yards. She had the impression of a bite taken out, of some black creature displacing the people at her shoulder. Her arm was torn from Neil's. A squad had charged from the side. Now a second came from in front. People fell around her. She was hurled back through them as though tumbling down rapids in a creek. A baton raked her side, another jabbed her thighs, and she made a whoof of terror at its penetrating head. A rush of protesters carried her down Molesworth Street. They were fragile, stunned, their unity gone. Ellie put her hands out and ran among the fugitives up Hill Street. She stopped outside the General Assembly Library and looked into the skirmishes on Molesworth Street. Neil had been torn away like paper.

'Get out of here,' someone yelled.

She went further up the hill, then drifted back. She wanted to go round the edges, pull him out of the battle, get him home. She stood under trees leaning over the footpath, wiped her mouth, tasted blood. She had no memory of hurting her face but felt her ribs stinging from the baton blow. The young policeman's face returned — such shining intentional eyes. She was appalled that she had been nothing to him.

'Get home, lady,' a man said.

'My husband's in there.'

'They're not arresting. It's best if everyone just goes home.'

She made her way up Hill Street to Tinakori Road, then went back. She could not leave him. Police outnumbered protesters, who walked among the uniformed men insubstantially. Further down, at Lambton Quay, the march was reforming. Amplified voices brayed, competing with each other. Ellie searched for Neil as darkness fell. She turned and went back to Tinakori Road, where people sat weeping on the kerb. Ellie started to run. Neil might be hurt somewhere. She had to be by the phone. John too — John might be home from his friend's place. She had to stop him coming out into this blood and danger.

'Ellie.' Neil was walking up Bowen Street. 'I couldn't find you.'

They held each other close, turning in a circle. 'Did you get hurt? Your mouth is bleeding.'

'It's nothing. I don't remember . . . Neil, your head.'

'Is it cut? I can't feel blood.'

'There's a huge bruise. Let me look at your eyes. You've got concussion.'

'No, I'm all right. Ellie, did you see? They can't do that. They can't just go charging into people. Jesus, we're a police state. That fucking Muldoon.'

'Neil —'

'I'm going to every one of them now. Every bloody match. They can't get away with this. Ellie . . .'

He turned and vomited into the gutter. Ellie held him. 'I'm getting you home and into bed. Then I'm calling the doctor.'

He took out his handkerchief and wiped his mouth. 'I need some water.'

'Come on home.'

He retched again, dribbling yellow slime from his mouth. 'If you think this is bad, remember what those fucking Boers are doing to the blacks. There would have been bullets flying in Molesworth Street.'

She helped him home and made him lie on the bed. She wet a flannel and washed his face, then felt the bruise behind his ear with her fingertips.

'I'm phoning the doctor.'

'No you're not.'

'What if you've got concussion, Neil?'

'I haven't. Anyway, no fascist thug is putting me in bed. Ellie, did you feel the groundswell in that crowd? I've never been in touch with that sort of thing. We've got to keep this protest going even if we lose.'

'So you can feel?'

'Shit, Ellie, no. Because it's right and the tour is wrong. And something's going rotten in New Zealand. Even if you didn't find that out tonight, I did. I'm going up to Palmerston North on Saturday.'

'No you're not. You're going to the British High Commissioner's for lunch.'

Neil blinked. 'Ah, yeah, that.'

'Remember how important you said it was?' She heard the sneer in her voice and did not like it but could not stop. 'Career-wise?'

'Shut up, Ellie.'

'That's some choice you've got to make, between yourself and you.'

'Ellie —'

'It's going to be interesting to watch.'

'Ellie, please —'

She snatched the flannel and held it to his mouth while he retched again. Later, contrite, she propped him up on pillows and brought him soup and toast; and when he woke in the night and placed his hand on her, she pushed him on his back and straddled him. His eyes grew huge, the way a woman's might, she supposed. 'Sshh,' she whispered, 'lie still, you've had a busy day.'

'Ellie . . .'

'No words.'

Oh, she thought, when they had finished, that was good. We were together; he was there. She wanted to keep him inside her but felt him loosen, so slid off.

Neil sighed. 'I thought it was only bad girls who got on top.'

'You thought a lot of things that were wrong.'

'I did, didn't I?'

Their breathing slowed. Their warm sides seemed to melt into each other, crushing their clasped hands between. She began to doze.

'Ellie?'

'Mm?'

'We'll go to that lunch on Saturday. What I'll do, I'll just go to the tests. Is that all right?'

'Whatever you say.'

'I love you, Ellie.'

'I love you too. Go to sleep. Wake me when you're ready again.'

'Ellie.'

'What?'

'I'm ready now.'

She felt him. 'Yes, you are. I must have been wrong about concussion.'

'Me on top.'

Ellie wondered if her eyes were huge.

The next night they went to the opening of Fan Anerdi's exhibition at the David Shea Gallery. Ellie took John along, hoping Audrey would be there. She was the nearest thing he had to an aunt.

They arrived early and circled the big room and the annexe, looking at the paintings. Neil brought Ellie a glass of wine.

'They're good,' he said. 'You can feel the tension.'

Ellie did not know what he meant. Between the colours? Between the shapes? She did not feel it. Fan's paintings disappointed her. She seemed to have made a half-hearted return to — was it cubism? Early Cézanne? She could not understand why hills and bush should be shaped like this. Brown, green, this way, then some other way. Solid blocks, oddly angled, running at the edges. She knew enough not to ask what Fan meant by it all, but felt she was entitled to *see*. She missed the colours Fan had worked with — colours that took your breath away. Missed yellow hills and brilliant trees and their recognisable interdependence.

'It's great how painters get better the older they are,' Neil said.

'Yes,' Ellie replied, wondering what she would say to Fan.

A small commotion sounded at the door. Fan came in, encircled by David Shea's arm. She looked trim, upright, and neatly, acceptably old. Her clothes had the brightness her paintings lacked. Ellie waited until others, many others, had talked to her, although they exchanged a tip-fingered wave.

'Where's Audrey?' John whispered.

'It looks like she didn't come.'

'Ellie dear, I'm glad you could make it,' Fan said. They embraced. 'And John.'

'You remember Neil?'

'He's the novelist. Hello. And hello again, young John. I hope you think my paintings are fun.'

'What are they?' John said.

'You look at them, you'll see,' Neil said.

John ignored him. 'We thought Audrey was coming.'

'So you brought yourself along for her not me?'

John became confused. 'Both of you,' he said.

'Ellie, come here. Come in David's office. I want to talk.'

Ellie followed, holding Fan's dry fingers in her hand.

'Is it something about Audrey?' she said as Fan closed the door.

'Yes. She's sick. She's ill. I shouldn't be here.'

'What is it?'

'Her diabetes. You knew she had that?'

'No. No.'

'Didn't you notice she never ate all those cakes she baked? She's losing her eyesight, Ellie. And she's —' Fan made a grimace of pain; held out her hand, palm down, and wobbled it — 'like that. I've had her in hospital. She should have died several times.'

'Who's looking after her?'

'I am, who do you think? Oh, you mean tonight? I've got a nurse. She's not much good but she can cope one time. I'm flying home in the morning. I wouldn't be at this stupid opening except I've got a contract fat David won't let me out of. But it's my last. They're no good, Ellie. You can see that.'

'Well . . .'

'I can't paint any more. How can I when Audrey's going blind?'

Ellie put her arms around her, wanting her to cry. Her own cheeks were damp. The door opened behind her.

'Get out, David. Buzz,' Fan said. She stepped away from Ellie and dried her eyes. 'Now he'll spread it that we're lesbians. Well, who cares?'

'I wish I could help you. Help you both,' Ellie said.

'Can you come over?'

'Fan, I . . .'

'Yes, all right, I know, you've got your man.'

'And John. And my job. But I'll come. I'll come soon. A weekend, would that help?'

'Visitors only get in my way. Don't worry, Ellie. She's been fussing over me for forty years, now I can do her. Just send your love.'

'I do. I do.'

'Good. Now let's go back. He'll be lucky if he sells any of these.'

'Neil likes them.'

'Jolly good. I hope you're happy with him.'

'Yes, I am,' Ellie said, knowing suddenly, sickeningly, that she was not. It was like standing on a step that wasn't there.

'What's wrong?'

'Nothing.'

Not happy with Neil but wanting to be, waiting to be. Audrey was proof that it would not happen. She and Fan looked at happiness differently.

'Do you mind if we go soon? I promised John we'd eat in a restaurant and it's getting late.'

They went back into the gallery.

'She loves John, you know. She'd love to see him one more time,' Fan said.

'I'll bring him over in the school holidays.'

They ate in a McDonalds, which delighted John. Neil, his eyes darting, was pleased too. 'It's like passing into the future.' He bit his hamburger, sending a squirt of sauce out one side. 'These things are good.'

Ellie felt as if there was no ground underneath her. 'You can have mine.'

'I will, Mum,' John said.

They shared it; shared her chips. She should have been pleased with their grinning squabble, but wanted to warn Neil: Keep away. He's my son, not yours.

Where am I going? she thought. She had not known that Audrey was her touchstone for love.

She telephoned Fan the next night.

'How is she?'

'It doesn't change. It won't change now except for the worse.'

'Can I talk to her?'

'No. She's sleeping. Write a letter. Wait on.'

Ellie heard voices — Fan's scolding, Audrey's a whisper.

'Ellie, is that you?'

'How are you, Audrey? Should you be out of bed?'

'It's a dull place to be. And I have to be sure that the rest of the house is still here. It's got a way of vanishing when you're locked up.'

'You're not locked up,' Fan's voice said.

'Is John there? Can I talk to him?'

Ellie fetched him from the TV room. He said hello, then listened. 'Are you sick?' he said, and listened again. 'Yes, goodbye.' He gave Ellie the phone.

'Audrey?'

'I'm putting her back to bed. Write a letter,' Fan said. She hung up.

'She says she's not sick, she's just off colour,' John said. He went back to his TV programme.

'Is that the old one with the hump?' Neil said. 'What's that called, lordosis? Or maybe that's the inward one? I should know these things.'

She wondered if he expected her to look it up. Audrey in the painting above the fireplace, a creature of planes and angles and of red and blue, transported her away from Neil and his words — his word concerns, his practice and practicalness, his information hunt, his sniffing nose for this thing and that, his flicking eye, his sharpness and consequent dreaminess — into a place of simple things: this colour, this shape, this woman Audrey.

She left him reading, and washed the dishes. She felt calm and still, unconcerned about what happened to her next.

The High Commissioner invited a selection of Wellington writers and their husbands and wives to a Saturday lunch to meet the visiting novelist Miriam Freeman. *Lounge suit*, the invitation said, annoying Neil. He did not own a suit of any sort and had to hire one. Ellie wore the dress she thought of as her best. The style and colours were out of fashion (which Neil, surprisingly, knew) but she felt comfortable in it. One of the best things about the feminist revolution was that you could wear what you liked.

Neil looked distinguished in his suit. He would be a handsome old man if he survived middle age. Triumphs were more likely to spoil him than disappointments. His face had the potential for fatness, which satisfactions would bring out. Today he was looking bony and intelligent. His Adam's apple bounced, a movement Ellie found sexy. Hair covered the damage to his head but the bruising on his ear had turned the top half yellow. The bottom was pink, with a thin lobe jutting like a supplicating hand.

'What are you looking at?'

'You, Neil. You look good.'

'So do you. If you'd asked me I'd have bought you a new dress.'

'Too late now.'

They sat in their car along the road from the High Commissioner's house. Neil did not want to be the first to arrive.

'I suppose I should have read this woman. Tell me something about her, quick. Is she a Jew with a name like that?'

'She's a working-class girl from Birmingham. Well, not a girl. She's in her forties. Five or six novels so far. Shortlisted for the Booker Prize.'

'I know all that. What are they about? What are their names?'

'I hope you're not going to pretend to have read them.'

'I will if I have to. People are always doing it to me. Come on, tell.'

'Girls kicking against the class system. And marrying bastards.'

'Give me something to say.'

'Oh, Neil. Say you like the way they slap their husbands down. Literally, I mean. One of them kicks him in the crotch. Then they take off.'

'In every novel?'

'Two of them. They're fun. Tell her you laugh. Keep your legs crossed.'

Two novelists and an arts administrator went in. Neil parked the car closer and they walked up the path. A woman, perhaps a secretary, welcomed them. Neil mistook her for the High Commissioner's wife.

'It's good of you to ask us,' he said.

·'Come into the drawing room,' she said.

The High Commissioner apologised for his wife being home in England. He introduced them to Miriam Freeman, a tall woman with angular shoulders and a concave chest — a starved sort of figure, Ellie thought — but a broad-nosed merry face, and eyes the colour of Angela Prime's but more lively. Got you, Ellie imagined Miriam Freeman saying. She wore a plain badly hanging dress with a biro fastened in the neck.

'We both write novels,' Neil said.

'What, you too?' Miriam Freeman said to Ellie.

'No, I meant you and me,' Neil said. 'Ha. Ellie doesn't write, she paints.'

'Oh, what sort of things?' Miriam Freeman asked.

'No, I don't, it's just an ambition,' Ellie said. She could not believe Neil had used her like this.

'Well, there's nothing wrong with ambition, Mrs Higgs,' the High Commissioner said. He was a nice man, silver and pink and alert and kind. His smoothness probably came from his training.

'Not Mrs Higgs. I've kept my own name,' Ellie said.

'Ah, I'm sorry.'

'Ellie Crowther. And I don't say Ms.'

Miriam Freeman looked at Ellie's hands. Not a ring in sight. Her own were the same. She grinned.

'I love the way social life has got so difficult.'

Ellie sat across from her and one along at lunch. She looked out through floor-to-ceiling windows at a swimming pool hooded for winter, and lawns and gardens nicely trimmed, with a grass tennis court at one side. There was bush beyond, on the lower slopes of Johnston's Hill. She wondered how much it cost to buy and maintain houses like this all over the world, and lay on lunches — delicious entrée, salmon, lovely wine, and no doubt even better things to come. How did Miriam Freeman like being waited on after her childhood in a suburb of Birmingham, two-up and two-down? That quick violet eye took in everything; but a sense of humour was necessary too. A sense of outrage would get in the way. Ellie remembered how funny her novels were. Neil should read them and lighten up — lighten up his own. He was being very still, very precise, and had nothing to say, three places along from Miriam Freeman.

'I hope you're getting some idea of our literature,' said Dennis Hood, the poet, sitting on her left. He had not worn a suit but a silver-grey jacket of the sort Indian politicians wore, fastened at the neck. It seemed to constrict his voice, which was BBC, more English to Ellie's ear than Miriam's regional.

'I'm not trying,' she said. 'I'm here for a holiday. But don't tell my publisher that.'

'Ha ha. You don't know us, though, until you've read our books.'

'Do you think so? I've met some interesting people so far. I had a good talk with a man reading a horse-racing guide on the plane coming down.'

'The names of race horses are poetry,' Dennis Hood said, baring his teeth in a lipless smile. He recited several in his lovely voice.

'I doubt if there's a winner amongst them,' Miriam said. 'What I'd like to meet is some sheep shearers. People like that.'

'Oh, they have exhibitions,' the woman from her publisher said. 'I'll arrange it.'

'No, I mean real ones. In the country.'

'Fleecos and rousies, that's what you want,' Ellie said.

'Now what are they?'

Ellie explained. 'I do research for Neil but he hasn't needed sheep shearing yet.'

'What else do you know?' Dennis Hood intoned.

'Apple picking. Waitressing. Living in a commune. I did fish packing for a while in Nelson.'

'A novelist needs to know one person in every trade and profession,' said Philip Dyer, a novelist.

'Have you really lived in a commune?' Miriam said.

'Yes. A sort of hippy one.'

'Free love and all that?' Philip Dyer said.

'Not so much. Not even communal living, not much. Just — being free.'

'And have you shorn sheep?' Miriam said.

'No, I was a fleeco. We had one gun shearer —'

'Will you write these words down for me? Is fleeco hard?'

'You drop down dead at the end of the day. Except you have to spend time picking wool out of your nipples.'

'No?'

'Oh yes. It's so fine it gets in the pores and it itches like mad.'

'Details like that are great,' Philip Dyer cried. 'I'm always asking my doctor stuff. And the guy who services my car.'

'So then you shower . . .?'

'One place we went there were only taps. Another one we took bits of soap down to the river. The best days are the days it rains. You can't shear wet sheep.'

'So what do you do?'

'Play cards. Talk. Sleep. Drive into town to the pub.'

'And you're all sort of living in the bunkhouse together? Guys and girls?' Philip Dyer asked. He sucked saliva back in his mouth.

'Different rooms,' Ellie said.

'So no romances?' Miriam said.

'No. You get good mates, that's all. What we did, Phyllis and me, we made the mistake of apple-pieing the guys' beds. Tying knots in their blankets and so on. We were pretty stupid.'

'What did they do?'

'Held us down and rubbed dags in our hair.'

Neil coughed. 'My mother used to have a phrase: That's not a table topic.' He tried to sound humorous but got out his words as though setting type.

Miriam winked at Ellie. 'I think I can guess dags.'

Alison Farquhar (another novelist) asked about the Booker Prize, about agents and publishers, film rights, TV rights, and Miriam answered brightly, woodenly — polished wood. Ellie looked at Neil. He was talking — woodenly too — to the High Commissioner's secretary on his right. His eyes turned to Ellie, stayed long enough to chill her, flicked away. She understood how deeply she had transgressed. Had met it before, this residual propriety, and deference (he hated it but could not shake it off) to people behaving in formal and fixed ways. Well stuff him, it's his problem, she thought. I'll say what I like. Later he would mock them: the High Commissioner, Dennis Hood, Miriam Freeman too, and praise Ellie for her outspokenness. For the moment, though, his icy look. Poor Neil.

Lamb was the main course, for Miriam. Dessert: pavlova (out of season), for her as well. They moved back to the drawing room for coffee. Ellie was cornered by Philip Dyer, who had reviewed *The Dark Before the Light* favourably and could not understand why Neil was annoyed. Ellie did not tell him — that praise from a lightweight was demeaning.

'It's hard to know how Neil works, that's why he's so fascinating,' she said, trying to put wet-mouthed Philip off. He fancied her. Would use his novelist's licence soon to talk about sex.

'Excuse me,' she said, and asked the secretary for the toilet. The word came out clearly and Neil, over the room, looked at her and looked away. So bodily functions were not allowed in the High Commissioner's residence?

She stopped in the corridor and looked at a painting that caught her eye — a bright room, a balcony, a woman in a red dress. 'Fan,' she said, delighted. Her neat black signature was down on the right. The woman was Audrey. Ellie felt as though her mind was washed, as though Fan was saying, None of that matters in there.

Miriam Freeman walked down the corridor.

'I hate these things. I bloody hate them,' she said.

'I'm sorry.'

'No, not you. The thing I'll remember about this lunch is nipples and dags.'

Ellie laughed.

'Can I beat you in here?' Miriam said, opening the bathroom door. She hoisted her skirt and sat down. '"She peed like a draught mare." A man wrote that, I'll bet.'

'He must have listened,' Ellie said, remembering Boggsie.

'He was probably married. Don't you love marriage?'

'I've never tried it.' Ellie looked at her face in the mirror — her light bit of lipstick holding on, her eye shadow, rarely used, improving her eyes. Neil was a lucky man, she thought, smiling at herself.

'Joke?'

'Oh, nothing. Sometimes I just like my face.'

Miriam flushed the toilet. Ellie took her place.

'I've read your novels. Do you want to hear things like that?'

'As long as you don't try and talk about them.'

'I won't.'

'I've offended Mr Neil Hicks. I haven't read him.'

'His name is Higgs. And he hasn't read you.'

'The bugger.' Miriam washed her hands. She peered in the mirror. 'Who'd look at me if I didn't write?'

In the corridor Ellie stopped at Fan's painting again.

'Yes,' Miriam said, 'it's rather good. Very Matisse.'

'It's very Fan. I know her. Fan Anerdi.'

'Do you really paint?'

'I play around,' Ellie said. She could only think of the phrase she'd used to Derek: 'I'm waiting for a button to be pushed.' This picture could do it. Or did it just give a final nudge? Had she reached the place?

'The worst thing you can do is waste your time. Your chance goes with it. Believe me, I know. I nearly missed,' Miriam said.

'Did you really kick a man in the balls? Like in your book?'

Miriam laughed. 'I got him with my knee. I wouldn't try it if I were you. He lay curled up on the floor and cried.'

'And you got down and washed his face before you left.'

'No, I made that up. Listen, Ellie. Is that your name?'

'Yes.'

'You become one thing or the other. Decide.'

'Thank you. I think I have.'

They went into the drawing room, where she smiled at Neil. Dear Neil, I do love you, she thought.

Soon a ripple — time to leave — ran through the guests. The High Commissioner apologised for the dull weather; otherwise he would have shown them around the garden.

'Hold on,' Miriam said to Ellie. She whispered to her minder, who fetched a book from her satchel in the entrance hall: Miriam's most recent novel, *Can You Hear?*

'How do you spell fleeco?' Miriam said, taking out her biro. She wrote with her tongue poking out like a child.

Ellie read the inscription in the car: *To Ellie the fleeco. Listen! Decide! Miriam.* She was pleased. Was warmed by it, even though it was impertinent. She did not need people telling her what to do.

'What's it say?' Neil said.

Ellie read it out.

'What does that mean?'

'Haven't a clue.'

'It's a bit bloody rude giving only one person a book.' Neil grinned. 'Old poofter Dennis didn't like it.'

'Nor do you.'

'You think so? You worked bloody hard for it, I'll say that.'

'What do you mean?'

'Shearing stories. I'll bet no one's ever said nipples in that room.'

'Not a table topic?'

'Someone had to stop you. We'd have had sheep shagging next.'

'Shut up, Neil.'

'She really liked the nipples, Miriam did. You know she's a lesbian, don't you?'

'Rubbish. She's been married. She's got three children.'

'Yeah, these old dykes use that for cover. You needn't think you got that book because you were so witty.'

'Stop the car, Neil. I'm getting out.'

'I notice she followed you to the toilet.'

She had to get away, not from his malice but from his stupidity. He pulled up round the corner from the tunnel, and Ellie grinned at the rightness of it as she climbed out: through the narrow place into another world. And here she was outside a new art gallery as well. Paintings in the window. Listen! Decide!

She walked down the Rigi, holding Miriam's book, feeling calm. Nothing dramatic, she thought. No kicking in the balls and tears of agony. No washing of faces. Just a withdrawal, quick and clean, and no hard words. She loved Neil, after all. Ellie stopped. What was she going to do with that? Decide! Carry it in her other hand, like Miriam's book? It was heavier, it would strain her, it would hurt. Ellie felt tears in her eyes. She blinked them away. In the end she would lay it aside, this love she couldn't help feeling — lay Neil aside. In the end, not know exactly where to find him.

He was drinking tea in the kitchen when she came in.

'Want one?' he asked, smiling shyly.

'Yes. I'll get it.'

They sat across the table from each other.

'Is John home?'

'In his room, I think.'

'Did he like the movie?'

'I didn't ask. Ellie —'

'I'm going across to Nelson on Monday.'

'No you're not.'

'Listen, Neil —'

'Jesus, Ellie, you promised me. Kevin and Siobhan are coming.'

'You'll have to look after them yourself.'

'No, I can't. I can't stop when I'm in a book. You said you'd do it. You've taken the holidays off for John, so I can't see the problem. What about the second week? Go in the second week.'

At this point she should say, I'm not coming back. But he would fall apart; she knew he would. He might even cry. She felt a deep unwillingness to hurt him, even though, in some odd way, he wanted it. In the end, hurt would be meat and drink to him.

'All right,' she said. 'Monday week. Now excuse me, I want to talk to John. And take off that suit before you put marks on it.'

He followed her, then turned into the TV room. 'The match is on. There'll be some protests,' he said.

They made love that night, and again in the morning. Ellie would miss the pleasure and tenderness and his increasing acceptance of being joined. On Sunday night she lay beside him, listening to him breathe. Her fondness for him grew at times like this, when he was present but away: when he was dreaming; or sitting with her but by himself, his mind not working but open to the things that pleased and haunted him and made him afraid. He was all three — pleased with himself, haunted by himself and afraid of what he might or might not do. What was going on in his mind when, coming out of his trance, he groaned, 'No, no'? When he uttered loudly, 'You stupid prick'? And later, 'Did I do that?' He would never confess to her what it had been. 'Nothing, nothing, just working things out,' he would say. Other things she guessed explanantions for. 'Dim bitch.' That was Betty. 'Sweets to the sweet' — some woman dead, some early girl-friend, if he had had one, or maybe his mother. And 'Out of the cradle, endlessly fucking' — a generation he was envious of. But what did 'Right of way' mean, with a slapping of his hands on the table? And 'Fried with onions'? Neil fascinated her. She would miss trying to work him out.

Would miss his fastening on some incident that she might mention from her life, some trivial thing: 'What did he say? No, no, the exact words. And what did you say?' At other times she could not understand his indifference. He would yawn and switch off, not only with her, with other people. 'But Neil,' she objected, 'don't you need to watch and listen?' 'What,' he said, 'the little guy standing in the corner taking notes? That's garbage, Ellie. I'm an inventor not an observer.' Yet there was so much he needed to know, and he turned to her more and more, starting to understand the uses he could put her to.

If she stayed with Neil she would become as made-over as her mother was by George. She would malform, she saw it clearly: adjust to his malformations until they became necessary to her.

So, she thought, I'm going.

In the morning he said, 'How about you getting them? I've got work to do.'

'Neil, these are your kids. How will I know them?'

He gave her a photograph: children with still faces. She wondered what damage had been done.

'I'm Ellie Crowther,' she told the hostess shepherding them.

'I don't have your name on my list.'

'Their stepmother,' she said, hating the word. 'Hello, kids. Your father couldn't come, he's busy writing.'

'Yeah,' Kevin said.

'This is John. You two will be sharing a room.'

The boys looked at each other, then away.

Ellie drove home through the tunnel, supposing Kevin, like John, would prefer it to round the bays. The girl, Siobhan, had not uttered a word. She sat in the front seat, hands tight in her lap, trying not to cry. Ellie reached across and touched her knee, and the child flinched. Bugger Neil, he should be here, she thought.

She banged on the blue door with her fist.

'Neil, they're here. Come out.'

His footsteps sounded, the door sprang open. Before he could speak, she said, 'Siobhan and Kevin,' as though introducing them.

'Ah, ah,' said Neil, in pain. He blinked rapidly; shifted from where he had been to here; stepped outside; kissed the girl, patted the boy's head. 'Hello, kids. You made it?'

'Hi, Dad,' Kevin said indifferently. Siobhan said nothing.

'It's great you've come. Hey, you're looking super dooper doo. We'll have some good times. The pictures, eh? But right now I'm working. Did your mum tell you that? I'll be up at lunch time. Why don't you go with Ellie and get settled in? Ellie, eh?' He turned to her. She could not tell whether he was ordering her or pleading.

'Come on,' Ellie said. She took the children into the house. 'John, show Kevin where he sleeps. Siobhan, love, come with me.'

She took the child into the spare bedroom and put her bag on the bed. 'Thirsty? Hungry?'

'No,' Siobhan said.

Ellie looked in her face but Neil was not there; probably she took after the mother in her wide forehead and round cheekbones and small mouth.

'Are you missing your mum?'

Siobhan started to cry. 'Yes.'

Ellie sat on the bed with her and put her arm around her.

'This week will go quickly, you'll see. We'll find all sorts of things to do.'

'I didn't want to come. She said I had to.'

'We can ring her. We'll ring tonight. Would you like that?'

'She said not to . . . she said to tell you about my inhaler.'

'Inhaler?'

'For my asthma. It's in my bag.'

'Do you know how to use it?'

'Yes.'

'All right, Siobhan. You get unpacked now, then come into the kitchen and we'll see what we can find for lunch. I'm just going to see dad. You all right?'

Siobhan sniffed. She took a handkerchief from her sleeve and wiped her nose. 'Yes.'

'You're a pretty girl. Has anyone ever told you that?'

Ellie went outside and down the steps. She did not knock but opened the door and walked in.

'Jesus, Ellie, I told you —'

'Shut up. Listen to me.'

Neil clasped his head. 'It's like getting hit with a baseball bat.'

'That's what you need. You never told me Siobhan was an asthmatic.'

'Is she having an attack?'

'No, she's not. She's got an inhaler. Why didn't you tell me?'

'I never thought. She knows how to use it. Ellie, what's the problem? I've got to work.'

'The problem is this. Your kids are here and you're not going to lock yourself up.'

'We agreed —'

'We agreed nothing. You're their father. You're going to spend some time with them. Otherwise I'll put them on a plane and send them home.'

'You can't do that.'

'Can't I? Try me. They'll love it, too. They don't want to be here. So what you do —'

'Ellie —'

'What you do is work in the mornings if you have to, and knock off at midday and spend the rest of the day with them.'

'No. No.' He slapped his palms on his notebook, making a biro jump off the desk. 'I've got to do this.'

'No, you don't. What you've got to do is spend some time with your kids. I'll send them back, Neil, I promise you.'

'Ellie,' he groaned.

'Lunch is exactly one hour. Let me know then.'

She went out and closed the door.

Siobhan had put her clothes in a drawer. 'It's a soft bed,' she said.

'Good.'

'I wonder where my old mattress went.'

'I hope there won't be too much dust,' Ellie said.

She took Siobhan to the kitchen and taught her how to make macaroni cheese. When it was on the table she took all three children to the front bedroom.

'Now, we're right over his head. The way to make him come up is running on the spot. Everyone ready? OK, run.' They made a sound like a train on a railway bridge. Neil's door slammed. He came up fast. Ellie met him in the kitchen.

'Lunch time, Neil,' she cried. 'Your day's work is done. This afternoon you're going to the zoo. Now, everyone, macaroni cheese.'

She kept her front of good humour for the rest of the week. They all went to the zoo, where it rained on them, and brought home packs of Kentucky Fried Chicken for dinner. Neil fretted. He never lost his temper but seemed to grieve for his lost time.

'You can never be sure you'll find the same words one day as the next. I might have lost good stuff forever,' he said in bed.

'You'll survive.'

'My novel —'

'So will your novel. No, don't touch me. I'm too tired.'

In the morning she spread sheets of paper on the kitchen table and painted watercolours with Siobhan. She let the boys make a domino trail on the living room floor with Neil's books; enjoyed the way they fell cheek to cheek round the room. She played Monopoly with all three, took them to the museum and sent them to the pictures in the afternoons, with Neil along looking after Siobhan.

'How do you like Kevin?' she asked John.

'He's all right.'

'Do you talk about things?'

'Not much. I'm glad he's going.'

'Why?'

'He says his mum's prettier than you.'

'Well, she might be,' Ellie said, sounding light.

'No she's not. I bet she's dumb. He says Neil's not my real father but I know that.'

'Good.'

'He's scared of wetas. Mum, you know when Neil says "Fried with onions"? Kevin told me what it means. There used to be this actor who said it. It's supposed to be funny.'

'Has Neil said it to you?'

'Sort of.'

'So, what is it?'

'This actor, they used to ask him how he liked children, and he always said, "Fried with onions."'

'I see.'

'Who is my real dad, Mum?'

Ellie had been waiting for this question. She was surprised he had reached ten before asking it, and had taken his silence as a sign that he was happy.

'A very nice man I used to know. We picked apples together. After that we lived in a railway carriage by a river. Then I had to go away and you were born.'

'A proper railway carriage?'

'Yes. I painted the roof.'

'Can I see it?'

'I'll take you there one day. We had our bathroom outside in the trees, with a copper to boil the water in.'

'What's a copper?'

Ellie explained. She described the gardens and the river.

'I wish I could have lived there,' John said. 'Why did you have to go away?'

'I didn't like some of the people who came. You know how people spoil things. It got spoiled.'

John thought. 'What was his name? My dad?'

'Michael Rowe. He was called Mike.'

'What did he do?'

'Odd jobs. He played the guitar. He prospected for gold.'

'How?'

Ellie told him about Mike's panning and his sluice.

'Can I see it?'

'It's probably gone.'

'Can I try panning?'

'One day. I'll take you there. I promise.'

'Neat,' John said. 'Where is he now, Mike Rowe?'

'I don't know. I haven't seen him since I left.'

'Can we find him?'

'I don't think so. I don't know where to look. And he's probably got a different wife. He might have children too, the way I've got you.'

'Does he know about me?'

'No. Do you want him to?'

'I don't care.'

Ellie pushed his hair back from his forehead. She hugged him, held him tight, and he responded then pulled away.

'I like Mike for a name. But I like Crowther better than Rowe.'

'Me too. I'm going to tell you a secret. Don't tell anyone. It's just you and me.'

'What is it?'

'We're going to Nelson on Monday —'

'I know that.'

'But what you don't know is, we're not coming back.'

'You mean never? Not even after the holidays?'

'Never. We're shifting for good.'

'Is he coming?'

'No, he's not.'

'Great,' John said. 'Hey, Nelson. Neat.'

'I don't know where we'll stay. Probably with Audrey and Fan for a while.'

'It's better than here,' John said.

232

Neil had taken Siobhan and Kevin to the tropical plant house at the botanical gardens. He arrived home grinning.

'That's a neat place.' (Ellie was amused to hear him using John's language.) 'I should have gone sooner. Can you go there one day and take some notes? The names of the plants is what I want.'

'What's wrong with Siobhan?'

'Ah. I thought she might be going to get her asthma. It was hot in there.'

'Did she have her inhaler?'

'I forgot.'

Ellie took Siobhan to her bedroom, where the child lay down.

'How long now?' Siobhan said.

'Sunday. Three more nights.'

'Can I whisper something?'

Ellie put her face down close. Siobhan held her hair in two hands. 'I like you better than him,' she whispered.

Ellie went to her bedroom. She thought she might cry. Fried with onions. A thing like that was only funny once.

Later she discovered why Neil had obeyed her all week.

'I'll look after the kids in the morning. I won't work.'

'Why?'

'Well, like I told you, I'm going to the tests.'

'Christchurch? You're going there?'

'Yeah.' He gave a tentative smile. 'Ferry and train. It'll be a big demo, Ellie. I've got to be there.'

'Of course you have.' She could have worked his reasons out but did not bother.

'I should be back in time to put the kids on the plane.'

'I can do that.'

'No, I'm their father. It's my job.'

'We'll see. You can work tomorrow morning, Neil. I don't mind. I don't want you missing any words.'

He looked at her sharply, uncertain whether she was joking or not. She smiled at him.

'You don't know how much I want your novel to be good.' Otherwise he was nothing; his life was wasted. And he would be too small to see.

She drove him to the ferry next day, kissed him goodbye.

'See you, kids. Be good,' he said to Kevin and Siobhan.

Ellie hoped there would be no fights on the boat. From the look of them, half the passengers were rugby fans and the other half protesters.

'Where are we going now?' Kevin said.

Ellie had run out of ideas. 'I don't know.'

'Mount Victoria, Mum,' John said. 'We can watch the ferry go out.'

Ellie drove up the winding roads. They stood on the hilltop and watched the white ship make its steady curve round Point Halswell. She remembered standing on Brooklyn hill watching the *Wanganella* leave with Dolores on board — like walking round a corner and never coming back. Neil would be back. They had a final scene to play. It excited and perturbed her, and kept her on edge through the rest of that day and half the next. From time to time she was even afraid. Neil might be violent: she hadn't found that out. Underneath it all she was calm. Leaving was a fact. She'd already left. And he could go on splashing around in the deep end of his life, where he belonged, where perhaps he made the only sense he would ever make; and she could get out of her shallow end — and do what? We'll see, we'll see, she told herself, elated and afraid.

She drove the children to the pictures, where the boys promised to take good care of Siobhan. Ellie went home. She poured a glass of beer and sat in a thin edge of sunshine in the yard, smiling at her garden and the slope she had half cleared. She fetched a cloth hat to shade her eyes but the sun dipped sharply and was gone.

If I was a real wife, she thought — and gave a laugh. A wife would be at the TV set watching protesters fight police, looking for her man. She no longer had to — and no longer cared whether Neil believe in what he was doing or was at the protest because Neil Higgs,

234

the writer, had to be. It might be a bit of one and a bit of the other. That was his way of being whole. Ellie yawned. 'Go for it, Neil,' she said, and sipped her beer. She did not want to think about him any more.

She squinted up the slope, where the vanished sun backlit the trees at the top. She would not have kowhais and tuis now. Or sit in a bower. Or paint the roof.

Footsteps sounded, climbing from the road. Derek came round the corner. 'Hi,' he said.

'Derek. I thought you'd given me up. Where've you been?'

'Around. There's absolutely no one in the streets. It must be the rugby.'

'It is. I suppose you're too young for a glass of beer?'

'Yeah. I promised Dad.'

'Never?'

'Never.'

'Coca-Cola then? I've got a house full of it.'

She brought him a bottle and he sat on the bench, drinking thirstily.

'Mum's had flu. I suppose I'll be next.'

'Have you been looking after her?'

'Yeah. Dad's not well either, so I've been, you know, home.'

'Did you walk all the way here?'

'Sure. I needed to get out.'

'What are you going to do, Derek? I mean with your life.'

'Don't know.'

'You can't stay there too long. You'll lose such a lot if you do.'

'I'm all right.'

He smiled at her as though it were true — and perhaps it was. She understood him even less than she understood Neil.

A slower set of footsteps climbed. Derek said, 'That's Dad.'

George came round the corner and stopped. He looked at them sadly.

'I thought this was where you came,' he said.

Derek stood up and showed his bottle. 'It's only Coca-Cola, Dad.'

'Put it down. Go and wait in the car.'

Ellie heard him panting after his climb. He supported himself with a hand on the weatherboards.

'George,' she said, 'you'd better sit down. Let me get you a drink.'

'No thank you. Derek, go on. Obey me, please.'

Derek put the bottle on his seat. 'Come on, then. I'll give you a hand.'

'I want to talk to Ellie.'

Derek touched his shoulder in a friendly way. 'Sing out when you're ready. I'll come up.' He nodded at Ellie, almost formally. 'Thanks anyway,' he said, and went down the steps.

'George, please sit down. You don't look well,' Ellie said.

'I can't sit, Ellie. I can't sit with you.'

'Why not? We liked each other once, didn't we?' She tried to help him to the bench but he straightened, raised his palm to ward her off.

'Do you think I'll contaminate you? Do you think I've contaminated Derek?'

George shook his head. 'No words, Ellie. No clever stuff. You reject and despise the love of God.'

'Not at all. I just don't think he exists. George, please, will you give Derek a chance? He's a bright boy. He's got a good mind. I haven't tried to teach him anything. I don't know what he believes. I just let him come because I like him, and so he can see there's more to life . . .' She shrugged.

'Than what? The Divine Word? No one needs any more than that. The inspiration of the Holy Scriptures. You want to lead him the other way. Ellie, do you know what you are doing? We've got immortal souls, all of us, and we're all sinners. But the Lord Jesus Christ died on the cross and every believer can be sanctified. You too —'

'You think I'm wicked?'

'I think the Devil has reached inside you. He's got his hand

236

gripped around your heart. There's everlasting punishment waiting for you. Ellie, come to Christ. He's standing on a cloud above the damned. They're writhing in the flames and He turns his back —'

'The poor man,' Ellie said.

'But He wants you. He died for you. Ellie, we loved you once, your mother and I, but that sort of love is not enough.'

'Of course it is.' Ellie was dazed as though from blows. She might be lying sideways and spinning in a void. His certainty seemed to lay down rules. She tried to remember who was important. 'Derek is too young to know what he thinks . . .' But that was wrong. Derek, in his way, knew more than she did. 'He's special, George. Have you talked with him?'

'Are you asking me if I've talked with my son? You ask me that?'

'I mean with more than religious stuff. Do you know who he is?'

'I do. Yes, I do. He's a sinner. He's lied to me and disobeyed me. Derek is no longer pure in heart. You've done that —'

'No.'

'— and he's in danger of losing his soul. No, Ellie, don't touch me.'

'Sit down, George. You're going to fall over if you don't.'

His poor head, she thought, looking down on its corrugations. Once he and she had been equal in height, but his sickness had eaten his flesh and shortened his bones. He was liver-marked and patched with bandaids where his skin had broken: a sick old man grieving for his son. I've got to let Derek go, she thought.

'Wait there.' She hurried down as far as the blue door, called Derek from the car parked at the gate, ran back.

'He's coming, George. I hope you'll get well. George!' she cried as he swayed and took a sideways step to right himself. 'Come inside and lie down. Please, you can't drive the car.'

He smiled, almost in his old shy way. 'I've been a professional driver most of my life.' He turned to meet Derek, then turned back. 'We still love you, Ellie. Your mother loves you. We pray for you.'

'Thank you.'

'Let me take your arm, son.'

'Don't let him drive, Derek,' Ellie said.

'He's all right. You're all right, Dad, aren't you?'

She followed them down the steps, stood on the footpath and watched the car move off — professionally, as he'd said. His sureness might undermine her if it were based on anything sensible. And where, where did Derek stand? Where could he move on to? Yet he had a stillness that she could sense only as happiness and an instinctive knowledge of other people — and of himself-and-other-people. She should worry about her mother and George, their health and peace of mind and what would become of them, and let Derek be.

She climbed the steps, poured his Coca-Cola down the sink, rinsed her glass, then drove to the cinema for the children. At six o'clock they watched the news and saw the riots. Ellie could no longer connect them with apartheid and South Africa. They were about here and now, and Neil was right to be afraid. She did not see him among the protesters, who were, many of them, as armour-plated as the police. She hoped he had come through without being hurt.

He telephoned the following morning.

'Ellie, I can't get back. Not till Monday.' He had been 'roped into' a strategy meeting. 'Plus that' he'd met a couple of writers and needed to talk.

'So when exactly are you coming?'

'Monday. I'm flying. I get in at 1.30. Meet me, eh? And look, Ellie, I'm sorry about the kids. You'll have to put them on their plane. Can you do that?'

'I think I can manage. Do you want to talk to them?'

'Yeah. Kevin.'

Ellie went to the kitchen and made herself a cup of tea. Now, so late, all she could be was amused. It made her fond of him — almost. She was glad she had not told him that the children would be pleased not to see him again. She laughed out loud. Had he really forgotten that she was flying to Nelson on Monday? Her flight went out half an hour after his got in. It was nice and neat. She could give him her keys.

'What did he say?' she asked Kevin.

'Nothing much.'

'Is he talking to Siobhan?'

'No. He wants me to say we had a good time.'

'To your mother? Did you?'

'It wasn't bad. He doesn't want me to say he was down in Christchurch.'

'Don't tell lies, Kevin, if you don't want to.'

She put them on their plane in the afternoon. 'Presents,' she said: an expensive box of watercolour paints for Siobhan, a T-shirt for Kevin. They had touched her for a moment, these children, and glanced off. She expected never to see them again.

She and John packed: two suitcases each, two boxes of books. The smallness of the pile on the living room floor alarmed Ellie. She must have collected more in her life than this.

When she added Fan's painting, wrapped in cardboard, there was enough — enough when you added what she carried in herself. This time, this move, she wasn't reaching out; she already had the thing she needed, although she wasn't sure yet of its name. She helped John wrap his insect collection as cabin luggage.

Ellie slept her last night in Neil's bed. She wished he was there to make love with one more time. Was that perverse? She had almost loved him — loved him in a come-and-go, a puzzled sort of way. She might have him with her for a long time — sore places that might catch her unexpectedly. Yet leaving did not hurt: it seemed like the first sip of a drink, like the pushing open of a door.

In the morning she telephoned her boss and told her she was not coming back — burning the library bridge. She telephoned her mother.

'I'm ringing to say goodbye, Mum. I'm shifting back to Nelson.'

At once her mother began to cry.

'No, Mum, it's not you. It's me and Neil. We've had enough of each other. And Nelson is kind of home to me.'

'I'm sorry, Ellie,' her mother wept. 'George is sorry too.'

'I didn't mean to upset him the other day. Mum, I wish I could help you. I wanted to . . .'

So they talked, closer on the phone than they had been face to face since Ellie was a girl. She promised to call from Nelson, and promised to write, and wondered if she would ever meet her mother again. It seemed certain she would never meet George (heart was his trouble, he needed a bypass), and not meet Derek until he was grown up.

'Goodbye, goodbye. I love you, Ellie. Give John a kiss for me,' her mother said.

They had talked for almost an hour, and not once mentioned the beliefs that kept them apart.

Ellie locked the house. She collected the mail, which included a gold embossed invitation for Ellie Crowther and partner to a gathering to celebrate fifteen years of Angela and Barry Abbots' marriage. She slipped it into her bag to reply to from Nelson and threw Neil's bills on the back seat. Damn, she thought, I didn't do a redirection order, and wondered what else she had forgotten. Breaking John's school friendships worried her most but he only shrugged when she mentioned it.

They drove to the airport and checked in the luggage, then ate lunch in the cafe, waiting for Neil's flight to arrive.

'Do you want to say goodbye to him?'

'No,' John said.

'Stay here, then. Get some more chips.'

What a good-looking man, delicious, she thought, as Neil walked down the long ramp to the glass doors. She grinned at him: I'm pleased to have had you, buster. Don't crinkle your eyes at me.

'Ellie, hi.' He kissed her — missed her mouth, got her cheek. 'Everything OK?'

'They caught their plane all right, if that's what you mean?'

'Ah, the kids. They're good kids, aren't they? God, what a weekend I've had . . .'

He talked all the way to the car, where Ellie handed him the keys.

'I've got my boarding call in twelve minutes.'

Neil blinked. 'Nelson. Shit, I forgot. Do you have to go?'

'Look at me, Neil. And just be quiet.'

He had the ability to focus, be savagely quick. His bag smacked on the asphalt, his hand with a sharpened thumb hooked on her arm.

'No, Ellie, don't. You'll kill me, Ellie.'

'Let go, Neil. I said, *Let go.*'

'You can't —'

'Listen to me. It's over. I don't need you and you certainly don't need me. You only need yourself, and sure, a woman now and then for bed and cooking. That's not me.'

'Ellie —'

'I'm going now. I'm not sorry I met you. We had some good times. But another six months of you, I'd have nothing left.'

She turned and walked away, then stopped and said, 'Everything's all right at the house. I've even cooked some macaroni cheese.' There was no need for that: she felt ashamed. Wanted some better thing to say. He looked so stricken and enraged — what a left-side/right-side man he was.

'Your novel will be good, Neil. But if you've got someone new, don't think you have to dedicate it to me.' Was sorry for that too. Everything she tried would come out cruel, so she walked away. Did not want to hear or see — but was sorry for him saddled with his deficiencies, and proud of the way he turned them to account.

The plane flew out into a northerly. Ellie saw the wharves and the city, with ships and cranes, tiny beetling cars in the streets, one of which might be Neil's — and tiny became right: it put him in proportion to the whole of her life which, up here, over the harbour, she was better able to grasp — although she felt a sudden sting, followed by an ache, in the part of her mind that kept to the smaller scale. Let go, she said, and the city slid behind. Ellie settled back in her seat.

They flew over the coast, the strait and sounds, then over cloudy mountains, and sank with a gravitational pull down to Tasman Bay. The plane made a wide curve, banking so she looked into the mudflats, then righted itself; and she saw the black Doubles and the yellow Dun and thought, I'm home.

She thought, I want to paint them. How do I do that?

Between times

1982. ELLIE WORRIES about John sharing a house with a blind old woman who is dying and dotes on him, and another with her fussiness magnified and her temper quickened. Fan might be thinking 'Fried with onions'. But John, when Ellie edges into the subject, says he likes old Audrey and old Paintbrush. Fan does not frighten him: he grins at her. Audrey turns him white and tearful several times, but that is mortality — John's apprehension of it — and perhaps it's love. The experience will do him good. Audrey is neither distressed nor afraid. Just before she slips into her final coma she whispers to Ellie, 'Silverbeet water is best.' She means for minerals, for John.

Audrey dies in midwinter, when it is dark and cold. Depressing times for Ellie, with Muldoon back in power and a puggy garden and grey seas and Fan not able to say, 'I want you to stay', and Ellie having nowhere to go. There seems to be nothing to paint or even draw. Audrey's death has not freed Fan for her studio. It's as if she has gone colour blind, she confesses one day; and Ellie wants to cry, 'Teach me', but cannot for it might seem that she agrees Fan is finished. It is plain that she will never go back to painting of the kind she once did. Teaching me, Ellie thinks: isn't that a way of carrying on?

She does not rid herself of Neil as easily as she had hoped. In the cold winter her memories are warm. It's delusional and she takes refuge in analysis, and when that fails in metaphor: the coupling of engine and carriage is one, mechanical; in another there's a bony hand inside her, locked hard on some vital part. His fist is a piece of shrapnel and she lives with it lumpy under her skin, like a soldier home from the wars . . . Nonsense, Ellie says. Crap, she says. She tries to cure herself by being brutal. Perhaps all I need is a good fuck.

Spring sets her free, and sets Fan free, makes them generous. Ellie feels that she is growing new parts. Fan sees the fresh green in the grass and feels the sun. The warmth on her skin is golden; and Ellie will stay with her as companion and housekeeper, pupil too. It is arranged. Neil's hand loosens and is gone, although Ellie thinks of him when she wakes in the night, with pity, affection, exasperation, respect for a part of him, contempt for another. A man in bits, she thinks as she goes back to sleep — his deeps too difficult, his shallows full of crawly things . . .

Ellie repaints the rainbow on the letterbox. She paints over Audrey's name with her own. 'Fan,' she says, 'you can start teaching me now.' 'Just like that?' Fan tries to snap her fingers and fails, which makes her cross. 'Yes please,' Ellie says. 'I'd like to start today.' 'Oh ho, would you?' 'Not what to paint, I know that. Just how.' 'How to hold the brush?' 'Oh yes, that especially.' Ellie laughs.

They work daily in Fan's studio. 'If you think you're doing painting straight away you can think again,' Fan says. 'I've been drawing all my life,' Ellie protests. 'You've been making marks on paper all your life.' They get on badly a lot of the time. 'No, Fan, not still life,' Ellie says. 'I want to see an apple like an apple,' Fan replies. 'If you think there's an easy way, I'd like to know what it is.' 'But I want to use colour. I want to do hills.' 'I want, I want,' Fan says, 'just how old are you?' So they go on, through that year and the next. Ellie paints the hills, she paints the sea, paints apple trees, pine trees, using watercolours and later oils. She is never satisfied but remains excited — a low-level excitement, filling with her confidence. They're like a floor she stands on, tongue and groove. Her question is how she can make something happen in her work. She understands well enough how to put paint on canvas — even Fan admits it, but says, 'These good things you do are accidental. Another day it might be something else, or nothing at all. You've got to learn to get what you want deliberately.' Ellie likes the idea of accident, but likes rules too. She wants to be open to one while held fast by the other.

1984. Muldoon gets drunk and calls a snap election. Labour beats him. Ellie claps her hands. 'Now,' she says.

1985. Ellie describes herself as a painter when people ask. (Artist is pompous and imprecise.) She's alone much of the time in the studio. Fan hopes she might do something herself but cannot work side by side with Ellie. Besides, her hand is trembling; she is suddenly, after an autumn sickness, aged to a little stick-thin desiccated elf. Ellie tries to give her space (John has taken Audrey's studio as his room, so she can't go there) by driving out to beaches, valleys, hilltops, photographing, sketching, but Fan is not working when she comes home. She sits in the sun and reads and listens to music — preparing all the while, Ellie believes, gnomic, irrelevant, maddening remarks. 'You are lost, my dear, somewhere between matter and spirit,' Fan says. 'Oh Fan, just tell me what I did wrong' — but Fan only smiles: 'It's the only proper place.' 'Fan, please. Did I do the under-painting not dark enough? Is that why it's just not there?' 'Time and interconnectedness,' Fan says, 'or colour and light. Which do you choose?'

Meanwhile politics, betrayal. Ellie is furious, eroded, devastated. She had thought the people she voted for were socialists. Strange objects appear in the foreground of her paintings: river boulders not worn by water, shapes deformed. Appear as if by chance, become deliberate: Douglas and Prebble, and Lange who lets them get away with it. No faces, no human attributes. Behind tangled gorges the hills are slipping, the hills are dead. Ellie knows these paintings are a mess. But they're an improvement too; she has moved past something that blocked her way. She does not show Fan but stands them face to the wall. Ellie works on . . .

1986–88 . . . and works on. She begins to understand the demonic single-mindedness that drove Neil Higgs but is better controlled. The hills in her paintings flatten out. She sees it as a response to the gravitational pull of the world in her head. What's inside changes what's out there, and vice versa. She is less angry and her colours, her composition, are better for it. She wrenches out allegory from her paintings — wrenches it out — wanting only nature, wanting the world, but knows that she is in nature herself, that what she believes and feels is natural too. A place for it? On the canvas. Where's the place? A painting starts from the roots up, she is learning. It implants a shape and you grow into it, discover where the perimeters are and the centre is — and Fan, in Ellie's head, cries, No, no. Ellie sends her away. She locks Fan out of herself, out of her work. She paints, day long, week long, flattened hills above empty plains, light streaming invisible from the sky, which is only a source, a smear of blue. Everything else is ochre and brown: the plain full of itself, the low hills *there*. She puts people in, simple brushstrokes, darker than the plain, featureless, leaning like burned matchsticks, with bowed heads, as they move obliquely, right to left, into the distance. She turns from it, walks away, closes the door and will not let herself go back, knowing that what is wrong will strike her like a blow, and not wanting it, not wanting the pain (although it will tell her what is right). Ellie walks in the garden. She pulls some weeds, carries a basin of waste water from the kitchen to the parsley bed (it's another dry summer), smiles at John doing homework in his room (when did he come home?), lays vegetables on the bench to prepare for tea; then goes back, confronts it, lets her eye move around, and nothing jars. It is complete. And it is good. She sighs and sinks on to her stool, overcome with pleasure.

'Fan,' she says next day, 'can I show you something?' Fan looks hard, and does not like it, but stretches her mouth and nods, recognising that this is what Ellie will do. I can never be as pure as Fan, Ellie thinks. She will be only half as good. But this is her way, this is her work. 'Political,' Fan says. Ellie is surprised. She thinks more of Fan saying 'time and interconnectedness'.

Ellie paints a series haunted by the world she knows. The Waimea plains bake in the sun, dry hills slope on either side (sloping up? sloping down? she cannot decide). The real world is a shadow behind the substantial one she makes on the canvas (Belgian linen: Fan has taught her to use only the best). People trek — purposeful or de-feated? — towards a distant place where a river runs, or might not run. Why the near diagonal? Why the figures undefined? She does not know — only knows it has to be that way or she isn't moved, she's not engaged. There's a question of balance and colour, but her mind will not respond: the painting itself is the answer she can make. And no, she insists, it's not allegorical or political; it won't take on distortions from meaning of that kind. Fan sighs when she looks. She concedes, 'You've got the light.' Ellie says, 'Do you mind if I just like your paintings, Fan, but don't listen to you any more?'

She has an exhibition in a gallery in Nelson — ten paintings, $150 or $200 each. *Crowther,* she signs them, perhaps too boldly, at the bottom left or right. Nothing sells at the opening, even though Fan, whose fame increases, comes along; but two red stickers go up on the second day and Ellie sells four paintings by the end. She takes the others home and stores them in the spare room, where Fan has a dozen of her own put away. There's a quiet singing in Ellie's head. She's a professional, and look at the company she keeps.

1989. 'In your nineties you turn into a freak,' Fan says. It's her way of saying that she's ready to die. 'Ellie, dear, let's talk about money,' she says. 'No.' 'Oh yes. I want you painting, not wasting your time in some silly job.' Fan owns the house and five hectares of land, a portfolio of shares (worth less than they had been because of the 1987 collapse — 'which seemed to amuse you,' she says acidly), sixteen of her own paintings, including ten she thinks of as her best, three Woollaston watercolours, an early McCahon (kauri trees, owing something to Cézanne?), a Louise Henderson, a tiny drawing by Dufy and a thousand books. It's all for Ellie. 'There's no one else,' Fan tells her. 'Nephews, nieces somewhere, they don't count. It's you and John.'

In midwinter she dies quietly: the end of her busy opinionated life. Ellie grieves; and grieves for George, who dies in the same month. Cries for him because he seemed to give his life away while Fan lived hers right to the end. George, her mother, Derek, make a complicated knot, but she and Fan are like two strands of wool turned around each other.

She speaks at a memorial service for Fan in Wellington, describes her life and Audrey's at Ruby Bay — the house above the orchards and the sea, the hard work in the studio, Fan's single-mindedness, her puritan hatred of 'lazy paint', her decisiveness even when she rested (her teacup did not tinkle on the saucer, it clanked), her belief in objects, landscapes, *things,* which, if painted right, can be effortlessly shared, her belief that a painting was 'a place to go', where, in forms and colour, a still centre can be found, her hatred of too much explanation. Ellie says that she has learned all she knows from Fan, but sees people thinking, Who is she? and, What does she know?, so steps down from the lectern for more important speakers, but is happy with what she has said; and thinks of things she might have added: that with Fan, through her own work, she has found again the clarity she'd known at fourteen; and that she has regained her past — which is strange because she's not aware of putting it in her paintings.

Fan's dealer, David Shea, overtakes her outside the church. He offers to take her on, show her work. Ellie says she's not sure she's ready for Wellington. She suspects David is after her Anerdi paintings and becomes sure of it when he talks about her duty to let them be seen. 'If you'd like to do a retrospective, David,' she says. But it's selling them he wants, not showing them. She tells him that nothing is decided. They part with smiles. Ellie flies home. She wants to keep all Fan's paintings all her life but wants to show them to other people. She walks in her garden, wondering about possession, pleasure, duty. She wonders how much she is worth. It's not the money that interests her. Change 'th' to 'k': worth is work. She decides that she will keep Fan's paintings, show them to whoever wants to see, privately and publicly, sell them one by one when it's necessary, and get on with paintings of her own — sell them too if she can.

Ellie walks to the back fence and looks down the valley at the coastal road and the little town. The sea is grey, the sky is grey: lovely colours, lovely light. She could skate on that surface and turn on the hidden horizon, slide back, head down, on the pearly sky. Drop on her feet again at her own back fence. Ellie laughs. She turns and looks at her studio and her house. She breathes deeply, bares her throat, opens her arms.

'Thank you, Fan,' Ellie says.

Gethsemane

ELLIE LEFT her flattened hills and forward-bending figures behind. It puzzled her that as she achieved freedom, thanks to Fan, she should find herself painting landscapes empty of people. She brought weight into her palette with blue and green, painting creeks and solid-seeming bush and steep hills remembered from Golden Bay — the range across the inlet from Collingwood, the Aorere with sharp elbows and deep groins. It took her half a year to become convinced that she was heading somewhere with all this. She tried impasto, which her subject seemed to ask for — more weight, less definition — but rejected it, finding in herself some of Fan's dislike of excess. Slowly she began to simplify — less fracturing, less jumble, cleaner lines — warning herself to stop before tree and hill became mere notation; but found that she wanted to go back the other way, to complicate — but with what? She waited for the missing element to declare itself, and painted meanwhile half a dozen pictures that pleased her sufficiently to show. She placed them in a pottery shop in Nelson but wasn't sure the people who bought them were not taken in by their combination of prettiness and threat. David Shea made no further offer of an exhibition, although he telephoned several times about what he called '*the* Anerdi collection', refusing '*your*'. Ellie continued to put him off.

She turned from her easel one day and found a man watching her from outside. He stood close to the window, with his eyebrows raised in a question; and Ellie, after the lurching of her heart and shrinking, almost blanking out, of her consciousness, thought, He's still a silly bugger, still doing it wrong. She took a deep breath, stilling her anger, and went outside.

'Hello, Mike,' she said, closing the door. She did not want him in her studio, or in the house, even on the section. He's got no claim. I don't even know him, she told herself.

'Long time, Ellie,' he said.

'Yes, it is. I don't like people sneaking up on me.'

'I didn't. Didn't mean to anyway. But I thought I'd try the back door, then I saw you painting away. Hey Ellie, do I get a kiss or something?'

She had two fears: that John would somehow turn up from Christchurch, and that Mike had Boggsie in his car.

'You should have telephoned. I'm in the middle of my working day. How did you find me?'

'I was driving through from Mot. I'm looking for work. Then I thought I'd take a look at the orchard — where we met, eh? I saw your name on the gate. So here I am. We still friends, Ellie? We had some good times once.' His smile showed the brown stub of his filed-down tooth.

Twenty years and all he's got is older, she thought. His hair was turning silver and was tied in a ponytail. There was a pathos in it she did not want to feel.

'Have you got anyone out in the car?'

'No, just me. It's nearly lunchtime, Ellie. I could do with something to eat. I'd have brought a couple of beers if I'd known I'd find you here.'

Ellie looked at her easel through the window. She felt another fear: that, jerked away, she would not find her place when she went back.

'Just let me clean my brush, Mike. No, stay outside.' She did not look at the painting; cleaned her brushes and palette, went back out. 'I'm sorry but I don't like people in my studio.'

'Sure. A kind of sacred place, eh?'

'No,' she said sharply, and led him into the kitchen. 'I've got some fish stew. Will that do?'

'Great. I'd love a beer.'

She got a can from the fridge and handed it to him. Poured stew from a basin into a pot, turned on the stove. She looked at Mike to see if John was in his face, saw nothing and felt a relief that made her smile. 'What have you been doing, Mike? After Good Life, I mean.'

'Do you want a full breakdown?'

'No. What do you do now?'

'Ah'm a travellin' man,' he said, showing his stump of tooth.

'Does that mean nothing? I'm sorry, I'm not trying to be rude. You told me you'd go into school teaching one day.'

'Trouble is —' he grinned — 'I can't stand kids.'

'No? Why didn't you get your tooth fixed, Mike?'

'Hey,' he said, not liking it but forcing good humour, 'I got my manhood, I got my health. What's a tooth? And one of them's still there anyway.' He began a grin to show her, then covered his mouth. 'You were always pretty stroppy. Let's just say I've got my priorities right.'

'Good times?'

'Yeah, good times. What's wrong with that?'

Ellie put bread and butter on the table. She laid plates. 'I enjoyed Good Life for most of the time.'

'Yeah, so did I.'

'How long did you stay?'

'Coupla months after you left. You stole my car!'

'Did you and Boggsie get your crop harvested?'

'Huh,' he said.

'What went wrong?'

Mike watched her cautiously. 'You don't know, eh?'

'No, I don't.'

'OK. Someone went in and sprayed all the plants. I thought it must be, what's their names, Annie and so on, but they don't use poison. Boggsie reckoned it was you. He was all for finding you but I called him off.'

'Thank you.' She tried to sound light. 'Where is Boggsie?'

'Dead.'

'How?'

'Sydney. He got in with some pretty heavy dudes. Boggsie always had some deal worked out. He thought he was sharp.'

'What happened?'

'They found his body, that's all. Burned in his car. You must have read about it.'

'No, I didn't. Do you mean he was murdered?'

'The cops thought so. They never caught anyone. Too damn clever, those boys across the ditch. Anyway. That was Boggsie.'

'Were you in Sydney?'

'I got out quick. I don't go for all that heavy stuff.'

Ellie went to the stove. She found that she was trembling, and did not know whether it was from horror or relief — Boggsie, who had haunted her, gone; but in that way, burned in his car. Mike frightened her too and she had to glance at him to discover he was no threat — except in a time-wasting, importuning way. She found a sudden grief in her for John, who was his son, and a confusion about what she should do. What would John want? Should she give him the choice of knowing, even if it hurt? Wasn't her duty more to keep him safe from Mike's world — from the squalor that he wore like a snail shell on his back?

'The old sheila that owns this place still here?' Mike said.

'No. She died.'

'Her name's on the gate.'

'I haven't painted it off yet. Stuff still comes for her.'

A tremor seemed to run through him, a subtle alteration. 'So,' he said, and drank from the can, 'what's the score, Ellie?'

'Score?' she said, although she knew.

'How come you live here?'

'Why shouldn't I?'

'Yeah, but I mean, who owns the place?' He grinned, watching her. 'You, eh? Nice going.'

She felt as if he'd thrown a bucket of dirty water on her. Instead of making her angry, it defined her: untouchable. She saw how far she'd moved, how Mike could never come close. Sure and self-possessed, she ladled stew into the bowls.

'I'm right, aren't I? It's yours,' he said.

'Yes, it's mine.'

'So, you'd be able, say, to put me up for a couple of nights?'

'Eat it while it's hot, Mike. Then I've got work to do.'

'Painting? Is that what you do?'

'Yes.'

'Those yours?' He waved across the bench at the living room.

'No, they were done by Fan Anerdi.'

'Modern stuff.'

'Fan was a modern woman.'

'I like that one you were doing better.' He swallowed a mouthful of stew, which had not been heated enough. Ellie left hers. She would put it back on the stove when he had gone.

'So, how about it, Ellie? You got a spare bed?' He stopped and seemed to shrink as a thought struck him. 'You haven't got a bloke, have you? That'd be my luck. Hey, you haven't, I can tell. Women get a certain kind of look.'

'Don't be cheeky, Mike.'

'Just cracking jokes. You know me.'

'I don't have a partner, but I might have soon.' Where did that come from? Invention? Prophecy?

'Yeah. OK.'

'And I'm expecting my brother.'

'I didn't know you had one.'

'I've got two. And a sister as well. My son's coming home.'

'I didn't know — kids?'

'A lot of things can happen in twenty years.'

She was sorry for him but not enough to do more than let him finish his meal. He ate another spoonful and pushed his plate away.

'You wouldn't have another beer, Ellie?'

She fetched him a can.

'So,' he said, twitching his shoulders, turning over what he might say.

'Where do you go from here, Mike?'

'Dunno. Travellin' man.' He tried to grin. 'I might try Good Life.'

'It's not there any more. It's turned into a religious place.' She smiled at him. 'Not your style.'

'No. Ellie, what say a couple of nights? Then I'd be gone. I could do a bit of work in the garden. I need —' he surprised her — 'need to be still now and then. Put myself together. I haven't had it easy, Ellie, I guess. If I can have some peace and quiet I can go on.'

It might have been half true, but the rest was bogus. Ellie saw it in his eyes as he watched for his effect on her. His couple of nights would turn into three or four. There would always be reasons. He would dig in and she might never be rid of him. Peace and quiet would graduate into lounging around and guitar strumming and beer and pot and sex. He'd want sex. Ellie wanted work, she wanted painting, she wanted herself.

Whatever you're going to do, do it now, she told herself.

'Sorry, Mike.' A refusal for her own sake, not John's. 'Have you finished eating? I want to get back to work.'

'Ah, Ellie, you've grown hard.'

'Not especially. I've learned what I want.'

'Don't you think there's too much selfishness in the world?'

'Oh shut up, Mike. Just drink your beer. How much money have you got? Do you want some money?'

It stopped him and changed his direction, although he said, 'You don't have to insult me.'

'I'm not trying to.' She got her bag from the sideboard and rummaged for her purse. 'There,' she said, tipping coins and bank-notes on the table, 'does that help?'

He swallowed and slid his eyes away. 'I've got to buy petrol to get away from here. So sure, I'll take it. You've turned into some sour old bitch, Ellie.' He scooped the money — fifty, sixty dollars — in one hand, put it in his pocket. 'Can I use your bog? Or do I have to piss out in the drive?'

'Down the hall.'

She put his bowl on the bench and tipped hers back into the pot. She wanted to get Mike out of her house. Get him out. He would make her dissatisfied with where she had been. She wanted her past solid and square, not marked and twisted retrospectively. She stood by the back door; stepped into the yard when the toilet flushed.

'Out here.'

'Can't wait to get rid of me, eh?'

'There's no work in Nelson, Mike. It's the wrong season.'

'Is that a way of running me out of town? I wouldn't have treated you this way, Ellie.'

'No, probably not.'

She saw him hunting for another insult. 'Sour bitch' had not been strong enough. Instead, his eyes filled with tears. 'Anyway,' he said.

'What?'

'Thanks for this.' He tapped his pocket, jingling coins. 'I'll have enough to get my car on the ferry now. Just about.'

'You're heading north?'

'Might as well.'

He did not know where he would be from one day to the next; but she held herself hard.

'Goodbye, Mike.'

He turned away, then stopped at the corner of the path. 'I don't care how you remember it, you were the best sheila I ever had.'

She went through the house and watched him from the veranda; saw him step over the gate.

'It's a bloody pity you turned out how you did.' He got into his rusty Toyota under the pines and drove away.

Ellie ate her lunch. She tore bread and wiped the bowl clean. Sour bitch? She saw how it might seem as true as 'best sheila' for him — and how 'best sheila' made him better off than her. She had no memory of a matching sort. But she had John. And, whatever the loss, she had saved herself.

She locked the house and drove into Motueka. Drew cash from the bank, did her weekly shopping, drove home hoping that Derek would have arrived. She wanted to be with someone, wanted to talk. He had phoned the week before to say he was passing through. His man's voice had surprised her, so strong had been her feeling that George and her mother had left him no way of growing up. The thought of seeing him had set up the same quiet humming in her that came when she knew that a painting was going to work. As for John coming home, that would not be until the university holidays in August, so in a way she had lied to Mike, allowing him to suppose that John was a child expected home from school. Clever, she thought, not liking herself.

There was no Derek waiting on the porch. She began to be angry with him, and calmed herself by sitting in the back yard in pale sunlight from across the bay, listening to the wind in the pine trees and the sound of cars on the coast road. She poured a glass of beer and drank it slowly, wondering about the slow ruin of Mike's life. She could not understand such easy choices, such lack of will. She tried not to feel guilty. She wanted to forget him.

Clouds came up and hid the sun. The sea darkened. Separation Point turned from blue to grey. Ellie went into her studio. The painting on her easel seemed insipid. She had meant it to be strong but all she could claim for it was that it was nicely painted. What was in it except a creek and rocks and bush and a hill? All these things had substance, yet no substance was there. She squeezed black paint on her palette and took a thick brush with stiff hairs. She dragged paint down the hill, not knowing whether she was crossing it out or adding something — a single thick line against the grain. She dragged a second time with a drier brush, broadening it and making the edges scratch, then let it fork and made a figure, a man, scarcely defined, only suggested, not requiring anything more, swell or bulb of head, or shoulders, feet. She let him fade in scratches at the edge, let him peter out, but saw how much he was present, how he inhabited the landscape. Even though I've ruined it, she said. Who is he? No one. Someone. Someone with a right to be there. He came from the bush and hill but equally from her. He wasn't Mike. Or Neil. Or John or Derek. Anyone. Not her father. He wasn't the new partner who had suddenly appeared in her conversation with Mike. Was he a man? Yes. Not a woman. She had known that as she dragged her brush against the grain.

Ellie took the painting down from the easel and leaned it face out against the wall. She took another, not choosing, from the dozen she had worked on recently (creek and hill), and propped it in place. She made the same vertical stroke, with her brush even drier, increasing the scratchiness at the edges; made the figure two limbed, walking not on the hill but in front of it, his footing unseen so he seemed to float, while the solid black (she increased it) at his centre, like a spine, anchored him deep into the land. She drew her breath; her quiet humming began, although another painting was ruined. She looked at it a long while, trying to feel, not understand. I'm *doing* this, she thought, it's not one of Fan's accidents. 'Be quiet, Fan.'

She put another painting in place.

Ellie worked late into the night, then ate and slept, and went out to the studio as soon as it was light. The paintings she had finished (ruined) stood against the wall: hill, bush, creek, black figure, some smaller than her first, some large (one was a torso blotting half the canvas out). She did not know what the right proportions would be — if there was 'right' — or if she would paint many or just one; but began, calm in her movements, with a new canvas (she prepared her own: soaked them and stretched them and put the gesso on); moved her brush loosely, smelling the piney solvent in the paint — creek, bush, hills again, visualising them without a figure but knowing he was implanted there. Who was he? What was he? She did not any longer want to know. Hold him back a while, he'll turn up in his own good time. All she wanted was for the paint to go on . . .

Ellie photographed her paintings and sent copies to a dealer in Auckland. Thank you, he replied, but I'm afraid . . . Silly cow, Ellie thought. She tried David Shea, who saw her for the first time as more than a female upstart hoarding Anerdi paintings she didn't deserve to own. Yes, he would show her work in a November slot that by good chance had become available. Would she prepare an artist's statement, please, and perhaps find a more appealing title than *Figure 1–10? Spirit of the Land* or *The Human Occupation* or *Do I Belong?* — how about that? Oh no, Ellie thought, no dressing up. (Fan would have called it 'spreading jam'.) What I've named it is what it is. She would not write an artist's statement either; quoted Fan a second time: 'I've never read one that isn't some sort of gorse hedge growing round a painting.' She wrote an autobiographical paragraph, giving little away, but allowed David to add: Friend and pupil of Fan Anerdi.

John had examinations and could not leave Christchurch, so Ellie went to Wellington alone. She stayed in Brooklyn with her mother and learned that Derek had by-passed Ruby Bay and gone to Golden Bay. He was living in a religious community.

'What's it's name?'

'Gethsemane.'

'But that's where I was. I mean, geographically. It was Good Life. Then some religious cult moved in when Terry and Rain left. What's he doing there?'

'I don't think it's a cult, Ellie. You've never been fair about what people believe.'

'Sorry, sorry. They're Anabaptists or something. New Testament Christians anyway. They don't like the Old. Earlyites they call themselves. That's the name of the boss. Robert Early.'

'Yes, I know. He's hardly "boss".'

'How does your church feel about them? And what's Derek

doing there? He doesn't believe that stuff.'

Her mother was vague — 'Just seeing what he thinks,' and, 'He'll come back. Derek knows there's only one true way.' Then she let her worry surface: 'Ellie, I can't go there. Will you go? Go and see?'

'They wouldn't let me past the gate.'

'Yes they would. Visitors are allowed. I think you should write first, though. Ellie . . .?'

'Well, I'll see. Would Derek want me? He didn't make any effort to call in.'

'He likes you, Ellie. You and he clicked, he said.'

'Ha, clicked. I'll think about it. I don't promise.'

She took her mother to the opening next night. She had sent an invitation to Neil and his wife, Amber Somerville, a radio journalist. (The novel that might have been Ellie's was dedicated to her.) They did not come. Angela and Barry Abbot came, bringing Hollis Prime. Ellie turned from a conversation and saw him standing inside the door, leaning on his stick. He's a sort of shadow man, she thought; although her heart gave a jolt as if something more substantial, a car or bus, had pulled up with a screech in front of her. She smiled at him — a minimal smile — then was engulfed by Barry and Angela. When she was able to look again, he had his back to her and was moving along her paintings.

'Is Hollis down here now?' she said.

'No, he's visiting,' Angela said. 'He doesn't like Wellington much, his ex-wife lives here. He advises Barry, doesn't he Barry?'

'He certainly does. He never stops,' Barry said, beaming.

'I saw where you gave up politics,' Ellie said.

'It gave me up. It chewed me up and spat me out. Ellie, these are great paintings. What do they mean?'

'Whatever you like.'

'I'm a simple guy. I need to be told.'

'Don't be boring, Barry. Which one shall we buy?' Angela said.

'It's a matter of where we'd hang it,' Barry said. 'Is this someone you know, this feller in them?'

Ellie supposed she should say something clever. Instead she was confused: he might be one person or a multitude. 'They've all got names, Barry. They're *Figure 1–10*.'

'You must spend a lot on paint, putting it on so thick.'

'I'm modest compared with some painters I know.' She wanted to be away from here — sitting in the twilight in her back yard with the trees and her cat for company. She excused herself and talked with other people, then joined her mother, who said, 'Does that red pin he stuck in mean a picture's sold?'

'Yes. Oh, good.'

'Eight hundred dollars.'

'He gets a third. Did you see who it was?'

'That man you were talking to. The one who smiles all the time.'

'Ah, Barry. I suppose Angela told him to.'

'Who are they?'

'I was with her at Willowbank. He's some sort of property investor.'

'Who's the funny woman at the door?'

Ellie felt her heart lighten. She was joyful suddenly, as though every one of her pictures had sold. 'Excuse me, Mum. It's Mrs Nimmo.'

'She looks like a baglady.'

'Doesn't she?'

A supermarket bag with something — clothing, shoes? — in the bottom. A fur coat with patches like mange. Rumpled socks, multi-coloured sneakers. A crocheted cap with wisps of white hair poking through. Serene face.

'Mrs Nimmo, I'm Ellie Crowther. I was hoping I got the invitation right, but I wasn't sure you'd remember me.'

'Of course I remember.'

'It's such a long time. It's thirty years.'

'You don't measure memories by arithmetic,' Mrs Nimmo said. 'You weren't a waste of time, Ellie, so it's yesterday.'

'Thank you for coming.'

'It's my second visit. I came this morning when the pictures were going up, so I could see them properly.'

'David didn't tell me.'

'The fat man? He shooed me out. Tried to. I don't shoo. This time I came to see you.'

'I'm glad.'

'I've never had one of my girls become a painter. Now these — did you think about them a long time, or just pick up your brush and start to paint?'

'Oh, both,' Ellie said. 'But I think about them now, all the time.'

'So there's more to come?'

'Yes. But I'm not sure what.'

'Where did you get him? Out of your dreams?'

'He just arrived. I don't know who he is or what he means. They were only landscapes at first.'

'And you let him stay. You took the risk.'

'Oh, I don't know. He might be a friend. All I know is I like the paintings. I think they're good.'

'Yes, they are. I'll come again one day when no one's here, if that man will let me. He wants you to circulate, look at him. Did the stil bistroel work?'

'It wasn't for me.'

'Your friend, you said. Did she take it?'

Ellie looked nervously at Hollis Prime. He was out of earshot, talking with Angela. She smiled at him fleetingly, then whispered to Mrs Nimmo, 'No, she didn't. She got cross with me. She was a Catholic.'

'Plenty of them have abortions, dear. I did myself when I was a girl.'

'You're not a Catholic, are you?'

'I was once. Perhaps I still am. Mine was with knitting needles on a kitchen table. It finished me for children, I'm afraid. So your friend had hers?'

'I don't know. She went away to Sydney . . . oh, what's that?' Mrs Nimmo's bag pressed on her knee. 'Good heavens, a cat.' She peered inside and made it out — a tabby crossed with Siamese lying on a bed of tartan blanket.

'He's old and sick. I'm sorry if he smells a bit. I suppose you thought it was me.'

'No, no,' Ellie said.

'Of course you did. Be still, Beria, I'm taking you home.'

'Who?' Ellie said.

'Oh, Beria. He murdered all my sparrows one by one. Merciless. Then he moved in, the way cats do. Now he's old and I can't leave him to die alone. So he comes with me. What can I do?'

'Have you given up politics? — Yes, in a minute, David. I haven't finished talking with Mrs Nimmo.'

'I haven't got time,' Mrs Nimmo said. 'Communism was a great idea perverted — by monsters like this.' She gave the bag a shake, which made the cat mew. 'I believe in original sin now. Not the Christian sort, of course. Although I do wonder what comes next. Life has been interesting but I'm getting just a little bit divorced. That's why it's nice to come and see this. Now, I must go. That's enough, Beria, you'll have your basket soon. Goodbye, Ellie.'

Ellie went to the door with her and kissed her cheek. 'Will you let me give you a painting?'

'No, dear, no. I've got no room. I mean in my head. You've no idea how nice it is just seeing one of my girls. That's enough.'

'I'm glad I had you for my teacher.'

Mrs Nimmo changed Beria to her other hand. She nodded and smiled and went away, but turned after a step or two and said, 'Oh, Ellie, I meant to say, don't waste too much time with Angela Prime. Not when you've got your work to do. Goodbye, dear.'

Angela caught Ellie as she crossed the gallery. 'What on earth did she have in that bag? It wasn't a cat?'

'Yes, it was. Called Beria. Hollis, it's good to see you. Thank you for coming.'

'What an extraordinary way to live your life. I think I can smell it,' Angela said.

'David will bring some air freshener. Thanks for buying one of my paintings.'

'Oh, I like them. Hollis says they're expressionist.'

Ellie turned to him. 'Don't put labels on them, please.'

His face coloured — a self-betraying face in spite of its stillness. She wondered if he was able to smile.

'It's just,' she said, 'I don't like words you throw like a blanket over things. Sorry.'

'I meant there's more than just technique.'

'Don't write off technique. There's lots of plain bad painting around.' I hate this sort of conversation, she thought. 'Excuse me, I'd better save my mother.'

Who was not in need of saving, was perfectly at ease, watching David fix another pin in the wall.

'What does a blue one mean?'

'On approval, something like that.'

'There's two red now and one blue. Is that good?'

'For someone like me, in Wellington, very good. A lot of exhibitions don't sell anything at all.'

She was pleased with her mother, more relaxed with her. Mrs Brownlee had taken care to look her best: new flat shoes, a piece of blue glass jewellery, blown into a bubble, nestling in an Indian scarf at her throat. Where did she get that? Her new freedom, easier smiles, were a mystery too. She seemed to miss out the step she had learned from George — that shuffling pause caused by reference to some body of law. Perhaps a new man had come along. Or — Ellie preferred this — with George gone (poor George) she was recovering herself.

They waited until the last person had left, and stood with David in the empty gallery. Ellie looked at her paintings and felt a shock: they're good. She turned away, believing she might cry.

'Three sold and one maybe,' David said. 'That's more than satisfactory, my dear.' (Her first 'my dear'.) 'I think I detect a little groundswell, maybe. The only thing you might have done — some fetching title, some, oh, grabber perhaps. People like things easy.

265

They don't care so much for enigmatic.'

'I'll try to remember,' Ellie said.

'The lady who bought that one —' Mrs Brownlee pointed — 'said she liked it because it seemed to mean all sorts of things.' She squeezed Ellie's hand as they went out. 'It's lovely to see you doing well.'

Ellie stayed in Wellington another day. She caught a bus down Brooklyn hill in the afternoon, and nosed around in bookshops and galleries. Then she walked along the waterfront to Oriental Bay, where the tide held its fullness before turning. It was a moment she had watched in inlets at Waimea and Collingwood, wondering how to catch the moment, like a deep slow breath, like a turning over in sleep — catch it in paint. I need my paintings to be human, she thought. Did that mean she must always put a person in? She walked along past Hay Street and Grass Street — names she liked — making for the steps leading down to the sea opposite the ugly hotel that spoiled the furthest part of the Parade. She wanted to take her shoes off, wet her feet — wash her feet. I don't mind message any more, she thought. (Be quiet, Fan.) I don't mind me in my paintings. Why should I? I suppose I'll always stick at $800: David should really let me go. The painters who were starting to make their names, all the new ones, were cool and clever, or clever and cruel, or witty and unconnected, and she could not go in any of those ways, would not want to, any more than be contented with colour and light. Yet she retained the happiness she had felt the night before when she had seen that her paintings were good.

'Ellie,' said a man sitting on a seat. He tapped with his stick on the pavement. Hollis Prime.

'Hello. Can I sit down?'

He made room. 'I always hesitate to interrupt when someone's as far away as that.'

'Was I? I suppose I was. Euphoria from last night. What are you doing here?'

'Looking at the Hutt. Have you ever been back?'

'Not really. Passing through. I've never seen the hostels again. Have you?'

'No. If I came back to Wellington I'd want a house up high.' He pointed his stick at Wadestown.

'I've got one where I am. I look down the hills and over the sea. Are you thinking of coming back?'

'One day maybe. Not for a while.'

'Are you still doing the same sort of thing? Tax law?'

'Yes. The same.'

'For Barry?'

'Among others. He —' Hollis grimaced — 'he fell in a hole. I'm trying to get him out. It's mainly get Angela out, I suppose.'

'What sort of hole?'

'I can't talk about it. It goes back to pre-1987, when everybody was getting rich.'

'And not too concerned about how. Equiticorp and all those others.'

He looked at her sharply and she said, 'I'm not saying Barry was like that. I've got some shares. They were left to me. Mostly Brierley.'

'Hard luck.'

'What should I do with them?'

'I really don't know.'

Ellie was amused by his stuffiness. 'I don't like shares. Money making money. It seems to me people should do it — with work, I mean, not shuffling bits of paper and punching keys.'

Hollis laughed. 'You've just wiped the stock market out.'

'Oh, good.'

He laughed again, but said nothing more, just tapped the toe of his shoe with his stick. Then he leaned back. 'It's nice sitting here.'

'Does your leg still hurt?'

Hollis smiled. She thought there was something sad in it.

'I remember your way of coming out with things,' he said.

'I thought polio got better. I mean, improved.'

'It does for a while. Then it gets — do you want to know?'

'Only if you want to tell me.'

'I'd rather find out about you. I haven't forgotten, Ellie. That night we drove down to Petone beach. Something nearly happened that night.'

'I might be the best sheila you never had.'

'I don't mean sex.' (What a serious fellow, she thought.) 'You set something going in me. I might have found something out.'

'What?'

'I don't know. Then of course Dolores got in the way. I couldn't help going after Dolores. So — I kind of closed up again.'

He disappointed her. This backward looking and romanticising made it seem as if he had some sort of limp in his mind.

'I think I might have disappointed you,' she said.

He squinted at her in the lowering sun. 'I don't think so. What are all the things you've done, Ellie? Have you got time?'

'You want my life?'

He looked at his watch. 'It's only half past three. Would you like a coffee? I think there's a place.'

'No, let's sit here.'

'Starting from when you told me what a ratbag I was, down on the wharves.'

That's just across the water. We've come in a circle, she thought; and then was reluctant. Wasn't it imprudent, perhaps dangerous, to give your life away in lumps the way he wanted? She was afraid, superstitiously, of what she might lose, and she said, 'My life's pretty boring'; then was angry with herself: No it's not. See, I've lost something already, saying that.

'I left school and got a job in a library. And lived in a flat and met some boys and travelled around.'

'Pretend you're painting it,' Hollis said.

It took her breath away. It was as if he'd leaned forward and touched her face. As if he had touched her intimately.

'You don't know anything about that,' she said. She began to say that painting was her job and nothing special, which was only half true, then fell silent as she understood that in her work she had regained her past in a way most people could not. She was not aware of putting it on the canvas, yet it was there, in what she chose, in what arrived unchosen, in her brushstrokes, in her palette. She reached a kind of deep acquaintance with herself. So she described her life to Hollis Prime and had the sense of working, making detail, but also of making huge strides, of stepping long over tens of years, until she was able to say, 'That brings me right up to last night.' She might have added, 'brings me up to now'.

'That's quite a life for pretty boring,' Hollis said.

'I didn't mean that.'

'I didn't think you did. Where did he come from, the figure in your paintings?'

'Oh, I don't know. I never knew my father. Maybe it's him. Or men I've known. Or something else. Maybe not a man. It could be me. Or what Mrs Nimmo talked about . . . No, cancel that. I learned how to paint from a woman who hated meanings. I don't want to go after them.'

Hollis worked a piece of asphalt free with his stick. He picked it up and lobbed it over the wall into the sea.

'I bought one,' he said.

'When?'

'Last night. The one where he takes up half the space.'

'I thought that was Barry and Angela.'

Hollis smiled. 'He was my frontman.'

'Why did you do that?'

'Because I didn't want to talk about it right then.'

'With me?'

'Anyone. I didn't want to have to explain.'

'Explain what?'

'It seemed a kind of warning about —' he shrugged — 'things that are going on. And where I am.'

She had wanted something more personal but still was pleased. 'I'm glad you chose that one. I like it best.'

269

'Good.'

'And I'm pleased you didn't buy it just because you know me . . . I could have given you a discount.'

'No way. You've got to make a living. Painting's your job.'

They sat a while in silence, watching a ferry move out. Traffic roared sporadically behind them. The sea slapped on the wall with a kind of exhalation then the hiss of retreat. It sent up a clean smell of seaweed. She turned her head as Hollis turned, watching the ferry.

'The Hutt,' he said, looking beyond it.

'As good a place as any, I suppose. You know — I think I saw you — the black figure, I mean. When you followed me over the sandhills down on Petone beach . . .' Then she told herself, Stop there.

He seemed to understand, not want to go on either. 'Long ago and far away,' he said, standing up. 'I'm catching a taxi back into town. Do you want to share?'

'No, I'll walk.'

They went towards Quayside restaurant.

'Things that are going on?' she reminded him. 'Where you are?'

'It's a long story. I might tell you one day.'

'Visit me in Nelson if you like.'

He looked surprised. His face began to colour, which amused her.

'Thank you,' he said. Then: 'What I said about Barry . . .'

'Yes?'

'I shouldn't have told you really.' He went redder. 'I don't mean I don't trust you, of course . . .'

'That's all right.'

'Barry isn't a crook. He's just a fool. A greedy one. But he's generous. He likes people . . .'

'He told me once he nearly cried when his friend hung himself.'

'And then he'd forget.' He stopped at the crossing where he would turn away. 'I want to . . .'

'What, Hollis?'

'I want to get it finished. All this.'

Ellie touched his arm. 'Come and see me.'

She walked towards the city and in a moment saw him pass in a taxi, sitting straight; not pretending not to see her but turning his problems over in his mind.

He's strange, she thought, he's all cramped up. Like a woman in a tight skirt trying to walk fast.

Ellie grinned; she laughed, feeling excited. But it was a rational excitement, wasn't it, and not schoolgirlish? She had not reproached him, had not needed to, when he had mentioned Dolores.

It was like brushing her hair and finding that a knot had come free.

Ellie stopped her car on a low rise and looked at the land across the river. Clearings had been cut in the scrub — wide ones shaped like ping-pong bats, long ones like flax leaves, running towards the foothills of the Quartz Range. She saw a tractor standing driverless on one of them, and wondered if it belonged to Gethsemane. Nine years ago she had driven down this metalled road to show John the railway carriage where she had lived. They had found the gate locked and the scrub cleared on the near side of the river. Men worked on the foundations of a building too big for a house — perhaps a meeting hall or a church. The clearing where the garden had been was turned into pasture, and the railway carriage was gone.

'I suppose they broke it up for firewood,' she said, imagining the roof in flames, with her first real painting coming to light under the tar.

They had driven further down the road and walked across the footbridge. She showed John the undercut bank in the river bend where two kayakers had drowned, and the waterfall on Salisbury Creek, but the scrub was too thick for them to find a way to the creek where Mike had abandoned his sluice. They turned back and drove to the head of the Heaphy Track where they walked a little way so John could bounce across the river on the first swing bridge.

Driving back past the commune she had thought, At least they can't get to the other side.

It seemed she was wrong. The green and brown clearings probed and licked between the gorges. The Earlyites must cross on the new concrete bridge below the bend, and have their own road leading into the ranges and more bridges built over creeks. The place where Mike had grown his marijuana was probably used for grazing sheep.

She drove on and found a gate with *Gethsemane* painted on it and no prohibition against entry. The name was strange, she had thought, driving over the hill from Ruby Bay. If she remembered her Divinity right, Gethsemane was the garden where Jesus was betrayed; where he was sorrowful even unto death and said, O my Father, let this cup pass from me. Why use it for a community where everyone followed him?

But where — Ellie stopped the car — was everyone? The place was deserted. Not a movement, not a sound. There were four houses, including Terry's A-frame; two large buildings, one hangar-roofed and double-storeyed; and half a dozen others — workshops, barns, storage sheds — built of green-painted corrugated iron. But no people, none in the gardens behind the buildings or in the orchard of silver trees — olive trees. Vehicles stood empty. Across the river the tractor sat unattended. It's like the *Marie Celeste*, Ellie thought. She felt she might be ambushed.

Then a man wearing black trousers and a white shirt came out through the double doors of the largest building and stopped on the forecourt, staring at her. He had the isolation of a survivor, the last person left. For a moment she thought he was Derek — but no, he was too thick in his build and pale in his hair. She drove across a cattle stop, along the drive and pulled up in front of him.

'Hello.'

He made no answer. A stern-looking boy, rather like a reborn economist. In a tie and jacket he'd be at home at No.1 The Terrace.

'My name's Ellie Crowther. I telephoned Mr Early and he said I could come and visit my brother.'

'Stay in your car, please.'

He turned inside, crossed a wide foyer and went through another door, closing it behind him. There was no sound except the murmur of her car. Ellie switched off the engine, hoping she might hear the river. Where had Robert Early hidden his people?

Doors concertinaed at the back of the foyer and suddenly the space was surging, full. The doors to the forecourt opened. Men in grey boilersuits, women in blue long dresses and white head-scarves, poured out, silent except for the chattering of their shoes. They broke around the car, went by on either side, giving Ellie no more than a glance. They made her think of Bruegel peasants on a village square — which was wrong, because the women's dresses were nun-like in their fullness and the men were hair-trimmed and closely shaved and clean. She tried to shake off the fear she felt. There was no hostility, but an absence of curiosity that she found unnerving. Many of the women were young. All looked placid and some were beautiful. Children ran and hopped and clung to hands. They too seemed incurious. The boys wore white shirts and black trousers, the girls long blue dresses and headscarves like their mothers.

How many? It seemed more than a hundred people had passed. They walked away, the women and children to the hangar-like building, the men to the vehicles and sheds. They must have come from lunch, Ellie realised. Everyone would gather for meals, even at midday, from the furthest corners of the farm. She watched for Derek coming out. Wouldn't he find Gethsemane like a school? He had hated school.

The young man reappeared with an older man at his side. He indicated Ellie and turned away.

'I'm Robert Early,' said the man. 'And you are Mrs Crowther.'

Ellie did not risk correcting him. A dogmatist. And 'Ms' or even 'Ellie' might get her expelled. 'It's good of you to let me come,' she said.

'Would you like to get out?'

Ellie obeyed, hoping that her floral culottes would not offend him.

He was dressed like the young man — white shirt, black trousers — while the older women coming from the dining hall were clothed identically to the earlier ones, except that some wore headscarves bordered in blue. It made Ellie look at their faces. Perhaps that was the idea.

'I was hoping I could see Derek Brownlee,' she said.

'I think he went out the side door. They're haymaking in the river paddock. I'll send someone for him later on,' Robert Early said. He was looking steadily at her face as though trying to read her. It forced her to talk.

'I used to live here once, in a commune called Good Life. I lived in a railway carriage down there.' She pointed towards the river, then fell silent, seeing that he had no interest.

'Verity,' he said to a woman standing close, 'will you check that Mrs Crowther is all right.'

The woman smiled, invited Ellie with a gesture, and led her through the foyer to a small room at the side.

'Would you undo your blouse,' she said.

'I certainly will not.'

'Please. We had a woman come here with a tape recorder once. It was hidden inside her jacket. Robert heard it click when the tape ran out. Poor thing.'

'What happened to her?'

'Oh, nothing. Robert sent her away. She was a journalist.'

'Did he take her tape recorder?'

'No. We're not scared of the world outside or what it might say. But we like to check. Please?'

Ellie pulled her shirt out, undid the buttons, raised her arms. She turned in a circle.

'Thank you,' the woman said.

'Do you all wear the same clothes?'

'Yes. They're very comfortable. Two dresses each.'

'With that expandable panel in front?'

'Only the married women. Child-bearing women.'

'How many . . .?'

'Me? I've got eight. And another one on the way.'

'Are you . . .?'

'I'm Robert's wife. He has other children by his first wife. She died. Grandchildren too.'

'Have you always been — I don't know what to call you.'

'Earlyites. No. I taught in a girls' school. German and French. Are you ready, Mrs Crowther?'

'How old are the girls here when they marry?'

'Robert will answer your questions. You can ask him what you like.'

They went back to Robert Early in the foyer. He smiled at Ellie, bending his head to reduce his height.

'Verity explained to you? That's good. The woman went away and wrote a story full of lies.'

'I think I read it.' Not a good story. The reporter was unrelenting in her disapproval, holier in her way than the Earlyites. Later on a television crew had tried to get in but were turned away by young men at the gate and reduced to taking long shots from the road. There were rumours of sexual abuse of children — but Ellie could not believe them, watching Verity walk away. She tried to remember: hadn't there been a police raid that had turned up nothing sinister?

Robert Early took her through the folding doors into a dining hall, where women pushing trolleys were clearing dirty dishes from the tables.

'How many people live here?' she said.

'Two hundred and seventy. I'll take you round, Mrs Crowther, and show you how we live.'

She followed him through the hall into a huge kitchen where half a dozen young women, wearing white aprons over their dresses, stacked plates into dishwashing machines, while others — Ellie did not count, but there were ten or fifteen — peeled and chopped vegetables at a long bench, measured flour, tipped it into mixing machines, fed a continuous oven — 'Built here, it's our invention,' Robert Early said — turned baked loaves out on trays to cool. One meal hardly finished and they're busy with the next, Ellie thought. She wondered if this was how these girls would spend their lives. None of them gave her more than a glance. She would have expected her clothes, if nothing else, to interest them.

'They all look so contented,' she said, although she might have chosen 'lulled, untroubled'.

'Yes, they are.'

'Were they born here? Or did they join?'

'Some were born before we shifted from the Manawatu. Others came from outside, like your brother. But you don't "join", Mrs Crowther, you surrender your whole will and life to Christ. "And the Lord added to the Church daily such as should be saved." Now, I'll show you our school and sewing shop and then you can see our family rooms.'

Ellie followed him through the senior schoolroom, where Verity was in charge of two younger teachers; then the infant room, the sewing room, the gardens; huge workshops servicing tractors and trucks and a helicopter — 'We've got some good mechanics so we take on contracts from outside.' He showed her a plant making methane gas from pig manure. Outside again, she heard machines working downriver and saw a haze of dust rising beyond a shelter belt of squared-off pines; smelled hay, which, familiar, helped her keep steady against a growing bewilderment at what Gethsemane was and who Robert Early was.

He took her up stairs over the dining hall. A corridor ran the length of the building, with doors on each side. A village of cots stood at the far end, watched over by a girl sitting in a chair. She put her finger to her lips.

Robert Early smiled at Ellie. 'They take turns at minding. They all learn childcare.'

'Boys too?'

'No, not boys. This one is empty, I think.' He opened a door. 'Each family has a room like this. You see, parents and children

276

together. Nothing is hidden or shameful in family life. But this is mainly for sleeping. The whole community is a family too.'

A king-sized bed with a coverlet of sky-blue flowers on a pink background stood under the window, and two sets of bunks against the walls. There were three chairs, a tallboy, a set of drawers, a narrow desk. Nothing else. The partitions stopped two feet from the ceiling. There were similar rooms on either side, Ellie supposed. She looked for pictures. None. Plastic flowers, pink and white, stood in glass vases. Bows made of ribbons perched like butterflies on the walls. Ellie had never seen a room so barren.

'Nice,' she whispered as Robert Early waited. 'But . . .'

'Yes?'

'Where do you go to be by yourself?'

He smiled at her. 'When a couple needs to be alone they go to one of the houses for a few nights. It rarely happens. There's no sin in procreation. Or did you mean singly? No, Mrs Crowther, there's no need for that sort of privacy. Christ must be shared not hoarded away. And the devil can worm his way in when you're solitary. Now —' he led her into the corridor and beckoned the girl — 'I'll get you some tea. This is my daughter, Harmony. There are sixty people along here —' he waved at the corridor — 'and all of them are descended from me. Tell them in the kitchen Mrs Crowther would like some tea.'

The girl hurried away.

'She doesn't like leaving the babies long. I've got a son and two grandsons and a great granddaughter in those cots.'

'Amazing,' Ellie said. She could not think of any other comment. Queen bee, she might have said, but that was a sneer, short of the understanding she strained after. What was the reason for this place and this behaviour? A pleasant strain of normalcy ran over something deeply abnormal and possibly dangerous. Yet she liked Robert Early — in a way, in a way. A handsome man, gifted with easy speech.

He took her downstairs and sat her at a table in the kitchen, where the women worked with economy — economy in their faces too. She drank tea and ate a shop biscuit — was she not fit to share food baked at Gethsemane? — listening as he talked, watching his face and friendly eyes. His head was round, almost perfectly, and massy if that was a word, furred with grey close-cropped hair and deeply scored with lines in the forehead and cheeks — like a chopping board, she thought. When he smiled he showed elderly teeth, like stained porcelain, each one a slab. His nose had been broken at some time and badly set. It was a high-specific-gravity head, set on a body that seemed too light for it. She was sure that he had lived through a crisis, remade himself, and his weightiness came from there.

'Gethsemane seems a strange name,' she said.

'Why?'

'Wasn't it where Jesus was betrayed?'

He looked at her with more than his professional friendliness: with interest. 'He's betrayed daily, every minute, out in the world. And he's known betrayal in here. We have had a Judas or two.'

'He asked God — take this cup away from me.'

Robert Early smiled, pleased with her. 'Do you remember what he said after that? "Nevertheless not what I will but what thou wilt." God's will, Mrs Crowther. He left the cup for him to drink. That is why we are here in Gethsemane, joined by Christ into his church.'

'Yes, I see.' She did not want any more of this. 'I saw some violins and cellos. Do all the children play?'

'They do. And sing. We have an orchestra and a choir.'

'What would happen if one of them got very good and needed teachers better than you've got?'

'We've got good teachers.'

'But if one was really gifted? Would you let her go outside and learn out there? Play professionally, I mean.'

'No.'

'Why not?'

'That would be to lust after the world.'

'I don't know. Isn't it like sharing a gift?'

'Nothing can be shared except in Christ. The wide gate leads to destruction and the narrow pathway to eternal life. You've heard the word "ecclesia"? It means the called-out ones. The world outside is Satan's world. Here we love and obey God. Our children play their instruments in praise of him, not for applause. It's really very simple, Mrs Crowther.' He watched her steadily for a moment. 'Entertainments dishonour God.' Then as suddenly as he had become interested he was bored, which she took as recognition: an unintended compliment to her. 'I've sent someone for Derek. He'll be waiting for you out by your car. Try not to keep him too long. We've got a lot of hay to get in.'

'Yes. Thank you for your guided tour.' She stood up and offered her hand. He took it, seemed surprised at the contact, let it go. She left him by the table, looked back from the door, saw him half-turning, as though uncertain, and thought, He's the boss, he's in command, but it's not enough. She went out through the dining hall and foyer, found Derek by her car and hugged him tight.

'Hey, don't crush me.'

'I've just been talking to Mr Early. Do you hate the world, Derek? Do you think I'm evil?'

'My problem is I don't hate anything. Which makes it pretty tough around here.' He stood back and looked at her. 'They've given me ten minutes. Walk back down with me.'

He was sweaty from hay-making, with runnels in the dust on his forearms and smears on his cheeks where he had wiped his palms. He pushed his cloth hat back and grinned at her. Ellie thought, He's made it, he's got through. She could not understand what he was doing in this place.

'You look fit,' she said.

'Yeah, I am. It's doing me good. I like that painting you gave Mum.'

'Thank you. It's an early thing. I'm doing better ones now.'

'You should paint here.' He jerked his hand at the hills.

'I did once. I lived here.' She stopped on the track across the paddock. 'Almost exactly on this spot. In a railway carriage. There was a bath outside in the rain. Look.' She ran three steps, prised a piece of orange-coloured brick from the ground. 'It stood on this. On bricks. Oh God, can I keep it?'

Derek laughed. 'Pre-Gethsemane. What did you think of Robert?'

'I'm not sure. I expected someone charismatic and he's not. But he's — powerful.'

'Sure. Charismatic doesn't go down. It's almost as bad as popery. The whore of Babylon,' he grinned.

'You're not staying, are you?'

'Don't know.'

'Will they let you go?'

'I might tunnel out. Hey no, relax. Gethsemane isn't dangerous, not like that. There's some things here I really like. They have fun. Singing, dancing. All in line. Pretty girls.' He grinned again, then was serious. 'Baptisms. Full immersion. I like that.'

'You don't mean it?'

'Sure I do. If I believed in it that's what I'd want.'

'But you don't?'

'No, I don't. There's too much else. Outside, I mean. You just can't say God's only here. Come and have a look at the river.'

They went down the paddock and along the broken bank. Only a few trees stood, isolated. Ellie advanced on the flat rock she had used as her private place. After a moment she tossed the piece of brick into the water and saw it sink and lie in the pebbles five metres down; appearing, disappearing as the current moved.

'No souvenirs, eh?' Derek said.

'No.'

'See the shingle bank?' He pointed down river. 'That's our baptising place.'

'I'd love to see one.'

'And over there by the waterfall, that's where the local hoons come. Two or three carloads of them sometimes.'

'What do they do?'

'Mooning. Dropping their jeans. Shouting stuff.'

'Can't you get them stopped?'

'Robert doesn't want to. It's not on Gethsemane land. It's the neighbour's place.'

'And it's the world.'

'That's right. It makes us —' he clenched his fists, tightened his shoulders — 'even closer. Why would we want to go out there?'

They came off the rock and walked across the paddock to the shelter belt. Two girls swinging empty baskets passed by. Their blue dresses billowed in the grass and their tight headscarves seemed to turn their round faces pink. Bruegel fitted this time — the image and the practices of Gethsemane ran together.

'I've missed afternoon tea,' Derek said. 'Listen, Ellie. Seventh day, ten o'clock — sorry, that's on Sunday but we don't use pagan names — anyway, ten o'clock, he's doing three baptisms down there.'

'Adults?'

'Oh, sure. You can't do children.'

'Because they're not old enough to understand sin. That's Anabaptists.'

'Yeah, OK. What I'd like — can you drive over and park along by the bridge? You can watch from by the waterfall. There mightn't be any hoons, they don't always come. When you see me walking up the bank, go back and wait by the gate.'

'You're coming out?'

'I won't have much stuff. Just my duffel bag. I know it's a long way to drive . . .'

'I don't mind that. But can't you just leave? Any time?'

Machinery burped and chugged beyond the trees.

'I've got to go. Yeah, I can leave. But I want to do it this way. It's easier for me. I wouldn't ask, Ellie . . .'

'Yes, all right. I'd like to see a baptism anyway. Ten o'clock.'

'I'll be at the back. No one will see me, not when Robert's holding someone under. Ellie, thanks. Thanks for coming.' He moved away, giving her no chance to hug him. 'If you're phoning Mum, tell her I'm OK. Give her my love.'

'I will.'

'But don't tell her about me leaving yet.'

She watched him walk around the end of the shelter belt, moving in his paddle-footed, left-seeking way, but surer than she remembered, much more strong; then went back quickly to her car and drove away. She did not want to meet Robert Early — did not want him looking in her face. He might see Derek's escape, which elated and frightened her, written there. She suspected him of having the power. And although he was mad — wasn't he? — and probably dangerous, she felt she might apologise for the young men's mooning, for their obscenities and ugliness — and wasn't that saying sorry for the world she loved living in?

Ellie painted another picture using her man made of earth and air, but it didn't work. No matter how she blackened him, he had no business there. This sudden going wrong alarmed her. 'I haven't finished with you yet,' she said, 'don't go away' — and tried to keep him by dragging her brush between his legs and making a penis, hoping he might gain and they discover a way to go, but all it did was dangle, even when she thickened it. She scrubbed it out — a joke, a schlong — and did no more that day or the two days after.

On Sunday she packed bread and butter and chicken legs and beer in a chillibin and drove over the hill to Golden Bay and down the Aorere valley to Gethsemane. The morning was windless, the sky lacquered, the trees so still their heads seemed moulded from clay and glazed and baked. Sharp leaves were picked out from the surface. She wanted things softer, and wondered if this hardness were premonitory.

Gethsemane was deserted, without sound. A chaffinch singing on the fence made a counter-silence. She sat by the gate a moment, listening and watching, then re-started the engine and drove down the road half a kilometre and over the new bridge leading into the hills. She parked in yellow grass off the shoulder. There were no other cars. She locked her doors in case hoons should arrive, then opened the passenger one and took her binoculars from the glove box. Images for paintings — an explanation she had never needed before: an apology to Robert Early. She climbed a fence and crossed a paddock empty of stock; took a rutted path towards the sound of the waterfall; broke through gorse and tea tree; came out among jumbled boulders where the creek ran into the river.

The shingle bank was further off than she had expected, but crossing the creek would bring her out on shelves of rock exposed to the Earlyites — who stood in an order that must be hierarchical: older men in front, young behind, women and children in the curve of the bank. They looked brave, Ellie thought, as if no other humans had a place in the world, but as if they must stand close together to survive. She righted herself, smiling at the exclusion she had felt; enjoyed their blue and white and black, their placing in the river bend, their pictorial justness and propriety, and was angry with herself for leaving her sketch pad at home.

She could not make out Robert Early among the men, or Derek among the younger ones at the back, but did not use her binoculars to search. She wanted to preserve the blocks of colour and see the river and its shore in their natural focus: the glossy white and black of shirts and trousers, the blue of dresses against the porous bank. She framed the picture with her hands, then saw Robert Early emerge and walk towards the water.

Ellie scrambled back to the shelter of the trees, sat half-hidden and put her binoculars to her eyes. He halted midway on the shingle bank, turned to face his people and spread his arms as though embracing them. When she had left him in the kitchen, he had seemed not to have enough. Now she felt the fullness he possessed — all these followers, all this land. He was preaching, haranguing, with the black square of his bible in his hand.

She moved her binoculars and found Derek in a group of three behind the women — probationers, she supposed, not yet admitted fully to Gethsemane. She saw how easily he could slip away once the baptisms began. She moved the binoculars — found several of the young men looking at her, in response to Robert Early's outflung arm. She shifted further into the shade, feeling guilty and ashamed — voyeur — but did not think he would recognise her in her dark green trousers, with an autumn-leaved scarf tying up her hair. He's using me for the evils of the world, she thought.

His voice came up the river but she could not separate words from the noise of the waterfall. Perhaps he was saying 'Jezebel.' Ellie shook her head. That's not me.

She did not use the binoculars again but watched as two men led a woman down the shingle bank. Robert Early spoke to her, softly, it seemed, intimately, then gave his bible to one of the men and walked into the river up to his waist. His lower half darkened underwater, his shirt stood rounded like a spinnaker. The woman waded to him. Her blue skirt billowed and she pushed it down, sinking it. He took her in the crook of his arm and called out again, ritualised words that came like dog barks through the sound of the waterfall. Ellie saw how helpless the woman was, yet felt her compliance as he bent her backwards with a hand on her chest. Her long hair fell from her scarf. He pushed her under the water and held her down — too long — while he cried out, cleansing her. What would the words be? Something about being born again and raised into the body of Christ? Whether mistaken or not, that faith was acted out in a ceremony reaching back in time. See how they stood together, watching the man in the river — watching 'then' as well as 'now'. Ellie envied them the continuity. But her place was over here, not bunched up in the hands of Robert Early.

He raised the woman. Her scarf had slipped from her hair and she pulled it into place, wading ashore. Men and women gathered round and hugged her. Robert Early waited, waist deep in the water.

Ellie looked for Derek. He was gone. She hurried through the trees into the scrub, found the track, started across the paddock. A car drew up behind hers, and two youths got out and climbed the fence. They came towards her, one ferrety and leathered, the other fat and pink. Ellie pulled her scarf off.

'Hey, lady, don't say it's over.'

If they came too close she would club them with her binoculars.

'Are you saved?' asked the pink one with a leer.

She passed them, slid through the fence, got into her car. Such feeble hoons. The world, even in Golden Bay, should be able to provide more convincing evil than that.

She turned the car and drove to Gethsemane. Derek was opening the gate. He smiled at her tightly.

'Get in,' she said.

'Hold on. Someone might be coming. I'm not sure.'

'Who?'

A woman came out of the building alongside the dining hall. She looked about her, blinded by the sun; saw Derek at the car; started forward in a lopsided run, holding up her skirt.

'She made it. Good on her,' Derek said.

'Who is she?'

'Have you got room? She's my friend.'

'Derek —'

'Don't worry. They'll be down the river half an hour yet.'

'I'm not getting mixed up in kidnapping.'

The woman was growing younger, turning into a girl, while her progress increased in uncertainty.

'I want her to get out the gate all by herself,' Derek said.

She came through with a moaning sound. Her face was unseeing, as if the world outside Gethsemane burned her eyes. She pushed out her hands to find her way. Derek caught them, one, two, like paper darts, and guided her into the back seat of the car.

'OK?'

'I don't know,' she panted.

'Take it easy. Breathe deep.' He slipped in beside her, closed the door. 'OK Ellie, it's all right to go.'

'How old is she?' Ellie said.

'Seventeen.'

'What's her name?'

'Paula.'

'Paula, listen to me.' She waited until the girl unclosed her hands from her face. 'Are you sure you want this? You want to leave here?'

Paula made a small explosion of breath.

'Was that yes?'

'Yes.'

'All right. And you're seventeen?'

'Yes.'

Ellie nodded.

'Wait,' Derek said. He got out of the car and closed the gate. Gave the name Gethsemane a pat. Ran back and got in beside Ellie. 'Let's go.'

She drove without speaking. The girl had thrown a swift look out the back window, then lain down out of sight on the seat.

'Shouldn't you sit with her?' Ellie said.

'I want to leave her alone. Do you mind being quiet, Ellie?'

She drove through Takaka and up the hill, where Paula sat up, looked into the valley and made a thin sound of pain, stretching her mouth. She lay down again.

'Does she need something to eat and drink?' Ellie said.

'No.'

'What about you?'

'Just keep going.'

'To my place?'

'Yes, that'll be good.'

'Won't they follow us? Try and take her back?'

Derek frowned and shook his head. He made a shushing sound.

They reached Ellie's house after midday. She imagined it would look welcoming, although she wasn't sure that she was welcoming herself; but Paula turned her head neither left nor right as Derek led her in by the arm.

'Bathroom?' he said.

'In there.'

He took Paula in, whispered for a moment, then came out and closed the door. Ellie carried the chillibin inside. She put it on the kitchen table and switched the kettle on.

'Tea?' she said, when Derek came in with his bag.

'Thanks.'

'Some chicken?'

'Yeah. Good.'

'Now, Derek, tell me what this is about.'

'She's leaving, that's all. Or trying to.'

'Did you talk her into it?'

'No. She came to me one day. She said she wanted to, and would I help.'

'Is she part of Robert Early's family?'

'No. One of the others. They joined when she was six. Up in the Manawatu. That's all I know.'

'I can't believe they won't try and find her.'

'They won't. She's been baptised, Ellie. Now she's lost again. They won't come chasing her. She's got to go to them. And repent. Until then she's —' he shrugged — 'castaway.'

'Do I get a chance to talk to her?'

'Not yet.'

The toilet flushed. Derek stood up.

'Is there a bedroom I can put her in?'

'For both of you?'

'No. She's not my girlfriend. I hardly know her.'

Ellie opened the spare room. The bed was made up. She drew the curtains back but Derek said, 'Better close them, eh?' He sat Paula on the bed. 'I'll be out soon.'

Ellie went out and closed the door. She drank tea and ate a chicken leg, stopping now and then as little surges of alarm ran through her. This Paula was a child, and she and Derek had abducted her. Someone must be hunting. They might have called the police. Then that alternative world imposed its images — Gethsemane. The man in the river, the women in their medieval skirts, the assembled

287

community on the bank — and it seemed possible that Paula was, as Derek had said, castaway. Cast away.

Ellie stood up and went out into the sun, into her garden. She walked past her studio and was momentarily shocked to see nothing on the easel; and was shocked then by Paula's life, which must be equally bare now that she had fled. But surely inside Gethsemane there had been a poverty even more terrible, a denial that left one stripped to the bone with only a few responses left. It was a prison — but there are monsters outside too, Ellie thought. Where could a girl like Paula go?

Derek came out the back door and crossed the lawn, bending under a peach tree.

'She's all right. She's going to have a sleep.'

'Does she need anything? A nightie? Pyjamas? She's got no clothes.'

Derek shook his head. 'She can't, Ellie. Thanks anyway. But she can't touch stuff. I mean out here in the world. She can't even look at it. Your paintings and ornaments. And your soap and stuff.'

'They must have soap.'

'Sure, but different. Everything is different. It's . . .'

'Filled with the devil?'

'Yeah, I guess. I think your pyjamas might freak her out. It's going to take time.'

'Are you frightened she won't make it?'

'Not frightened. I think she had to see the world.'

'She's not doing much of that.'

'No. And when she's seen it and knows she can live here, or she can't . . .'

'Are you saying she might go back?'

'Yeah. Maybe. Part of it is, she's seventeen. She's late getting married. She said no when her parents chose the first guy. Robert doesn't like that. She's not going to be able to do it again.'

'What will happen?'

'If she goes back? Well, her name's scratched out of the book. I

288

mean the Book of Life, up in heaven. So she's got to get it written down again. Go through it all. Repentance and baptism, all that. I bet bloody old Robert'll hold her down a long time. She'll have the men's committee as well.'

'What's that?'

'The group of leaders. It's a kind of inquisition. She'll have to confess all her sins and abase herself. It's like an exorcism. It goes on all day long. All night too.'

'You can't let her, Derek.'

He shook his head. 'I can only do what she wants me to. I brought her out. I'll help her as long as I can. I'll even marry her if she wants me to. But if she says she's going back I'll take her. You can be quite happy there, you know. There's lots of happy people.'

'Robert Early isn't.'

Derek looked startled. 'Do you think so?'

'He hasn't got enough.'

'Oh, sure. More souls for salvation.'

Ellie did not mean that. She did not know what she meant. The thought of allowing Paula — whom she did not know, had scarcely seen (a chubby face, poppy-red cheeks) — allowing her to fall into Robert Early's hands stabbed her like a tortured nerve. She said, 'Tell me what she needs. Underclothes she needs. God, I'll buy her bloomers if that's all she can wear.'

'Ellie —'

'We've got to keep her from going back.'

'It's Sunday. There's no shops selling bloomers, whatever they are. I'll take her shopping when she's ready to go. The best thing we can do now is leave her alone. Just let her come out slowly, if she wants to.'

Paula did not appear that night. Ellie made a bacon quiche, and Derek took some to her in her room. In a moment he was back. 'I'll take mine in as well. Sorry, Ellie. She can't eat alone.' Ellie wondered if she would be able to sleep alone after the family stalls at Gethsemane. She washed the dishes, tried to read, missing her Sunday paper; put some harmless music on the player; sat with the lights low by the window, watching the brightness fade off the sea and stars wink on the edge of seeing. Her worry about the girl dissipated and she began to wonder about herself: was she lonely? Was her work, which had satisfied her fully, enough? Did she need, like Paula, to run away, find something new and dangerous, even if she turned and ran back home?

Ellie poured herself a whisky. She pulled on a jersey and sat outside. Were these real questions, or was it simply that for the moment she could not paint? She had come to the end of her shadow man. Was she missing him or just waiting for what, or who, came next?

'I think she'll stay a few days,' Derek said, coming out.

'How do you know I don't charge board? Sorry, I'm joking. Come here, Derek. Give me a hug. Now, do you drink? I don't have Coca-Cola any more.'

'So she can stay? We don't have any money —'

'That's all right. As long as you like. Will fruit juice do?' She brought a glass out to the yard and they sat in adjacent chairs, looking through the crooked half-lit trees.

'Do you think you'll fall in love with this girl?'

'Me? No chance. When I said I'd marry her, I meant if it would help her stay outside.' He smiled shyly. 'There were a couple of others there I liked better.'

'Did you do anything about it?'

'They were married, even though one of them was younger than Paula. They can marry at sixteen. As long as they've got "the flowers of their age".'

'Which they would have at sixteen.'

'I don't know much about all that.' Derek blushed. 'If I'd stayed there I would have got married. I don't know who to.'

'Why not Paula?'

'No.' Derek was quiet for a moment. 'The trouble is with her, she likes girls.'

'Did she tell you that?'

'I'm not actually sure one hundred percent. But I think she does.'

'And there's no room for lesbians at Gethsemane. So what does she do?'

'Gets married. There's no other way.' He grimaced. 'Work and worship and prayer. Community. She'll probably survive better there than here. I don't think she can make it after living tied to old Robert since she was six.'

'Does Robert know about her?'

'He knows everything. She'll have a hard time but she'll get by. She'll get married and have kids and live and die. She'll even be happy, as long as she's got Robert and Christ.'

'It won't work, Derek. It's unnatural.'

'That's what the world says, not Gethsemane.'

Ellie gave her room to Derek so he would be close if Paula needed him. She slept in Audrey's workroom among John's trays of spiders and moths, and was glad to be out of the house. She worked preparing canvasses in the day, not knowing what she would paint on them. Paula was up at dawn, walking to the back fence, barefooted in the dew. Was shoeless a good sign? She still wore her headscarf, with her hair trailing down her back. Later in the day, when Derek, removed by several paces, walked at her side, she kept it knotted in a bun.

Ellie enjoyed her work. She almost forgot her visitors. On the third day an idea began to take shape. She saw it the way she'd seen that fragment of brick in the river — appearing, disappearing, misshapen by the current. She cut sandwiches for lunch and left them on the table. Paula had still not spoken more than half a dozen words to her or looked in her face, but Ellie's need to 'save' her had disappeared. She would do it if she could say, 'Stay' or 'Go' or 'Run, hide', but did not want involvement any more. Let Derek try. She took a sandwich into the studio, ate half of it, sat with her pad on her knee and started to draw. One page. Two. Three. Four.

'Ellie.' Derek's head came round the door. 'Am I disturbing you?'

'No. What is it?'

'Can I borrow your car? I want to take Paula into Motueka. She needs some things.'

'The keys are on the table by my bed.'

'Thanks. Ellie?'

She waited.

'I haven't got any money. Can you lend me some?'

'Bring my bag.' She wrote him a cheque. 'It's cash. Take it to my bank. Is it enough?'

'Yes. I'm sorry it's like this. We won't be here much longer.'

'As long as you like. I told you.'

He went out but came back straight away. 'It's important, this trip, Ellie. She'll have to go into shops.'

'What about her dress? I'll lend her one.'

'She won't wear it. We'll go to an op shop. She can buy one.'

'Underclothes?'

'She's washing them in the basin and putting them back on. We'll buy a pair.'

'Good luck.'

She sketched again but something had got in the way. Her idea had been coming clearer from page to page: a torso, square; a pushing arm, a shape in folds of cloth underwater; a face with seamed cheeks and stiff-lidded eyes; a wide-open mouth from which might issue a column of sound. There was too much Robert Early. The picture should not be personal. If that girl washing her underclothes and putting them on wet could not have a place, then he, with all his features, should not.

Ellie puzzled what to do. Get rid of his face? She ran her pencil through it but did not know how to start again. She went into the kitchen, slapped her pad down on the table, then went back to the studio for her half-eaten sandwich. She leaned on the fence by the orchard, watching thinners work in the trees. Later she cleaned the fowl house, shovelling buckets of manure from underneath the perches. There were paintings inside her but they wouldn't come out. She could not see beyond those hippopotamus eyes and open mouth, that man with huge creative drive but nothing to create. She felt his faith and anguish. Yet he was not the subject she was trying for. Things were out of balance. She must find a way to make him only part, not all.

The car came up the drive under the pines and turned neatly into the garage. George must have taught Derek to drive — one good thing. She carried a bucket of manure into the herb garden. Derek walked across the lawn to join her, while Paula, in her blue dress, went into the kitchen.

'She couldn't do it,' he said.

'Go into a shop?'

'Not even get out of the car.'

'What did you do?'

'Parked down by the sea at Ruby Bay.'

'Talking?'

'Not much. Paula hasn't got much she wants to say. She was shivering and crying most of the time. I don't know how to help her when everyone walking past is damned.'

'And she is too?'

'Yes. She's evil. She's going to burn. So am I.'

'I don't suppose I could talk to her?' She watched the girl standing by the kitchen table. 'Oh my God.'

'What?'

'She's looking at my drawings.'

Ellie ran across the lawn into the kitchen. Paula squawked like a chicken and jumped away. She ran along the hallway, threw open the front door, ran outside.

'No, leave her,' Derek cried, holding Ellie's arm.

'I'm going to talk to her. Shit, Derek, I've had you in my house for three days. I've got a right.'

She went on to the front veranda and saw Paula running towards the patch of swamp. Saw her trip and sprawl, then sit, headless, knees wrapped in her arms.

'Stay here, Derek. I'll bring her back.'

She went through the swinging gate and walked down the paddock.

'Paula,' she said softly.

The girl made a reflexive shrinking. She gave a sharp moan and closed her arms more tightly.

Ellie sat down.

'I'm sorry,' she said, thinking, There's no place for this child. I can't even put my arms around her. 'I didn't mean you to see my drawings. But I'm a painter. That's what I do.' It sounded so selfish, so unconnected, that she gave a shiver like the girl. 'Paula, I don't know what you should do. But come back to the house now. Derek will look after you. And you can stay as long as you like. I'd like to talk with you about all sorts of things.'

She put her hand on Paula's arm. The girl uttered a thin scream as though she had been scalded; and Ellie, her face suddenly streaming with tears, said, 'I'm sorry. I'll go.'

She walked, labouring, up the slope, passed Derek without looking. She went through the house and through the fruit trees, sat in the long grass by the back fence. Soon she heard the car drive away and could not help thinking, Yes, that's right — although she instantly rebelled and, confused, shifted again: that thin thread of Paula's life, should anyone dare snap it unless they had some substantial garment to weave her into? And I don't, Ellie told herself, I just have me. And my work, she added fiercely. And John as well. And it's enough. But what could I have done for her?

She dried her face. The tears had surprised her — and now, considering them, she moved almost to the point of consternation. What did they mean about herself? That she, her work, John, were *not* enough? I need to be painting a picture, that's all. It will come. I know it will.

Failing with Paula did not count because there had been no other possible end.

She sat at the breakfast table trying to listen to 'Morning Report'. Those voices, serious, informative, sometimes joky, were her usual company at breakfast. She wanted them to tell her where Derek was. Had there been a car crash, a drowning, a shooting? Did they have guns at Gethsemane? Had there been a burning at the stake, a crucifixion? It had seemed possible as she lay awake at 2 a.m.

She looked in his room again. His duffel bag was on the chair, so he meant to come back. There was little trace of Paula in the other bedroom: a dented pillow and a wrinkled mat, that was all.

Ellie sat on the living-room sofa, looking at the drawings in her pad. Robert Early was ordinary. She had given him a maw like Jonah's whale but in the morning light it was a mouth, large, cartoonish: a mouth. How had she done this? How had she come to try for what wasn't there? There's too much me in it, she thought, and not enough Fan. And what had possessed her to leave the pad lying on the table for Paula to find? She took it out to her studio, put it inside and locked the door.

The car came as she took the covered walkway back to the house, and she hurried down the side path and waited at the gate. Derek was alone. She hugged him. 'You're all right?'

'Me? Sure. Just tired, that's all.'

'Did you take her back?'

'Yeah, she's back.'

She made him coffee and sat him at the table.

'We stopped at one of the lookouts on Takaka hill. I wanted to give her a chance to talk, but she wouldn't talk.'

'Not about me? My drawings, I mean.'

'Not anything.' He pushed away his coffe mug and laid his head on his arms. 'I'm tired, Ellie.'

'What happened?'

'We sat in the lookout, then I had to go for a pee. Then she went too and I thought that was good. Normal, I mean.' He sat up. 'We stayed in the car while it got dark. You can see Rabbit Island and most of the Waimea plains, and Nelson on the other side — you've seen that view. Then the lights started showing: there's more than you think. Nelson was like a ship, and there were little towns, and strings of lights, and car lights moving along roads, and the more there was the more she had to go to Gethsemane. So after a while I took her.'

'Was Robert Early there?'

'No one was. It was all dark. They go to bed at ten o'clock. So we parked and waited all night. She slept a bit. So did I. Dawn was like — it was sort of bloodshot, but then it went soft. Nice colours. Like it was saying, Yes, all right.'

'So she went in?'

Derek nodded.

'Did you?'

'She didn't want me. I was —' he grinned without humour — 'like you. You and me are outside the gates. Some men were going to milking by then and women were going to the kitchen. Someone ran upstairs for Robert and he came out. No one said anything, just watched her walking past. She went into the hall and Robert turned and followed her. The others got busy with what they were doing, and that's all. I drove away.'

Ellie made toast. She boiled two eggs and watched him eat.

'So,' she said after a while.

'Yeah, so. I'm sorry I took your car for so long. I wouldn't blame you if you'd called the cops.' He stood up. 'Can I have a sleep for a couple of hours?'

'You can sleep all day.'

'No.' He was going into Nelson and catching the Picton bus and getting on the ferry to Wellington. 'Surprise for Mum.'

Ellie did not argue. While he slept, she telephoned Nelson and booked him a seat. After lunch she drove him in.

'Have you got enough money?'

'Sure. I didn't spend any. I'll pay you back, Ellie.'

'Please don't. It's a Christmas present. What will you do in Wellington?'

'I've got some friends at the City Mission. I can probably help with something there. She seems a long way away, doesn't she?' He meant Paula.

'Yes, she does.'

'It's a funny thing.'

When the bus had gone Ellie visited a friend. Had a look at the exhibitions in the Suter Gallery, did some Christmas shopping, mostly food (John had asked for money as his present), then drove home. She changed the linen on both beds, and thought calmly as she smoothed them down about what she might paint next. Nothing before Christmas, I'll take a break. Then she might do someone in a blue dress — but who and where she did not know. She would do a baptism too. But wait and see. Nothing was banging for admission.

She was pleased that Derek and her mother would be together at Christmas time.

She had John for only two days. Although she could have arranged an apple-thinning job for him, he stayed in Christchurch counting bats or wetas in Peel Forest, and staying close to some girl, Ellie suspected. He arrived on Christmas Eve, driving a Volkswagen, a beetle car, which belonged to Kerri — 'That's with an "i". It's nice having a girlfriend who's got wheels.' She was coming by bus on Boxing Day and they were taking off to walk the Abel Tasman track, then going on to do the Heaphy as well.

'Why didn't you tell me?' Ellie said; heard the complaint, almost whining, in her voice; turned away, said forcefully, 'You should have said. I needn't have got in so much food.' Hated that too — so impersonal, such a lie. She turned back and took his head like a ball in her hands, laid her cheek on his, and felt the pleasure of loving him, in spite of disappointments and that cold little judgement: He's ordinary. She felt again his gift for happiness, and that was not ordinary but exceptional in a way, although it depended — didn't it? — on not thinking too hard or far. Mike's legacy?

She fed him ham, with new potatoes and peas from her garden, and home-made pavlova and home-grown strawberries, and they drank wine from the vineyard down the road; then John switched to beer and Ellie to malt whisky — an early present to herself — and they both got more than a little, midway drunk.

'Who was he anyway? Mr Mike Rowe?' John said.

That was sobering. Ellie said, 'Are you sure you really want to know?'

'A ratbag, eh?'

'No, no. I loved him. He was funny and clever and . . .'

'Yeah, "and"?'

'Loved a good time. He was good-looking. He played the guitar and made up songs.' She could not think of anything more to say about Mike; was inclined to go back and qualify 'loved him' with 'almost'. Qualify 'clever' too. 'You know his name. You can track him down.'

'No way. I've got no hang-ups, Mum. I don't believe in all this bullshit about knowing who I am. I know all right. And where I come from. That's from you. Let's drink to us.'

She did not tell him Mike had called earlier in the year or that he did not know he had a son. There were questions she wanted John to ask, now that they were talking about his father. He did not ask them but got more drunk than she liked to see and went to bed.

On Christmas morning he slept late. She bullied him out at ten o'clock, drove him to Ruby Bay and made him swim — threw him into the sea, was how she put it to herself — and was tempted to tell him that she had swum here naked with Mike twenty years before. Something sounded in time with the memory: not so much a sigh of completion as the muffled clicking of a wheel as it set itself for its next revolution. She would like to think about it, this single momentous click, but had no time, let it slip away, as John started turning driftwood, looking for the things that lived underneath, which he knew and identified and explained. Ellie loved his interest and eagerness. It was in these tiny creatures that his chance lay to make himself grow. Again she heard the slow wheel click.

'Who's Kerri?'

'Just a girl. Go easy on her, Mum.'

'Of course. Why wouldn't I?'

'She's a bit nervous about meeting you. Famous artist and all that.'

'Me? I'm not. I'm anonymous.'

'She doesn't know much about painting, so — you know . . .'

Oh yes, I know, Ellie thought. Pretend it's not important, just something I do to fill up the time. 'Does she count sand hoppers too?'

'She's doing law. Her old man's a lawyer. She's pretty bright, Mum. OK?'

Yes, OK. She would go easy. This girl was probably number one in a long line. Ellie had better learn how.

Back home they gave each other presents. His to her: Picasso in a series called *Artists by Themselves*. She was pleased. He had tried. Hers to him: a cheque that must be twice as large as he had expected, he went so pink; some record tokens; half a dozen T-shirts (he lived in T-shirts); last of all (she went into the spare room and carried it out), a painting by Fan Anerdi, done in her colourist, post-impressionist phase.

'That's for me?'

'Do you like it?'

'I don't know. I'm not much on painting, Mum, but it'll remind me of old Fan.'

'I'll keep it here for you.'

'Sure. Sure. It might get beer spilled on it in a student flat.'

'When you do take it, John, you've got to look after it. And you're not to sell it. Not ever.'

'Is it worth something?'

'Probably about twelve thousand dollars.'

'Shit,' he said.

He met the bus in Nelson in the afternoon, and drove home with Kerri, a tall girl with a nervous habit of bobbing her head — why do I always want to weigh people's heads? Ellie thought — but a pleasant imperfect face: nose with a bend in it that made her look as if she needed protection, thick black eyebrows, long slightly flattened lipsticked mouth. 'Hello,' she said breathlessly.

Ellie felt an instant sympathy. It forced her to look at John in a new light. She would not have thought he had enough maleness in him yet to damage a girl. 'Come inside. Do you need the bathroom?' (Perhaps her bobbing was caused by that.) 'John can bring your pack.'

'Oh, no —'

'Oh, yes. It's good for him.' She wanted to say, Take care, don't trust him, and pull John aside and say, Don't you dare hurt her. He carried her pack into his bedroom.

But out of the toilet, relieved and freshened up, Kerri surprised her. She bobbed and was breathless only for a short while, then began to use a willed directness.

'We'll have to go early because we want to get a good way up the track. It's going to be full of Germans and Swedes.'

'Yes, John told me.'

'We'd be grateful if you could drive us to Marahau. It's better if I leave my car parked here.'

'I'll look after it.'

'And Mrs Crowther. Ellie. We don't have much time, so could I see your studio before it gets dark?'

Ellie wondered if learning how to take command was part of legal training. Kerri no longer seemed like a girl who would let her boyfriend borrow her car while she rode in the bus.

Ellie drove them to Marahau next morning, setting off as the sun came up, and was home again by seven o'clock. Took advantage of the coolness to work outside: topped up the tui jars with honey water, nailed new pickets on the front fence, a job she had hoped John would help her with; then sat drinking iced tea in her canvas chair in the shade, smiling at Kerri's yelps of sexual pleasure sounding through the wall last night, and the pair of them muffling each other's laughter with their hands. They thought, of course, that she wouldn't approve, but she approved. Have fun, she thought. But please be kind to each other too.

She had finished lunch, and was thinking about going back to her sketches of Robert Early in the river to see if she could find out what was wrong, when she heard the quiet popping of gravel in the drive, then, in a moment, a car door slam. 'Bugger,' she said. People sometimes came like this in holiday time, thinking that her studio was a showroom or that she kept Fan Anerdi's paintings on view. She had tried not answering the door but several had simply walked around to the back, and one young man, sent by David Shea, had poked his head in the kitchen window and grinned at her.

Ellie sat quietly at the table. 'No, I'm sorry,' she would say, and close the door. (Directness was something she could give Kerri lessons in.) Footsteps sounded on the veranda. The loose board creaked. Knuckles on the door, neither commanding nor tentative. Ellie sighed. She stepped softly on the lino and peered up the hall. A man showed darkly, framed from the waist up in the glass panel, reminding her, almost like a blow, of her shadow man. She shook herself, shook him out. She had finished with him, he was gone.

She padded down the hall in her bare feet, and knew who he was before she opened the door; was instructed by head shape and blurred features and, equally, simultaneously, by an undeniable sense that the time was right. She felt a deep accommodating pleasure.

'Hollis,' she said.

'Hello. I was passing, so I thought . . .'

'Come in. Come in.'

So familiar and I hardly know him, she thought.

'I've just finished lunch. Would you like some?'

'Ah, I've eaten. I bought a pie.'

A pie, a pie. It delighted her; took her back to his leather jacket and brylcreemed widow's peak and pink car.

'But I wouldn't mind a cup of tea. I'm —' he followed her into the kitchen — 'I'm sort of drifting round Nelson a couple of days. I've got a rental.'

'You're lucky this time of year.'

'Yeah, well.' He looked shame faced. 'Through the firm.'

'Ah, the firm' — thinking with no hostility, no feeling at all, that if it could set up abortions it could certainly do rental cars.

She made an effort, climbed out of the past; and was easy, welcoming, full of pleasure, sitting him down, putting on the kettle. He got up straight away and wandered into the living area, looking at the paintings.

'You don't mind me treating your house like a gallery?'

'Everyone does. Why are you looking round Nelson?'

'Well —' He turned from Fan Anerdi, came back to his chair. 'Can I opt for a beer instead of tea?'

They sat outside, shaded by the grapevine on the trellis.

'I'm mainly looking at bits of land. Not with an agent — now's not a good time. Just blocks of ten hectares, twenty hectares. I don't even know if they're for sale.'

'For your firm?'

'No, for me.'

'To do what with?'

'I'm shifting out of Endacott Prime. I'm —' he shrugged — 'changing tracks.'

He wanted to grow wine — plant some grapes, sell the crop for a couple of years, see what came after that, see if he could learn. It sounded banal to Ellie, a trendy occupation, a rich man's dream: sitting in his wicker chair overlooking his estate, sipping a glass of his own red as the sun went down — then it was transformed by a kind of poor man's hunger in his face. That bit of land was a dry place he must occupy and make his own.

'Shouldn't you be looking in Marlborough or Martinborough? Nelson's second rate. For wine, I mean.'

'No, I don't think so.' He named some wines that she agreed were not second rate (a small dishonesty: she did not know), then talked about climate and soil, a lawyerly summary that she wished would end. Hot days, cold nights? Gravel and clay? Ellie wanted why and when.

'Have you seen anything you like?'

'I've been driving past the wineries so far. Not going in. But I'd like to be away from other places. Down by the sea.'

'Would you like me to chauffeur you? It's my neck of the woods.'

'I'd love company.'

She took him along back roads leading down to inlets. He looked and was quiet, disheartened, she thought, by finding cows and apples everywhere, and on a piece of land lying perfectly for the sun, olive trees newly planted, less than waist high. But he marked the map he had fetched from his car and wrote in a notebook while Ellie drove slowly so as not to jolt his arm.

Later they went down the Waimea plains and came back to the coast through the Moutere valley. They stopped at vineyards, where Hollis bought wine, wanting to try everything, red and white. The car tinkled like sleigh bells as Ellie drove home.

'You'll stay for dinner? I've got food in abundance.'

'And I've got a plethora of wine.'

We must be scared, talking like this, Ellie thought. She did not know if they would be lovers that night; had the feeling it might be too soon. She did not have her footing; felt a movement under her as though she were standing on a mat on a slippery floor.

She gave him the meal she had given John, with ice cream instead of pavlova. They drank a bottle of sauvignon blanc, not chilled enough.

'Come and walk in my garden,' she said. 'We'll have coffee later.'

They walked to the back fence, where a breeze from the sea was changing the warm evening into cool night. The sun was down, leaving the Arthur Range red rimmed. Over behind Nelson, where lights made an experimental blinking, Mount Richmond and Mount Fishtail thickened and increased. The sea held a final luminescence. It did not seem like water but liquid air. Ellie felt the largeness of the place she lived in: the plunge down from one range, the smoothness and scope of the sea, the concave upward sweep to the opposite skyline; felt everything between: encrusted towns, contoured hills, roads and solitary houses, orchards properly arranged, inlets lapping unnoticed, out of control.

She breathed in deeply.

'What?' Hollis said.

'I'm glad I live here. That's all.'

'Yes, you're lucky.' He was quiet. 'Maybe there's a place for me down there.'

'I'm sure there is. You haven't told me why, though. Why you're leaving your job.'

'Well,' he said, and stayed leaning with his arms on the fence. She thought he might straighten up, withdraw and go away, but at last he said, 'I'm sorry I gave up smoking. I'd light a fag about now.'

'Is it that bad?'

'Some people might say I've made it all up. But what it is — I got ashamed.'

She waited, then said, 'What of?'

'Me, I guess. I'm fifty years old, and what am I doing with my life? Working out ways for greedy bastards to get out of paying their taxes. That's what I do, Ellie. It's what I've been doing mainly since you saw me last.'

'Since Dolores?'

'Yeah, since her. I don't know whether this is as bad as that.' He made a painful grin, not meeting her eye.

'Is what you were doing — is it legal?'

'Yeah, it is, by about a millimetre. One more step, just a little one, and you've gone too far.'

'Like Barry?'

'Yeah, like him. But I got him out of it, did you know? They didn't proceed.'

'Congratulations.'

He looked at her sharply and seemed about to reply, then let his breath out heavily and stared at the darkening sea. Ellie waited.

He said, 'You sit with these pricks and they're saying "I" and "me" all the time. And "mine, it's mine", and you're getting a fat fee, so you start saying it too. Me and mine. And you see ways of doing it that are so damned clever you forget what game it is you're playing. You work out all the shifty bits without looking at them. You say it's only business and you learn a kind of Alzheimer's about the things you've done. I was good at it, Ellie. Good at doing it and good at forgetting. I'm just about the best there is — a technician, yeah. But the sweet thing is that millimetre, staying inside. I haven't done anything I could get in prison or get struck off for. But I'm striking myself off. And I'd strike off most of the guys I was working with.'

'You don't have to see them any more.'

'I wasn't like that always. I was just a tax lawyer, starting out. I was helping people minimise, companies minimise. But the last ten years — everybody got so fucking greedy, and they don't want to know whether it's avoidance or evasion. It's like sex, Ellie. You get urges and you can't stop.'

'Well, they all came tumbling down, all over the place.'

'Not all of them.'

'And you have stopped. You're getting out.'

'I was like a man without a shadow. I was standing in some puddle, I don't know . . . There were other things.'

'Like what?'

'Leveraged buyouts. Junk bonds. That sort of thing. Have you heard of them?'

'No.'

'There's all sorts of tricks. There's loopholes you can drive a cattle truck through as long as you give the wheel a twist now and then. If that doesn't work, you set up a kind of labyrinth and go through there.'

'You're out of it.'

'Yeah, with so much money — big fees, Ellie. I don't know whether I can use it for buying land.'

Was he saying he could not make good wine using dirty money? She touched his hand.

'Yes you can.' Because he had confessed, because that brought its own absolution? She did not believe it would be so easy, but wanted to believe he had taken a step. It was painful seeing someone so ashamed. Exhaustion must have come close to emptying him out — but he'd had enough strength left to make a gamble: come to Nelson, search for a piece of land, come to her.

Ellie was aware of her blood coursing. Aware of arteries and joints and throat and mouth. She felt that she might stop him wasting away. But slowly, she thought. Say ordinary things. Don't go fast.

She looked over the garden at her house. The open door threw light into the fruit trees.

'Come on, I'll make some coffee,' she said.

They sat on the sofa side by side, with Fan's paintings gleaming like jewels, half in and half out of the light. She had never thought of her house or herself as empty, yet there were places in her into which he flowed. She wondered if that were delusional, or sentimental, even silly — and unnecessary at her time of life, with work that filled her, completed her, although it depended on what someone, somewhere, had called 'a maniacal inner solitude'. She had that: a possession, a treasure, and would not have it disturbed. Yet there were empty places, and here was Hollis Prime.

He asked if she still painted the shadow man and she said no, she was moving on to other things but was having trouble; could not go ahead because of something she hadn't seen properly yet and a balance she had not arrived at.

'Do you keep on working? Work your way through?'

'Yes, I will. But I'm waiting for a little while. There's a part that needs to click into place. In the meantime, I could paint pictures, I suppose. And they'd probably sell. Hills and trees. I'm good at those. But with the shadow man I moved away from landscapes, that sort of thing. I want my pictures to be human.'

'And nothing abstract?'

'No, no. I've got to have real things or else I'm lost. I want people and hills, and creeks and valleys. And I want a connection with whoever looks at them. Fan would have hated my stuff. But it's right for me. I'm almost frightened sometimes that the things I draw in my mind seem like a language, yet when I get to painting them the meaning gets lost, as if I haven't moved past simple notation, found the image.'

'Found the myth?'

'Why yes, I suppose. Image or myth or symbol, but something that people looking at the paintings share. Without effort. From a kind of deep acquaintance. That's what I get from certain paintings when I look. Even Fan's, who really is, you know, much better than me . . .'

Ellie talked. She had not explained her work before — how it concentrated her into a moment of time, into the colour and the stroke of the brush; how it opened like a flower and declared itself complete; and how all her self was absorbed into it until the moment when the picture was huge and weighty and whole and there was nothing of her left, just for a moment, before the one shrank to its proper size and the other came streaming back, restored. When she painted, Ellie said, she was herself yet overcame some excess of self. And when she lost a picture, when it failed to work . . . She held out her hand with the thumb folded under: 'I feel I don't have an opposing grip.'

She told him about her visit to Gethsemane and Derek's rescue of Paula, and Paula's return; and would have gone on to describe Robert Early in the river — but stopped, saw the danger, and was almost dizzy with her escape. That was no one's. It was hers, and other people must not know of it until she had seen it properly and painted it. She felt sorry for Hollis, excluding him, but almost triumphant with self; and she saw him clearly: a man with a disappointed life, whom she liked for some reason, without restraint, and whom she might even come to love.

She sat looking at him, thinking of the shape of his head. Drawing Robert Early, she would sketch a ball; but with Hollis it would be a box. He was sharpened at the temples, with a corresponding sharpness at the back —

'Ellie?'

'I'm sorry. I was thinking of something else. Do you want to stay the night, Hollis? I've got a spare bed.'

She felt that with her talk and his confession they had done something just as intimate as making love, and it was enough for now. From the way he behaved so easily — phoned his hotel in Nelson, cancelled his room — he felt it too. He brought in his bag from the car. She made him use the bathroom first, walked on the lawn among the trees, and when she went back inside he had gone to his room. His light went out as she locked the doors.

Ellie went to bed. She heard Hollis turning where the night before Kerri had yelped. He'll have to pay for his hotel room, but maybe the firm will do that, she thought. She turned out her light and realised as she went to sleep that he hadn't brought a walking stick with him, and she hadn't noticed if he still limped.

They ate breakfast together and it seemed to her a bit like under-painting, forcing pigment into a canvas with a spatula. She spoke, he spoke. At their next meeting, perhaps they would start to paint their picture.

'What's the joke?'

'Oh, nothing. I'm just thinking.' Almost said, It's a consequence of living alone, but said instead, 'I do a lot of it.'

He left her three bottles of wine; said he'd like to visit again, perhaps in February or March. 'What I was saying last night —' he looked at his hand — 'I guess I've got the monkey grip, eh?'

'You'll make it,' she said, and finding they were eye to eye, kissed him on the cheek.

He smiled and reddened, threw his bag into the back seat and drove away.

Ellie watched the car move slowly under the pines: saw Hollis's neck and squared-off shoulders, his blue summer shirt — and thought of Robert Early, standing up to his waist in the glassy water. It was as if she'd stepped to a neighbouring window and seen the same view differently, for the first time. So — it almost blinded her — that was how she must do it: the man in the river no longer drawing everything into himself. He stood right of centre, where the eye would start and where it must stop, but now there were people balancing him; the shingle bank held its proper weight, the trees and hills took their place by right. She saw the colours she would use to hold him still — stop Robert Early getting away with all the things he wanted . . .

She did not watch Hollis all the way down the drive but strode back through the house, plucked her studio key from its nail, and hurried under the trellis and across the lawn.

Her tuis were swooping. She understood their greed.

Between times

1991–92. 'A FELLOWSHIP more quiet than solitude': Robert Louis Stevenson. It is like that with Ellie and Hollis, although now and then they disagree. The orchard of young olive trees down by the inlet is for sale, and she wants him to buy it and do olives instead of grapes — something different, with more risk, more adventure — but he won't, it's wine he wants, his own label in the end; and before that, decisions — what varieties of grape, in what proportions, how the rows should lie — and work, putting in the posts and wires, planting the vines, watching them, protecting them in their dangerous first year. 'All that,' he says, with a reflexive twitching in his hands. Ellie sounds the phrase dismissively, but lets it go. His desire is stronger than her impatience. It's important not to quarrel over what can't be changed. They lie side by side after making love. She hears his breathing change as he goes to sleep, and feels how she has altered in her fibres — it's more than just the physical satisfactions of love — and knows that at last she has the lover she has wanted, a friend with whom she talks all day if she's inclined, and lies breathing with all night. 'No longer another person in the troublous sense': Stevenson. Oh, that's right. How right. Ellie smiles as she goes to sleep.

He stays a while, goes away — winding things up at Endacott

Prime — comes back, leaves again. Auckland puts a frown on his face but at last it's done, and in that week he buys the land he wants, across from Bronte on the Waimea inlet. His pupils dilate as though he's recognised a lover, and Ellie sees she'll have both less and more of him — less of his time but more of Hollis, because some part that had collapsed begins to fill out, unwrinkles as though he has stepped into the sun. She'd like to paint him.

She paints Gethsemane through those two years and has eleven paintings at the end: 'Baptism 1–7', and two called 'Flight' and two 'Return'. (Calls 'Return' 'Surrender' at first but then decides on neutrality.) They make a narrative — and how Fan would have hated that. She finishes as the builders frame Hollis's new house, as his year-old vines begin to flower. He looks at her work and she at his, and they praise one another — and disagree, not for the first time, about where she will live. He'll build her a studio down by the water; she can watch the tide come and go as she paints, and anyway isn't it time for a change? But Ellie will not leave her house and land. No, no. She touches his cheek, kisses him. 'Let's just be happy with what we've got.' They are only five kilometres apart. 'We'll wear out that piece of road. We'll always be together,' she says.

1993. Her exhibition sells out, which is rare. Ellie visits Wellington for a final look at Gethsemane (and because her mother has a 'friend' she'd like her to meet). She walks around the empty gallery. David Shea parades with her until she sends him away. How did I know that? she thinks, looking at Robert Early. Know to paint him from the back — his billowing shirt and hooking arm and angled neck, with a single rounded line for cheek and jaw: the water sliding, his buttocks and legs stratified; and the woman no more than a patch of blue deep down, except for her white headscarf turning like a fish: 'Baptism 1'? She moves back from number two as it moves from her: the woman still submerged, Robert Early smaller, the bank of pebbles solid along the top, the men's shoes gleaming, their trouser legs standing like tree trunks in a row. I made that one beautifully, Ellie thinks. He raises the woman in number three, holding his black bible in an upthrust hand. (Who's to know that in real life he gave it to one of the men?) They (twelve if you count) stand watching, sombre eyed, while the skirts of the women make a sky-blue sky, as if they're seen through feathered eyes. So the paintings go, shrinking the Earlyites into their paddocks and hills until, in number seven, the baptised woman walks tiny as a beetle up the shingle bank, Robert Early waits in the river, and another woman runs towards the gate where a red car waits.

How did I do it? Ellie thinks.

She's not so pleased with 'Flight' and 'Return'. A bit Victorian: the girl (only Ellie and Derek know who she is), seen across the paddock from the gate, stands on the concrete forecourt, not knowing where to run; and then, 'Flight 2', with skirts held up and one arm out, makes her stumbling run towards the gate. There's scarcely any detail in her face. Behind her the hills go up to the sky, with paddle-shaped clearings brown and yellow in the scrub. (Ellie has resisted the temptation to put a driverless tractor in one.) Then 'Return': skirts more narrow, headscarf tight, Paula walks in the dawn towards the dining hall. Men stand in the paddocks like isolated posts, watching her. (Seven if you count but there's no significance in the number.) The final painting shows her sliding away, a smear of blue, behind the glass door, while a man (Robert Early) turns to follow.

Not bad, Ellie thinks, but too much story. All the same, she goes away deeply satisfied.

She visits Derek at the City Mission: sees his innocence and gravity and wants to praise him. Takes a bus to Brooklyn where she meets Steve Sholto, a Londoner, retired taxi driver, lapsed Catholic ('A God-botherer? Me? You're joking, lass'), who has been her mother's lodger and is now her 'friend', and will be her husband before long. Mrs Brownlee glows. She drinks a glass of beer and blushes red at his jokes. Ellie flies home. There's no danger of Hollis taking her over like that. And why? She could dress it up but finds it enough to say, Because I'm a painter.

1994–98. Five years at the start of which Ellie unaccountably slows down. She tires easily, can't climb hills, sleeps after lunch and wakes exhausted. Wonders if it's a forerunner of menopause, and how bad that will be; but what it is — she's relieved, almost elated to know — what it is (she savours those three words, which foretell a cure) is a fibroid in her uterus, sucking her strength away. If it had haemorrhaged there would have been trouble, especially if she'd been out sketching somewhere alone. She might have bled to death; and Hollis goes pale, his own blood draining from his face. She sees him as she wakes from her operation (hysterectomy) and thinks — so unutterably tired — I don't mind if I die; but wakes again and sees him and is pleased in a slow suspended way that she's alive. They seem to exist in a clearing they have cut from the tangle of their lives, and she decides, We'll stay here, yes we'll stay.

She spends whole weeks, then whole months at his house, painting in a sunroom he converts to a studio, but goes back to her own place when she's ready to be alone — when she feels she's getting close to some image that she wants to declare. Hollis leaves her by herself up there — or, as he sometimes says, out there. Her paintings are full of the pressure of the tides. She paints the ebb as well as the flow and the rich emptiness of the inlet when the last film of water is gone and the sand sucks light into itself. These paintings make her happy. Nothing she has done before has made her feel so happy. It doesn't need to come from only trouble, she thinks.

But the big event of these years is Fan Anerdi's retrospective. Ellie lets all her paintings go, including the one she has given John and the two hanging in Hollis's house, and helps the young man who writes the biographical piece and the catalogue raisonné. (He's the grinning fellow who poked his head in her kitchen window.) She insists that Audrey be given her proper place. 'A long supportive friendship' is how the young man puts it. He wants to add 'equivocal' but Ellie says no, she'll withdraw her paintings if he does. She allows 'fulfilling', and still feels Audrey has not been granted her due. The exhibition goes to the four main centres and several provincial ones, including Nelson, and the house seems bare. Ellie sees her own paintings for the minor works they are but refuses to think of herself as small. There are times when she feels as large as anyone who has ever painted, and she looks inside her head at that line-up of Earlyites on the shingle bank — black trousers, white shirts, faces immobile — and feels her kinship with Goya, who lined up a firing squad of soldiers and prisoners for execution in that way. She runs through her own retrospective, right back to that painting in tar on the carriage roof, and feels a kind of terror: What if I'd never met Fan?

John and Kerri don't marry but live together. They have two children, then begin to like each other less. Kerri leaves him and is married inside three months and gone to live in Australia. Ellie is surprised at the tepidness of her grandmotherly love. It's John she loves. Her grandchildren will probably be as happy in Melbourne as in Christchurch and will like whatever his name is just as much as John — but her own child, will he recover? She watches him for signs of grief getting out of hand, but he settles quickly into a loose light contentment with himself, with the new woman he finds, and the one after her. There's a serious diminishment, Ellie feels — but then, did he ever have much weight?

In her worst moments, moving beyond intellectual judgements on her son, she seems to hear him rattling like a handful of dried peas in a can or — how much worse it seems — in a cardboard packet. She had hoped he would love his work as much as she loves hers, and believes that it interests him deeply at times — so how can he use his special knowledge in making little lightweight runs against her happiness? He seems to think she's out of touch and ill informed and somehow escaping from reality in her painting. So he must show her: Does she know that there's a blowfly with taste buds in its feet and when you see it walking on a turd what it's really doing is testing for a feed? How wonderful; clever fly, Ellie says. So he tells her about the Gordian worm that lives in wetas, eating them away but leaving their vital parts untouched. They drive them like a driver drives a bus, John says, and dry them out so that they seek water, where they drown; but water is where the worm's got to be, the smart little bugger, for the next stage of its evolution. Ellie can look at that clear-eyed; look at people too, who behave just as badly to each other, with the addition of cruelty and pleasure. Would John like some examples? He waves his hand dismissively. She makes him impatient with this sort of flying off from the subject every time. He makes her sad. He should have had a man in his life, even Mike.

Hollis's father lives in a nursing home in Wellington. He doesn't know Ellie and doesn't know Hollis most of the time but is clear about the voyage he never made around the world, solo in his yacht *Surprise*, the ports he stopped in and the storms he weathered. He's a happy old man, living a rich delusional life. 'It was midnight and a car stopped at my gate. Keith Holyoake. "Harold," he says, "I don't know what to do. You've got to advise me. Should I commit our troops?" I told him no but he wouldn't listen. Couldn't afford to offend the Yanks. Trade, you see.' At other times it's Norm who knocks at midnight, or it's Rob. 'I told him it was suicide to call an election but of course he did. Too much gin. That was Rob.' He holds Ellie back as she leaves: 'You can see the moon in the daytime, can't you?' he says. Ellie says yes. 'I told him you could but he called me a liar. He pulled me out and strapped me. You can, can't you?' 'Yes, you can. It's out there now.' 'I told him that but he wouldn't look. He strapped me in front of the class.' Tears run down the old man's cheeks. Hollis wipes him dry.

Several months later Harold Prime dies. The family scatters his ashes on the beach at Breaker Bay. A southerly drives huge seas on to the rocks, and spray streams inland. Ellie watches from the roadside as Hollis and his older son walk down the beach. Angela and Barry follow with their pregnant daughter and her child. Hollis hangs his walking stick on his arm and offers the carton like chocolates. Ellie approaches. She wants to be part of it but wants to watch. Angela takes a handful of ashes fastidiously. Throws it underhand into the wind. Grit stings their faces and grey ash streams through the group. 'I've got dust in my eyes,' Angela cries. 'That's not dust, lovey, that's your daddy,' Barry says. Hollis says, 'Throw it with the wind.' They release handfuls of smoke, which blows across the road into the hills. Ellie will paint this: black rocks, broken sea, people triangular in streaming coats, ashes smoking away. She wonders why Hollis is using a walking stick.

His vineyard is healthy: Tidal Flat (a name Ellie approves of — she designs a label to go with it). He still sells some of his grapes to established producers but has built a cellar and hired a wine-maker, sharing him with another small estate, and this year ('97) will release riesling and sauvignon blanc. Ellie tastes them: fresh and clean. But why is Hollis so tired just as he is set to succeed?

'I've been waiting for it,' he says.

Post-polio syndrome. She has never heard of it. He explains: after the illness some of the nerve cells partly recover. New fibres and filaments transmit the messages. So the victim carries on with his life (in Hollis's case limping from his slightly shortened leg). Then as you start ageing the new pathways wear out, become overgrown — 'choose your metaphor', Hollis says — and your trouble starts all over again: a sort of flaccid weakness, then sudden deadly fatigues. Mysterious pains, and pain referred in the butt and thigh. Loss of mobility and loss of balance. 'Bitching and bad temper,' Hollis says. 'I'm sorry, love.' Ellie almost cries, But it's not fair. 'What can we do?' she says instead. 'Live with it. Keep going. Pull my horizons in.' He looks from the patio across his vines. They're netted to protect the grapes from birds — ghost rows. 'If I can't do much work here, at least I can manage it.' He tries to grin. 'I'll still be boss.' 'Yes,' she says, 'of course you will. But treatment, I mean.' He tells her pain-killers, and massage and mudpools up at the hospital in Rotorua. 'Will you tell me when I need to come and live here?' Ellie says. She believes that he won't ask, so holds herself ready to recognise the time.

Which is midwinter, when he is forced to change his stick for crutches — not the sort fitting in the armpit but shortened ones halfway up the arm. He goes along with a clacking sound, as though renewed, although it's more her moving in that causes his cheer-fulness. Ellie is surprised not to grieve for the place where she has passed seventeen years of her life. She pictures a kind of knitting of her flesh into house and land, expects a tearing, imagines the sound of it, the pain; but there's none of that and she can't help being disappointed in herself. She's converted, she thinks sourly, into a bride: her house and kitchen, her husband, her man. Then she starts enjoying herself. She walks the boundaries with Hollis, at his pace. She climbs a stile and slaps along barefooted in the rushes, seeing mud crabs scuttling for their holes. She sees how the vineyard resembles a bird, one wing high (the riesling), one low (the sauvignon blanc). Looks at the neighbouring paddocks Hollis is hoping to buy for pinot noir. Red, she thinks, and tastes the colour. Perhaps she will start painting in crimson and maroon. She walks up and down the rows, counting them and thinking that the regularity is rather nice.

Straight lines bring control, but remember that the shape is a bird.

Tidal Flat

ELLIE WATCHED FROM the sunroom as Hollis walked up the new path to the riesling. He had mowed it the day before, trying out the modified controls on the tractor. Instead of going straight up, he'd cut an easy dog-leg so he would manage on his crutches. She watched his progress anxiously. He pushed himself too hard and seemed to have a dark enjoyment of his pain. He reminded her more and more of the boy she had first seen forty years before, sitting in the rain by the tennis court. He had been a singularity — but no, she protested, he's not any more, not sucking everything into himself.

She took her pad and started sketching him on the path, not solid but shot through with light, a tripod shape; then ran heavy strokes through it and dropped it on the floor — too sentimental. She tried again. A pair of moons in the daytime sky: Hollis and Ellie — but that was childish, it was rubbish. She scored it through, took another page: vine-fields tilted left and right, triangular planes. A path ran between them, finding its curve by gravity. Figures, not moons, hung in the sky, a boy and girl, while trees, forced into a slant, stood on one side and a sheet of rain on the other. Now she could put Hollis in, walking with his crutches on the path, and Ellie Crowther matching his step, the older figures slanting like the trees towards the right — which must be the future while left had to be memory? Surely, then, they should be two-faced?

Ellie tore the sketch out and crumpled it up. This was not her way. It was not her manner. She laid her pencil on the table and went down the brick steps to the yard to find an object warmed by the sun, that she might turn back to front without the fear of finding something there. It had been a trick at first, then became a habit. She called it a refreshment break or a comfort stop; but if she had used it when the shadow man appeared, would she have gone on with him?

She went out through the gate and walked along the front of the vine-rows. A rose bush flowered at the head of each one, not as an early warning of disease but because Hollis liked their colour. The grapes, sauvignon blanc on this lower level, were looking healthy, squeezing each other for room within each bunch and starting to blush on their rounded cheeks. Over in the shed Chris Latta, who did the heavy work Hollis couldn't manage, was hauling out nets. The riesling would be covered first. Starlings and blackbirds had already appeared and would be feasting before long.

Ellie walked between the rows to the edge of the water. She took off her sandals and waded in the rushes, disturbing tiny fish that vanished with a flick. Then she sat in her dinghy — her Christmas present from Hollis — waiting for the creeping tide to free it from the mud. She wanted to feel that moment of release, like being lifted minutely into the air. The house above the vines seemed to float on green waves. The door of her sunroom — she wondered why she could not call it studio — stood open. Ellie felt no temptation to go there. What would she paint? Hollis and Ellie, boy and girl, beside a tennis court in the rain? A woman sitting in a beached dinghy? Hills? Look at the Richmond Range. Look at the Barnicoat. Mount Starveall, Mount Malita. Why did she no longer need to paint them?

Ellie said, 'I'm not going to start worrying yet.'

There was no special virtue in hills (she had learned that when she had flattened them) and perhaps her preoccupation came from growing up with a range on either side. She should have felt shut in, but that had never been the case for they seemed to lean outwards instead of over her, say 'out' not 'in' — and that was why they took on extra meaning perhaps. Ellie laughed. There was so much to say 'perhaps' about. Perhaps the inlet tides, which she had painted for a season, were the tides of her life going in and out — men coming and going, Mike, Neil, Hollis, and that great inflowing tide of her years with Fan. Perhaps, perhaps. She had made good paintings, that was the certainty she had.

Ellie knew her place, compared with Fan, and with all those others who had worked and signed their names. She was confident in her social life, quick and sometimes loud with her opinions, and seeing her, hearing her, people gave the smile that said, 'Who does she think she is?' They supposed she saw herself in the foreground, one of the row of heads along the front, while Ellie knew she made a matchstick figure at the back — out at the far edge of the plain. They did not know how happy she was there. She'd found herself, had done her likeness, earned her place. Good paintings; yes, they're good, she thought.

She had tried painting John when he came at Christmas time, but could only get him when she sat him in the dinghy and pushed him through the rushes away from shore. A sketch had turned out to be enough; it was now, in a way, historical — John without oars — because later, as they sat on the landing, with tepid water lapping about their feet, he told her that he had located Mike Rowe and called on him.

He smiled at Ellie and seemed for the first time in years his proper age.

'How was he?' Ellie said carefully.

'Good.'

'Was he surprised?'

'He was blown away.'

'Pleased?'

'He seemed to be, when he got used to it. He wasn't very pleased with you.'

'Is that an understatement?'

John laughed. 'He reckons you're a phenomena.'

'Phenomenon.'

'Yeah, but I'm telling you what he said. I liked him, Mum.'

'Are you going to see him again?'

'Yep, you bet. We're having a beer when I get back to Christ-church. He lives — do you want to know?'

'Yes.'

'He lives in a caravan in a back yard. I think he's got something going with the woman in the house.'

'That'd be Mike. Did he have any message for me?'

'Just "Gidday". He said to tell you he's a painter too.' John laughed again. Mike had plainly delighted him. 'He drives one of those machines that paints white lines on the road.'

John took his Fan Anerdi painting when he left. He said, through the window, before he drove away, 'It's good seeing you and Hollis. You go together, eh.'

Like you and Mike, Ellie thought. She felt no jealousy, but little pleasure either — for that, it seemed, would be possessive, and she did not want John, the child, but wanted to watch him grown up, and applaud, tentatively, hopefully. Thank you, Mike.

That same day she and Hollis had rowed across the inlet to visit a potter friend on the other side. Coming back, she told him about John and Mike, and he laughed and said, 'I thought he seemed a bit more together.' He had talked about his worries for his sons, both of them getting nowhere in their jobs, and one drinking too much and betting too much. Angela, too, worried him, useless (her word) in her big house while Barry, out in the world, tracked about obsessively, hunting for deals.

Ellie rowed to the top of the inlet, then swept down to the vineyard on the falling tide.

'Maybe we should do some travelling, while there's time,' Hollis said. 'Burgundy, eh? Tuscany?'

'I want to stay here.'

He grinned. 'Me too. I just thought I'd better make the offer. OK?'

'Yes, OK.'

'I reckon this place will keep us busy till we die. Look up there' — the vines as green as saplings, the sweep of the plain (invisible but never out of reckoning), then the mountains with clouds like scoops of ice cream on the tops, and the sky — 'all of that,' he said, 'and you squeeze a dozen barrels out of it, and it's enough.'

He was losing money and would go on losing it for a good while yet, but refused to worry, dreamed only in seasons, vintages, and looked ahead to his own pinot noir — the glass uplifted like the Holy Grail. It did not stop him being practical. She had never known anyone so hour by hour and job by job.

He's first rate and imperfect, she thought — we both are. But, perhaps (again) only because we're together and have been apart. Words confused her; definitions were instantaneous but then lost shape as memory and desire, past and future, fitted them into the lives she and Hollis had lived and wished to live, where their usefulness was lost. Together? Apart? How inadequate when what she had meant was as large as their forty years of knowing each other yet as particular as the dipping of the oar blades in the water. 'Together' had a meaning altered each day from its meaning on the day before — but one of the things she must do was resist hearing the argument between increase in Hollis and herself and decrease in time. Daily changes were the things to note — dry air, white paddocks, ripening grapes. She must not think too far ahead to next year's calendar on the wall.

It had been her resolution, which she had kept and broken since that time. There were daily changes in him — more pain, stronger pills and, since Christmas, a trip to Rotorua, with another planned. She had learned to massage his legs. And now there were the modified controls and the crooked path.

Ellie got out of the dinghy. She walked along the shore to the Tidal Flat boundary and followed the fenceline up to where the riesling grew. Now she was level with the roof of the house. Where was Hollis? She went past the rows, looking down each one. He hated her worrying over him and watching him. What reason could she give for being here? That she had nothing to paint, so had come outside to pluck some leaves, let in the sun? 'Hollis?' Over beyond the house, beyond the sheds, she heard the sound of a motor — not the tractor but a throatier sound. It came from the entrance to the vineyard, by the gum trees, and was suddenly switched off. She walked down the slope, following the new path. A breeze hissed in the grass on either side. Stubble collapsed under her feet. She saw where Hollis had trodden and his crutches scraped the earth.

Ellie walked through her sunroom, through the lounge and out the front door. She went along the driveway to the sheds and saw that the vehicle that had made that throaty roar was a Volkswagen like the one Kerri had owned. It was pulled up in the yard beside piled-high nets on the trailer — an ancient car, rust eaten, painted green. The driver's door, newer than the rest, was bright orange and had 'Coco Cleaners' stencilled on it. The boot lid was tied down with an old brassiere. It made Ellie think of Mike, in spite of the name on the door.

She looked in the shed. Chris was hauling out more nets. She went around the corner to the cellar. Hollis and a woman were standing outside, he in the hunched stance his crutches forced on him, she facing away from Ellie, with one hip jutting and a cigarette burning at the end of her tilted arm.

Ellie thought: It's Dolores. She approached. Hollis looked at her briefly, then back at the woman, who turned. Sharp eyed, sallow faced, crinkle faced. She sucked on her cigarette and blew out smoke. Not Dolores. In spite of her weathered cheeks, too young.

'Ellie,' Hollis said. He swallowed. 'This is Mrs Johansen. She's —'

'Debbie,' the woman said. 'Mrs and I don't agree.'

'She's Dolores Wood's daughter.'

'Yeah.' Debbie laughed. 'A virgin birth.'

'And she says she's mine.'

'I don't just say it. I am,' Debbie said. 'Does your wife shock easy? But —' she made a calming gesture — 'I haven't come looking for a fight. The first thing is just to say hello. No harm in that.' Again to Hollis: 'Is she your wife?'

'We're not married,' Ellie said. 'We're partners though. And I don't shock easy. I knew Dolores. I shared a room with her.' She looked at Debbie Johansen steadily. 'You look like her.'

'I was her double growing up.'

'How old are you?' Hollis said.

Debbie smiled. 'Yeah, I thought we might get some arithmetic. 1960 I was born. In the Royal North Shore Hospital in Sydney. I don't know when you and Mum were having your good time but my guess is round about July 1959. Am I right?'

'Where's Dolores? How is she?' Ellie said.

'Oh, Mum. She's fine. Still living in Sydney. Last time I called she was still there.' The woman was sending narrow glances at Ellie. 'How come you and her were sharing a room?'

'Have you got a birth certificate?' Hollis said.

'What? Oh, yeah. It's in the car. It doesn't name you as my dad though. That's Raymond Oliffe, now deceased. Do we have to go through all this? Look.' She went to the car, quick, long striding. Ellie stood beside Hollis. She freed his fingers from their grip on the crutches and held his hand. Debbie Johansen came back with a folding purse. She took out a curved photograph.

'That's her and I reckon that's you.'

They were standing in front of Hollis's car. She was leaning into him with her arms around his waist. His right hand held her shoulder like a ball. Leather jacket, widow's peak, thin face grinning. How milky, how serene and expectant Dolores' face. It was not the way Ellie remembered her.

'Am I right?'

Hollis handed back the photograph. His face was composed,

smiling slightly, but Ellie, her arm inside his, felt his heart thumping.

'How long have you known about me?' he said.

'You specifically? Not long. But I always knew poor old Dad wasn't my dad.' She dropped her cigarette and ground it out. 'They got married a couple of months before I was born. He was twenty years older than her. He was some kind of saint. Do you really want to know all this? I thought you might hug me or something.'

Chris Latta started the tractor and drove away.

'Come up to the house,' Hollis said.

They walked side by side, Debbie Johansen getting ahead, febrile in her step, then slowing down.

'Mum didn't say you were crippled.'

'I had polio when I was young,' Hollis said.

'Before you knew her?'

'Yes, before.'

'You'd think she would have said.'

'What did she say?' Ellie asked.

'Not much. I found that photo. It's got the date on the back, did you see? 1959. So when I asked she just said, A man in New Zealand. She wouldn't say your name or anything. It was like you were dead. In fact one time I asked if you were. She just said, Rich people don't die. So I got "rich" out of her. Good-looking from your photo too. That was pretty nice for a girl of sixteen. I started figuring out ways I could find you. But when I ran away I forgot about all that. I was having too much fun at first and then too much bloody strife.' She had moved half a dozen steps ahead, but stopped and grinned back. 'I suppose I'm not every man's dream of a daughter, eh?'

'You ran away?' Ellie said.

'Yeah, from Woollongong; that's where we lived then. Up to the Cross. You don't want my history. I stayed out of the worst sort of trouble, I'll tell you that.' She paused on the path to the front door. 'This is some house. A vineyard too, eh?' She looked across the vines at the inlet and said, 'You're pretty lucky having this. Mum would have liked it. She's never got as much as she thinks she's entitled to.'

'Come in,' Ellie said. She led the way into the sitting room. 'Sit down, please. Would you like some coffee?'

Debbie sat down. She looked in a startled way at the paintings on the walls. Said, 'I'd rather sample some of the wine you make. If that's OK?'

Ellie brought an opened bottle from the kitchen and poured three glasses.

'I don't know what we should drink to,' Debbie said. 'Do you?'

'No,' Hollis said.

'This is not a confrontation, that's all. So, happy days?'

'Just drink it,' Ellie said. 'And let's talk properly. Hollis didn't know Dolores had a baby, you should know that.'

Debbie sipped her wine. She lit a cigarette. 'Because,' she said.

'Because what?'

'She got sent across to Sydney to have an abortion. She told me about it not so long ago. She drinks too much. It kind of frees her up and she lets things out. She said that's how rich people handled things back then. Send the girls away on, what's its name, the *Wanganella*?' Debbie blew out a stream of smoke. 'I suppose I'm lucky to be alive.'

'Listen —'

'No, stay out of it, Ellie,' Hollis said.

'Yeah,' Debbie said, and took a mouthful of wine, which made her choke. Ellie, nearer than Hollis, banged her back. She did not like the smell coming from the woman.

'Thanks,' Debbie gasped. 'Hey, I didn't come to fight. Where's my smoke?' She took it from the edge of the tray. 'Like I said, it's not a confrontation. And I didn't come for money, if that's what you think. You can keep your money. Or to hear him say he's sorry. Not for a bit of affection either.' She turned to Hollis. 'I just thought a guy like you, lawyer and all that — you were one, weren't you?'

'Yes.'

'— might be able, I don't know, to give me some help. I need someone with a bit of nous and you're related.'

Hollis lowered himself into his straight-backed chair. Ellie saw

327

him tensing with each throb in his leg, but now was not the time to bring him a pill. She wanted to put herself between him and this woman; wanted to slide between them on runners like a door. Hollis was on the point of some declaration which she must prevent. It could not be of love, it must be of guilt, and that would trap him in some unnatural stance. Too many years had gone by: responsibility should not be asked to travel that long way back. Sorrow would be better. Sorrow was not affected by time. She said, 'We'll help you if we can. But you mustn't expect too much, after forty years.'

Debbie Johansen made a delicate suck. She was clever with her cigarette: timed and punctuated. She picked a non-existent tobacco thread from her tongue. 'We?' she asked.

'Yes, Ellie. It's not we, it's only me,' Hollis said. In spite of that he kept his lawyer's manner. 'If you can tell me how, I'll help if I can,' he said to Debbie.

'Yeah. Good.' She sipped her wine and ran her tongue along her lip. Nervous, Ellie saw, and in some kind of controlled desperation. Coming here must have been a throw.

'I've got a son,' Debbie said. 'He's your grandson. His name's Dion and he's twenty-two. Yeah, wait on. I was only seventeen when I had him. And I wasn't married. You might say I took after Mum.'

'Where is he?' Hollis said.

'I'm coming to that.' She stubbed out her cigarette, lit another. 'He's a good kid. He was never any trouble. But he's bi-polar. Do you know what that is?'

'Manic depressive,' Hollis said.

'Yeah. Mostly manic. When I said no trouble I meant he takes his medication. He's bloody bright. He could be a lawyer like you. But there's times when he just gets so fed up he goes away. Vanishes. And that's when he really gets down. I reckon it's more than body chemistry. It's — deep. It's, What's the use? He wants to stop. He wants to die. They take him in for treatment — rehabilitation, that sort of stuff. But they don't keep them in there these days. Anyway, he doesn't belong, he belongs out. So, he comes. And the whole thing starts all over again.' She drank some wine and gave an uncertain smile. 'Some story, eh?'

'Where's his father?' Ellie said.

'He hasn't got one. Never had one. Never will.'

For one terrible moment, almost hilarious, Ellie saw Mike. 'Birth father? He must have had one of those.'

'Either one of a couple of blokes. I never followed it up, there was no point. And don't say Johansen, it wasn't him. He was a Kiwi and we came out here. He's history.'

'Is Dion in Australia?' Hollis said.

'No. The West Coast.'

'Down south? That's where you live?'

'Does it matter? I live in Auckland. *We* live in Auckland. I was over in Sydney visiting Mum. That's when she told me that abortion stuff. And your name. She's almost an alcoholic, if you must know. Dion was OK when I left but when I got back he was gone.'

'What part of the West Coast? You want me to trace him, is that it?'

'No, I've traced him. He wrote me a card from Greymouth saying he was all right. He kept in touch and then he stopped. Wouldn't answer, that sort of thing; and I knew what that meant so I went down there. Flew down, Christchurch, Greymouth. It's bloody expensive. And don't think I'm asking for money either.'

'No,' Hollis said.

'He was gone. It was a sort of transient house. Full of what would have been hippies once. You know, kids. I got it out of them that he'd gone to another house in Otira. Where the tunnel goes in. It's a kind of ghost town. So I went there. He was gone again, but this was just one bloke and one girl and they wouldn't say where. I told them who I was and what was wrong with Dion but they kept on saying, It's his choice. I couldn't get anything, even when I said I'd call the cops. All they said was, Call them. So . . .'

She was close to tears. She stubbed out her cigarette and gulped her wine; squeezed her eyelids shut.

'Take your time,' Hollis said. Was that what lawyers advised or was he a father?

'I walked around the houses. Jesus, what a place. They're mostly empty. Ever banged on empty doors, rooms with nothing in them? There's one crummy cafe in an old pub. I asked in there but they hadn't heard of him. If I'd had a gun I'd have gone back and shot those bastards in that house. But all I could do was sit and wait for the bus. Three sodding hours sitting on a bench.' She lit another cigarette, waved smoke away, looked at Hollis. 'While I was there I started thinking about you. I made up my mind on the plane going home. You weren't hard to find. So here I am.'

'What do you want me to do?'

'Come with me and find him. I need someone who swings a bit of weight. They know where he is. You can say you're a lawyer. If you say the cops, they'll know it's for real.'

'All right,' he said.

'You will?'

'Yes, I'll come.'

Ellie detected a lightening, a kind of unknotting in him.

'Debbie,' he said.

'Yeah?'

'I want Ellie too. Will you come, Ellie?'

He was saying to her, in this way, 'you and me' — restoring it.

'When?' she said.

'When, Debbie?'

'Soon.' She was crying; had scrabbled a handkerchief from her blouse and was wiping her eyes. 'Sooner the better . . .'

'Are you all right?' Hollis put his hands in his crutches, trying to rise.

'I thought you'd say no. Thought you'd kick me out. I would have bet on it. 'Scuse me a minute. Where's the toilet?'

Ellie showed her. She came back to Hollis. 'Can you make this trip?'

'I have to.'

'I know you have to. But can you, I said. And yes, I'll come.' She stood beside him and pressed his head into her breast.

'It's not so far. We'll take the Cruiser.' He freed himself. 'Ellie, I don't just want you for the driver.'

'I know.' You and me, she thought. 'This boy sounds in a bad way.'

He nodded. Sorrow, a haunted sorrow, on his face. That made a safer pathway for responsibility. Guilt, remorse, whatever — keep them out.

'I think we should go tomorrow. We should start early,' he said.

'Can Chris manage everything?'

'I'll talk to him.'

Ellie picked up her wine and sipped. 'She is who she says she is, Hollis. There's no doubt. She's —' raddled was the word she might have chosen; said instead, 'She's had hard times. But she's got Dolores in her face.' She was uncertain whether she should say the next bit, and swallowed more wine. 'You're there too.'

'I don't care who she looks like,' Hollis said.

'No.'

She was uncertain what the cost would be to him of not liking Debbie.

'I think she should stay here tonight. Debbie —' as the woman came back — 'Hollis thinks we should go tomorrow, is that all right? We've got plenty of room here, so you can stay the night.' Then, seeing Debbie draw back, she checked herself.

Let Hollis, she thought.

He said in a courtly way, 'We'd like to have you here. Dion can stay too, when we bring him back.'

'No way. I want him in Auckland. That's where we live. Is there any need . . .' She made a nod at Ellie, asking if she had to come.

'It's hard for me to travel unless we're in our own car. Ellie's the one who drives that. Anyway, I want her.' He smiled at Debbie. 'I don't know how I should behave with you. How do you act with a daughter you've never seen? You said a hug.'

331

Debbie shook her head. 'I was needling you. You've done OK. I can get a hotel room in town.'

'No. Stay here. Please,' Hollis said.

'Get your car and put it in the yard,' Ellie said. 'There's a bed made up.'

She wanted to give Hollis time alone, and went out with Debbie, then waited on the steps while she fetched her car. 'Is that you? Coco Cleaners?' she said.

'Yeah. I pranged my door. Dion painted that on when we got the new one.'

'You do cleaning?'

'House cleaning. Do you want some done?'

'No, no,' Ellie said, then saw that Debbie was joking. 'Why Coco?'

'I dunno. It sounded good. It's French, isn't it? You reckon house cleaning's good enough for the lawyer-man?'

'Don't call him that,' Ellie said.

'You look out for him, don't you? I can't say Dad.'

'Call him Hollis. He won't mind.' She swung between resentment of and sympathy for Debbie; and had, too, a physical revulsion. Not only a sweat smell (but she'd had a long drive), also the mephitic odour heavy smokers get. Dolores had smelled of sweat, as most people did in those days, coming in from work, but later on of soap suds and hot water and — Ellie remembered it for the first time in years — lemon tea with sugar when dressed for going out. Sweetness and astringency.

Debbie lifted her bag from the back seat of the car. 'When did you share a room with Mum?'

Ellie explained, and told Debbie she'd written to Dolores but had no reply.

'She's never mentioned you,' Debbie said. She jerked her head towards the sitting room. 'Did she pinch him from you? Or maybe it was the other way round?'

'It wasn't like that. Come inside. I'll show you the bedroom.' She left her there unzipping her bag. Hollis was still sitting in his chair — perhaps a little punchdrunk, Ellie thought.

'All right?'

'Yes, I'm all right.'

'I'm going to my studio so you can talk to her.' She was puzzled that she had said 'studio'. 'If you want me, call out.'

She tried sketching Dolores, then Debbie, but couldn't get either. Tried the bi-polar boy, making him up, but found she was doing Hollis in his leather jacket and bitter smile. She went outside and sat on the steps. Hollis was new made. She'd made him over, or so she'd thought, and that was why she'd never told him there was no abortion. It did not fit in with their lives. I'm not feeling guilty any more than him, Ellie said.

The tide had turned since she had walked by the inlet. The dinghy was drifting at the end of its rope. Soon it would tip sideways on the mud. Ellie smiled. She must try not to be afraid.

Later she saw Hollis walking up his new path. Chris was unloading the last nets from the trailer. He had three polytech students arriving in the morning to put them on. We shouldn't be away for more than one night, Ellie thought. Everything is going to be all right. She went into the sitting room and found Debbie smoking. How many packets does she get through in a day?

'Hollis tells me you're a painter,' Debbie said.

'Yes, I am.'

'Are all these yours?'

'No, they were done by a friend of mine, Fan Anerdi.'

'Are they modern art?'

'Well, they were done quite recently so I suppose they are.'

'I like that one over there. Did you do that?'

'Yes, I did.'

'What's it called?'

'Just "Figure 10". Hollis bought it. Why do you like it?'

'Dunno. You haven't made him real but you can tell he's dangerous. I've known guys like that. Johansen was like that.'

Ellie looked hard at the painting. He never has been just a shadow man, she thought. Muscle and bone, not earth and air. I wonder when he'll come back.

'That was the last one I painted. It was ten years ago. I went on to other stuff after that.'

'Can you make much money doing painting?'

'Not very much. Probably not as much as cleaning houses. But I had some luck.'

'Yeah, Hollis. The lawyer-man, eh? My mother got the dirty end of the stick. No offence. Anyway . . .'

'Yes, anyway?'

'It's not her I care about any more. I just want to find Dion. I won't cause you any more trouble after that.'

Barrelling the Landcruiser down the long straights took Ellie's mind off the night before. They had gone to bed early and lain with fingers intertwined, although she would have liked him closer than that. He said, 'Did you know she wasn't having an abortion?'

'Yes, I did. She told me that night on the wharf,' Ellie said.

'What exactly?' There was neither withdrawal nor tightening in his hand.

'Just, she was a Catholic and she couldn't do it.'

He was silent.

'I would have told you, Hollis. But too much time had gone by.'

Still quiet. Then he said, 'Too much time.' It seemed to be a statement not a question but she could not tell if he was agreeing. 'Now my daughter's here,' he said.

'Yes, she is.'

'I want to help this boy.'

They did not talk after that. His fingers relaxed and he went to sleep. Ellie lay awake a long time. She heard Debbie pad past the door to the toilet. Time, she thought. This person, his daughter, had been born, and grown up and had a child of her own, and now she cancelled all those years with a single step, colliding with a huge weight of blood and significance; and asking the question, Had she, Ellie, Hollis's lover, his 'wife', denied him with her silence the chance of being what he should have been? The uncertainty entered her dreams. She turned and ran on falling paths and opened easy doors but could not find him.

Now her concentration made her forget. She enjoyed driving the Cruiser, liked its weight and steadiness, and the sense she had of being inferior yet superior, like John's Gordian worm in charge of a weta. Hollis sat beside her with his hands in his lap. Debbie, fresher than the day before — blouse and jeans — sat smoking, always smoking, in the back. They passed through Murchison and stopped in the layby outside Lyell for morning tea. Ellie had made a thermos of coffee and sandwiches.

'All right?' she asked Hollis.

He gave a nod: Nothing I can't handle.

'Where are we?' Debbie said.

'There's some ruins up in the bush. There used to be a gold-mining town,' Hollis said.

'Jesus. Now it's trees.' The silence seemed to bother her. She relaxed when a convoy of cars sped by.

Ellie wondered about them heading south. She had overtaken traffic and been overtaken all the way from Nelson, more than she'd expected for a Saturday. She asked about it when they stopped in Reefton.

'It's the Wildfoods, lady. Down in Hoki,' the garage man said.

'It's a festival,' Ellie told Debbie. 'Bush food, that sort of thing.'

'Huhu grubs and wild pork,' Hollis said.

'There won't be any beds in hotels. Nowhere on the Coast.'

'So we'd better find him today,' Debbie said.

They ate fish and chips in Greymouth, then headed down the coast road to Kumara Junction.

'I came through here on the bus,' Debbie said. 'It's about another half hour.' She moved nervously in her seat. 'What if these people have gone to this Wildfoods thing?'

'We can only ask,' Ellie said. She smiled in the mirror. 'Try not to worry.'

Debbie's single thought was to find her son and make him safe, using Hollis and whoever else she had to; and mine, Ellie thought, is to keep Hollis safe — which Debbie knew. An unwilling sympathy existed between them.

The hills closed in and the mountains hid themselves. Ellie found the country oppressive. You needed to get up high, stand on the tops, let your eye travel out — the long coast on one side, the plains on the other: that was how she imagined it. Down here in the valleys, no wonder this boy Dion got depressed.

'There,' Debbie said, 'that's the pub. You turn before you get to it. Down there.'

A settlement of abandoned railway houses. Somewhere up the gorge the tunnel went in, running nine kilometres under the alps to the wide yellow river valley on the other side — a world as open as this was enclosed. She drove across the railway line and turned into a broken-edged street. How scrawny and pathetic empty houses became — like old men in hospitals, stripped to their underpants. Weed-grown paths, dead flower beds, a lopsided set of Venetian blinds, hurricane wire curling off roadside fences, a dog on a chain — alive at least, barking and wagging its tail.

'There. Stop there.'

Ellie stopped off the road. They got out and Hollis slipped his hands into his crutches.

'Sore?' Ellie whispered.

'I'm all right.'

'Her name's Charlie. He's Jeff,' Debbie said. 'I've just thought, maybe Dion's come back.' She rattled her pocket, looking afraid. 'I brought his lithium.'

Ellie went ahead and opened the gate. She crossed the lawn and calmed the dog. When she looked again, Hollis and Debbie were talking to a woman at the door.

'You didn't need to bring all these extras,' the woman said. 'Anyway, we told you, he's not here.'

'But you know where he is,' Debbie said.

'What if I do?' She was tall, high shouldered, thin chested, wearing a limp green petticoat as a dress. 'He said he didn't want anyone coming after him.'

'I'm not just anyone, I'm his mother,' Debbie cried.

'So? If he'd wanted you to know he would have said.'

'Can we talk to your husband?' Hollis said.

'Who are you?'

'I'm Dion's grandfather.'

'He never said anything about you either.'

'He's a lawyer. We can make you tell,' Debbie cried.

'Calm down, Debbie,' Hollis said. 'Look,' he said to the woman, 'Charlie, is that your name?'

'What if it is?'

'If we can just come inside for a minute . . .?'

'No, you can't. You'll wake my baby. I've only put her down ten minutes ago. And you,' she said to Ellie, 'get away from the dog. He's ours not yours.'

'Charlie, we're not here to upset you,' Hollis said. 'Maybe you can ask your husband to come out.'

'I haven't got a husband, I've got a partner. And he's down at Hokitika at the Wildfoods, OK?'

Ellie approached. 'How old is your baby?'

'Who wants to know?'

'Charlie,' Hollis said, 'I know you think it's Dion's choice. But he needs our help. He's got manic depression, do you know what that is?'

'Everybody gets depressed,' Charlie said.

'Not like this. It's a sickness, it's like cancer or diabetes; it doesn't leave you things like choice. He needs his medication. Was he taking pills here?'

'No, he wasn't.'

'How was he?'

'A bloody wet blanket. He just sat and stared at the wall. Look, I'm not telling you where he is. He was Jeff's friend, not mine, and I'm not involved. Go down the Wildfoods and ask him.'

Ellie said, 'Did they leave you behind? Is that the trouble?'

'They didn't want a baby in the car. Him and his mates. If it's any of your business,' Charlie said.

'Is Hokitika on the way to where Dion is?'

'What's that got to do with it?'

'We can give you a ride down there if you'll tell us where to find him.'

Charlie stood still.

'We've got room in the car. Hokitika, is that where he is?'

'No, he's not.'

'But down that way?'

Charlie shot her eyes from one to the other. She gave her shoulders an angry twist. 'They're turds, all of them, leaving me.'

'We can take you. Maybe we can even bring you back.'

'I can get my own ride back.'

'So,' Ellie said, 'shall we wait?'

'How do I know you won't dump me halfway?'

'A woman with a baby, sure,' Debbie said.

'We won't,' Ellie said. 'You can tell us where Dion is after we get there if you like.'

Charlie's eyes moved quickly again. 'Wait here,' she said.

They went back to the Landcruiser. Charlie came out of the house and locked the door. She still wore her petticoat but had put a pink crocheted jacket over it. She had a daypack on her back and her baby in a sling on her breast. The dog howled as Ellie drove away.

When they reached the Junction, Hollis took a road atlas from the glovebox and handed it back. 'Can you mark it for us, Charlie? Where to go? Here's a biro.'

'When we get there, I said.'

'You'll save time. It's half past two. You'll miss the stalls.'

338

'I can just tell you. It's a shack out on the coast, past Harihari. I've only been there once, so I don't know if it's got a name. And I don't know if he's still there. He went more than a month ago.'

'Who owns it?'

'I don't know. Jeff used to stay there whitebaiting. You go up the river to get across. All he did was tell Dion how to get there.'

'Mark it on the map,' Hollis said. 'And draw the roads. Come on, Charlie. No one's going to tell on you.'

She unslung her baby and drew lines, marked crosses, then wrote directions inside the back cover. Ellie drove slowly into Hokitika. The streets were lined with cars, and noise in a crackling lump lay over the showgrounds. She stopped at the gates and Charlie got out, put on her pack and snatched her baby. She slammed the door and went away without a word.

'How do we know she's not lying?' Debbie said.

'I don't think she is,' Hollis said.

'How long will it take to get down there?'

'Harihari's about an hour. It depends on how rough it is once we're off the main road.'

Ellie drove out of Hokitika, crossed the long bridge over the river, and headed south. Hollis took the atlas from Debbie and kept it on his knee. South of Harihari he said, 'Watch out for a road on the right.'

'What name?'

'She couldn't remember,' Debbie said. 'Halfway to Whataroa.'

'We're halfway now,' Hollis said.

'Nothing but bush,' Ellie said. 'Here's something. Shall I go down here?'

It was little more than an opening cut in the trees. Two ruts led away, separated by weeds.

'She said it was pretty hairy,' Debbie said.

'"A mailbox in the ferns",' Hollis read. 'It's got to be this.'

Ellie drove the Landcruiser into the opening. She locked the hubs. 'How far did she say?'

'She didn't. Not far. There's some old bloke lives down here in a bach.' Debbie was leaning forward between the headrests. 'Dion must have walked in from the road. Why come to a place like this?'

Why not? Ellie thought. It was ideal for being alone. She drove slowly, not wanting to jolt Hollis. The Cruiser was higher than a road car but weeds and bracken scraped its underside. It dipped and reared through ruts and potholes. She tried to hear the sea above the grinding of the engine.

They emerged from the bush as though from twilight into day. Sand dunes spread out like a no-man's land. The light from over the furthest one was brilliant with refraction. That could be a reason for coming here: Dion might crave light — a kind of natural lithium. Ellie drove more slowly. The track looked as if no vehicle had been along for months. Her impression of a no-man's land grew stronger. The up and down of the dunes made shell holes and trenches. A grey heaviness one way, yellow light the other: she began to see the colours and shapes as paint.

The track turned right along the back of the dune fronting the sea.

'There should be a bach soon. There. I think we should ask,' Hollis said.

'I'll go,' Debbie said. She was out of the Cruiser before Ellie stopped, and through the opening in a fence of driftwood twisted in wire. She ran to the front door of the bach and knocked.

'Are you all right, Hollis?' Ellie said.

'Yeah, yeah.' Then he smiled, apologising for his abruptness. 'I'll take something when we get there.'

'Promise?'

'I promise. Thanks, Ellie. Thanks for driving.'

'What if we don't find him?'

'We keep on looking.'

Debbie got back in the Cruiser. 'No one home. Let's keep going.'

A labrador dog appeared on top of the dune. It barked once, then looked behind. The man who climbed up — head, shoulders, torso, legs — paid no heed to them. He came down the dune with sliding steps and walked along the side of the track. Ellie drove to meet him. He was an old man, stringy where once he must have been heavily muscled. He wore a red singlet, corduroy trousers, a baseball cap, and had a sack of driftwood slung on his shoulder.

'Hello,' Ellie said.

'I'm not home Saturdays,' the man said.

Hollis leaned across. 'We were wondering if you could give us directions.'

'Where to?'

'There's a whitebaiter's hut. We're looking for a young chap who might be living there.'

'What's he done?'

'Nothing. This lady's his mother. She needs to see him.'

The old man gave Debbie a sour stare. 'I run away myself when I was his age,' he said.

'You've seen him, then?'

'He's sick,' Debbie said. 'He needs his pills. I've got them here.' She showed the bottle.

'What sort of sick?'

'He's manic depressive. We're worried he might do himself some harm,' Hollis said.

The man put down his sack. 'I don't go much on interfering.'

'Is there a shack? Is he there?'

'I seen a young bloke. Five six weeks ago. He was askin' where the whare was, so I told him.'

'Have you seen him since?'

'Asked him how long he was stayin'. He didn't know. I told him he should keep north of the creek because south is mine. I guess he done that. I haven't seen him.'

'Do we keep on driving?' Hollis said.

''Bout a mile. Don't ask me in kilometres. Whare's on the other side. Go up where it stops being tidal.' He nodded at the Cruiser. 'This thing'll get you across.' He hoisted his sack.

'Thank you,' Ellie said.

'Skinny kid. Looked like he thought he might burrow there underground.'

Ellie drove again in the hollow behind the dune. The Cruiser lurched, making Hollis grunt with pain. She went slower, with dips and curtseys, leaning like a yacht. Bush moved in close; the dune petered out; a long beach appeared, losing itself in haze. Ellie took the Cruiser on to hard-packed sand. She followed an inward curve to the mouth of a creek.

A tin shed, little more than a box, stood behind flat dunes on the other side. The door was ajar as though someone had passed in or out — but long ago, Ellie thought. She drove up the side of the creek into stringy bush. Branches slapped the windscreen and scraped the roof. Nothing had travelled this way since last year's whitebaiting season, she was sure. The Landcruiser might be too wide to get through.

'We're going away from it,' Debbie said.

'No,' Hollis said. 'There's the ford.'

Red water from some swampy source flowed on shingle into a tidal pool. Ellie drove across in low gear. The sand came further inland on the northern side, with tussock grass hardening it. She wound and dipped towards the sloping roof of the shed, then crawled through a hollow between mounds and brought the Cruiser to the half-open door. *Andy's whare* read a sign burned into a board. The walls were so eaten with rust she felt she could nudge them flat and drive on over the top. She turned off the engine. The grumbling of the sea began.

Debbie got out. The half-open door seemed to unnerve her.

'Wait on,' Hollis said, fitting his arms into his crutches. Ellie had meant to get his painkillers from the bag in the back but felt herself drawn beside him to the shack.

'There's no one,' Debbie said. She held the lithium bottle squeezed in her fist — an explanation, a charm to force her son to appear.

The door had scraped a crescent in the floor. Ellie forced it open. 'Anyone here?'

There was no window and she could scarcely see; then something pale, a plastic bucket, caught her eye beside an iron stove. There were bunks against the far wall, with mounded clothes on the lower one and a tongue of mattress lolling from the top. A smell of urine pushed like a live thing into her throat.

Debbie edged past her. She made a step, then crouched and hissed, dropping the pill bottle. She ran, half her normal height, to the bottom bunk. The boy, Dion, lay underneath the tangle of clothes, his hands like two white balls of wool on top, his face framed in beard and hair. Ellie thought he was dead.

Debbie fell on her knees. She touched Dion's face, stroking it flat palmed, then laying her cheek on it. 'He's alive. He's warm,' she cried over her shoulder.

Ellie ran to the Cruiser and brought back a torch. She went again for water and a pillow and a blanket.

'He's dehydrated,' Hollis said. He looked in the bucket. 'Empty.'

Debbie had grown calm. She took the bottle and trickled water into Dion's mouth. He made a faint coughing sound, then a cat-like mewing.

'Be careful he doesn't choke,' Ellie said.

Dion half opened his eyes. He closed them.

'I'm here,' Debbie whispered. She turned her face at Hollis. 'He's been starving himself to death.'

'We've got to get him out,' Hollis said.

'No. Don't shift him. He'll die.'

There was only a whisper of life in the boy. His skin had a pallid sheen, yet was dry; his face was the hollow face of newsreels. He looked as if his bones would break if they lifted him.

'Stay with her,' Hollis said. He went out to the Cruiser. Ellie followed him.

'You can't drive,' she cried.

'I'm telephoning. If this bloody thing will work out here.' He punched 111 on his mobile. 'Not getting through. You'll have to drive out. We need a doctor and a helicopter. God knows, he might be dead by the time they get here.'

'Let me take the phone. I'll try when I'm out on the road.'

'Make sure they send paramedics at least. Go fast, Ellie.'

She drove back over the ford and along the back of the sand dune. The old man was standing in his doorway.

'Do mobile phones work from here?' Ellie cried.

'I wouldn't know.'

'Where's the nearest doctor and police?'

'Whataroa for police. There's a district nurse at Fox.'

She drove out to the road and tried the phone but got only silence. Looked at the map: Harihari was closer but Whataroa had the policeman. She was there in twenty minutes. Found the constable, told her story: Dion would die. His mother was a nurse (had Debbie said something the night before about working as a nurse aid once?) and was certain he would not survive being brought out overland; so, a helicopter, a doctor, paramedics, hurry please. Then she went outside and sat exhausted in the Cruiser. She had been driving for ten hours. The constable came out for more directions, went back inside. Ellie ate the sandwiches left over from morning tea and drank lukewarm coffee from the thermos. She should take food and drink back to the whare for Hollis and Debbie. And Hollis would need his pills, which were here with her. Why hadn't she thought?

'I'm going back,' she said, looking in at the constable.

'The Greymouth rescue heli can't come, so they're sending one from Christchurch. Park beside the whare so they can see you. Are you OK?'

'Where can I buy something to eat? Not for me, for the other two.'

'I'll bring an emergency pack. I'll only be ten minutes behind you. Take it easy, eh?'

She arrived at the whare, where Hollis stepped out like a man from a prison cell.

'There's a helicopter on the way,' she cried. 'The policeman from Whataroa is bringing some food. Hollis, your pills, you need something.'

'I'm all right.'

'Oh shit, don't be stupid. Take your pills. Killing yourself won't help him.'

'He's not going to make it, Ellie. You can hardly feel him breathing. I think if he even opened his eyes it would use up everything he's got.'

She had never seen him cry. It was silent, as though, like Dion, he had no strength left. Ellie felt overwhelmed with his loss. She took him to the Cruiser and made him sit in the back seat; made him swallow a pill and drink some water. The constable arrived and went into the whare. Hollis struggled out of his seat and followed. Ellie waited outside, watching for the helicopter over the hills. It came from behind her, down the beach, made a wide swoop and settled on a tussock dune behind the whare. Two men got out, met the constable halfway down, talked briefly with him and went inside. In a moment one ran back to the helicopter and carried equipment down. The pilot brought a stretcher. Hollis came outside.

'What are they doing?' Ellie said.

'Putting him on a drip.'

'Is he going to make it?'

'They don't say. She . . .'

Ellie waited. 'You mean Debbie?'

'I've never seen anyone so . . . I think if he dies . . .'

'What are you going to do, Hollis?'

'They're taking him to Christchurch. There's room for two of us.'

'All right.' Ellie took his face between her hands. She kissed him carefully, a soft pressure. 'I love you, Hollis.'

He struggled to speak, then nodded in a way that answered her. She smiled. Enough.

'Will you be careful?' she said.

'Yes. Where will you go?'

'Down to Franz and see if I can find a bed. I'll drive home tomorrow.'

'I'll phone you when we know something.' Hollis freed his hands. His crutches fell behind him, criss cross on the sand. He hugged her but she felt that she was holding him up.

The paramedics carried Dion to the helicopter. Debbie walked alongside with the drip-bag and clamp. Her lightness and her leaning reminded Ellie of Hollis. The boy was nothing like, with his naked eyelids and fallen mouth. He was generic.

They had always been there, waiting for Hollis to look around.

Ellie picked up his crutches. She went to the Landcruiser for the bags and carried them up the dune to the helicopter.

Instead of driving south to Franz Josef, Ellie turned north. The sunset thickened and the long slow evening turned to night. She drove into Hokitika, which more than any town she knew made her think of frontiers. Even with crowds in the streets and drunks on balconies and music punching from doorways she could feel the huge emptiness beyond the dark.

She had meant to get a meal and drive on, but sitting in the restaurant — a French name, French food — she understood that she had pushed herself far enough; and that thinking, Home, straight home, while driving out through that no-man's land of dunes, had been delusive. Home was Fan's house on the hill, and Ellie could not live there any more. She felt her eyes fill with tears. I'm tired, she thought, I need to sleep. Home is at Tidal Flat with Hollis. I've got my studio. It's not a sunroom. I'm happy there.

She used the toilet, washed her hands and face, then drove towards the river mouth and found a place to park in the line of cars. People walked to and from the beach. Watching them, she wondered if Dion would live or die. How exhausted he must have been, going into that hut and forcing the door closed as far as it would go. Like that boy in Lower Hutt who had hanged himself. And how they had been waiting, Debbie and Dion, unseen at the edge of Hollis's life. Would they help him complete himself, as she could not, or would they just bewilder him?

She locked the Landcruiser and walked to the river mouth. A long sandhill hid the sea from the town. She climbed up and saw a line of driftwood fires, more than she could count, on the beach. They made a row of stations, each one paler, as far as the northern edge of the town.

Ellie went down the sandhill. She took off her sneakers and walked between the fires and the sea, which ran soft waves around her ankles. People called to her, moving in the shadows behind their fires or kneeling close with faces lit up. They offered beer and food but she walked on until she found a fire that had been left. She sat looking into its red heart where the wood combusted: deep and rich, natural, chemical. She felt that she might pick it up and mould it in her hands. Heat from the flames dried the tears on her face.

She walked back to the Landcruiser and made a bed on the back seat. The pillow smelled of Dion. She turned it over and dozed uncomfortably as people went by and cars started up. A torch shone on her and a Quasimodo face flattened on the window. A woman shrieked. The mouth spread its lips and smeared away. Ellie turned her own torch on her watch: one o'clock. She slept then, deeply, and found that it was ten to six when she looked again. She wondered where Hollis was — at the hospital, at a hotel? Had he slept?

She ate some chocolate and an apple and drank water from the bottle she had filled at Ross. The public toilet was filthy from the night, so she drove out of town to a layby and used the bushes. She washed from her bottle, then settled down to some serious driving. Outside Greymouth she picked up a hitch-hiker, a girl smelling of unwashed clothes and marijuana. She was heading to Nelson to pick apples.

'You can go on the back seat and sleep if you like,' Ellie said.

She drove through Reefton and Inangahua and stopped for

morning tea in Murchison. The girl was murmuring in her dream, so Ellie left her and sat in the tearoom alone. Somewhere around here Carol, her friend from twenty-five years ago, lived on a farm. Happily, happily, Ellie hoped. She remembered Carol's grief, remembered her own loneliness, then Neil, then Fan, then John and Derek. Hollis came at the end of the line. Where was he?

Ellie sat still, forgetting her sandwiches and coffee.

The fires burned on the beach, making their stepped-down progress into the dark. She saw how their colour weakened as they went away; saw people sitting close, with faces lit up and clothes almost white — no competing colours. Figures stood at the back of them, indistinct. Could she paint them? Paint the night? She had never tried. And that fierce blaze, that consuming light? Oh yes I can, Ellie thought.

A figure moved between the firelight and the luminous waves: a man like a shadow, walking on the beach. She had been expecting him. Hello again. Do you have more substance now, blacking out, biting out the rim of the fire?

Ellie smiled. Oh yes I can.